The Wychford Murders

The Wychford Murders

PAULA GOSLING

PUBLISHED FOR THE CRIME CLUB BY
DOUBLEDAY & COMPANY, INC.
GARDEN CITY, NEW YORK
1986

All of the characters in this book
are fictitious, and any resemblance
to actual persons, living or dead,
is purely coincidental.

Library of Congress Cataloging-in-Publication Data

Gosling, Paula.
The Wychford murders.

I. Title.
PR6057.O75W9 1986   823'.914   86–11498
ISBN 0-385-23551-8

CHAPTER ONE

"The DCI is here."

The small crowd of police and forensic officers parted, as a tall, angular, well-dressed man scrambled down the bank and came across to the roped-off area. His expression was intent, and his eyes were everywhere, taking in the terrain, the activities of the police on the spot, the position of the corpse, and possibly the barometric pressure adjusted to sea level. Luke Abbott's reputation preceded him. If you were a crook, he was a relentless enemy. If you were a colleague, it was good to stand behind him. (He appreciated your support—and that way you wouldn't get hit by whatever was flying in his direction.) He was one of the younger detective chief inspectors in the region, and he'd achieved that position with a combination of professional skepticism and dogged persistence in solving his cases. He just kept going until he got to the end—and he almost always got to the end.

He'd been assigned to this case in a hurry, but took his time assessing all that he wanted to consider at the scene. Finally, his grey-blue eyes came to rest on the area medical officer. "Well?" he barked.

The MO shrugged. "I need time for tests . . ."

"Come on, Cyril . . ."

The MO tried to scowl, but failed. "Damn you, Luke, you're always so damned determined to get an answer. You make me say things I regret afterward."

Abbott grinned, and waited. Cyril usually gave him something to start with. It might not be big and it might not be important, but it was *something*, it made the motor start and the gears mesh, and that's all he asked. A toe in the door, even if it was the corpse's toe, would do.

"Female, middle-aged, grabbed from behind, throat cut," Cyril Franklin said, tersely. "No struggle, unconscious almost immediately, died in minutes from blood loss."

"Any idea about the killer?"

Cyril shrugged. "Victim's not particularly tall or particularly well built. Killer was probably taller—certainly not shorter. Five foot nine, say, maybe more. Right-handed. The esophagus is cut through as well as both main blood vessels. That's not easy. When the head is tipped back like that, both main vessels slide in behind the esophagus, which protects them. Could have been a woman with a very, very sharp knife—or a strong man with a dullish one. I'll be able to tell you more after microscopic examination of the edges of the wound. Speed was as important as strength, here. Came up behind her, put an arm under the chin, lifted and cut, probably all in one motion. She never had a chance to run or defend herself. The killer wouldn't have gotten much blood on him—or her. It was all over in a minute."

"That's *how.* I want to know who and why," Luke said.

"That's *your* job, my friend, not mine," Cyril Franklin said, with obvious relief. "I just take them apart and put them back together again."

A stocky, dark-haired man came up to stand beside Abbott. Paddy Smith was his sergeant, long overdue for promotion. Abbott had just signed his fourth personal recommendation, and he hoped the promotions board didn't have any more excuses left. An old enemy had been blocking Paddy's way, but the man in question had recently been indicted for fraud, much to everyone's relief. What would happen to Paddy's ambitions as a result was yet to be revealed.

"They found her handbag in the bushes over there." Paddy produced a plastic bag containing an open handbag, its contents spilled out. "Purse empty, no loose money. Lipstick, pressed powder compact, eyeliner, so on." He manoeuvred the items through the plastic bag. "Little address book, diary —looks like she mostly used it for shopping lists." He fiddled some more. "Cards, here—library, cheque card, some kind of ID." He turned it over. "Name, Beryl Tompkins, worked for the photoprocessing plant as a cleaner, apparently."

"Could be someone else's handbag," Abbott said. "We'd better have a look." They went over and Franklin lifted the canvas sheet. The picture on the ID card from the plant was in black and white, which made comparison with the whey-white face of the dead woman easier than it might have been. Franklin looked up at him, waiting.

"Okay," Abbott said.

"You don't suppose she was some kind of spy, do you?" one of the local men asked. "I hear they do a lot of work for the Ministry of Defence over at that plant."

Abbott looked at the dead face. The features told him nothing, but the clothing spoke of a conventional woman with ordinary tastes. Beryl Tompkins, secret agent? Did secret agents have library cards and wear hand-knitted cardigans? He doubted it, but the KGB was supposed to be good at that kind of detail. He made a mental note to contact the Home Office, but he felt the solution to this killing would prove to be far more prosaic. "Was she raped?"

"I don't think so, but sometimes they rearrange the clothes—after. I told you, I need tests." Franklin sighed, heavily. "I don't think you'll have to dig deep for the motive on this one. No money in that purse, is there? People around here mostly get paid on Thursdays. Whoever did it was strong, deter-mined, quick—and cold-blooded."

"Why do you say that?" Abbott asked, quickly.

Franklin shrugged. "Stands to reason, doesn't it? Just cut her throat and dropped her where she was. No attempt to cover her up or drag her away or hide her. Just left her lying here on the path, as if the poor woman was just a piece of old rubbish he had no more use for."

Abbott smiled, gratified. "There," he said. "I knew you'd come up with something." He turned on his heel and started to walk away.

The medical officer stared after him. "What? What did I say?" But Abbott just waved a hand and went on. "Breezy bastard," Franklin muttered, and then he grinned at a near-by constable. "Somebody ought to nail his shoes to the floor, that one."

The constable looked a little shocked. "Sir?"

"Nothing," Franklin said, going back to the corpse. "Nothing at all. Come on, Beryl, old girl. Time somebody looked after you, and I'm afraid it's going to be me. Sorry, and all that, but . . ." He shrugged. "My job, you know."

The constable turned to one of his colleagues. "Do you suppose he talks to them all like that?" he whispered. The colleague, a younger man, fixed him with a beady eye.

"If he does, I reckon he's hard up for conversation," he said. "They ain't none of 'em going to answer back."

"She was a reliable woman, very uncomplaining, although the work here is hard, for the money." The personnel manager of Jiffy Photoprocessing leaned forward, confidentially. "I believe her husband has been out of work for some time, now, and she was the sole breadwinner for the family. I know she did other cleaning jobs, but I never enquired too closely about them. I think for some of them she was paid in cash, you see, avoiding the taxman. Considering her position, it was little enough extra, God knows, and they needed every penny. I'm not the kind to carry tales, but I thought the less I asked the less I'd know, so to speak, and the less I could be expected to tell— if you see what I mean."

"I see." Paddy made a note, as Luke leaned back in his chair. He glanced around the office. Obviously the job paid well, for the room was spacious and well furnished. The personnel manager, a large sleek man named Grimes, was apparently fond of military history—presumably his own—for the walls were covered with framed photographs of his service days. Groups of uniformed men in front of various places and pieces of artillery proclaimed what this particular daddy had done in the war. There were also family photos on his desk and on the bookcase beneath the window, but they were few compared to those on the wall.

Grimes saw him looking at them, and smiled. "I was in the photographic section during the war," he explained, proudly.

"I see," Luke said. He could also see that Grimes was prepared to elaborate on this, so he hurried on. This was no time for reminiscences of How I Won the War with My Box Brownie. "Did Mrs. Tompkins have any special friends, here, among the cleaning staff?"

"Oh, she was well liked, Inspector, you could certainly say that. Yes, Beryl always had a cheerful word for everyone. I know one of the women, Hilda Stanwick, was her particular friend. Would you like her address?"

They thanked him and took it down. After phoning to make sure she would be at home, they drove away from the photoprocessing plant and down the hill toward Woodbury, which was a small village about a mile away.

"You're from this area, aren't you?" Paddy asked, as they approached the village.

"From Wychford itself," Luke said. "But it's been a long time since I was here. There have been a lot of changes in . . ." He paused. "My God, eighteen years! Hard to believe."

"A lot has happened to you in those years," Paddy said, as he turned, following the personnel manager's rather vague directions. "University, marriage, the boys, moving up to DCI, learning all you know from me . . ."

Luke smiled. "More true than you think. They say you can't go home again, and I suppose it's true. The Luke Abbott who left Wychford full of high hopes all those years ago isn't me."

"No," Paddy agreed. "You're the raddled, cynical old copper, beaten down by the forces of crime and disorder, soured and—"

"Oh, shut up," Luke said, amiably. "I'm not all that soured. Just a little turned around the edges." He looked around at the huddled houses of Woodbury. "*This* place hasn't changed. It was always a secret from the tourists. Wychford took all the traffic, and made all the money. I always wanted to bring Margaret back here, but once the twins arrived, there was never a moment we could call our own." His face grew grave as he remembered how few moments he and his wife had ultimately had, shared or otherwise. Their closest time had been during the terrible months when she put up her brave fight against cancer—a fight she eventually lost. He wondered if he would ever win his own fight against the ache he still felt at her loss, and the way her memory shone out of the boys' eyes.

"Is this it?" Paddy said, recognizing the pain in Luke's face, and wanting to distract him.

"I reckon so," Luke said, looking out at the row of terraced cottages. "Number twenty must be the one at the end."

Mrs. Stanwick proved to be a heavy-set woman who smoked continuously. That might have been the explanation for her red-rimmed eyes, but Luke thought otherwise. Her front room was crowded with furniture and dazzled the eye with conflicting patterns. Every surface shone with polish, and she herself was tightly tidy in her flowered dress.

"Poor Beryl." Mrs. Stanwick sniffed daintily into a crisp white handkerchief that still had the traces of a stick-on price tag clinging to one embroidered corner. Stuffed into the waste bin beside the fireplace of the little terraced house he could see a mass of discarded, rumpled tissues. "If only it hadn't been for my veins."

"I beg your pardon?" Paddy asked, momentarily caught off balance.

"My veins." Mrs. Stanwick extended a fat, mottled leg. "They were playing me up something terrible last night, and so I didn't go into work. Beryl and me always walked down together to catch the last bus but one after work, regular as clockwork. I carried the torch, well, you need one along there, and Beryl, she pushed aside the bushes, like, because of me not being able to stand spiders and that? I don't know why she went down there alone, should have gone around the road, even though it is longer. Did she have a torch?"

"We didn't find one," Paddy said, making a note.

"No? That's odd. You could break an ankle quick as a wink on that path, without a torch. Not a proper path, anyway, just a way we go through down the field and that. Maybe she did go with someone else. Maybe it was a man went with her and turned funny along the way. Oh, dear." Her eyes rolled at the thought.

"Was she friendly with any of the men at the plant?"

"Beryl? Oh, no. Oh, no, not at all. Beryl wasn't the type to encourage that sort of thing. Anyway, we didn't go into the plant, much. We did reception, the labs, and the offices, Beryl and me did. Mr. Grimes, the personnel manager, he give us the offices because of my veins and Beryl's bad back, said it was lighter work. Well, and it was, not like that nasty business down on the plant floor, all them chemicals and such . . ."

"Who does that work?"

"The other girls. Younger, most of them. They don't care, that lot, only rough work they do, not fussy enough to do offices. Beryl and me, we didn't mix much with them. No, she must have tried it without a torch, all on her own. I blame myself that she's dead. I do. She counted on me, did Beryl, and I let her down, and now . . . now . . ." Tears welled up in Mrs. Stanwick's eyes and overflowed her already chapped cheeks. The new handkerchief collapsed into a ball under the assault, and Mrs. Stanwick searched her pockets for tissues. "I'm sorry, I'm sure," she apologised. "I do feel her death, so. She was a lovely, lovely woman." Mrs. Stanwick sighed deeply. "I'll have to go around by the road, now, and every time I pass the path I'll think of Beryl, lying there, alone . . ."

They eventually escaped the trembling bulk of Mrs. Stanwick, after assuring her that life was like that and we never know what's ahead, do we, and she shouldn't blame herself, nobody could have known.

They will do it, these idiot women, Paddy grumbled to himself. Go down the damnedest dark ways just to save a step or two. Then he thought of Mrs. Stanwick's veins and was a little ashamed. A policeman's lot was not the only unhappy one.

Especially where feet and legs were concerned.

Mrs. Stanwick had told them about Beryl Tompkins's other two cleaning jobs—for a Mrs. Dyson in town, an elderly lady who lived alone, and for Mr. Pelmer, the chemist. She had shared the latter job with a Mrs. Teague, doing alternate afternoons. Mrs. Teague was one of the "other girls," who worked at Jiffy Photoprocessing, doing the plant area, although she was older than Mrs. Tompkins and Mrs. Stanwick. She did the rough work at the chemist's, too. ("Beryl dusted the displays," Mrs. Stanwick confided to Paddy. "Beryl knew how to keep things nice. Not like some.")

A painful interview with Mrs. Tompkins's bereaved husband confirmed her goodness and her fastidiousness. Mr. Tompkins, a large, slow-thinking man, felt bad about the fact that he had not gone up to the factory to meet his wife the night she died. He'd wanted to go when she phoned him to say that Hilda Stanwick hadn't come in, but she had told him not to, for someone had to stay home and keep an eye on the children. They weren't a family to let their children run wild or be left. The children, a boy of fourteen and a girl of twelve, sat wide-eyed and stricken into silence on the sofa. Their clothes, though well worn, were clean and tidy, as was the house itself. Everywhere Paddy and Luke looked they saw evidence of love and care—and a sudden, cruel emptiness. Obviously Mrs. Tompkins had been the heart of the family, and now that she was gone, they were lost and bewildered.

Luke knew that feeling only too well.

"Of course, when the time for the last bus had come and gone, I began to get worried," Mr. Tompkins said, in his slow, deep voice. "I called the plant, but the watchman said everyone had gone. I called the hospital, thinking of an accident, like, but they said no. Finally, at midnight, I called the police. Around seven this morning, they come to tell me." His eyes began to overflow. "They was kind, like—I knowed one of them from the pub and all, but . . ." He shrugged, unable to express the pain he obviously felt.

Paddy and Luke exchanged a glance, silently agreeing there was no work here for them, save uttering those few empty words that would bring neither comfort nor explanation.

Mr. Tompkins saw them out, carefully closing the door to the sitting room, where the children stared unseeing at a muttering television set. "They didn't tell me—mebbe they couldn't—was she . . . was she raped?"

Paddy had to look away from the agony in the man's eyes.

"No," said Luke, firmly. "As far as we can tell, her wage packet was all that he was after. Mr. Grimes told us she was paid yesterday, as usual. There was no money in her handbag when we found it."

"Oh, God," Mr. Tompkins said. "It was little enough she got paid. To be killed for it . . ." But there was relief in his face. Luke felt as if he had fed a crumb to a starving man.

"We'll keep you informed, Mr. Tompkins," he said.

"When can we . . . when . . ."

"The coroner will be in touch with you sometime today or tomorrow morning," Luke promised.

They left the house and walked silently to the car. Paddy looked around at the street of small but charming houses. "This really is a lovely area."

Luke unlocked the car without glancing up. "It used to be," he said, bleakly.

CHAPTER TWO

Jennifer Eames stood outside the chemist's shop and looked up the High Street. There was a storm on the way. The afternoon was darkening, but late autumn sunlight still poured down on the golden stones of the buildings, giving the entire scene a strange, two-dimensional quality. As if the whole street were a set for some play or film. What would it be called?

She glanced at her wristwatch. *Darkness at Three Forty-seven?* Something like that. A damp breeze tugged at her jacket, and she could smell rain in the air over the traffic fumes and the bitter tang of the marigolds in the flower-bed a few feet away. She'd promised to meet Frances in the Copper Kettle at four.

"Oh, Dr. Eames!" Jennifer started, and turned. It was Mr. Pelmer, the chemist. "I'm glad I caught you—I'm afraid you forgot to sign this scrip for old Mrs. Biddle." He held out the form, and Jennifer felt herself flushing as she took it from him and fumbled in her shoulder-bag for a pen.

"Sorry, Mr. Pelmer. I must have been distracted by something . . ." She found the pen and put the paper against his window to sign it. The pen had to be shaken several times before it would agree to write uphill in this un-seemly fashion.

Mr. Pelmer laughed heartily. He was a small man with a large shaggy head. He reminded her of a seaside donkey. He apparently believed a loud laugh was a sign of masculinity. It tended to startle those who were not used to it, and occasionally caused alarm in strangers, but Jennifer was becoming re-signed to the sudden bray. She might as well, she thought—she'd be hearing quite a lot of it in the years ahead.

"Why, that's nothing," Mr. Pelmer informed her with further deep chor-tles, as if medical mistakes were a prime source of comedy. Perhaps, to him, they were. "Your uncle was a devil for signatures. I could always tell what time of day he'd written a scrip. In the morning they were quite legible, but by evening surgery he was so fed up with all his patients' moans and groans that they were often no more than a couple of scribbles and a straight line for his name. I used to tell Mrs. Pelmer, it was *me* prescribing for his evening patients, not himself." He stopped laughing. "No disrespect intended, of course." Mr. Pelmer was testing the ground. He looked at her, speculatively.

"Of course," Jennifer agreed, handing back the prescription form.

"He's a fine man. We miss him, terribly," Mr. Pelmer continued. "There'll never be another . . . that is to say . . ."

Jennifer smiled. "I agree. Many of his patients have told me the same thing. There'll never be another like him."

Mr. Pelmer gave her an odd, sideways look. "Fortunately," he said.

Jennifer refused to be startled into betraying her charming and unrepentantly eccentric uncle, the recently bedridden Dr. Wallace Cadwallader Mayberry. "Was that the only unsigned scrip?" she asked, brightly. "I must get on—I have quite a few house calls still to make." Now, Jennifer, don't start that, she told herself. You have two house calls, that's all. Just two, and lucky to get them.

"Ah, yes. I heard Mr. Teague was poorly, again," nodded Mr. Pelmer, sagely. "That will be the Mixture As Before, no doubt. I'll have it ready." He beamed at her, and winked, all help and unknown secrets shared.

"Good afternoon, Mr. Pelmer," Jennifer said, and walked away before he could continue. Smug old fool, she thought, knowing it probably *would* be the mixture as before, unless her uncle had misdiagnosed. There was always that possibility. Over the last years, arthritis had slowly inhibited his activity and efficiency. He'd taken on a younger partner, David Gregson, but ever since her divorce he'd kept on hoping Jennifer would give in and "come home," as he'd put it. Since it had been Uncle Wally who'd inspired her to become a doctor in the first place, she supposed he'd always known her capitulation would eventually come. Secretly she hoped he'd give up the idea, for she was ambitious, and had her eye on a consultancy in internal medicine. Whenever she came down for a visit he'd speak of the practice and the patients as if they were already her own. She would smile and then firmly change the subject. Perhaps he realised it was not what she wanted, perhaps he didn't want to call in her affectionate obligation. It remained a kind of stand-off between two stubborn but loving personalities.

Then about a year ago, he'd started writing and phoning her, asking, then begging her to leave her hospital post in London and take over his country practice. At first she'd been annoyed that their unspoken nonaggression pact was being broken. She'd made vague promises, postponing the fateful day, hating herself for the procrastination. But gradually something in his voice and letters started alarm bells ringing in her doctor's brain—that cold, objective place where analysis and ego stand shoulder to shoulder, looking out on a wayward world. In a sense, Jennifer had been almost relieved when his mild stroke came along. Her diagnosis had been correct—and it made her break from London and frustrated ambition much easier.

But not easy.

Having lived in Wychford until she was fourteen, there was some sensation of coming home. The town *looked* much the same, but the people had changed, and herself most of all. She was not an innocent girl now, but a trained physician annealed in the wards and corridors of a London teaching hospital. Or so she kept telling herself.

Her first problem on her return remained her biggest problem—Uncle

Wally's partner, David Gregson. He viewed her as a consultant might view a junior houseman—someone to do the dull work, not yet a proper doctor. They had clashed several times already, and she could not foresee the situation improving. She knew she had a quick temper, but she also knew she was a damn good physician. She felt Gregson's resentment was unfair, and that his consistent refusal to share the responsibilities of the practice was tantamount to cutting off his nose to spite his face. He kept using words like "temporary," and talking of the time when Dr. Wally would be able to return to work. But that was impossible and they both knew it. He maintained the pretense ostensibly to keep Wally's spirits up, but more for his own reasons, she suspected. He didn't want to accept the inevitable, any more than she had wanted to accept it. But here she was, and here she intended to stay. The past months had told her she probably would have made no more than a competent consultant—and a woman needed to be far more than competent to get anywhere—but now she had a chance of becoming a very good GP.

She turned into the Copper Kettle and took one of the corner tables for two. A few minutes later, Frances Murphy entered, waved, and came over. Wearing a green coat and a bright red scarf, she reminded Jennifer of a fine, ripe apple. She was a pippin within, too—her basic sweetness overlaid with the sharp tang of an ironic turn of mind. She had a newspaper in her hand, and dropped it onto the table while she undid her coat, took it off, and then replaced the cutlery she'd swept onto the chair with it.

"Would you believe it, there's been a murder!" she announced, dramatically. "In Wychford, of all places!" Frances had been born in County Cork, and the accent still clung to her words, giving a delicious roundness to her *r*'s and a faint lilt to her sentences. (Since she was on the plump side, however, references to her round *r*'s were not welcomed.) For the rest she was black of hair, fair of skin, and white of smile. She was a physiotherapist and had only lived in Wychford a few months herself when Jennifer returned. They had become good friends on the sound basis of being able to make one another laugh, but murder wasn't that funny.

"This will certainly startle Aunt Clodie," Jennifer said, picking up the newspaper. "She always maintains Wychford is the dullest town in Britain."

"They ought to twin it to Calglannon, then," Frances said. "The dullest village in Ireland, distinguished only by the excitement caused one day by my mother's pressure-cooker exploding. I can still see her with the carrots in her hair." She beamed at Jennifer. "Do you ever suppose they have any of that lardy cake left?"

"I thought you were going to start a diet this week," Jennifer said, absently, absorbing what details the *Chronicle* had concerning the murder.

"No, that was last week," Frances said. "This week I'm going on a bender. Or is it blinder?" The waitress came over and she ordered tea and cakes for two, having ascertained that the lardy cake had been demolished earlier by some tourists. "Who was it that got killed, then?" she asked, trying to read the paper upside-down. In her off-duty hours, Frances was trying to become a writer. She'd had a couple of stories published, and was currently working on a novel. Everything was grist to her mill, and if natural curiosity was an indicator of writing talent, Frances was bound to be a success one day. "Beryl Tompkins," she spelled out, slowly. "Oh." She sat back and looked distressed. "Oh, dear."

Jennifer glanced up at her tone. "You knew her?"

"Yes. You should, too. She's in your practice. Dr. Gregson referred her to Dr. Blythe, and we've been treating her at the clinic. Four degenerate discs."

"I don't think *I* ever saw her." Jennifer tried to place the name and couldn't. "Was it before I came?"

"Perhaps it was," Frances said, vaguely, leaning back for the waitress to put down the tea-tray. "I was trying various treatments, but she said they weren't doing her any good. Of course they weren't, I told her, as long as she kept up her work at that factory, pushing that great divil of a waxing machine around. But she needed the money, she said. Poor woman, lying there, murdered in her second-best shift."

"How do you know that?" Jennifer demanded.

Frances looked at her reproachfully. "Well, it says she was coming back from her cleaning job, doesn't it? She'd hardly wear best for that, now, would she?"

"No, I suppose not." The thought of the woman being found murdered in her old clothes made it seem more sad, and cruel, somehow—even her dignity had been slaughtered. It was like Frances to pick up that small detail. She glanced through the rest of the story. "It says she was killed on a path that runs from the photoprocessing plant down to the highway. And that her throat was cut from ear to ear."

Frances was pouring out the tea, and nearly missed the cups. "The plant is just up the hill from the hospital," she said, thinly. She put down the pot, and took a long drink of the scalding tea. "I'm glad I've kept the car, after all," she said, with a gasp.

"You mean you're still driving it?"

"And why shouldn't I be?" Frances demanded.

The thought of Frances in charge of a car always made Jennifer plan her own journeys carefully. Frances hated machinery of any kind, and the enmity seemed mutual. If ever there was a human being with whom machinery did not co-operate, it was Frances Murphy. Regularly, her small car leapt forward without warning into traffic bollards and walls. Trees had been known to leave the forest simply to force her into ditches. At work, sun-lamps melted plastic couches or went sulkily into eclipse, and whirlpool baths whizzed themselves into foaming maelstroms that overflowed onto everyone's shoes. At home, her oven lay cold and dark, or burned unmercifully every scone or pie she attempted. For Frances, wide-eyed in an inexplicably malevolent world, television sets fused, irons scorched, hair driers frizzed, and tin openers went for her thumbs. She said it was either fairies, or the Revenge of the Twentieth Century. On the whole, she favoured the fairies.

"Better a flat tyre than a cut throat, I suppose," Jennifer conceded.

"Better neither," Frances said, picking up another cream cake and glancing across the street. "I see Mark Peacock has closed early again. The tourists must be flying back to their star-spangled nests."

Jennifer followed her glance. At Peacock's Antiques, the lights were out and the "closed" sign hung, slightly askew, on the door.

"That's odd," she said, but offered no more.

Frances, warned off by her expression, changed the subject. "How goes the war between you and David Gregson, then?"

Jennifer was startled. "What made you think of him?"

"It wasn't that I wanted to think of him, it's that I *didn't* want to think about that poor murdered woman," Frances said, resolutely folding the newspaper and dropping it onto a chair beneath the table. "Still on speaking terms, are you?"

"Oh, yes, but through clenched teeth," Jennifer said. "It would be easier if he didn't live in the house with us. As it is, we have to be polite to one another at meals, as well as discussing the business of the practice and conferring on patient care. God, it's hard work."

Frances tsk-tsked companionably. "His patients think the world of him. He's always been very nice to me, very helpful. I don't understand why you don't get on with him. He's been marvellous with your uncle, you know."

Jennifer sighed. "I know he has. That just makes it all the more difficult, because it must just be *me* that's wrong. But, dammit, it *isn't* me. It's him. He's not being *fair*. Or sensible. I'm a good doctor. I can be of enormous help in the practice, but does he use me fully? He does not. If I were Wally's nephew instead of his niece, I'm certain it would be different. The plain fact is, he's a woman-hater."

"Didn't his marriage break up recently?"

"Yes. But I don't see why he should take it out on *me.*"

"You're handy, and you overreact," Frances observed. "Why not?" She pushed the plate of cakes toward her. "Have the last cream doughnut. It will give you strength."

"I need all I can get," Jennifer agreed. *"Especially* if people are going to start getting murdered around here. A few more close encounters with David Gregson's bloody wounded ego, and I may turn killer myself."

CHAPTER THREE

"Mark, you mustn't! I forbid it!"

Mark Peacock looked at his mother pleadingly. "It's the only way, the only hope we have of holding on to this place. You don't want to move into a poky little flat in some seaside town, do you?"

His mother shuddered. "Hardly. But letting strangers in . . . it's too ghastly. I don't want them here, they wouldn't be the kind of people *I'd* choose to invite into my home. It's taking money for hypocrisy."

"Money is what it's all about, Mother." Mark felt hopelessness taking hold, yet again. It was not the first occasion they'd had this conversation, but he wearily prayed it would be the last. Time was running out. "I've sold exactly three antiques this week, for a total profit of less than fifty pounds, and with winter coming things will only get worse, not better. You can't go on living this myth of the lady of the manor when we haven't got enough in the bank to cover the first mortgage, much less the second. Once our available capital fell below that level, the bank manager began giving me the eye and holding up my cheques."

"Mark!" Her horror was genuine, if overdramatised.

"I didn't say he bounced them, just that they were a little slow in going through," Mark said. "But bouncing them isn't far away, and somehow I'd always pictured myself as the father of bouncing babies, not cheques."

"You're not even married."

"That's hardly my fault—you've never approved of any of the girls I've been interested in, you've gone out of your way to discourage any . . ."

His mother was momentarily distracted. "Since you persist in going out with totally unsuitable girls, I can do little else. I don't know why we sent you to those expensive schools—they don't seem to have instilled any values in you, whatsoever. A man in your position . . ."

"I have no 'position,' Mother, other than a half crouch engendered by the increasing burden of this house," Mark said, petulantly. "If it weren't for that ridiculous will of Father's, drawn up when I was a *child* . . ."

"You're still a child," his mother snapped. "You have a fatal attraction for shiny toys. The least little tart catches your eye."

"Jennifer Eames is hardly that."

She looked perturbed, suddenly. "Is *that* who you're thinking of, then? I thought . . ."

He looked defensive. "What? You thought what?"

She turned away. "One hears things, dear. One is not *totally* out of contact with the village, you know."

"No, I don't know anything of the kind," he snapped. "Would you care to elaborate on that?"

She started to speak, then apparently thought better of it. "No, dear, I wouldn't. Boys must have their toys, I suppose. I thought you had finished with Jennifer Eames, anyway." It was a question.

He clenched his fists. "We've both been rather busy, lately. That doesn't mean anything. Her professional life is . . ."

His mother snorted, delicately. "Delving into the inner recesses of perfect strangers is hardly work for a lady."

"My God, you're impossible, Mother. Like something out of an E. F. Benson novel. Do you maintain these antediluvian attitudes intentionally, as some kind of prop to your public image, or do they just spring out of a lifetime of willful ignorance?"

She chose to disregard this. "As for her family—hardly our kind of people. I believe her father threw up a steady if unimportant position in the Civil Service to 'find himself' and now spends his life daubing second-class paintings in some fishing village . . ."

"Her father is a fine water-colourist who lives in St. Ives and is a member of the RA . . ."

She rolled on. "And her mother 'weaves' or something similarly rough-handed. All sandals and beads, no doubt, like those hippies up at the craft centre." She eyed him covertly to see if these darts had gone home, and was annoyed to see him wearing a look of patient resignation. Time to change tack. "Her aunt is on the church committee with me, of course. She was a Debenham before her marriage. I find her acceptable, although a little erratic. All the Debenhams are. But that uncle of hers!" Outrage overcame judgement, as it so often did. "Dreadful man. Dreadful!"

Mark's mouth twitched. "Just because he told you a few home truths . . ."

"Don't be ridiculous." She dismissed the subject.

"You want me to marry some hideous female from some so-called good family, who will honk around me telling me what to say and remind me what fork to use. Well, I won't. It would be my final surrender and, dammit, one like you is enough. What I really need is a strong-armed red-cheeked country girl who isn't afraid to get her hands dirty. Just keeping the rats down—the *real* rats, that is, not the Inland Revenue—is wearing me out."

His mother, a small expensively dressed woman with curly grey hair and fluttering hands, shivered elaborately and gracefully. "*Not* the rats again, darling. Please."

Mark felt like striking her, and might have, if he'd thought it would have any effect, or get through the wall of fantasy she'd built around herself. At fifty-six Mabel Peacock Taubman was fighting a steady holding action against time as it affected her body, her mind, and her surroundings.

Peacock Manor was a massive and gloriously beautiful house set in several acres of Cotswold gardens, the eastern border of which gave onto the grounds of a recently converted monastery. Much care had been exercised to keep this latter operation out of sight, and it was only over the strenuous objections of Mrs. Taubman that the Monkswell Craft Centre had come into existence at all. She had claimed that it would destroy the "ambiance" of Peacock Manor, but, in truth, it would have taken a great deal more than a craft centre to do that. The manor, with its golden exterior and airy interior, was a monument to the nameless architect who'd fashioned it centuries before. It was said Capability Brown had had a hand in the designing of the gardens, but Mark had found no mention of such an association in the house records, which were complete and a collector's item in themselves. An architect himself, by inclination as well as by (uncompleted) training, he found the house a constant source of inspiration and comfort. But whereas his mother saw it as a fit setting for herself as well as an indicator of social status, he saw it whole, and clearly.

It was destroying them.

Like some beautiful, loved, but useless animal, it was literally eating them out of house and home. Taxes, utility rates, maintenance—it was gnawing away what little available capital they had left.

The difficulty was that, according to his late father's will, his mother held the purse-strings until such time as he married and produced an heir. Therefore, as far as she was concerned, the money and the house were hers in trust, and she didn't intend it to go to just any Thomasina, Deidre, or Harriet. She was a capricious woman and had not been forthcoming with her approval for a wife. That, too, was a provision of the will, for she had dominated Mark's father before him fully as much as she dominated her son.

Mark had left university when his father died because Mabel had no idea how to run the estate. Perversely, she wouldn't hand things over to professional management—or, in her word, "strangers"—and had demanded Mark's return. It was yet another strand to the web she'd woven around him. Mark had to beg her largesse for the life of the house. She played a coquettish game of "not understanding finance," and made terrible scenes over any manor expenditure, unless it was on herself. Not that the house wasn't worth the effort. Mark would have wheedled his life away for the house, but the present situation was hopeless—and so, it seemed, was any possibility of his mother's perceiving it. The simple truth was, they had to do something drastic, or sell.

"A conference centre is *not* like an hotel, Mother," Mark went on, sulkily. "Companies bring their senior management to them to have discussions or to take concentrated courses . . ."

"A *school?* That's even worse . . ."

"No, love. Like . . . like . . ." He floundered in his mind, trying to the correct description, one that would both penetrate her obstinacy her conceit.

ving house parties," he finally said. "It's true, we wouldn't know the people *personally*, but they'd hardly be poor or uninteresting, because we'd charge them the earth to come here, wouldn't we? And someone like yourself, who knows the correct way of doing things and so on . . . well, it would make all the difference, you see. You'd have a staff to attend to all the physical details, you know—cooking, housekeeping, and so on. You would merely act as a gracious hostess, preside at the dinner table, answer any questions about the house . . . that sort of thing," he finished, lamely. Her back was to him, and he couldn't tell what she was thinking. "They'd be top-drawer people, Mother, cabinet ministers, perhaps, industrialists, people from the arts . . ."

"Like a salon?"

"I beg your pardon?"

She turned, and he saw, with relief, that it *had* penetrated, at last. Moreover, she seemed suddenly taken with the idea. "In France, during Napoleonic times, women in society often had salons where the famous came to meet and talk together. Some of the women became famous themselves, Madame de Staël, for one, and that other one—no, she was someone's mistress or a model or something—anyway, is that the kind of thing you mean?"

"I suppose so. Mostly it would be week-ends or single weeks, so the rest of the time the house would still be ours—or as good as ours, aside from the servants—and life would be pretty much as before. We'd just be entertaining more, that's all."

"Your stepfather wouldn't like it."

Mark shook his head. "Actually, it was Basil's idea in the first place. Just a casual thought, but I saw the possibilities immediately, and we've talked it over quite a bit."

"Basil approves?" This seemed to startle her.

"Of course. My God, you know how he loves the house—perhaps even more than we do. He practically croons over every nook and cranny—I've caught him stroking the stones from time to time." His tone was determinedly light. "And talking to them."

"Don't be ridiculous." His mother almost smiled. She found her second husband's enthusiasm for Peacock Manor charming. It was, she was certain, just a reflection of his love for her.

"Well, you know what I mean. He says it's worth any effort to avoid losing it to strangers. He's right. But we will lose it, Mother. I'll have to sell, soon, if we can find no other way. It's *my* house, remember."

"You can't sell it out from under me, Mark!"

"Ah, but I can, Mother. I simply would rather find another way." He had intended to scare her, and he saw by her expression he had succeeded. He stood up and went over to look out the mullioned windows at the sweep of uncut lawn. "Anyway, I'm grateful for Basil's support, even if it's all words and no action."

"He's trying to make money for us . . ."

"But not succeeding. Let's face it, Mother, he's a delightful fellow, but no great shakes at business."

"One could say the same of you, my darling boy." Her voice was sweet, but her expression was not, and Mark knew he'd gone too far. Criticising her precious second husband was strictly a no-go situation.

"Basil would also be an asset here, you know," he went on, a trifle desperately. "He looks terrific, plays good golf and tennis, can mix with all sorts, and people take to him. They really do."

"Yes, of course they do," his mother said, impatiently. "You don't have to lay it on so thickly, darling. I *am* considering your little idea, you know. It might not be as bad as I originally thought."

Mark winced inwardly at the "little" tag being attached to the plan he'd been nurturing for the past year or so, that of turning Peacock Manor into a commercial concern. Discreetly, handsomely, of course—but a business all the same.

It was ideally located in the Cotswolds, with the benefit of a direct rail link to London. Admittedly the service left something to be desired—only four up and four down trains a day—but they were morning and evening, timed for commuting. The network of motorways also reached within five miles of the town, which was approached on all four sides by decent and beautifully routed minor roads. True, there was usually a traffic jam at the Martyr's Bridge, but Peacock Manor was isolated from all that. It was, in fact, the ideal place for the tired businessman to rest and relax.

Eventually Mark intended to add a small golf course to the tennis courts they already possessed (but which needed resurfacing). Perhaps even a squash court or two in the cellars, which were extensive and, at present, largely unused. Wisely, for once, he held his tongue about these envisaged "improvements," and stuck to the point.

"I think I could make a great deal of money, make Peacock Manor famous —in the right way of course—and, in general, get everything on a permanently sound financial footing. Eventually, perhaps, we could even accumulate enough capital to stop the thing." Over my dead body, he added, silently.

"Show me those plans, again. The ones for the bedrooms, I mean."

Mark made for his study. "I have them right in here," he said, eagerly.

Slowly, smiling to herself, his mother followed him. Looking at something was no commitment, and it would pacify him for the moment. Tomorrow she'd take another look at that damned will.

CHAPTER FOUR

Jennifer's last call was in the new housing estate, to check on Tricia Baldwin's new baby, who had been "poorly in the night." However, it was immediately clear that Darren Patrick was in fine fettle, plump and gleaming with health in his pram. That was more than could be said of his mother, who looked pale and exhausted. Gently, Jennifer asked questions while writing up her notes. The baby got her down, sometimes, Tricia admitted. She was worried because she had lost her temper at him that morning, and had shouted loud enough to frighten him—as well as herself.

Jennifer grinned. "I'm glad to hear it," she said. "Getting cross is perfectly normal. If a new mother tells us she occasionally has the impulse to chuck her baby down the stairs, we know she's probably going to be all right. The ones who worry us are those who have irritable babies and yet insist fervently that everything is 'just perfect.' They might snap, one day, and do some real damage. Nothing is ever perfect with a baby in the house. Babies are annoying, self-centred egotistical little creatures. You'd get angry if an adult behaved the way they do, wouldn't you?"

"I suppose I would." Tricia gave Jennifer a sideways glance. "Sometimes he gets on Fred's nerves something awful. When he can't stand it any longer he just storms out of the house, and walks around for hours. He says the sound of the baby's cry makes him feel crazy, and it's true. Last night, his eyes just went blank and he walked out of here like a robot or something. He didn't come back for hours and hours. Does what you said go for fathers, too?"

Was this the real reason she had asked for a house call? Jennifer suspected so, especially when the baby was so patently healthy. Poor girl, she'd been frightened by her own husband. Jennifer knew the feeling only too well. She was instantly sympathetic, while privately making a mental note to check Fred Baldwin's records for signs of instability when she got back to the surgery. No sense having a mother and baby at risk.

"Certainly, fathers can get upset, too. But he goes out, doesn't he, rather than hurt the child? He gets rid of his anger by walking around, using up the energy the anger generates. I think that's a good solution. I imagine you often wish you could do the same—walk away. Am I right?" She looked closely at the girl. After a moment, Tricia Baldwin blushed, and nodded.

"I did, once, and left *him* holding the baby. I mean really. When I came back they were both asleep on the sofa and the television was just blaring away."

"And no harm done to either," Jennifer smiled. "Don't worry. I can see you're a fine mother. He's a lovely, healthy baby. I suspect the trouble last night was a tooth coming in. I'll give you a prescription for something to help him through it. I sometimes think parents suffer more than babies when teething time arrives. If you think this is bad, wait until he starts chewing the furniture! They can be as bad as puppies!"

Tricia laughed, at last. Jennifer tickled Darren Patrick's stomach gently and he gave her a quizzical glance. Should he cry at this final outrage or not? He'd just been fed, and it was very comfortable there in the pram. On balance, he decided to let it go, and fell asleep.

"Is that you, Jennifer?" came a voice from the sitting room.

"Well, if it isn't, you'd better have the locks changed, Aunt Clodie," Jennifer called out, putting down her case and hanging up her jacket. She went into the sitting room and kissed her aunt, who was seated at her embroidery frame placed in the bay window to catch the last of the late afternoon sun.

"Don't be flippant, dear," her aunt murmured, mildly, inserting another French knot with practised ease. "It will give you sciatica."

Jennifer halted halfway to the sofa. "How can being flippant give me sciatica, for goodness' sake?" she demanded.

Aunt Clodie bit off the end of her silk thread. "Because sooner or later someone will kick you up the backside for it," she said, bending down to extract a different colour from the skeins in her workbasket.

"And I had to ask," Jennifer said, flopping onto the sofa. "Have there been any calls since I left?"

"No, dear. Nothing. The world seems to be quite healthy, today."

"Not completely. There's been a murder." She tossed the evening paper over to her aunt. "Rather a nasty murder, as a matter of fact. One of our patients, apparently. Frances knows the woman—she was treating her for a bad back."

"Dear Frances—she's been such a godsend with your uncle." Clotilda glanced down at the paper where it lay beside her feet. "I shall read about it after dinner, when I feel stronger."

Jennifer took a long, deep breath and kicked her shoes off. "David allowed me four house calls this afternoon. Mr. Teague, Mr. Kretzmer, Mrs. Tippit, and Mrs. Baldwin. He took all the rest."

"Perhaps he's trying to spare you."

"Oh, come on," Jennifer snapped. "I know you like him, but really, Aunt Clodie, isn't it about time he trusted me with more than boils and babies?"

"He will, he will. If only you wouldn't fly off the handle the way you do . . . I know that disconcerts him."

"He just closes down like a clam and walks away. He's a pompous, smug, impossible bastard!" Jennifer hit the arm of the couch with a balled fist, wishing it were Gregson's head.

Aunt Clodie sighed. "Why are all the attractive men such stinkers? It seems to be a law of nature. The minute I met your uncle I thought he would be fun because he was so ugly. After all the conceited, pretty men I'd known, he was a great relief. Mind you, there's fun and fun," she added, with some asperity. "The dear old fool."

Jennifer gazed at her aunt with love and amusement. Aunt Clodie had been a flighty girl, by all accounts; the reigning beauty of the county and a social butterfly, but with a whim of iron. Marrying Wallace Mayberry had been something of a rebellion. The subsequent years of living with her adored but impossible husband had instilled in her the kind of patience known only to sufferers of chronic pain or poverty.

"I had tea with Frances in the Copper Kettle. Mark Peacock had closed his shop early for some reason. All worn out by fleecing the American tourists, I expect."

"Don't be sarcastic, dear. It will give you lines in the face." Clodie plunged her needle into the linen and out again. "Mark may have many faults, but dishonesty isn't one of them." She looked up and their eyes met. "At least, I don't *think* it is." For all her soft appearance, Clotilda Mayberry, née Eames, was possessed of a first-class mind, and had a good instinct for people. "Mark is such a charming man, so cultured and intelligent, I wish you'd . . ." She stopped. Aunt Clodie also possessed a sharp eye, and could see that Jennifer was not in a mood to be cajoled about Mark Peacock. She wondered, not for the first time, what had caused the rift between them. When Jennifer had first arrived, she and Mark had seen quite a lot of one another. Then Jennifer had gone up to London for a week to finish off the selling of her flat, and since she had returned, Clodie was certain she had seen nothing of Mark at all. It was very puzzling. Meekly, she went back to her embroidery.

"Maybe I could poison David Gregson," Jennifer mused.

"Don't be silly, Jennifer. That's another thing that upsets David, I'm afraid. When you say such wild things."

"Well, you know what I mean. Anyway, I've got poisoning on the mind, at the moment. I actually found myself suspecting poor Mrs. Teague of giving her stinker of a husband arsenic this afternoon."

Her aunt considered this, as if she had been asked to solve a crossword clue. "She works as a cleaner in several places. One of them is Mr. Pelmer's. Another is the photoprocessing plant. They use a lot of chemicals, there, I should imagine. She could get hold of all kinds of things. Who knows?"

They stared at one another across the top of the embroidery frame for a long moment, and then Jennifer sighed. "We've got to stop doing this, Aunt Clodie," she said.

"It's not as if it were the *real* thing," her aunt said, glancing down at the newspaper on the floor with distaste. "*Our* little conjectural diversions are quite harmless."

"I'm not so sure they are," Jennifer said, swinging her feet down and sitting up. "It's your fault, you know."

"I suppose so," her aunt said, resignedly. Aunt Clodie was an inveterate reader of mysteries and thrillers. She made up for the dullness of her life with constant conjecture about "things in the village." Funny looks, a word overheard, and so on. Bent over her embroidery frame, her mind free to wander, she imagined murders everywhere. Oh, it was a game, of course it was a game —and one that was hard to give up, since it harmed no one.

Jennifer shared her Aunt Clodie's taste for fictional mayhem, and, when she'd come down from London to take over her uncle's practice, it wasn't long before Aunt Clodie revealed her private obsession—trying to figure out who would like to murder whom, or, indeed, who might have murdered whom, or was planning to murder whom, or who was in the process of . . .

And so on.

Had Jennifer carried things too far, this time?

"You don't *really* suspect Mrs. Teague, do you?" Aunt Clodie demanded, worried enough to leave her stitching for the moment. A long strand of scarlet trailed from her upheld hand, as she regarded Jennifer in some dismay. "I mean, you wouldn't really *do* anything about it, would you?"

"I'd have to do something if the tests revealed arsenic," Jennifer said. "I'd have to report to the police that *someone* was putting the stuff into Jack Teague. I wouldn't make any specific accusations, obviously—that's *their* job —but I'm sure I'd be expected to report it to *someone.*"

"But wouldn't you have to tell Mr. Teague, first? Before you went to the police?"

"I don't know," Jennifer admitted, slowly. "If she killed him outright it would make it much easier, of course." She stopped. What was she saying? Clodie had got her going, again. It really was too much—and with a real killing in the neighbourhood, in poor taste, as well. But when she thought of Mrs. Teague—those dark, resentful eyes, that tight little mouth—oh, well. Reluctantly, she put her shoes back on and stood up, relinquishing the comfort of the sofa and the fireside. "I'm going to have a quick bath before evening surgery," she grimaced, slightly, "where I will sit and listen to all the patients going in to see Dr. Gregson."

Her aunt watched her go out—such a delightful girl. So sad to see her wasted like this, working with sick people, running herself ragged, with her big brown eyes and silky hair and lovely legs unappreciated. Wally might have been a trial, but at least he'd always *appreciated* his wife. Jennifer deserved better, especially after what she'd gone through with that ridiculous ex-husband of hers. Clodie had had great hopes of Mark Peacock, despite his ghastly snobbish mother. (She, who had little to be snobbish about, having been a Norwood before she'd captured poor gentle Major Peacock. Erratic family, the Norwoods. First the grandmother running off with that bizarre Italian nobleman who kept trying to fly off the top of things in weird contraptions that invariably crashed, then the mother who drank and kept a pet monkey. And wasn't there talk of a mad uncle, locked away between the wars? Of course, who could say what was madness, these days? They did such wonderful things with drugs, now.)

Clodie brightened, thinking of drugs and more. Perhaps Mrs. Teague *was* trying to kill her husband. Perhaps Jennifer's hunch would prove correct, and she'd go to the police, and there would be a tall, handsome detective assigned to the case, and . . .

Devoted Reader was off, again.

"Uncle Wally?" Jennifer knocked and, hearing a gruff command from beyond the panel, opened the bedroom door and put her head around the edge. "Is the doctor in?" she asked.

"No, he's out" said her uncle from the bed. "But your uncle is here."

"Oh, good." Jennifer came in and regarded with affection the large figure that lay mounded under the embroidered counterpane. "Never could stand that crabby old GP, anyway."

"He was a bit of a pain," Wallace Mayberry conceded. "Too much on his mind, that was his trouble. Had a good day?"

"Not too bad." She gave him a very brief outline of the day's two surgeries. It was his considered opinion that Jennifer was a sound doctor, but "soft." She was glad of his advice on many of the cases—people he'd treated for years, and whose idiosyncrasies were as familiar to him as his own. His right arm and leg were still weak, but his mind was as sharp as ever.

"I saw ten patients today. David Gregson saw twenty-three," Jennifer grumbled. "You'll have to speak to him, Uncle Wally, you really will. What's the point of my being here if I'm not carrying my share of the load?"

"Speak to him yourself," Uncle Wally said, good-naturedly. "He's not an ogre. Sit down, discuss it, work things out."

"He's not reasonable," Jennifer objected, somewhat childishly. "He hates women, I'm certain he does. Maybe he's afraid I'm a better doctor than he is."

"David is a fine physician," Uncle Wally said. "Wouldn't be my partner if he wasn't. And he doesn't hate women at all, although after what that wife of his put him through, he'd have a perfect right to be down on the sex. He's just—a little conservative." He sighed, and looked out of the window. "Weather closing in, I see. Autumn here at last."

Normally her uncle would have led her into a spirited discussion about the practice, but today he seemed content to let the subject go without argument. For a moment Jennifer was concerned, and then she remembered that this was one of the days Frances came to treat him. "Feeling tired?" she ventured.

He roused himself to a mild echo of fury. "Tired? *Tired?* The wench is a sadist, do you know that? She loves having me at her mercy. Ghastly woman. Fire her."

Jennifer grinned. "Out of a cannon?"

"Preferably." He smiled back, wearily. "She wants to put me on a bicycle."

For a moment Jennifer thought she hadn't heard correctly, and then she smiled. "An exercise cycle, I presume."

"Well, I'm hardly about to go wobbling down the drive, am I?" Uncle Wally grumbled, more amiably. "Although I wouldn't put that past her, come to think of it. She was saying something about fresh air and sunshine. Very nasty stuff, that. I wouldn't mind, you know, except she is so *damned* cheerful, I want to swat her. May God forgive me for every elderly patient I ever told to 'snap out of it' or 'get up and about more.' How they must have wanted to tell me to go to hell."

Jennifer knew how Frances had to steel herself to confront the old man each time she came to treat him, and smiled to herself. Uncle Wally was improving steadily under her gentle tyranny, despite his complaints.

"I'm an old man, I'm tired, it does me no harm to lie here and rest."

"Liar. You know better. And you've been resting for months, now," Jennifer said, briskly. "I think an exercise bicycle is a very good idea. Twenty miles a day should be enough to start with."

"*She* reckoned fifty. Said she'd connect it to my telly and I could provide my own electricity for watching old films all afternoon."

The thought of Frances connecting anything to anything nearly made Jennifer laugh aloud. "Good film on this afternoon," her uncle went on, changing the subject enthusiastically. "Don Ameche inventing the telephone. He . . ."

Jennifer broke a rule and interrupted her uncle. "Do you think Mr. Teague's wife is capable of poisoning him?" she asked.

Her uncle looked at her reproachfully, still being full of old Hollywood's magic, but considered the question. "Up to her old tricks again, is she?" Uncle Wally asked.

"You mean all those enigmatic notes I found in his file about gastric . . . ?"

He waved a hand. "Over the years, I'd say three or four times. I sent him for X-rays, barium meals, gastroscopy, the lot, as you saw in the notes. Then I hit on arsenic."

"What did you do?"

He shrugged. "For right or wrong, I left it, because I tell you, honestly, I couldn't make out whether she *meant* to kill him or just to pay him back for making her life hell. The doses were very small, you see, not lethal at all. But I managed to let her know *I* knew what she was up to. He improved dramatically. It weakened him, though. Didn't get around to beating her up again for some time. Had some sympathy for the woman, but murder . . ." He shook his head. "Not supposed to do it, you know."

"I know," Jennifer said, drily. "On the other hand, you're not supposed to beat your wife, either."

"I should have beat mine," Uncle Wally said, dourly. "Then maybe she'd come up here and visit with me more often."

"That's not fair," Jennifer told him. "You're quite capable of going down in your wheelchair. The lift works perfectly. You could even walk if you had a mind to and took it slowly. Anyway, when she *does* come up here, you complain that she interrupts the best parts of the films. It's a wonder she hasn't poisoned *you!*"

His face lit up. "Do you suppose she has? One of those rare South American poisons out of those damned murder mysteries she's always reading? Might explain a lot of things."

"Uncle Wally, much as you would like to blame your illness on someone else, the fact is that all your life you ate too much, smoked too much, drank too much, worried too much, and did too little about it. A stroke is getting off lightly, if you ask me. I would have expected apoplexy at least, particularly during one of those Sunday lunch-time political arguments you used to get into at the Woolsack."

"How is the Woolsack these days?" he asked, in an attempt to divert her from yet another lecture on healthy living.

"Still standing, despite the loss of your custom," Jennifer retorted. "Dinner's nearly ready, I understand. Count yourself lucky I haven't got time to read you the Riot Act. And don't you *dare* smoke that cigar you're hiding on an empty stomach, you old . . . you old worm!" She gave him a friendly scowl as she went out.

"Worms can turn, you know," he muttered, darkly. But he grinned at the closing door, and moved the cigar from under the bedclothes into the bedside table drawer.

For later.

Dusk slowly claimed the lovely town of Wychford with its shadows.

Little by little it changed from a gold and green patchwork to black velvet and diamonds: streetlamps, headlamps, lights from every size and shape of window—all twinkled on the slopes above the murmuring chuckle of the now invisible River Purle. The trees along its banks whispered together, their conversation drifting up the fields and over the hedgerows to the wooded heights beyond.

In the cottages and homes of the old town, lamps cast their glow outward across fading gardens and leaf-strewn lawns. The long line of traffic in the High Street had at last disappeared. The softness of the summer's end was being nipped by the chill of autumn, and night was coming on.

At Peacock Manor, the houseman was carrying in the predinner sherry; while at the Mayberry home, the evening meal was already on the table. Dr. Mayberry's tray had been carried up to him, and he was cutting roast beef and watching an old Will Hay movie on BBC 2.

Mr. Pelmer, having stayed open late to fill any prescriptions from evening surgeries, had locked up at last, and disappeared. In his windows spotlights shown down on laxatives, tonics, cosmetics, perfumes, and adhesive plasters, but the shop behind this lavish display was dark.

In David Gregson's modern house, set high in the surrounding hills, an old clock clicked and sounded the hour. The clamour of its bell echoed through all the shining, empty rooms.

At the new housing estate, children were being rounded up for baths, and babies (including a still lively Darren Patrick Baldwin) were being fed, winded, and proudly presented to weary fathers just home from a long day's work.

The four rooms of Frances Murphy's little flat filled with smoke as the oven happily, busily, and thoroughly burnt the casserole she'd set the automatic timer to cook for dinner.

At the Monkswell Craft Centre, a party was beginning. Hilarity, wine, and nonsense held sway. People came and went, laughter was heard, and there was quite a bit of sexual by-play in the darker corners of the place. This came under the heading of artistic expression, and was more or less tolerated. To have protested would have labeled one forever "non-creative," a fate not to be borne.

It grew late. And later, still. Slowly, the lanes and streets of the town grew quiet. A slight mist rose from the cooling fields and hung over the River Purle. An owl hooted and swept low over the dark meadows, watching for prey. The bell in the tower of St. Mary's church struck one. The people of Wychford were safely home and at peace.

Save two.

On the second curve of Swann Way, below an elderberry bush, one was lying dead.

And another was running away.

CHAPTER FIVE

Luke Abbott and Paddy Smith were in the dining room of the Woolsack when the landlord came over to them. They had stayed over to pursue their enquiries concerning the death of Beryl Tompkins. Abbott was just about to ask for more toast and coffee, but the landlord spoke first, and said there was a phone call for them.

When Luke returned to the table, the coffee cups had been refilled and fresh toast was in the rack. He scowled at them.

"That was PC Bennett. We have more work to do," he said.

"Oh?" Paddy went on buttering toast. Another set of damn forms to fill in, presumably.

"There's been a second murder. Here in Wychford itself, this time. Another woman with a cut throat."

Paddy stared at him. "You're joking," he said, around a mouthful of toast and strawberry jam.

"I only wish I were."

"Bloody hell. Same method?"

"According to Bennett, exactly the same. Body was found about twenty minutes ago, on the towpath beside the river. If I remember my local geography, the path from the photoprocessing plant crosses the highway, drops down the hill, and eventually joins the towpath." His face was blank. "Cyril is on his way. I guess we'd better be, too."

"Looks like we could be here a while," Paddy said, carefully. "Maybe you'll have time to look up some old friends."

"Old friends or old fiends?" Luke asked.

"I wasn't going to suggest it," Paddy commented, swallowing the last of the scalding coffee, and standing up. "I never said a word."

"You didn't have to," Luke said, getting up, too. "Every time we attend a homicide, these days, the word is there in the back of my mind. Isn't it in yours?"

"Psycho?" Paddy asked. Their eyes met.

"That's the one," Luke agreed.

They came out of the Woolsack and looked down the graceful slope of the High Street. The rain of yesterday afternoon had cleared the air, and overhead a wide V of migrating geese arrowed across the blue sky. A few of the trees showed that frost had passed by recently, for leaves at their tops showed yellow and red. There was condensation on the windows of the car, further evidence that cold weather was on the way.

"Maybe I should have packed warmer clothes," Luke said. "I have the feeling I'm going to need them."

CHAPTER SIX

It was halfway through morning surgery that Jennifer first heard about the second murder. Kay, their secretary and receptionist, brought the news in with her coffee.

"We've lost a patient."

Jennifer looked up, resignedly. "Mr. Wymark? I've been expecting the hospital to call—"

"No. Win Frenholm."

Jennifer's look of resignation changed to one of astonishment. "But she was here only yesterday. She wanted me to—" she stopped, suddenly. "I suppose she's gone over to Mitchell, or Larrabee. Lord, I must have really upset her, after all."

"Not half as much as the person who cut her throat upset her," Kay said, dropping the bomb at last.

"*What?*"

Kay nodded. "My brother's wife's sister's boy is on the police. They found her this morning out along the towpath. Under an elderberry bush. Poor cow. She wasn't exactly my cup of tea, but nobody deserves to go like *that.*" Kay crossed her thin arms across her chest and regarded Jennifer with some interest. "What did you do to upset her, then?"

"Nothing," Jennifer said, hurriedly. "Nothing that matters, now. My God, that's two murders, isn't it? That one over in the Woodbury area, and now this one."

"Both with their throats cut, too. Looks like there's a nutter on the loose. Aside from you and me, that is." Kay's usual bantering tone was a little thin, this morning.

"Was she sexually assaulted?"

"I don't know, he didn't say about that. Only that it had happened, like. Not supposed to say anything, come to that, but I stopped there on my way in here with a pie for his mother as she hasn't been feeling up to much after her op, like, and he did just mention it, in passing." Kay shivered. "Makes you sick to think about it, one cut and wham, you're finished." She gave Jennifer an odd glance. "Sometimes your uncle used to be called out by the police. Any chance you'll get tapped on the shoulder?"

"No. I gather they usually call Larrabee, now—his son is a police constable. All he does is certify death—nothing else. If it's a suspicious death, they send for the scene-of-crime people from the Regional Forensic Laboratory and a Criminal Investigation Department team from the Regional Crime Squad, as well."

"Now how the devil do you know all that?" Kay demanded.

Jennifer sipped her coffee and smiled over the top of the cup. She would have dearly loved to say through reading all those mysteries of Aunt Clodie's, but it was much more fun to appear omnipotent. "Good heavens," she murmured, mischievously. "Do I know something local that you don't?"

"Fine thing if you do," Kay said, with a pretense at outrage. "I'm supposed to do the gossiping around here, not you. Are you trying to do me out of a job or something?"

"God forbid," Jennifer said. Kay Hall had been her uncle's secretary and receptionist for the last ten years. She was endlessly energetic, intelligent, funny, and knowledgeable about the people and ways of Wychford and the surrounding countryside. A tall, angular woman in her forties, with a mass of blond hair, Kay was possessed of a quick tongue and a warm heart. She had trained as a nurse, but married soon after and had never gone back. Running the Mayberry (now Gregson and Eames) surgery suited her down to the ground, for she could fit it in with her family life.

"Shame you won't get in on it." Kay spoke with the objective regret of a true news-gatherer.

"I've got quite enough on my little plate, thanks very much," Jennifer said, finishing her coffee.

"Not if we go on losing patients like this," Kay said, taking up the cup. Jennifer got the impression that Ms. Frenholm wouldn't be missed. Kay was not one for hypocrisy. "Won't catch *me* out after dark till he's caught, nor Debbie, neither, unless her father or brother's with her." She gave Jennifer a hard look. "And what about night calls, that's what I want to know? What about you traipsing all over with your little bag and nothing else but a great big smile? You want to stop that, straight off. Could be a drug addict, you know, something like that. Addicts usually want money to buy their junk— but sometimes they go after the stuff itself. Lots of doctors get mugged for dope, you know. Why . . ."

"I'll be careful," Jennifer promised. "I'm not exactly eager to get my throat cut."

"Could have fooled me," Kay muttered to herself, meaning to be over-heard. "The way you talk to Dr. Gregson, sometimes."

"Hey!" Jennifer called out, but Kay had made a quick exit, knowing her arrow had gone home. She was uneasy because of the tension between the two doctors, and wanted them to get along better. Jennifer was sorry about this, but she couldn't see any way around the problem at the moment.

She pressed the buzzer for the next patient to be sent in, and resolutely cleared her mind for receiving symptoms and complaints. But when the door opened, it wasn't a patient who entered. David Gregson came in and closed the door behind him, then stood looking at her.

She looked back, noting the grey in his thick light brown hair and the piercing green eyes that transfixed men and enthralled women. All women except Jennifer and his estranged wife, that is. Jennifer thought him cold and unsympathetic, although she had to admit, grudgingly, that he was a good physician, particularly in diagnosis. Furthermore, his patients were fiercely loyal to him, which told her that the warmth she couldn't detect had to be there, somewhere.

"Yes?" she asked him, finally.

He left the door and came a few steps toward her desk. "This murder—" he announced.

"Yes?"

"I don't like the sound of it. Two women now. I'd rather you weren't the third. I'll take all night calls until the man is caught."

"Nonsense," Jennifer said, briskly.

"It's not nonsense, it's common sense," Gregson snapped. "If you weren't such a damned feminist . . ."

"I'm not a feminist, and I'm not an idiot. I'll be cautious. You don't let me take many calls as it is. Night-time is the only time I see anything interesting. Otherwise you leave me all the boils, bunions, and . . . and . . ."

"Bruises?" he suggested, with a half smile. "I'm sorry it seems like that, but the truth is, those are mostly the kind of things *I* see, as well. That's general practice. Working in the hospital, you only saw the referrals, the sharp end of medicine. It's more basic out here. Think of us as the lymphatic system of medicine—we filter out the boring bits. It isn't often we get something spectacular."

"Such as Mr. Crittendon?"

"I called you in on that," he reminded her, gently. Mr. Crittendon was a local man who had come in with raging malaria, caught on a selling trip to the Far East. Malaria is hardly endemic to the Cotswolds—and Mr. Crittendon had been a textbook case.

Jennifer relented. "Yes, you did. I'm sorry, David, I don't mean to sound resentful, but . . ."

"But you feel it? Fair enough. So do I. After all, most partners in a practice would have some say on who came in when another partner retired, wouldn't they?"

"Uncle Wally hasn't exactly retired."

He looked at her in pity. "You know as well as I do that he must stop now. All this talk of coming back and taking up the reins is so much self-indulgent nonsense. Even if he could stand the pace physically, his mind couldn't take the strain; nor his spirit, the pressure. He's finished, Jennifer, and we both know it. Obviously he will be invaluable on a consultative basis, but . . ."

"How nice of you to admit that much." Jennifer said, stung by his brusque stating of a fact she knew to be true. "I thought you were going to go on pretending forever."

Gregson ignored that. "He was a brilliant physician in his time, but he's tired, Jennifer. Very tired, now."

"In which case, you'll be senior partner and will want to find someone more to your taste to replace him, no doubt," she said, acidly. "A little awkward, don't you think, seeing as you are living in his house as well as working in his offices?" It was unfair and she knew it, but he always rubbed her the wrong way.

"There is another alternative," he said. "I could be the one to leave, letting you take over, instead. You'd like that, wouldn't you? Everything to yourself?"

"No," she said, evenly. "I wouldn't. I am not capable of carrying a practice this size on my own, but I *am* capable of carrying half of it. If I were allowed to, that is." She let go of that argument and tried another. "Anyway, Uncle Wally needs a man around to talk with."

"And you?"

Something in his eyes compelled her, so that she couldn't look away. "I enjoy a colleague to discuss things with, yes," she admitted. "It was something we always had, at the hospital. I find general practice kind of . . . scary, sometimes, to tell the truth." When he looked at her like that she found it impossible to do anything else. "I mean, making a diagnosis in a bedroom on your own, with only your eyes and ears and touch to rely on—it's awful. Frankly, sometimes, it scares me to death!"

"So you admit it?" Something in his eyes softened. "Maybe you'll make a better GP than I thought. We're all scared, Jennifer—alone in those bedrooms, with some anxious parent, husband, or wife watching you, thinking you're a God when you're just a man—or woman—trying hard as hell to remember the twenty-three alternative conditions all those damned symptoms add up to. Or worse, trying to find a way to tell them that it adds up to something really nasty. When I came here Wally told me being a GP was the toughest specialisation of all. He's right."

Jennifer smiled. "He used to tell me that when I was a kid trailing around after him on his rounds." She looked at him, again, not quite sure if he were being sarcastic or not. "Are you really scared, sometimes?"

"Yes."

"Thanks for telling me, then. I'd begun to think you were the original iron man."

He shrugged, as if he were suddenly embarrassed by having admitted so much to her. Or even by spending more than two minutes there in her office. "I haven't got time to discuss this fascinating conflict of character and interests with you. We both have patients waiting. I will take the night calls. You can have most of the day calls. You won't *believe* how many boils there are on how many backsides, this time of year."

He was gone before she could protest.

Two sore throats, four "feeling poorlys," one sprained wrist, one impending breakdown, a measles, a "frozen" shoulder, an insomnia, and a confirmed pregnancy later, she was "free." Free to write up her notes, fill in and sign repeat prescriptions, and pick up her list of house calls, that is. She was about to leave when the phone rang.

"It's the police," Kay said, with her hand over the receiver. "Apparently, Barry Treat had to go over to identify Ms. Frenholm's body, and he's collapsed in a heap. They wanted to send for an ambulance, but he's asking for you. Care to dance?"

"I'm on my way," Jennifer said.

"Ghoul," Kay said, grinning, and relayed the information.

"Let us pray it doesn't reach the national papers, that's all I can say," Mabel Peacock Taubman said, turning away from the window where she had been watching the activities of the police on the far bank of the river. "I told you bringing all those hippy types right onto our very doorstep was asking for trouble, didn't I?"

"What does it have to do with the artisans at the centre?" Mark spoke so sharply that he startled her.

"Why, she was one of them," his mother said, rallying. "The milkman told me she was one of those pot-making people. You know her, too, if I'm not mistaken," she added, cuttingly. "No better than she should be, of course. She worked with two men—that should tell people something."

"Tell them what?" Basil asked, lazily. After an initial glance, he'd taken no interest in the busy scene across the way. "She may have worked with them, my dear, but she didn't necessarily sleep with them. If you mean the two I think you mean, I believe they're both gay, anyway."

"Gay?" Mabel snorted. "I don't see what's gay about homosexuality—sordid and disgusting is what it is."

The two men glanced at one another. Mark raised his eyes to the ceiling, as if asking for deliverance, and Basil shrugged. "Times change, my dear. These things are perfectly acceptable, now."

"Not to me," Mabel said, firmly. "The bizarre sexual combinations and recombinations of that group over at the centre are enough to fill a hundred revolting novels of the type that sell so well today. You know that's true, Basil. I don't know what possessed me to agree to the thing in the first place, right on our doorstep."

That phrase was a particular favourite of Mabel's—"right on our doorstep." The fact that they had no neighbours within half a mile in any direction was beside the point. Whatever happened in Wychford happened to *her*, and was almost always an affront. Not for the first time, Mark glanced at his mother and his stepfather and wondered what, if any, passion passed between them. Basil was a good ten years younger than his wife, and even to a son's kind eye, Mabel could not be said to be a ravishing beauty. She had kept her figure with assiduous attention to diet and exercise, wore excellent clothes, was cleverly made-up (her complexion was a source of great gratification to her), and had her hair dressed in the height of matronly fashion, but there was really no disguising the fact that the years had passed. They made an attractive mature couple, it's true, and they seemed devoted to one another. But he couldn't imagine them in bed together, or doing more than brushing cheeks. Nor did he want to imagine it. Especially not while he was eating breakfast.

"Well, I'm sure they'll catch whoever did it quite quickly," Mark said. "There was another murder like it in Woodbury a couple of days ago."

"Good Lord," his mother said, taken aback. "I didn't know that."

"Oh, yes you did, my dear," Basil said, around his fourth piece of toast and marmalade. "I showed you the editorial about it in the evening paper yesterday."

"Another woman?"

"Oh, yes."

"Were they—" she paused, delicately. "Were they . . . interfered with?"

"The paper didn't say. I suppose so—although I think there was some mention of handbags being missing."

"So you can't really call it just a local murder, can you?" Mark said, cheerfully. "It seems to be a travelling phenomenon."

His mother fixed him with a basilisk eye. "I don't consider this to be a matter for humour, Mark. Why, this second girl was murdered just across the river from us. A matter of a few hundred yards—"

"Plus another hundred yards width of water."

"Well, I shan't take a step out that door until this madman is caught. No woman is safe with such a monster about."

Mark opened his mouth, but resisted the obvious jibe. He glanced over at his stepfather. "You'll miss your train, chum, if you don't get a move on. Want a lift to the station?"

Basil looked up from his newspaper, and his eyes went to the long-case clock on the wall behind Mark. "Good lord, I had no idea. So much for my morning stroll." He moved his eyes to the window. "Not that the weather looks all that friendly. Thank you, Mark, I'll take you up on that."

"Where are you going, Mark? You don't open the shop on Thursdays. I thought you were going to drive me into Milchester this morning," his mother said, fretfully. "You know I need a new gown for the Carslake wedding."

"Yes, I do know that, Mother," Mark said, standing up and dropping his napkin beside his plate. "I also know that to pay for it I will have to arrange to sell something I love."

She looked at him in surprise, then made a dismissive sound, rather like a small detonation behind the teeth. "Don't be ridiculous."

"Actually, I have to go into town, but I'll be back within the hour, so your trip to Milchester is still on, don't worry."

"And what am I supposed to do while you're off in town?"

Mark was following Basil out the door. "Meditate on the meaning of life. It will do you a world of good."

When Basil came back, hatted and coated, to give her a goodbye kiss, she spoke angrily. "You must speak firmly to Mark, Basil. He's getting absolutely impossible, lately."

"My love, he'll hardly listen to *me*," Basil said. He was a tall, slender, distinguished-looking man of fifty. His looks had been a very valuable asset on the London social circuit. An early and short-lived marriage had established his heterosexual credibility, so his continuing bachelorhood had been put down to either a broken heart or reluctance to repeat this early mistake. His easy manner and charm had meant he was much in demand, and it was with some dismay as well as astonishment that "society" and Nigel Dempster greeted his sudden marriage to the "unknown" Mabel Peacock, widow of uncertain years but apparently the possessor of certain means. One less around the right tables, they said, and they were correct. Despite expectations to the contrary, Basil had remained faithful to his wife and his duties, retaining his modest position in the City and behaving himself impeccably. "Mark thinks me a shallow idiot, you know," Basil said to his wife, with rueful amusement. "He's simply impatient to get this scheme of his off the ground, my dear, and resentful of your standing in his way. Perhaps you ought to give in to him, after all."

She looked at him reproachfully. "I never thought I'd hear you say that."

Basil sighed. "And I never thought working in the City could be so exhausting and unrewarding."

Her sympathy was instantly aroused. "Is it so terrible, then?"

"Not terrible, my dear. Just damned *dreary*, that's all. And the journey back and forth . . ." He shrugged. "Ah, well, small price to pay, I suppose.

Still, Mark's scheme *would* mean I could stay here with you all the time. Such a lovely prospect ought to be worth a bit of sacrifice, don't you think?"

"Sacrifice, indeed," Mabel snapped, then relented as she looked at his disapproving expression. "I am thinking about it, Basil, actually. Really, I am."

He brightened. "That's the way. Think it through. That's all the boy asks."

The boy appeared in the dining room doorway. "Ready?"

"Coming," Basil said. He bent to kiss his wife again. "See you on Saturday, my dear. I'll catch a morning train."

"You're not staying in town *again?*" Mabel asked, in sudden dismay.

"Needs must, my sweet. Dinner with the directors tonight, big conference first thing Friday morning. Must be fresh and bright," Basil said. "It might go on to all hours, and will probably end with another dinner out. I don't particularly relish the milk train. I'll stay at my club, as usual. Tell you what, I'll bring you a pressy to make up, all right? 'Bye, darling."

Mabel stared at the doorway resentfully, and heard the front door slam on their low-voiced conversation. She looked around the empty dining room, and found no joy in the satinwood panelling or the silver on the sideboard. She stared at the cold toast on her plate. "Bloody hell," she said.

CHAPTER SEVEN

The Wychford "cop shop" could easily have been mistaken for a small college or public school building by some passing stranger. Built along Georgian lines, it stood at the top of the sloping High Street, under the benign protection of several huge chestnut trees.

Inside, however, it could have been mistaken for nothing else. Gutted and redecorated in the mid-seventies, it featured worn dark green linoleum, cracked tan plastic upholstery, ribbed glass, and chrome. A gesture toward public relations had been made in the reception area with the addition of two large "Swiss cheese" plants, but their growth had been so uninhibited that they reminded one unpleasantly of the tangled webs woven by deception. It was, however, as clean as tired ladies could make it each night, and did *not* smell of disinfectant.

It smelt of computer terminals.

Jennifer identified herself to the constable at the desk, and was conducted through a blank door, down a blank corridor, and into a small room where

Barry Treat sat shaking, hiccuping, and refusing hot sweet tea proffered by a cool sweet WPC.

"Oh, God, Dr. Eames, it was *ghastly!*" he shrieked, the minute Jennifer came through the door. "She was absolutely drained, one could see right through her hands, those lovely, gifted hands, so still, so, so . . ."

"So forget it," Jennifer said, brusquely. She had been administering to Mr. Treat's bodily frailties for some months, now, and had learned that he responded best to a firm hand and no nonsense. When she went on, however, her voice was gentler. "I know viewing the dead is upsetting, but what you saw wasn't really your cousin, you know. It was just something she left behind. It's terrible, and a great shock, but you have to pull yourself together and not give in. You have a sensitive nature. You'll only do *yourself* harm with hysterics, and there's no point in that." Over Mr. Treat's head the WPC gave her a thumbs-up sign. "Why didn't you want to go to the hospital, anyway?"

"Oh, God, I hate the places," Mr. Treat moaned. Jennifer's plain talking seemed to have ended the hysterics, but self-pity threatened to replace them. "My mother died in a hospital, my father died in a hospital, my closest, dearest friend died in a hospital, people go in and never come out, I can't . . ."

"I get the picture, Mr. Treat," Jennifer said, opening her bag. "You're not keen on hospitals." She found what she was looking for and began to prepare a disposable syringe. Treat glanced up and turned green.

"Is that necessary?" he quavered.

Jennifer looked down at him and sighed. "You don't like injections, either?" He shook his head, a small tear slipping from one of his long eyes. He had clownishly large features in a small face, his chin swamped by nose and eyes. He wore elfin clothes in brown and orange; smock, silk shirt, tight trousers, pointed leather boots. There was something fey and child-like about him—and he knew it. She snapped the syringe and threw it in the bin, then found some tranquillisers. She gave him two, and quickly wrote out a prescription for a few more.

"Get this filled on the way home," she said. "Or would you be better off going to work?"

"Gordon will be expecting me," Treat said, feebly, putting down the paper cup of water the WPC had given him.

"Are you all right to drive?"

He gave a great sigh of suffering, but it was obvious he couldn't wait to get out to his partner and tell the dramatic all of his morning's experiences. "I'll manage," he said. "One must go on, mustn't one?"

"Oh, indeed, it's the only way," Jennifer agreed, not unkindly. His manner was unfortunate. For all his posturing, she could see that he was genuinely upset. Most people would be, in similar circumstances, and creative, imaginative people more than most. "Have you finished with him?" she asked the WPC.

"Oh, yes, ma'am," the girl said. "It was only for identification. He was fine at the scene, but when we came back here to fill in the statement . . ."

Mr. Treat stood up and fixed her with a glare. "I don't like police stations, either," he said, and, gathering his tattered dignity about him, he strode out. His exit was marred by a brief tussle with the door, which opened inward instead of outward, but eventually he won. His footsteps went lightly away, faster and faster.

Jennifer closed her bag and looked at the WPC. "Anything I can do for you? You look done in."

"Thanks for the offer," the woman grinned. "If it's not the company, it's the hours. We don't get many murders around here. It was pretty unpleasant, but I haven't actually fainted, yet. No doubt I'll save up and do it right in front of the chief inspector, knowing my luck."

"Oh, I think you'll cope all right," Jennifer said, following her out into the hall. "This is the second one, isn't it?"

"There was a similar one in Woodbury, yes," the WPC said, cooly.

"Any connection between the two?"

The girl looked at her, reproachfully.

"Sorry," Jennifer said. "I shouldn't have asked."

The WPC sighed. "You aren't the first, and you won't be the last, Dr. Eames. I'm afraid most people will jump to the same conclusion." She paused in the doorway. "Blimey, there he is now."

"Who?"

"The DCI—detective chief inspector. The big one."

As they emerged into the reception area, two men were talking to the constable manning the desk. The taller of the two turned, casually, and then stared. Jennifer stared, too.

"Jenny Eames? What the devil are *you* doing here?" he demanded.

The last time Jenny had seen Luke Abbott had been at a school cricket match the day she'd left Wychford. He'd looked splendid all in white and padded up, arguing with the umpire, his bat whirling dangerously as he gestured. The older man had looked thoroughly alarmed, she remembered, and probably with good cause.

In the intervening years he'd grown taller and leaner, learned to polish his shoes, no longer had scabs on his knuckles, and had developed a nice line in smiles. The buccaneer's moustache he wore looked right on him, as did his well-cut three-piece suit. However, she sensed—even in that moment—that his brash adolescent spirit had been tested by some terrible pain to produce a deeper strength and sensitivity than he had ever shown as a boy. He had been her hero, then. She had expected him to become a professional sportsman, or a lawyer, or a doctor, or even prime minister. But not this.

"Detective Chief Inspector?" she gasped. "You?"

"What's wrong with being a policeman?" he demanded, rather defensively, all too aware of the eyes and ears around them. "Perfectly respectable profession."

"Oh, yes, I agree. Absolutely." Her mouth quirked. "I just wondered how you got promoted so far. With your temper, I would have expected you to be constantly in the doghouse—or whatever the police equivalent is."

He grinned. "I've been there once or twice. As it happens, I've learned to control my temper and have risen through my own dazzling brilliance. What else?"

"I hesitate to think." She glanced around the reception area. "One thing hasn't changed, I see."

"What's that?"

"They're all still scared of you."

"That's because he's a big mean bastard," came a laconic voice from beside them. It was Luke's sergeant, his amused expression giving the lie to his statement. "What was he like as a kid, then?"

Jennifer looked at Abbott, who gazed dangerously back. "A *skinny*, mean bastard," she smiled. "Very breezy when in a good temper, very nasty when not. People tended to go around him in wide circles."

"Mmmm. Still the same, then," Paddy nodded, grinning.

Abbott glanced at the constables watching them from behind the reception desk, and cleared his throat. This whole thing was getting out of hand, in addition to which, he had a job to do.

"Well, it looks as if we're going to be around here for a while. Maybe we can get together some evening."

"That would be nice. I'm living with my aunt and uncle—I've taken over his practice." Abbott nodded, as if he'd already known that—so his surprise hadn't been at seeing her, but at seeing her in the police station. Jennifer hesitated. "Win Frenholm was one of our patients," she said, carefully. The change in him was sudden and total. She was no longer an old childhood friend recognised and indulged for a social moment or two. She was pertinent to his investigation.

"Oh?" he said. "Had you seen her recently?"

"As a matter of fact, I saw her yesterday morning," Jennifer said, a little disconcerted by the sharpness of his glance and tone. "She was on Dr. Gregson's list and normally saw him. But we do an open surgery in the mornings, seeing patients as they come in, and yesterday she specifically asked for the "lady doctor." When I talked to her it was apparent why—she wanted an abortion."

"And did you agree to help her obtain one?"

"I explained the customary procedure," Jennifer said. "I also suggested that she discuss it with the father, first. She said he wanted nothing more to do with her, and that suited her just fine."

"Did she tell you his name?"

"No. She was pretty upset—she seemed to think I could do it for her there and then, on my own. When she heard about having to get other opinions and all the rest of the rigamarole to have it on the National Health, or paying to go private, she went a little crazy. Then, after a minute, she went quite cold. It was eerie to watch, really. She began to ask me about blood tests to prove paternity, all that sort of thing. Her mind seemed to be going a hundred miles an hour. She was an extraordinary girl in many ways—totally egotistical, I'd say. Even ruthless. And yet, with that angel face of hers, she could probably con anyone into believing her to be a sweet, innocent child. She said she knew who the father would be. She said he could afford—"

"*Would* be?"

"She said, 'I know who he'll be, the poor bastard.' "

"Then she could have been referring to the child."

Jennifer thought about that. "I suppose she could have been, at that. As a matter of fact, I asked her what she meant, but she just gave me an enigmatic look and said she'd be back in a day or two with it all 'worked out.' "

"She said this yesterday morning?"

"Yes."

"And then she was murdered yesterday evening," Paddy observed, quietly.

"But, surely . . ." Jennifer began.

"What?" Abbott asked.

"The other woman—in Woodbury. Wasn't it the same kind of killing? Isn't it the same killer?"

"That's exactly why we're on our way out there," Abbott said. "It makes you wonder, doesn't it?"

CHAPTER EIGHT

Luke Abbott viewed the body of Win Frenholm with dispassionate interest, as a surgeon might. It was no longer a person but a problem.

"Attractive girl," he said, quietly. She'd been about thirty, with long blond hair and a slim delicate figure. Small regular features in a fine-boned face. The blankness of death gave no indication of her personality. Jennifer Eames had said she was egotistical, even ruthless, and could probably make people believe anything. Apparently somebody hadn't been charmed. Her clothing was individual and somewhat "arty"—but the colourful top and trousers were clean, well kept, and, he guessed, quite expensive.

The woman in Woodbury had been much older and no longer so obviously attractive. "She was pregnant, by the way," he said, to no one in particular.

Cyril Franklin, on his knees in the grass beside the body, looked up at him in surprise, wondering if Abbott had developed second sense.

Luke smiled. "Her doctor told me she'd been after an abortion." His eyes noted details. "Wound goes from left to right, one cut, clean, powerful, probably a right-handed man coming from behind." Cyril sighed, took off his black-rimmed glasses and began to clean them as Luke continued to state the obvious. "No defence cuts on the palms of the hands, no torn fingernails, nothing to indicate a fight of any kind."

The girl's clothes were blood-soaked, particularly down the right side, but, as with the woman in Woodbury, they were not disarranged or torn. "Killed where she was found?" Paddy asked.

"I'd say probably," Cyril pointed with his spectacles. "Regular outline in this pool of blood. It congealed around her. Not as much blood as you might expect from the size of the wound, but she was pretty skinny."

"Same as the other one?" Luke asked, too quietly.

Cyril was silent for a moment, looking at the girl, his glasses dangling from one hand. He didn't want to answer that, any more than Luke had wanted to ask it. Eventually, he put his glasses back on, and nodded. "Could be."

"I want to have a look around," Luke said, and turned away from the cruelly drained husk on the ground. Easier to view a place. Easier not to get angry, that way. After a few steps, he turned back. "There's one thing you could do for me, if you wouldn't mind." He told Franklin what he wanted.

"My God, you're a cold bastard," Cyril said. Then he grinned. "I should have thought of it myself, of course."

"I want the whole works, mind," Luke said. "Anything at all you can discover might be a help."

"It shall be done, oh Great One, even unto the last molecule," Cyril said. "Should be fascinating."

"Kind of a cold bastard yourself, aren't you?" Luke observed.

"Cold hands, warm heart."

"Of course," Luke nodded, and turned back to Paddy, who was waiting on the path.

Swann Way was the respectable part of the old towpath beside the River Purle. It had been tidied up, renamed, and some houses had been built there in the thirties, with lawns leading down to the water. There were still old boathouses along the bank here and there, and the remains of docks visible in the water, but after the war they had mostly been allowed to fall into disuse and then ruin, as the big old houses became a drag on the market. The river was now back in fashion, but the towpath was thought by the new residents to be a bit of a bother. It meant strangers, not fairies, at the bottom of their gardens.

Since the war the River Purle hadn't seen much through-traffic, for many parts of the course that connected it with the Thames were narrowed or silted too shallow for large family-sized boats. Only small craft could use its full length, and there were some stretches of it only dedicated fishermen saw, now. The towpath had more or less disappeared along most of it, but Swann Way was clear because the locals used it as a shortcut between the town and the new housing estate. It was just beyond this clear stretch that Win Frenholm's stylishly booted foot had been seen protruding from beneath the bush where she lay on a crimson bed of her own blood.

The area was now blocked off by the police. Several gawkers were hovering, and a boat was drifting nearby. The two men in it were ostensibly fishing, but had their eyes fixed on the towpath and the activity there.

"You can see more or less what must have happened," PC Bennett said. He was the local constable assigned to liaise with the CID, and he was nervously eager to prove his worth. "He got her just as she reached the end of the shortcut and before she turned up the rise toward the town. Afraid the towpath's no good for prints—the council in its wisdom just put down a load of fresh gravel last week. No way of knowing whether she realised she was being followed and was running, or if she never knew he was there until he jumped her. The gravel is thick enough to hide anything like that."

"Anyplace where he might have waited for her?" Paddy asked, turning to look back up the towpath. "That old boathouse, for instance? You checked it out?"

Bennett nodded his head. "We've had a real good look at all of them, sir, as far back as the housing estate. Most of them are just falling apart or only used for rough storage, if they're still intact. We found a few places where fishermen have sat for the day, but no marks that might have been made by the killer, we don't think. Our best guess is that he followed her down the path from the housing estate itself."

"Anyone in those homes up there report a cry, running feet, anything?"

"Not so far. We're doing a house to house, naturally."

"Naturally." Luke's voice was quite neutral. "Who found the body?"

"Oddly enough, one of her business partners—chap named Barry Treat. He was taking the shortcut into town, saw her foot sticking out. He recognised the boot right away, apparently they're hand-made by one of the craft workers up at the centre." Bennett consulted his notebook. "Said he felt a 'premonition,' because he knew it was hers. Went a few steps on, stopped when he saw the blood, then ran for the nearest phone. He was all right at first, then collapsed at the station. High-strung chap," he added, austerely.

"You say he's a business partner?"

"He's a second cousin, actually. Only living relative, I understand. She had one of the craft shops out at Monkswell with him and another chap, name of Gordon Sinclair. Potters, they are. Were. Well, the other two still are, I mean." Bennett's aplomb slipped, momentarily, as he scrabbled to clarify things. "They also shared a house on the estate—but there was nothing funny. Well, there was. But not with the girl."

"With the two men?"

"Possibly. Only guessing, of course."

"Oh, come on, now, Bennett, I can take it."

"Both as queer as coots, sir," Bennett said, with a relieved smile.

"So not likely to have been the father of her unborn child."

"Christ, no!" Bennett instantly regretted his vehemence. "I mean—"

"Go on."

"Well, they don't make any bones about it, sir. All flags flying, so to speak."

"I see. A great many flags, or just a few?"

"Sir?"

"I was just wondering about camouflage, that's all. But I can't see any reason for it, in this day and age. Just a thought. Rather a coincidence that *he* should find her. You say this Treat is a relative?"

"Second cousin. Aren't any others, apparently."

"So he inherits her all? Or was there a will? Or perhaps a partnership agreement?"

"We haven't gotten that far, yet, sir."

Paddy grinned. "What? Five hours gone and you haven't gotten that far, yet?"

"Sir . . ."

Luke smiled, too. Bennett seemed a decent lad. "Carry on, Constable. You're doing fine. I'm just going to take a walk up the towpath, before that raincloud over there decides to burst. Coming, Paddy?"

They crunched along beside the river, which lived up to its name and murmured peacefully between its banks, overhung on the opposite side by large willows. Beyond them was a narrow band of wild growth, and beyond that, a sweep of lawn. "Peacock Manor, over there, Paddy. We passed it on the way in—big, splendid place with a circle drive, all leaded windows and ivy. I had big plans to grow up and buy the place with my millions, one day. Son of the house was about my age, went off to the best schools and all that, while I attended the local grammar. He played the toff on holidays, so I beat the hell out of him, one summer. No trouble to us, afterward. Not a bad chap, just . . ." His voice halted, but he went on walking.

"Just what?" Paddy asked, trying not to slip down the bank where the water had undercut the path.

Luke smiled. "Just bloody rich," he said.

"At the present rate of outgoings, I'd say another year or eighteen months will see you irretrievably in debt. It's a terrible thing, Mark, and I hate saying it, but there doesn't seem to be a way out. The money from the land sale for the housing estate was only a stop-gap and to finish off those death duties. Unless you're prepared to sell more land . . ." Heatherington, the bank manager, raised his hands and let them fall.

"I suppose another mortgage is out of the question?"

Heatherington looked at him over the top of his glasses. "Isn't that a bit Peter and Paul? If you had a regular income, Mark, or even if your stepfather's income was a bit *more* regular . . . the bank *might* consider it. But, in the present circumstances, no, I'm afraid not. Surely you don't *need* that land between the house and the river?"

"Of course we don't *need* it," Mark agreed, a bit savagely. "But it's part of what makes the house so special. I showed you the plans for the conference centre. That area would be landscaped for a small golf course. If we sell that off, the conference centre would lose a valuable asset and drawing card."

"What about the land in back of the house, then?"

"I suppose we could sell off that top parcel, Fox Run. It's over the round of the hill, out of sight of the house itself. The local hunt would set up a howl, of course, but I can't go under just to see a lot of animal lovers in red coats have their little entertainments, can I? Do you think we could find a buyer for it?"

"I happen to know a national conglomerate is looking in the area for a suitable site," Heatherington said, slowly.

"Site for what?"

"A hypermarket."

Mark paled. "Anyone else looking?"

"An electronics firm, perhaps. And a couple of speculative builders. I'll look around, shall I?" Assured of some business and the continued solvency of an old and valued customer, Heatherington became more expansive. "I don't suppose you have your eye on any heiresses, do you?" he smiled.

Mark Peacock raised an eyebrow. "Don't think I haven't considered it," he said. "But I find it hard to be quite *that* cold-blooded about saving the manor. If one wafts into my line of vision, fine, but I refuse to go fortune-hunting." Unlike Basil, he thought to himself. And look what *he* got, thinking Mother was so wealthy. The house fooled Basil, as it fooled so many others, Mark himself included, in a way. Ah, but he loved it. Loved it enough to stop seeing Jennifer Eames before he found himself well and truly in love with her, and willing to throw sense to the winds. She was a super girl, but he could hardly expect her to take on him, his mother, Basil, *and* the worry about the manor. Besides, he didn't for a minute think she would have him. If only Mother would let go of the reins, he thought. If only I were stronger and could tell her to go to hell.

"Well, I'll leave it with you, then," he said, standing up and extending his hand toward Heatherington. "As soon as you've located a possible buyer, let me know." The bank manager assured him that it would be soon, and they parted.

Outside, in the street, Mark took a deep breath. Rain had come and gone while he'd been in the bank, and the newly washed air was fresh.

He started toward his car, and saw Jennifer Eames coming out of the chemist's shop opposite. Waiting a moment, to say hello if she crossed the street, he saw her glance his way, and then walk on, her head high.

Mark felt something twist inside him. He got into his car. Basil Taubman turned and raised an eyebrow. "Well?"

Mark watched Jennifer get into her car and drive off, then jabbed his key toward his own ignition, and missed. "We'll probably have to sell off Fox Run," he said, angrily. "He wouldn't give us any more time. Sounds like there are several possibilities—such as a hypermarket."

"Mabel would never stand for *that*," Basil said, visions of a possible scene conjured up before his horrified eyes.

"That's what I'm counting on," Mark said. "If I point out to her that this is the only alternative, it might swing her over to the plan, and she'd sign the damned papers at last."

"How much time do you have?"

"Oh, Heatherington has to do some homework. Now I've told him I'm willing to sell—or intimated I am—he's apt to be quiet for a month or two. Also, his wife is socially ambitious, and they'd like to stay on Mabel's good side. They assume, you see, that there is one." His smile was wry. "We can hold things off, but eventually . . ." Mark slumped back in his seat. "You've *got* to convince her, Basil."

"I'll do my best," his stepfather said, and smiled. "I've been known to have my little successes in the past."

Mark stiffened. "Never mind the past. It's the future we're concerned about, here."

"Point taken, dear boy," Basil agreed. "And now, if you'll drop me at the station, as advertised, I'll do what I can toward paying the bills. All right?"

Mark glanced at him. "All right. Thanks."

Basil shrugged. *"De nada.* I want things to work out as much as you do. I love the house, too—it is my spiritual home as well as my physical one. I've *told* you that, many times. I'll do anything I can to keep it. You *know* that."

"Yes, I know." His stepfather's psychic vagaries about the house sometimes verged on the embarrassing, but he was grateful for any support. Mark turned the ignition and started the car. First the station, then back home. He drove recklessly toward Martyr's Bridge, cutting in front of a lorry and causing it to slam on its air brakes. He went over the bridge too fast, and had to brake wildly to avoid a tour bus parked on the opposite side.

Soon it would be time to take Mother to Milchester.

He would have preferred a warmer destination for her.

"The first thing we want to do is try to find out who the father of her child was," Luke told Paddy, who was making notes. "Obviously we talk to her cousin and his friend, then her other friends, and try to build up a picture of her."

"And the papers? What do you want me to release to the papers?"

Luke considered. "Tell them there are certain similarities between this killing and the one in Woodbury, but don't elaborate. If I know them, that's all they'll bloody need. I don't want to give anything away." He looked at Paddy, who raised an eyebrow.

"Well, both were women and both had their throats cut, those are certainly similarities," Paddy said, shrugging. "But you know they're bound to start putting together some kind of Ripper thing."

"Maybe that's just what we've got," Luke said, bleakly.

"I thought you didn't want to talk about that," Paddy reminded him.

"I don't. Cyril didn't—as I'm sure you noticed. But you're right, it's something we have to consider. We *also* have to consider the possibility of a copy-cat killing—which is why we have a lot of legwork ahead of us, to see if we can find reasons either to connect these women, or to separate them into having individual reasons for being murdered. If it *is* a copy-cat killing, it won't do either murderer any harm to think we're looking for a maniac. It might lull them into being careless about alibis and such. Alternatively, if we *are* looking for a maniac, he may surface, eventually. They often do."

Paddy frowned. "By killing again, you mean?"

Luke nodded, his face grim. "And again. And again. And again."

CHAPTER NINE

Monkswell Craft Centre was a low grey stone rectangle set back some two hundred yards from the main road. A large but tastefully lettered sign indicated the turn-off onto a gravelled road which led to a rather unevenly surfaced parking area on the far side of the buildings. Luke and Paddy left the car there and picked their way down the flagstoned path that led through the low arch in the wall.

The old cloisters had been beautifully restored, and the open central area paved over. The aged stonework was mottled here and there with white and green lichen, and the graceful pointed arches of the covered walkway were complete again. Carved stone rosettes bracketed them one by one, and at each roof corner of the inner square a small gargoyle stuck out a tongue at the devil. Simple hand-made benches had been placed around a fountain in the middle, providing seating for shoppers or patrons of the small coffee shop that had been placed on the site of the original kitchens. At the moment the fountain was rather redundant, as it had begun to rain again, and the drops that were projected upward were swamped by those coming down. Rainwater gushed from the gargoyles into small basins below their chins, and their mischievous expressions had taken on a sullen air, due to the glistening overlay of moisture. No one sat on the benches, and the pigeons (for there was clear evidence of pigeons) had gone somewhere dry to roost. The scene was bleak, set for a party to which no one had come.

All around the inner side of the old cloister walkway, however, brightly lit windows revealed the various craft shops and their wares. Chunky, amusing sweaters from the Knit-Wits, wrought iron and tinsmithing at Clangers, silk flowers at Rosie's Posies, hand-dipped candles at Off Our Wick, homespun shawls and clothing at Get Weaving. In addition to these rather archly named endeavours there were other artisans at work who simply had their names and crafts over their doors—a carpenter making pine furniture, a stained-glass artist, a portrait sculptress, a leather worker. Win Frenholm's shop had belonged to the first category—it was called The Three Wheelers, and its small display window was crammed with rather odd pots and plates.

Luke, wincing at some of the more gaudy specimens, looked through the glass shelving to the shop beyond, and saw two men in close conversation. They were holding hands.

The smaller of the two had been crying—so, presumably, he was the sensitive Mr. Barry Treat. The other, a rough-hewn type in a clay-spattered pullover, had to be Gordon Sinclair. He was scowling down at his partner, his eyebrows drawn darkly together under his overhanging thatch of grey hair.

Luke turned to Paddy. "Do you know, I think I'd like a cup of coffee, first. How about you?"

"Always a good place to start," Paddy acknowledged. They went down to the snack bar and entered its steamy fragrant interior. A long counter with stools ran down one side, in the American style, and five small round tables took up the rest of the space. There were checked plastic tablecloths on the tables, and small pots of artificial flowers in the centre of each (courtesy of Rosie's Posies?). Luke's nose told him baking was done on the premises, as did the homely look of the pastries and cakes displayed under glass on the counter. He also deduced that bacon had been cooked that morning, and that the coffee was fresh. In short, here was something special—not the usual stewed tea and damp buns. Three women, seated at the rear with their heads together over empty cups, glanced up at them and then at each other. Luke nodded and sat down at the counter with Paddy. The man behind the coffee urn emerged and took their order. He was bald and comfortable-looking, with a tattoo showing beneath the edge of his white short-sleeved T-shirt.

"Two coffees, please, white. Bit far inland for you, isn't it?" Paddy asked.

The man grinned, showing old-fashioned false teeth somewhat the worse for wear, and drew coffee from the big urn that reflected his porcelain grin. "You might say that," he agreed, amiably.

"Here's to the Merchant Marine," Luke said, approvingly, toasting the tattoo with his coffee cup.

"That's it. Something to eat with your coffee?" the man asked.

"No, thanks very much," Luke said.

"Pie looks nice," Paddy said. "I'll have a piece of that."

"Made it myself, this morning." The man cut a large wedge of the sugar-crusted apple pie and presented it to Paddy with a flourish. "You'll like that, you will. Dutch recipe. Give you a bit of energy on a day like this." He regarded them thoughtfully. "Come to interview the two in the pottery, have you?" he said, after a moment.

"What gave us away?" Luke asked, not denying it.

"Eyes," the man said, leaning on the counter. "With the police, the eyes are never still. Always watching, you are. Just in case someone starts something, I suppose. Bad view of life to carry with you, gentlemen. Very cynical. Shame about the girl."

"You knew her?"

"Know them all," the man said. He raised his voice, slightly. "Police, here, ladies—come about Win."

"Damn," Luke muttered into his cup. He turned and gave the ladies a wide, white smile, which was not returned. "Afternoon, all," he said, and then mentally kicked himself for sounding like Dixon of Dock Green. It was a trap he always tried to avoid. He could hear Paddy choking quietly on his pie. "Shut up," he muttered, and increased the voltage on the smile. "Do you mind if I join you?"

The three women were wildly disparate in appearance. One was tall, angular, and white-haired; one was small, dark, and plump; the last was a real Titian-haired beauty.

"I suppose you might as well," the older woman said. Her eyes were faintly pink, as if she might have been crying some time earlier. "Could we have more coffee, Sam, please?"

"Right away," said the bald man.

Luke settled himself in a chair beside their table. "I'm Detective Chief Inspector Abbott," he said.

"Abbott of the Yard?" asked the red head.

"No, Abbott of the Regional Crime Squad," he smiled. "I admit, it lacks a certain tone. Do you all work here at the centre?"

"We're the Knit-Wits. That's Mary Straker," said the red head, indicating her dark-haired partner. "I'm Annabel Leigh. Hannah Putnam, here, is the portrait sculptress."

"I saw some of your work as I passed through, Miss Putnam. I particularly liked the small figure at the back."

Hannah Putnam's harshly lined face took on a more amenable expression. "Old Tom?" she asked. "Only thing worth showing. Thank you."

"Hannah does kid's heads during the summer to keep her alive while she does her own stuff in the winter," Annabel volunteered. "That's how most of us work. We get a little burst around Christmas, but summer is our main selling time. Things are quiet, now, as you see."

"They won't be for long," Paddy said, coming over with his coffee. "I understand your local paper comes out mid-afternoon. You might find yourselves busy very soon after."

"You mean ghouls?" Hannah asked, with distaste. "I suppose that is inevitable."

"Won't be entirely a bad thing," Luke said, easily, leaning back. "They might well spend some money while they're here."

"No publicity is bad publicity," volunteered Sam, from behind the counter.

Hannah Putnam turned in her chair to fix him with a hard stare. "That is not in very good taste, Sam Ashforth."

He was unabashed. "Still true, though. Ray Moss was saying this morning he had some old sketches he did of her, he was going to get them out and frame them up, ready for trade. You've got a head of her, too, Hannah, I know you have. Could sell it at a good price, now." He was aware of their disapproval, and his tone became defensive. "Look, we're going down the drain, here, even if none of you will admit it. She didn't do much for us while she was alive, God knows. Let her do some good when she's dead." His expression was truculent, a prophet patronised in his own country.

Luke kept his face neutral. "I didn't notice the name Ray Moss on any of the shops. Is he one of the craftsmen, here?"

"He's a lithographer and printer. If you go through the tunnel opposite the archway, you'll find his studio in a long barn beside the cloisters. I think it used to be a granary. Most of us have some of his things up in our places. We sell them for him and take a small commission. He doesn't mind being watched, that's one of the conditions under which these places are let to us, but he hates dealing with the public directly." There was something in Annabel Leigh's voice that intrigued Luke.

"Is he good?"

"His work is exquisite," Hannah Putnam pronounced. "It is all he lives for. As an artist he is a model to us all." She paused. "As a human being—less so."

Mary Straker leaned forward and spoke for the first time. "He is huge, and gross, and when he eats he always leaves a little food in the corners of his mouth. He is disgusting." She looked a little startled at her own boldness, and sat back in her chair, grasping her coffee cup in both hands.

"I see. You say he has some sketches of Win Frenholm?"

"She modelled for many of us at one time or another," Hannah explained. "As Sam said, I have done a bust of her. Also a full-body study. She had wonderful bones, perfect proportions, and could stay still for long periods. These days, so many of them fidget. It is an art in itself, being still. She had that."

"You didn't like her." It wasn't a question. Hannah Putnam regarded him steadily for a moment.

"I expect you will find all this out in due course, and I see no reason for hiding it. No, I didn't like her. I loved her. It was a love she did not return. She had the cruelty that occasionally accompanies great beauty. She gave herself to many men, for they were always after her, and it pleased her to see them crawl. She hated men, but that didn't mean she loved women. Only herself." The older woman spoke with great dignity. Luke felt sorry for her, and was impressed by her forthrightness. She made no excuses, had no pretenses. Despite her age, she herself had an undeniable beauty. Her spare figure was dressed simply in a black sweater and trousers, and she looked him straight in the eye. After a moment, Annabel Leigh put her hand over Hannah's, and spoke with careful emphasis.

"Win Frenholm was a bitch, and you're going to find a lot of suspects out here, I'm afraid. I wish you luck, Inspector. In the year we've been here, she made a play for my husband, and for Mary's. I could cheerfully have killed her myself. But I didn't. We had a party here, last night. Most of us attended it. Win did, too. A sort of end-of-season let-your-hair-down. She circulated, disappeared, returned, circulated, disappeared again, returned again, then went for good. It was a pattern she had. Perhaps the last man she seduced could tell you what you want to know. We can't."

"I see," Luke said. "Well, I thank you for your frankness." He stood up. "If you'd be kind enough to tell Sergeant Smith, here, all the details you can remember about last night, I'll go have a chat with Mr. Moss."

He left Paddy getting out his notebook, and emerged again into the damp shadows of the cloisters. He followed the stone walk around to the tunnel and came out in front of the Granary Press. The big double door was open, and he went in to the sharp smell of acid, chemicals, ink, and hot machinery. He supposed it was all part of the lithographic process. At first the long, cavernous room seemed empty, but he spotted a broad back hunched over a workbench at the far end. "Mr. Moss?"

The figure jerked upright and turned. In the harsh overhead light, Ray Moss resembled a bad-tempered bear roused from an incomplete hibernation. Thick straight hair hung over his bearded face, and black eyes burned through the fringe as he glared at the intruder. "Well?"

Luke showed his warrant card. "I'm Detective Chief Inspector Abbott. I'm investigating the death of Win Frenholm. I understand you knew her, and I was wondering if you could tell me anything about her?"

Moss snorted. "I could tell you where every mole on her body was, if that's what you mean. She was a scrawny bitch, but what meat she had was prime."

"That isn't exactly what I meant." Luke was surprised to find himself annoyed by the rawness of Moss's reply. He was hardly a protected species, himself, but the brute smell and attitude of the man was somehow shocking. He seemed to have no spiritual dimension at all, but simply to exist as an animal exists, for and of the flesh. And yet, as Luke went forward, he saw examples of what was presumably this same man's work on the walls, and found it equally unsettling. Instead of explicit pornography or bold colour graphics, they were the most delicate of flower studies, still-lifes of hedgerows, bracken, tiny animals, stream beds, birds. "I meant what *kind* of person she was, and whether you spoke to her last night at all. I believe there was a party here?"

"I didn't go to the goddamn party. I was working. I'm working now," he added, pointedly.

Luke glanced down at the workbench and saw about a dozen sketches in the same delicate hand that had done those on the wall. It was not difficult to recognize the likeness of the dead woman he'd seen a few hours before. "I see. You're matting those for sale, are you?"

"What if I am?" Moss's voice was threatening.

Abbott shrugged. "I'd have thought you might like to keep them. As a remembrance, perhaps?"

"If I *wanted* to remember I might. I haven't got an alibi, if that's what you're after. I was here alone until after midnight, and then I went upstairs to bed." He indicated a rough ladder-like staircase leading up to a hole in the wooden ceiling. "I keep a bed here, in the loft. Not supposed to, but nobody says anything. Cheaper than renting some other place to sleep. All I want is my work, so what use is some goddamned flat or house to me?"

"No use at all, I don't suppose," Luke said, calmly. The man's simple physical presence was a kind of threat, and he was not surprised Moss rarely sold any of his work himself. Customers would have been terrified of him. "I understand she came and went several times during the party. Did she come to visit you during one of those absences?"

Moss had a sharp Stanley knife in one of his huge hands, and he was cutting conte board to matt the sketches. The knife stopped moving, lifted momentarily from the cardboard, and then, very delicately, returned to its task. "No," Moss said.

"Are you cer—"

"I said no."

And you're lying, Luke thought to himself. He looked at some of the sketches that were already matted and covered in a thin clear protective film. "How much are you asking for that one?" he asked, indicating a chaste nude study of Win Frenholm. She was three-quarters turned away, sitting with her knees clasped to her chest, the fine curve of her spine and the smooth shadows of her back taking the light. Her head was turned toward the viewer, and while there was no sexuality in the pose, there was a kind of challenge in the face to which few men would fail to respond. Her long hair was caught up high on her head, but strands had escaped and drifted over the nape of her neck and her shoulders. It was exquisite.

"Fifty quid," Moss said, brusquely.

"Would you take a personal cheque?"

Moss turned and regarded him with some curiosity. "You want that?"

"It's very beautiful," Luke said, truthfully. "I have a good place for it in my flat, where the afternoon light would strike it at exactly the right angle. Yes, I would like it."

Moss seemed disconcerted, and looked away. "Why?"

"I think it might remind me of the reason I became a police officer in the first place," Luke said, simply. "She was alive—now she's dead. Her life was stolen from her. Whoever she was, whatever she was, that's wrong. That should be punished."

Moss considered this. "What about at night? Where would the light come from at night?"

"I have a Chinese lamp, rather low and to the left." Luke waited.

"A cheque would be fine." Moss walked away, as if he didn't want to see it being written. "Just put it on the shelf above."

"She did come here, didn't she?" Luke said, as he wrote. Moss made a kind of noise, half sob, half snarl. He kept his back turned.

"She came. I had her. She went. She was like that. She . . . let me, when she felt like it. When she was bored. Sometimes she laughed at me, said I smelled, said I was revolting. I didn't care what she said, as long as she let me touch her. She was . . . perfect. Every inch of her. Perfect as a flower."

Luke tore out the cheque and put it carefully on the shelf above the workbench. He picked up the sketch. "What time did she come? What time did she leave?"

"She came about seven, left before eight. Went back to the party, I guess. I could hear the noise."

"And you didn't go, yourself?"

"I wouldn't waste my time on most of them, bunch of arty-farty amateurs. Maybe three real artists here, that's all. People who *care* about their work, people who don't just turn out what's trendy, what's saleable."

"Artists have to survive, too."

"Only to work," was the angry reply. Moss still had his back turned. "Anything else you got to ask?"

"Not at this moment, no. I may be back."

"Oh, feel free to drop in anytime." Moss's tone, a parody of politeness, returned to its former growl. "I'm not going anywhere."

Abbott met Paddy Smith halfway back down the tunnel. "Well?" Paddy asked.

Abbott felt subdued by his encounter with Moss. "She was with him from seven to eight." He held out the picture, tilted it so the grey light from the rainy afternoon was not reflected by the Pliofilm cover. "He's twice my size, has no gift for words, is heavily furred, and growls like a bear. She laughed at him, insulted him, consorted with him—playing her version of the princess and the monster. However, that's how he felt about her." He turned the sketch for Paddy to see.

Paddy whistled, softly. "Poor bastard."

Luke nodded. "Time to see the grieving cousin, I think."

CHAPTER TEN

Insistent hammering on the door of The Three Wheelers eventually produced Gordon Sinclair from the rear of the shop. Scowling, he opened the door and spoke through the gap. "We're closed today."

Abbott produced his warrant card. "I'm sorry, but I'm afraid it's necessary."

"Couldn't it wait until tomorrow?" Sinclair wanted to know.

"I'm afraid not." Luke smiled and looked expectant.

"Bloody Bolshevik," Sinclair muttered, but he unchained the door and let them pass within, rechaining it behind them. For good measure he pulled down a blind and hooked it at the bottom, and turned to face them. "Come in the back. We're working."

His freshly spattered smock had already told them that. They followed him between the display cabinets. Paddy's eye chanced to fall on a price tag, and he nearly stumbled. One hundred and fifteen pounds for a lamp base? A lime-green-and-purple lamp base? With . . . things stuck on it? Or had they possibly grown there, like fungi? They certainly resembled fungi. Poisonous fungi, at that.

He knew something about art, was rarely certain what he liked, but he knew what he didn't like, and that definitely was it.

Through the curtains at the back, they found a large workroom with (true to the name of the shop) three potter's wheels. Drying racks filled a lot of the space, and a huge kiln took up most of the rear wall. Sinks and workbenches completed the picture of an active, if small, pottery.

A small bedraggled figure was seated behind one of the humming wheels, poking dejectedly at a pot which was obviously going to be a big hit as it was lopsided and had a tear down one side. Paddy sighed, and felt very non-U.

"Police, dear," Gordon Sinclair said, going over to Barry Treat and placing an encouraging hand on his shoulder. "Buck up."

"Oh, God!" Barry said, and swept the pot off his wheel with a dramatic gesture. "Oh, *GOD!*"

Paddy, leaning against a workbench, sighed heavily, and agreed with J. Alfred Prufrock. He should have been a pair of ragged claws, scuttling across the floors of ancient seas, instead of an overworked cop having to talk to a couple of raving queers about a murder. An interview with Mr. Treat was not going to be one.

Luke ignored the melodrama, as if it were a natural part of existence. He smiled at the two men. Treat brightened slightly. Sinclair glowered, clarifying the relationship instantly. Luke therefore concentrated on Mr. Treat.

"I'm sorry to intrude at a time like this, but I'm sure you're as anxious as we are to catch the murderer of your cousin, Mr. Treat."

"Of course he is," Sinclair said, impatiently.

"And although it will be difficult, I'd be very grateful if you'd go over the events of last night and this morning with me."

"Is that really necessary?" Sinclair interrupted. "He's given a statement to the police already, surely that's enough for you to be going on with."

Luke kept smiling. "Ah, yes, but that was just the local police who, though admirable, are not exactly experienced in the investigation of a murder."

"And you are?"

"I am. A macabre occupation, but mine own."

Paddy turned away so they would not see him smile. Luke was getting into the role now—playing up to them without mocking them. It was an art at which Paddy himself had never excelled. Straight in and straight on was his way. Luke was the chameleon. Luke was the dancer.

"Very well," sniffed Barry Treat. "No, Gordon, don't fuss, I'm all right. If it will help, I'm prepared to do what I can. After all, she was my . . . dearest cousin." He produced a deep sigh and visibly braced himself. "What do you wish to know?"

Luke pulled out a stool and settled himself elegantly, flipping open his notebook with an efficient flourish. Sinclair, upstaged, retreated sulkily to a workbench where he began slamming clay down again and again, making a nonverbal contribution with every thud.

"First of all, I believe Miss Frenholm lived with you?"

"We shared a house, yes. It was really like two flats, the way we did it up, although not really—if you know what I mean. Gordon and I had the rooms upstairs and Win the downstairs, sharing the kitchen and so on. It worked very well."

"It worked," muttered Sinclair. "Just."

Treat gave him a look and then turned back to Luke. "Gordon was just that wee bit jealous of the friendship I had with Win," he confided. "But, after all, she was my only relative. Her parents took me in when my parents died, and then she went on looking after me when they were taken. We went to art school together, worked in the same ghastly china factory when we graduated, and so on. Then I met Gordon and we had the chance to come here. Naturally, Win came along."

"Naturally," grunted Sinclair.

"Gordon, you never said you minded," Barry Treat protested. No reply, but a further series of thuds. "Anyway, we came here. Win was charming and a *great* asset when it came to selling our work."

Sinclair snorted and slammed down the clay with a great crash. "She was a promiscuous bitch, Barry, and you know it. If he's going to tell you fairy tales, Inspector, you'll be wasting your time. I'll tell you what you want to know. We lived in the same house, all right, but she was rarely there because she slept around so much. We can't tell you who her playmates were, I'm afraid. Last night was one of the rare occasions when she came back with us—I presume she was tired out after playing around with Moss and Timothy and whoever else was interested. Her contribution to community feeling, presumably." The venom in Sinclair's voice practically dripped.

"Timothy?" Luke asked. "Would that be Gary Timothy, the glassmaker?"

"Yes, he was one of her regulars. And there might have been a borrowed husband or six. When Win got tight she got insatiable. My God, she even made a pass at *me*, once."

"What?!?" shrieked Barry Treat.

"Oh, don't get upset," Sinclair said, with a momentary tenderness in his voice. "I just laughed her off. Well, it was ridiculous, she was . . . not normal. She was just an oversexed bitch who liked to play games with men. She went around searching for the Big O, as they say. But whatever kicks she got at the party can't have been enough, because she was on the phone within a few minutes of getting back to the house. I heard the ting as she put down the receiver. About ten minutes later she went out."

"What time would that have been?"

Sinclair considered. "About midnight, or so."

"Not a very late party, then?"

"It might have been, but we left around eleven-thirty. We're not late birds," Sinclair said. "I was surprised when Win left with us, as a matter of fact. She was behaving a little oddly—odd for her, that is. Oh, there were the in and outs with men during the party, yes, but there was something more to it. There was a kind of frantic quality about her, you know? I saw her using the phone a couple of times, too, during the evening. I guess she finally reached who she wanted when she got home. Maybe it was her killer. Maybe she knew she was going to die, and that's why she'd gone so hot and heavy all night. Sort of a last fling?" He made a face. "I guess that was a bit over the top, even for me. But she was *not* the same as usual. It wasn't for laughs."

"She was pregnant," Luke said. "Did she tell either of you?"

"Pregnant? Win? She never even . . ." Sinclair began, in some surprise, but Barry Treat gasped.

"You mean there was a baby? That a baby died, too? A tiny life within her . . . oh, God, how cruel. We might have had a little family, Gordon, a little baby to love."

This was too much, even for Luke. "She apparently planned to have an abortion," he said, brusquely. "We think she intended to meet the father last night to discuss his paying for it. Any idea who he might have been?"

"None," Gordon said, glancing at Barry, who was now trembling with a new emotion—frustrated motherhood. "Look, is there much more?"

"I'm afraid so," Luke said. "I understand Mr. Treat found the body this morning?"

"Oh, GOD!" shrieked Barry. "I want to forget that."

"You were going along the path to town . . ." Luke persisted. Gordon gave him a dirty look and went over to put an arm around Barry. "Why was that?"

"To . . . to get some milk," Barry hiccuped. "We'd forgotten to put out the thing for the milkman, and we were out of milk. There's a little shop by the bridge as you come up from the towpath. I ran because Gordon wasn't awake yet and I wanted to . . . make his tea . . . and I saw her boot . . . and . . . then her leg. At first I thought she was *in* there with someone—you know, in the bushes. But her foot didn't move. I went a little closer, and saw the blood . . . and then I ran. I didn't look anymore, I just ran to the little shop and the man called the police and they came and I had to go back, and it was Win . . . I told them I thought it was Win and it *was* Win. It was Win . . . and she was . . ." He gave a kind of gurgle and went pasty white. Sinclair supported him as he swayed.

"For Christ's sake, what more do you need?" he rasped.

"Who owns this shop?"

"I do," Sinclair said. "I own the house, the shop, everything. If it's inheritance you're thinking of, forget it. Barry gets nothing but grief from Win—as always. At least that will stop, now that the bitch is dead. I might have killed her, but not Barry. *He* thought she was wonderful."

They let themselves out of the pottery shop, Paddy with relief, Luke with resignation. "Two down, and the rest of the world to go," he said. "We've got two victims—one sensible faithful family woman, and one promiscuous tart. Where's the connection, Paddy? What the hell did they have in common?"

"They both met the wrong man at the wrong time," Paddy said, pointedly.

"You think so?"

"I'm afraid I do," Paddy said. "I'm afraid what we're chasing is a psychopath who kills women at random. I'm afraid he'll kill again."

"I'm still not convinced of that. And I'm certainly not sure about the random," Luke said, grimly, and headed toward the car.

CHAPTER ELEVEN

The physiotherapy department of the hospital was overwarm and overcrowded. Grunts and gasps of effort arose from various curtained cubicles as treatments were carried out. An occasional "ouch" pierced the ear. Above this mixture of sounds, as neutralising as piped music, there was the hum of small machines and a rhythmic splashing from the direction of the hydrotherapy pool.

Jennifer found Frances in her office. She was peeling wax from her shoes with intense concentration. Jennifer's hi startled her, and she whirled around on her swivel chair, which tilted and nearly dumped her under the desk.

"You have a license to drive that thing?" Jennifer laughed as she leapt forward to steady her friend.

"Suspended," Frances said, gamely righting herself and preparing to take the chair on again if it chose to continue the fight. Outnumbered, the chair remained still, but seemed to exude an aura of menace. She eyed it cautiously, and elected to stand. "What brings you out here?"

"Kay's car is in the repair shop again and her husband is in ward six having his bunions corrected at last, so I drove her out. Also I wanted to ask you to come round to dinner, tonight. I need a little moral support."

Frances held on to Jennifer's shoulder as she replaced her dewaxed shoe. (The warm wax bath had overflowed while she was dipping a patient's arthritic hand—just another of life's little adventures.) "Why? Not that I need a reason to leap at Mrs. Louis's cooking whenever asked."

"Well, I'd like to say it's because you're such charming company, which you are, but really it's to even up the numbers. The police are coming to dine."

"I beg your pardon?"

"Unbeknownst to me—or to Aunt Clotilda, for that matter—my dotty uncle has been keeping up a correspondence with Luke Abbott for years. He helped Luke straighten himself out after his father ran off, and they've kept in touch ever since, through college and everything. He rang him up as soon as he knew he was in town, and invited them both to dinner tonight."

"Both?"

"Luke and his sergeant—Paddy Smith."

"I can see why you want a few more on your side," Frances acknowledged, with a grin. "What's the betting that your uncle has every gory detail out of them in nine minutes flat?"

"No bet," came Kay's astringent voice from the door. "*My* bet is that he kept in touch with Luke Abbott merely to have a line into Scotland Yard, the old busybody. Newspapers never tell the whole truth, he used to say."

"And then he'd send you around to find out all the details, right?" Jennifer laughed.

"I have my uses," Kay smiled back.

"She has an intelligence network of friends and relatives that covers the whole county," Jennifer told Frances. "What would you like to know?"

"Who owns that little cottage in the woods opposite the craft centre?" Frances asked promptly.

"Mr. Ebenezer, the cobbler," Kay came back, just as quickly. "Why, thinking of buying it?"

"Is it for sale?"

"I'll ask him—let you know," Kay promised.

"See?" Jennifer chuckled. Then she grew serious. "Kay, did you know Luke Abbott?"

"Sure," Kay said. "What do you want to know about him?"

"What happened with his father, exactly?"

Kay sighed, and leaned against a filing cabinet. "Ran off with some girl from Milchester, broke his wife's heart. I know it's an old-fashioned phrase, but your uncle said that was the God's truth, in her case. She actually developed heart disease and died about two years later, when Luke was—let me think—about fifteen, I suppose."

"I never knew that," Jennifer said, thinking back to the Luke she had known, then. It must have been right around the time she'd had such a crush on him.

"Oh, yes. He wasn't the type to parade his troubles, but he looked after her all through her last illness. Real devoted to her, he was, took her death hard. He was supposed to go into care, but your uncle intervened, found him a place with a family in town, so he could finish his schooling. Luke was a little wild for a while, but he settled down once your uncle stepped in. They were real close until Luke went up to university. I know they wrote to one another quite a bit, for a while. Then Luke joined the police, got promoted, got married, and I don't know much after that."

"Luke Abbott is married?" Jennifer interrupted, her voice tinged with wistfulness.

"Was. I think his wife died a couple of years ago," Kay said. "Why—were you interested?"

"No, of course not. That is . . ."

"Hah! What goes on here?" Kay said, and she and Frances fixed Jennifer with inescapable glares.

"Nothing," Jennifer said, lamely. "I was only asking."

"No woman ever 'only asks' about a man," Kay said, firmly.

"Is he attractive, Jennifer?" Frances asked.

"No. Yes. Well . . ."

"If he looks the way he did when he left for university, he's not too bad," Kay conceded.

"Well?" Frances persisted.

Jennifer wilted. "He's not too bad," she admitted.

"Which means *I* get stuck with the other one, is that it? What did you say his name was?" Frances asked, rather bleakly.

"Paddy Smith," Jennifer told her.

"Oh, God—sounds like an Irishman," Frances mourned. "Will I never escape the divils, even here?"

"Seems a damned foolish time to go socializing, when we've got this case on," Paddy grumbled to Luke, as they drove up to High Hedges. It was a big rambling house of the local golden stone, heavily ivied, with mullioned windows and a sweep of lawn on three sides. A small sign saying "Surgery" pointed to a smaller door on one side of the main entrance. "Very nice, very *Country Life*, and me with only my old tweed suit."

"The Mayberrys aren't like that," Luke said, stopping the car and looking up at the welcoming glow in the windows. "Dr. Wally is the closest thing I've got to a family. He was damned good to me—for me—when I was younger. I wouldn't be here if it weren't for him."

"Do you mean he's the killer?" Paddy asked, wryly.

"No—but *I* might have been. Or in jail myself, instead of putting people there," Luke said, seriously. "I think maybe that's why I've had what success I've had—I'm a crook at heart. Dr. Wally saw that and turned it around in me. We used to go fishing a lot, talked for hours—we were very close. Then, when I went to university, we slowly lost touch. Well, I moved on, I suppose. Grew up. We were down to exchanging a note with our Christmas cards, but I always felt he was here, ready for me any time, ready for a talk on the riverbank. I'm sorry that it wasn't affection that brought me back. It should have been. He's a remarkable man."

But Luke's first sight of his old mentor told him that here, too, there was change. Once upright, unpredictable, and full of energy, the old man was now weary and bent over in his wheelchair by the fire. Nevertheless, his eyes were still fine and bright, and he gave Luke a thorough inspection, scowling at the moustache.

"Don't like the soup-strainer," he grunted.

"I'll consider shaving it off," Luke said.

"Only consider—no promises?"

"I'm not the promising kind," Luke laughed.

"So I recall. And who's this with you, glowering around like a suspicious collie? We don't have any weed or snow here, young man."

"I beg your pardon, sir?" asked Paddy, startled.

The old man turned to his wife. "Isn't that the right word?"

"Uncle Wally, stop that," Jennifer admonished him, with a smile. She was delighted to see how he'd brightened up when Luke had entered the room— she'd brightened up a bit, herself, as a matter of fact.

Luke introduced Paddy to the old man, and then Jennifer completed the formalities, leaving a stricken-looking Frances talking to an equally uncomfortable-looking Paddy beside the fire. When she went over to help David Gregson with the drinks, she noticed his hands were shaking. She looked at him out of the corner of her eye, but there was nothing in his face except a strange blankness. She could understand Frances and Paddy feeling awkward, but what on earth could be the matter with David? He caught her looking at him, and flushed.

"Have I got toothpaste on my chin or something?" he muttered.

"No, of course not. Are you all right?"

"I'm fine," he said, brusquely, and turned to hand out the glasses. She watched him for a moment, then shrugged and turned to the guests. If he wanted to go on shutting her out, so be it. She'd waste no more time on him.

After a moment, Clotilda came in and beamed around her. "Dinner will be ready shortly, as long as Mrs. Louis doesn't lose her nerve," she told them, and collected a drink from David as she went past. He looked after her, glanced around at everyone, and then went back to his intense study of the bookshelves. Jennifer sent him a scolding glance, but he paid no attention.

Clodie was in her element. It was the first dinner party she'd been able to have since Wally's illness, and she was determined it should be a success. She bustled around, busy with the task of putting everyone at ease—a talent which she had in abundance. The mix was a little unusual, but with luck, all should go well.

As long as Wally behaved himself.

Clodie's optimism lasted until half past the dessert.

They'd covered the changes in Wychford since Luke was last there, Wally's stroke, Jennifer's divorce, the death of Luke's wife and how he'd managed to look after their twin sons since then, Clodie's work for the church committee (she was making a tapestry for the altar), Frances's search for a house and weren't prices awful, Paddy's hoped-for promotion, David's move to this house and how it would improve the efficiency of the practice, and then, quickly (seeing fire in Jennifer's eye), the weather.

Wally hadn't had much to do with the weather, lately, having been confined to home. Besides, he felt that sufficient attention had been paid to generalities and personalities. Avoiding Clodie's eye, he plunged in. "So, who killed these women, then?" he demanded of Luke. "Got your man, yet?"

"We're working on it," Luke said, austerely.

"Got any good clues? Any leads?" Wally persisted.

"A few."

"Oh, come along, Luke," Wally said, slightly nettled. "You can do better than that. You're among friends, here."

"Stop it, Wallace," Clodie said. "You know perfectly well Luke can't discuss a case while he's investigating it."

"Poppycock," Wally said. "There's no reason why he can't tell us how he's going along. _We_ won't talk to anyone about it."

"He can't be certain of that."

Uncle Wally began to go red in the face. "Well, thank you very much. I haven't been a doctor all my life without learning how to keep a secret or two, have I?"

"Such as a certain lady trying to poison her husband with arsenic?" Jennifer put in, quickly. "What would be the official position on that, Luke?"

"Are you serious?" Luke looked across the table at her, gratefully.

"Quite serious." She outlined the story of the Teagues, calling them Mr. and Mrs. X. Uncle Wally, knowing himself vulnerable on this count, calmed down slightly as she talked. When she had finished, Luke considered, but Paddy spoke.

"Attempted murder is a crime."

"So is wife-beating," Frances said, instantly. "It sounds like self-defense, to me."

"Rather a drastic form of it," Luke smiled across at her. "I don't know what the lawyers would make of it, mind, but as far as the police are concerned, we can't arrest without a complaint being made. We can bring a case ourselves, of course, but someone would have to give us the information required to make the case sufficiently strong to expect a prosecution."

"You mean you'd turn a blind eye to attempted murder?" Clodie demanded.

"Self-defense," Frances affirmed. Her outrage concerning this point of women's rights had brought a flush to her cheeks and a spark to her eye. "No man has the right to beat his wife and make her life a misery. No woman should have to put up with it. She has my sympathy, entirely. I'd give him arsenic, myself, the rogue."

Paddy turned and looked down at her. She was a different woman altogether than he'd originally thought. It was as if a sparrow had suddenly decided to sing. "The trouble would be if she put in a pinch too much and knocked him off," he told her, gently. "Not quite like overseasoning the roast, is it? We could hardly turn a blind eye to a corpse, I'm afraid."

"Well, of course not," Frances said, becoming flustered under his steady gaze. When he'd walked in she'd noticed immediately that he resembled Cornel Wilde, her childhood hero, and from that moment on, she had been too stricken with shyness to speak more than a few polite monosyllables to him. Of course, he couldn't be expected to know that he brought back to her all the warm dark excitements of the cinema on a Saturday afternoon. She was certain he merely thought her awkward and peculiar. Lord knows she *felt* awkward and peculiar. She was not accustomed to the police looking like this. If she leaned forward and ripped open his shirt, would there be a blue uniform under it?

"What's wrong?" he asked, suddenly discomfitted in his turn by her change of expression.

"Nothing," she said in a strangled voice, returning to her lemon soufflé, praying she would not choke. Not thirty minutes had gone by and she was already considering ripping off his shirt. Frances Murphy, what would Sister Ursula say to you, now, if she knew of your evil thoughts? Wicked girl. Frances swallowed a giggle, choked, reached for her napkin, and knocked over her wine. It ran over the tablecloth like a fast-moving snake, and down onto Paddy's knee. He jumped back, knocked against Clodie's elbow, and triggered the sudden ejection of her spoonful of soufflé into Luke's lap.

The ensuing activity, which involved leaping up, apologising, and the swift application of napkins and salt, effectively sank the question of arsenic and Old Bill, but it did not divert Uncle Wally.

"She was a bit of a tart, you know," he announced. Everyone froze. For a wild moment, Jennifer thought he was referring to Mrs. Teague, who was thin, slatternly, and sly.

"Who was?" asked David Gregson, who had remained seated during the flap, concentrating on his dessert. For an instant it seemed as if the two men were alone in the room and all the fluttering was as of distant theatricals, of little or no interest to them.

"Murdered girl. The second one—down by the canal. Frenholm, her name was. One of our patients, as it happens. Had to treat her for VD about six months ago, just before my illness. She had to name her contacts, of course. Took two pages. Don't know where they find the energy, these young people. Exhausted me just writing them down."

"I'd appreciate a look at that list," Luke said.

"Privileged information," Uncle Wally said, promptly. "Mind you, I wouldn't say no to an *exchange* . . ."

"Why, you old devil," Clodie said in annoyance. "You had that up your sleeve all the while."

"I can get the information from the Department of Public Health," Luke said, mildly, sitting down again after checking his chair for any stray spots of soufflé. "Would take a few days, of course."

"Well, a few days could make all the difference," Uncle Wally said, encouragingly. "After all, he might strike again tonight or tomorrow night."

"Who?" Frances asked, mortified by the furore she had caused, not giving a damn, now. What worse could happen than already had?

"Why, this monster, this killer who's roaming about with his little knife at the ready," Uncle Wally said. "Two women, throats cut, must be the same chap. Psychopath, probably, hates women . . ."

Jennifer involuntarily looked at David Gregson, who chose that moment to look at her. He went pale, then flushed, and looked away quickly.

"We don't know it's the same man at all," Luke protested.

"Aha!" Uncle Wally said, gleefully.

"We don't know that it isn't, however," Paddy added. "We have only started our investigations."

"Rubbish," Uncle Wally said. "You know. You *always* know. Why, Luke, you wrote me yourself once that most murders can be solved within the first forty-eight hours."

"Most murders, yes. Most murders are family affairs, so to speak," Luke said.

"But there's a new kind of killer surfacing, isn't there?" Clodie asked, quietly. "What they call a serial killer? Someone who just kills for thrills and moves on . . . kills strangers."

"Another American import," Uncle Wally growled. "Not here."

"What about the Yorkshire Ripper? Or the one in London who stuck them down the drains and under the floorboards?" Frances asked. "Is that the kind of thing you mean?"

"Their motives were sexual," Jennifer said. "These women weren't raped."

"Weren't they?" Uncle Wally pounced, and glared at Luke, as if it were his fault if they'd escaped that particular horror.

"I'm certainly not convinced that the same person killed both women," Luke said. "We're waiting for the post-mortem reports." He handed his empty plate to Jennifer, who had stood up to clear for cheese and coffee. "At the moment there seem to be no obvious suspects or motives in the death of Beryl Tompkins, whereas in the case of Win Frenholm, there are almost too many. Jennifer was kind enough to tell me the Frenholm woman was pregnant, so I've asked for a full scan of the foetal blood. If the pregnancy was a direct or even an indirect motive for her death, having a match for the father might help us to narrow down the number of suspects."

"Could you convict on that?" David asked, in an odd voice.

"No, of course not. But it would add, could add, to the weight of evidence. It might give us a pressure point with the suspect, when we have him, as well. It's a long shot, of course, but long shots can occasionally be accurate. I can't really say anything more at this point."

Uncle Wally, initially enthused by these snippets of inside information, now regarded him with disappointment. What had seemed a fresh spring had suddenly dried up, for it was obvious from Abbott's tone that he'd said all he was prepared to say. "You've changed, lad. You really have."

Luke met his eye. "I hope so," he said, evenly. "I am a detective chief inspector, Doctor Wally. If I haven't learned my job by now, I shouldn't have it, should I?"

David Gregson spoke abruptly. "I suppose it's rather like the case of the wife poisoning her husband. You need a corpse to prove the nature of the crime. Two similar killings might be coincidental, but three—not so likely. So, what you're really waiting for is a third murder, isn't it?" His voice was reflective. "That would settle whether it's a case of serial killing or not, wouldn't it?"

"We'd rather work on what we have," Paddy said, firmly. "Two dead women is more than enough for us, thanks."

"Yes, of course. But it *would* make it clearer, wouldn't it?" David went on. His tone was scholarly, objective, but it struck cold all around the table. "You'd know, then, wouldn't you? I mean, you'd be certain, then?"

"All we'd be certain of is three women dead instead of two," Luke said. "There are such things as copy-cat murders, you see. I'm rather inclined toward that probability at the moment."

"But where do you draw the line?" Uncle Wally persisted. "I accept that if a second murder is committed that looks like the first, you might say *that* was a copy-cat killing. But David has a point. Surely the obvious conclusion would be that the same person had killed three times? In which case, doesn't it stop being copy-cat killing and start being something much worse? Or are you seriously saying that if you had a third murder you'd consider the possibility that it had been committed by a *third person?*"

"No, I'm not saying that." Luke's voice was becoming steely. "In fact, I'm trying very hard not to say anything at all. At the moment I have two murders to investigate, one over in Woodbury . . ."

"That's only a mile away over the hills," David interrupted.

". . . and another here in Wychford," Luke went on, through clenched teeth. "My God, man, two women are dead—isn't that enough for you? It's the media who like to produce these kind of scares—it sells newspapers, but it doesn't solve crimes."

"Luke," Paddy said, quietly. "It's only conversation."

Luke, with a great effort, calmed himself. "Yes, of course. Sorry." He managed a smile at Clodie. "Apparently it's bothering me a little more than I thought." He turned to Wally and David Gregson. "You must get that problem in medicine, too."

"Sometimes," Wally said. "Does you credit, Luke, to care about things. But it can get in the way."

"I know that, sir, believe me."

Jennifer could see that he was in a difficult position, and suggested in an overbright voice that they all help themselves from the cheese board while she got the coffee. Clodie said something to Luke about the weather, and Frances began what seemed to her an inane conversation about house-hunting and its attendant difficulties. The women, in short, did their duty and tried to keep things light, sensing that boredom was probably the best way to avoid blood on the linen.

David Gregson, reaching for the biscuits, murmured something to Uncle Wally, who had begun to sulk. The old man looked startled for a moment, looked at him for a long time, then nodded. He asked no more questions of Luke, or anyone else, after that, and it was left to the rest of them to keep the conversation going.

Clodie, watching her husband down the length of the table, saw that he was tired, now. Perhaps it had been too soon, after all, to expect him to face this. He'd seemed lively at first. Too lively by half. Now he was grey-faced, and slumped. He kept looking at David Gregson, and then down at his plate.

He hardly touched his cheese.

CHAPTER TWELVE

"I suppose you wondered why I didn't call you after you came back from London?" Mark Peacock put down Jennifer's drink and seated himself opposite her with his own.

"I assumed you didn't want to call me," she said with a smile. A careful smile, not too light, not too anything. "Our friendship wasn't on that kind of basis, was it?"

"I didn't let myself call you, because I was afraid I might be getting in too deep," Mark said, with every appearance of frankness. "My situation wasn't exactly ideal. "Vis-à-vis the house and my mother and—everything."

"Sorry, I don't follow."

"It doesn't matter. The point is, that's all changed, now. She's finally agreed to let me go ahead with my plans for the manor."

"You mean the conference centre plans? That's marvellous, Mark. I'm really pleased for you." And she was. Something in him had changed, seemingly for the better. There was a bright and almost manic light in his eyes, a vigor where before he'd been subdued and bitter. Either way she had to admit he was an unnervingly attractive man, physically. The stormy sexuality of his frustration had been replaced with a strange sense of power and excitement. As before, when she was with him, she had to remind herself that this was not enough on which to build either a romance or a life. She had been well aware of Aunt Clodie's eager hopes for a "good match," and quite steadfast in her own determination not to make the same mistake twice. She'd married for sex once before, and ended with subjugation.

Never again.

That did not, however, preclude an interesting relationship between two consenting adults, and that had seemed in the offing, before she'd gone to London a few weeks before. When he hadn't called her on her return, she'd assumed that he'd lost interest. She'd been sorry, as there were not all that many attractive available men in Wychford, and it promised to be a long, lonely winter. There was no denying her ego had been a little bruised, as well. But she'd had no regrets—and no intention of calling him, either. So, when he'd rung the surgery this morning and asked her to lunch, she'd been wary, even reluctant.

But, after all, one had to eat lunch somewhere.

He was waxing enthusiastic, now, the fire burning bright in him. "We're going ahead with the conversion work immediately. Hickson, the builder, is already putting up the scaffolding. I've had him on stand-by for months, ever since I began to think Mother was weakening." He took an impatient swallow of his drink to wet his throat. "I have Basil to thank for it, really. It was he who put the final pressure on her, gave her an extraordinary song and dance about how he wanted to spend more time with her, if you can believe it."

"Perhaps he does."

"And perhaps he's afraid his job in the City is getting a bit shaky," Mark said, with rather more insight than she had heretofore thought him to possess. "Of course, steeped in those wretched romances she reads all the time, *she* believed him. She'll do anything for Basil—thank God he sees it my way." A peculiar look came across his face. "I must say, he was pretty damned convincing, last night. Very impressive. At any rate, Peacock Manor is about to start paying for itself—and just in time, too. Things were getting pretty close to the knuckle."

"Were they?" Jennifer was surprised. It never occurred to her that people like the Peacocks could have financial worries. "Well, I'm very, very pleased for you, Mark. I know how much the project means to you."

"And to you," Mark said.

She frowned. "I don't understand."

"Don't you?" he asked. For some reason she couldn't fathom, he seemed disappointed in her. As if she'd missed a cue. He put his drink down and contemplated it for a moment, cleared his throat, seemed to make up his mind, and raised his eyes to hers. "When we're a going concern, we'll be having groups of people to stay, as you know. Although we're not legally required to have one, I would like to have a physician available for our guests should, God forbid, the need arise. I'd like that physician to be you. Would you consider taking an annual retainer to be the official medical consultant to the Peacock Manor Conference Centre?"

"Oh." Now it was her turn to feel disappointed, for which she roundly admonished herself behind a bland smile. "Why me, Mark?"

"Well, this is going to be a very distinguished operation. I think, with your looks and charm, you'd be a definite asset to us. It would involve a little more than strapping the odd sprained ankle, of course. I'd need your advice on fitting out a small medical room, which exercise and treatment facilities to install, sauna, jacuzzi, and so on. We'd have to work together quite a bit, before the opening. Would you mind that?"

"Of course not. But surely . . ."

"What?"

"Well, wouldn't your mother object? I have the impression that she doesn't approve of women doctors. Or perhaps it's just me she doesn't like."

"Mother will have nothing to do with the administration side of the manor," Mark said, firmly. He picked up his drink, put it down, picked it up again, and took a swallow. When he put it down, it was with a small crash. "You want the truth, don't you?"

"Yes, Mark, I do."

"It's the only way I can see more of you without getting up her nose," he said, rather like a small boy admitting a minor misdemeanour. "You're right, she doesn't approve of you. She doesn't approve of any girl for me, frankly. I've had to knuckle down to her in the past, but if this thing works out, and I know it will, then what she thinks and says won't matter, any more. I didn't care enough about anyone to fight her, before . . . but I do, now." He looked at her reproachfully. "I thought you knew that."

"You're a grown man, Mark, surely your life is your own."

"My life, yes. My income, no." He stopped as the girl from the bar came over to tell them their table was ready. They moved into the dining room and settled themselves. Despite the change in locale, Mark apparently felt the need to continue his self-justification. "I admit it, I've done her bidding for the money. What did it matter? My career was stonewalled, anyway. I've been too weak to break away, or too lazy, probably. All I've ever cared about is the manor. But now . . ."

Jennifer began to eat, automatically. Some part of her was hungry and needed sustenance, the rest of her was numb. She couldn't believe that Mark was saying these things to her, when for weeks she'd been convinced she'd been just another trophy on his watch-chain.

"I'll be honest with you, Jenny, because I think you deserve it," Mark was continuing. "I want to see more of you. Eventually I hope to make our relationship a great deal *more* than just professional. I can't do that, yet. I know Mother is difficult—sometimes downright impossible. And I admit I've always given in to her in order to have an easy life. But this project is something I'm willing to work hard for. And the same thing goes for us. I've stayed away from you these past few weeks quite deliberately—to see if what I was feeling was really as strong as I thought it was. I know now that it is. I've been lazy and weak, but I intend to stop that. I don't want you to get away, Jenny. Give me a chance. Help me stand up straight, at last."

She believed him. She was certain he'd never been this honest with a woman, because he was so awkward about it. She'd never seen him awkward or uneasy about anything, before. And she wasn't altogether sure she wanted to see it, now.

"I'll have to talk it over with David," she said.

"What?"

She'd thrown him, she really had, and this gave her a good feeling. His assumption that she'd been just waiting to be asked rubbed her the wrong way. Hadn't any woman ever hesitated before his charms, before? Probably not. It would do him a world of good. "I meant the thing about being your medical consultant. It's a business matter, Mark. I *am* part of a practice, you know. It may be that it would have to be a joint undertaking."

"I don't want Gregson, I want you. Would you have to ask his permission to marry me, as well?"

"Are you asking me to *marry* you?"

He looked exasperated. Unaccustomed as he was to public speaking, he was very aware of her clear voice and its carrying quality against a background of largely male conversation. Fortunately a political argument was in progress, and nobody was paying them the least attention. He began, "I thought I explained that . . ."

She relented. "Yes, you did. Sort of. Look, Mark, you'll have to forgive me, but to coin a cliché, all this comes as a bit of a shock." She sighed. "I thought we'd been out and had some pleasant times together, and that was the end of it. Nothing you ever said or did gave me any reason to believe that I was special to you in any way. Now you suddenly come along and profess deep feelings . . . what am I supposed to think? What am I supposed to do?"

"You went to bed with me."

"Of course I did," she snapped. "You're a very attractive and exciting man and I'm a healthy, normal woman."

"Do you go to bed with every attractive man you go out with?" he asked, neutrally. It sounded more like curiosity than resentment.

"No, certainly not!" There was no point at all in trying to explain to him how it had healed her to have a man prove to her that she was still attractive after the divorce. He'd been her medicine. An antibiotic against the infection of self-doubt.

He smiled suddenly. "Neither do I. Sleep with every woman, I mean," he added, hastily. "So, I wasn't wrong about you. Or us."

"Let's just say you were and you weren't. What I do with my body is one thing, what I do with my life is quite another."

"You mean now that I've given in to your desires you don't respect me any more?" he asked, all innocence.

She looked up, quickly. The bastard, he was laughing at her. Served her right for underestimating him. Ah, but he was so attractive, sitting there. And he had such nice hands. And such a nice mouth. And underneath the teasing he was quite, quite serious. She had to respect that.

"Eat your lunch," she told him. "It's getting cold."

"Is that supposed to be some kind of coded response?" he asked, dutifully picking up his fork but doing nothing with it. "Does 'Eat your lunch' stand for 'Yes, Mark' by any chance?"

"It stands for no nonsense," Jennifer said, with a smile. "And for 'I'll think about it.' " She glanced at the clock. "And for 'My God, it's after two o'clock and I have the antenatal clinic this afternoon.' Your mother's right, women doctors are *not* the thing. No grace."

"It's my mother who's still the problem, isn't it?" he demanded.

"Not at all. I just need time to think, that's all," she said, her mouth full of Haddock Mornay.

"I thought . . ." he began, then stopped. He was quiet, watching her bolt her food. "Perhaps I should have thought a little more," he finally said, with a trace of bitterness. "I can't say I blame you. You wouldn't want her always there, would you?"

"Sorry?" She was finishing up her wine. The pregnant ladies would be arriving, and Kay would be running out of excuses.

"Nothing. What about tonight?"

That stopped her. "Tonight?"

"We could have dinner."

"Oh. I don't know . . . ring me after evening surgery, would you?"

"You've got surgery this evening, too?"

"Yes."

"You work too hard." Mark scowled. "Gregson expects too much of you."

"And about time, too," Jennifer said. "Thanks for the lunch, Mark. And . . . the rest. I'll ring you."

"When?"

"As soon as I can. 'Bye." She kissed him on the cheek, kept moving, and left him looking after her, frowning. When he realised other people were staring at him, he sat down. When the waitress brought the cheese board, he cut off a large wedge of cheddar with a savage swipe of the knife, nearly frightening the poor girl to death.

He apologised, smiled, and asked for a brandy.

What a gorgeous man, thought the waitress, who was new to the area, and she rushed off to do his bidding.

After an exhausting afternoon with the nervous mothers-to-be of Wychford, Jennifer came in panting for a cup of tea. Her aunt was in her usual place before her embroidery frame. She received the news about Mark Peacock with surprising calm. Even a little skepticism.

"Now, why does he suddenly re-enter your life, I wonder?"

"Because I'm gorgeous, desirable, exciting?"

"No," Clodie said, uncompromisingly, trailing pale pink through the linen to form another flower petal.

"Thank you very much," Jennifer said, wryly.

"Of course you are *all* those things, dear," Clodie went on, vaguely. "Certainly. But to ignore you for over a month, and then to more or less *propose* . . ."

"He didn't propose, he just sort of mentioned it as a possibility. Anyway, I thought you *wanted* him to propose," Jennifer interrupted, feeling her news was not being received in the proper manner. Why wasn't Clodie excited? For that matter, why wasn't *she* excited, herself?

"I wanted you to be happy," Clodie said.

"I am happy," Jennifer said. "And anyway, there isn't any commitment about it. He simply said that he wanted . . ."

"To keep you on a string for his personal gratification and delight," came a voice from the other side of the room, and David Gregson stood up from where he had been dozing in a chair in the bay window. His face was as rumpled as his clothes, and his hair stuck up at the back like a boy's. "To say to his precious clients, look what a clever boy am I, to have this beautiful woman doctor as part of my operation. How liberated. How handy, especially when you see the way she eats out of my hand."

"David, that was unkind," murmured Clodie, who sounded as if she were trying to stifle a laugh.

"Very amusing." Jennifer could feel anger rising. "Do you often eavesdrop on people's private conversations, or is it a new hobby you've taken on to fill the vacant hours?"

"Clodie knew I was there," David said. "If the devastating and desirable Mark Peacock has been so hell-bent on his project for so long, why didn't he mention this consultant thing to you before?"

"He may have. God knows the idea of the conference centre was his main topic of conversation every time we went out. I don't remember whether he mentioned the possibility of my being part of it or not," Jennifer said, uneasily. "Anyway, that's not the point."

"The point is, any professional commitment you make is a matter for all of us to consider. Your first responsibility is to the practice, you know."

"I *know* that," Jennifer said. "I was going to tell you about it the first chance I got."

"Of course you were. And to think that last night I assumed you were smitten by the poor man's Sherlock Holmes. I should have known the trouble lay closer to home." David turned to Clodie. "You see? It just proves the point I've made before. You spend thousands of pounds and hours training a woman to be a doctor, and you might as well be throwing it down the drain. The minute a man comes along and crooks a little finger at her—off she goes. It's all in the hormones. It's pathetic!"

"Just because you couldn't hold onto your *own* wife . . ."

"Jennifer!" Clodie said, in a shocked voice.

But Jennifer had eyes only for David Gregson. "*If* you had been listening closely, you would have noticed I accepted neither Mark's offer of a private retainer nor anything else. I am very aware of my responsibilities to the practice and to our patients. This is something that is way in the future, anyway. I had every intention of discussing it with you and Uncle Wally, and I told Mark that. Furthermore, I do *not* let my hormones rule my mind, but it seems to me you do. Of all the biased, chauvinistic, pig-headed men I've ever known . . ."

"No doubt you've *known* quite a few . . ."

"David!" Aunt Clodie was getting ruffled—and getting nowhere. The two of them might have been alone in the room.

"Cheap shot, doctor," Jennifer snapped.

"Not the first one fired in this room," David said, with maddening calm. Only his hands betrayed him, fists behind his back. "What retainer was he suggesting—or were *you* going to pay *him?*"

"We didn't talk about money." She was sorry this had started.

"You surprise me. I was under the impression Peacock talks about nothing else."

"Mark is a very cultured, intelligent, charming—"

"Poltroon," David interrupted.

Jennifer stared at him. "A what?" she finally managed.

He had the grace to look abashed. "Poltroon."

"A perfectly good word," Aunt Clodie observed. "Your serve, Jennifer."

Jennifer was looking at David Gregson oddly. He stared back, and began to look uneasy. "Is poltroon the best you could come up with?" she asked, feeling sudden, inexplicable laughter welling up inside her, despite determined efforts to remain angry. He looked so untidy and dishevelled, standing there, and she had a sudden image of a little boy whose marbles had been stolen. He was so cross he was funny.

"Well, it was short notice," he said, defensively. "I've been reading Dumas."

"I see. That explains everything, of course."

"Of course," echoed Aunt Clodie.

He stared at them both, saw their amusement, and felt foolish. "I'm afraid I'm too tired to be clever," he finally said, with a trace of bitterness. "I leave such things to you ladies. Meanwhile, it's getting late and I have some work to do before dinner. If you'll excuse me—" He started for the door.

"David," Jennifer said, in a conciliatory tone. He stopped but didn't turn around. "Mark's not really bad, you know," she said to his back, surprised at her desire to placate him. "He can't help being who he is or what he is. The retainer question is something we can deal with when and if the offer becomes real. In the meantime, as long as I continue to do my work responsibly, what I make of my personal life is just that—personal. I might point out that men, too, are subject to emotional strain, and can occasionally carry it over into their professional life. When you consider the suicide and drug-dependency statistics for doctors, the cases brought up before the General Medical Council, all men . . ."

"Touché," David said over his shoulder, in a tone that said he was finished with her and the conversation. Jennifer stood looking at the empty doorway.

"You won that round," Aunt Clodie observed. "He expected you to explode, and you didn't. At least, not very much. I count that quite a triumph for the cause, Jennifer."

"Yes, quite," Jennifer agreed, in a tight voice. "I may be going out with Mark tonight, by the way. I haven't decided, yet."

"That's nice, dear," Clodie said. She was scowling at her embroidery. That flower wasn't right, at all. Not at all. The whole thing would have to come out and be done again. She raised her eyes and began to speak, but saw that Jennifer, too, had left the room.

"Get on with your work, you silly old woman," she told herself. "Let the young ones sort out their own problems, just as you did yours, once upon a time." She worked and pulled and fiddled with the embroidery. But it wouldn't come right, because her mind kept wandering off onto other things. "Silly old woman," she muttered, again. But it wouldn't stop.

Evening surgery went on rather later than Jennifer had expected, and when she finally rang Mark it was too late for dinner. She grabbed a quick sandwich in the kitchen, and then met him at the Woolsack for a drink.

For some reason he thought the fact that she had called him had been a capitulation, and the drink only a prelude to a resumption of their affair. When she made it clear that she had no intention of ending the evening in some hotel bed, he began an argument that was settled only by her leaving abruptly. Twice in one day was perhaps too often to leave a man scowling, she thought, as she drove home alone. If nothing else, that should help you make up your mind about him. Did she want to be married to a six-foot schoolboy? On balance, she thought not.

She collapsed into bed, exhausted, and fell almost immediately into a deep, dreamless sleep. It didn't last.

Someone was shaking her shoulder. She muttered and rolled away, burrowing under the bedclothes, aware that cold air lay outside, waiting to grab her.

"Jennifer! Dammit! Jennifer! Wake up!" The tone was urgent, and the voice was David Gregson's. My God, an emergency, she thought, and swam upward from the depths of sleep toward his face, misty in the dark above her.

"What is it? Mr. Deever, again?" she mumbled, struggling to keep her eyes open.

"No, it's not Mr. Deever," David said, bleakly. "It's your boyfriend. It seems his mother has been murdered. They rang up for a doctor. Do you want to go, or shall I?"

CHAPTER THIRTEEN

They had rigged some lighting by the time Luke and Paddy got there. Clouds of frozen breath wreathed the heads of all the uniformed men standing around. The night was bitterly cold, and many of them stamped their feet and clapped their hands in an effort to stay warm while waiting for the formal investigations to begin.

No cloud of breath hung over the mouth of Mabel Peacock Taubman, but a faint haze could be seen above the gaping wound in her throat, for there was still warmth in her body.

She lay at the foot of the long lawn that swept from Peacock Manor to the river. She wore a flowered silk dress and a coat that lay beneath her. Her arms had not been in the sleeves, Luke observed, so she must have had it over her shoulders. She had come out for a reason, a compelling reason, but hadn't expected to be long about it.

"We thought it might have been the dog, sir," PC Bennett said, when Luke had had a look around. "She might have come out to call it or something like that, wandered down the lawn and got caught out."

"They have a dog?" Luke asked.

"Yes, sir, they do. Her son says he came home and found the front door wide open, the dog roaming free and behaving strange, like. Kept running toward the river and then coming back, if you get my line, as if he wanted to be followed. Mr. Peacock checked the house and saw his mother was gone, so he got a torch and went after the dog. Says he thought she might have taken the dog for a walk and sprained an ankle or some such . . . found her, like this. Very close to his mother, was Mr. Peacock. Took it hard. We rang the doctor to come to him."

"I see. Thank you. Has the coroner been notified?"

"Yes, sir, on his way." Bennett knew the drill by now. Getting quite used to it, he was, with all these murders.

Mark Peacock sat in the hall, his face white, his hands clasping the heavily carved arms of the straight-backed chair that faced the door. When Luke and Paddy came in, he did not even look up. Luke had to walk over and speak to him twice before he stirred.

"Mr. Peacock, I'm Detective Chief Inspector Abbott. I'm sorry about your mother, and I'm sorry to have to bother you at a time like this, but there are some questions."

"She's dead," Mark said. His voice was flat and toneless, as if he were just reading the news.

"Yes, sir. I'm sorry."

Mark looked up. "It doesn't make sense, you know."

"Sir?"

"Her being out there, all alone. She said she wouldn't go out, you see. She was alone in the house, tonight. We have no live-in servants, Basil is up in London. I went out for the evening, and she said she'd stay inside, because of this killer, but she must have gone out, after all. She didn't have to go out for Barkis—he comes when you call him. He's a good dog. Why did she go out?"

"I don't know, Mr. Peacock." Luke looked around. The hall was beautifully furnished and brightly lit, but it was hardly the place to conduct an interview. Outside there were voices and the sound of engines and footsteps as the forensic investigation team arrived. Inside there was only oak panelling, black-and-white marble tiles, embroidered Jacobean draperies, several oil paintings, and Mark Peacock. There was a movement by the chair, and Luke corrected his listing: there was also Mark Peacock's dog, a liver-and-white spaniel, sitting uncertainly against the wainscoting, its worried eyes turned up toward its master. "Is there somewhere we can talk, sir? Somewhere perhaps a bit more private?"

"What?" For the first time since Luke had entered, Mark Peacock seemed to become aware of his surroundings. "Oh, yes . . . of course." He stood up, wavered slightly, then righted himself. His eyes focussed on Luke. "I know you," he said, after a moment. "Don't I?"

Luke nodded. "I grew up in Wychford. Luke Abbott."

Mark stared at him for a moment. "You gave me a thrashing one summer. As far as I can remember, I deserved it. Is that right?"

"It seemed right at the time," Luke allowed. "In retrospect, I think I went a little over the top."

"I've never forgotten it," Mark said, still in that strange, distant voice. "My mother wanted to . . ." he stopped, abruptly. "This way." He turned and went through a door to their right, the dog at his heels, leading Luke into another beautiful room. Embers burned low in the grate of a huge fireplace, before which was drawn up an armchair. A tall lamp was beside the chair, and a small table, on which was an empty teacup and a metal biscuit box containing a multi-coloured assortment of tapestry wools. A small embroidery hoop was on a footstool before the chair as if it had been dropped there when its owner got up, the needle thrust through a partially completed lamb. Mark stopped short and looked at the chair. "You see? She was listening to music and sewing—that was how I left her." He gestured toward a carved chest which stood open. Luke could just see the glow of a red light within, showing that the stereo equipment housed there was still turned on. He went over and looked down.

"The Pirates of Penzance," he read off the label of the record on the turntable. From the cover of the album propped against the back wall of the chest, a pirate leered at him, teeth clenched around a curved dagger. Luke reached out and gently turned the pirate to face the wall. The knife was a little too relevant for comfort.

"One of her favourites—it's the complete production, dialogue and . . . and . . ." Mark Peacock's voice caught for a moment. "That was how I left her," he repeated, slowly. "Why would she go out?"

"What time did you leave?"

Mark looked distracted. "It must have been about eight. I just gave her a quick kiss and said I was going out for a drink, but I'd be late, so she mustn't wait up for me. She had a habit of waiting up for me." He tried to get himself under control, took a sudden breath, and started to shake. "Oh, God." He sank down on the sofa and buried his head in his hands.

The door opened and Paddy came in. "Doctor's car just coming up the drive," he said, softly, glancing at the now sobbing man on the sofa.

"Fine," Luke said. "I think it would be better if we waited. Tell someone to get in touch with this Taubman at his club. And see if you can find some coffee or something in the kitchen, will you? My eyes are full of sand already, and it looks like a long night, again."

"Are you arresting him?"

Luke stared at Jennifer in astonishment. He hadn't expected the doctor to be her, and he certainly was unprepared for her abrupt question. *"Arresting* him? What made you ask that?"

"I don't know," Jennifer said. "I just got here and I don't even have matching shoes on." She gazed in surprise at her feet. One blue pump and one brown pump.

"I don't want you here, Jennifer," Mark suddenly announced, his sobs momentarily abated. "There's a killer around here. This is no place for a lady."

"She's no lady, she's a doctor," Luke said.

"Still the golden-tongued devil, I see," Jennifer said, icily. "But he's right, Mark. I'm here as a doctor, not as your . . . not as anything else. Luke wants to ask you some questions, and you're upset."

"I'm quite capable of answering questions," Mark said, huffily. "There was no need to call you or anyone else."

"When the police called Dr. Gregson they said you'd fainted," Jennifer pointed out.

"Even so." Obviously Mark was embarrassed. "You told me that Gregson was taking all the night calls."

"He is, but he thought . . ." Jennifer paused. "Please let me help you, Mark. You said today you wanted me to help you stand up straight, remember? You need to do that, now."

"Mother's dead," Mark said. "Mother's gone, and Mother's boy has to stand on his own two feet, now." A stricken look went over his face and he began, suddenly, to laugh. It was a terrible sound, and he looked at them as if he couldn't understand it, himself. As if something were inside him, laughing, and he couldn't stop it. His eyes were astonished, wide and horrified, but his mouth went on laughing and laughing . . .

Jennifer slapped him once, twice, but it did no good. The sound of his laughter increased in volume and started to rise into hysteria. She reached for her bag, extracted a disposable syringe, and quickly prepared a sedative injection. Paddy, seeing what she intended, pushed up the sleeve of Mark's jacket as far as it would go, and held it until she was finished. Mark's terrible laughter continued for a minute, and then, suddenly, stopped. His eyes shut and he slumped against the sofa.

"You didn't have to knock him out," Luke said, reprovingly.

"I didn't expect to," Jennifer said, slightly startled. She glanced at the glass ampoule from which she had extracted the drug, to reassure herself. "No, it's all right. I expect he'll come round in a minute or two. It's the shock—that's all." She felt for Mark's pulse, smoothed the blond hair gently back from his clammy forehead.

A muscle jumped in Luke's cheek, and he spoke rather brusquely. "I understand you were out with Mr. Peacock this evening," he said. "I thought doctors weren't supposed to socialise with their patients. Or doesn't that apply to lady doctors?"

"Mark is on Dr. Gregson's list, not mine."

"Rather a fine point, isn't it?"

"Perhaps."

"Why didn't Dr. Gregson come, himself? He is taking the night calls, isn't he?"

"Yes, he is. I suppose that under the circumstances he thought I'd like to be with Mark. Mark and I have been—quite close. Also, since I would probably be here for some time, it left him free to take any other emergency calls. I really didn't take the time to enquire into his motives—I was just grateful for his kindness."

"I see." Luke's voice was carefully neutral. "According to the houseman, Mr. Peacock and his mother had an argument before he left the house this evening. An argument about you."

"Oh?" Jennifer kept her eyes on Mark.

"Yes." Luke's smile was tight. "He said there had been arguments before. About you."

Jennifer sighed. "Mrs. Taubman didn't . . . approve of me. Me, or my profession, or both."

Luke nodded. "Apparently she used the phrase 'over my dead body.' Any comment?"

"She was a very melodramatic woman, fond of making scenes," Jennifer said. "That was one of the methods she used to get her way."

"Did Mr. Peacock mention this argument to you?" Luke asked.

"No. It can't have been important."

"I see."

Jennifer stirred, uneasily. "Why aren't you outside, with the others, prodding about and looking for fingerprints and all that kind of thing?" she demanded. She felt oddly frightened by Luke. He seemed strange and distant, and she found it hard to reconcile the charm and vulnerability he'd shown at the dinner table the other night with the brusque and intimidating person he was now. Mark looked so defenceless, slumped there, with these two great hulks looming above him.

"There are specialists to do that," Luke said, gently, sensing her resentment. "We're supposed to assess their results, and question suspects."

"There. I knew you suspected him," Jennifer snapped, her worst suspicions confirmed. "Mark was with me until nearly eleven."

"Eleven? Are you certain that was the time?"

"Yes. I looked at the clock as I left."

"When *you* left? You left separately?"

"I had met Mark there, so I had my car with me."

"I see." He made a note of this.

"So he couldn't have had anything to do with it."

"I didn't say he did," Luke told her, mildly. "What are you getting so excited about?"

"Oh . . ." Jennifer could feel tears dangerously close. "First David, now you . . . I'm just sick of it, that's all."

"Sick of what?" Paddy asked in some confusion. Luke just watched Jennifer as she again brushed Mark's hair back from his forehead and then sat down beside him proprietarily.

"Oh, people not trusting Mark just because he's rich and handsome." Jennifer grumbled.

"Poor guy," Luke said, in a wry tone. "My heart bleeds for him."

Jennifer's eyes blazed up at him, then, slowly, the fire died. She even managed a small laugh. "You know what I mean," she said, ruefully. "It just came out funny, that's all."

Mark stirred beside her. "Jenny . . ." he whispered.

"Yes, Mark, what is it?"

"Basil . . . somebody should tell Basil. I need him here."

"Who's Basil?" Luke asked.

"Basil Taubman is his mother's second husband. Mark's stepfather, I suppose, although it's hard to think of him that way. He's not exactly the fatherly type," Jennifer said.

"Where is Taubman?" Luke asked Mark.

Mark's eyes were dreamy, his manner vague. "London. Basil stayed at his club in London last night and tonight because of some meeting or other," he told them in a slow drawl. "Somebody should tell him she's dead. Ding-dong, the witch is dead." Silently, tears began to well up in Mark's eyes and overflow down his cheeks.

Abbott, looking at him, felt a kind of withdrawal in himself. The man even looks handsome when he's grieving, he thought. It didn't seem right, somehow, and yet something in him sensed that the grief, at least, was real.

"I don't think this is going to get us very far, tonight," Paddy said. "Let's put him to bed and talk to him in the morning. Don't you agree, Doctor?" He looked at Jennifer. She couldn't read his eyes, but she thought there was some kindness in the suggestion. More to the point, some sense.

"Yes. That would be better for him."

"I want to talk to him now," Luke said, flatly. Paddy looked at him in surprise; Jennifer, with irritation.

"Can't you see he's upset and under the influence of drugs?" she demanded. "He's not responsible for anything he says."

"Which might make it all that much more interesting," Luke said. "What are you so afraid he'll say, Jennifer?"

"I'm not afraid of anything he might say," she told Luke angrily. "I'm just afraid you'll bully him into saying something that could be misinterpreted."

"My, my—he does seem to inspire motherliness in his women, doesn't he?" Luke said. "Big boy like that should be able to look after himself, shouldn't he?"

"That was a rotten thing to say," Jennifer snapped.

"Yes, it was," Paddy agreed. "She's right, Luke. You should know nothing he says now could be used in evidence. Leave him till morning." Paddy was puzzled by Luke's emotional reaction, and put it down to old emnities, or perhaps new interests. Jennifer Eames was a very attractive woman, and Margaret Abbott had been dead for two years. Luke hadn't liked hearing that

Jennifer was involved with Mark Peacock. And he'd apparently never liked Peacock, himself.

They'd been wrong to send Luke down here. The usual policy was dislocation—sending in strangers. Perhaps they'd felt that twenty years would have made Luke a stranger to his home town. Perhaps they hadn't realised the old connection existed—murder enquiries hardly allow time for an in-depth study of a detective's personnel file before assignment. Or perhaps, and most likely, there hadn't been anyone else available at the time. Nevertheless, it was already making things difficult. If he hadn't recognised that, he wouldn't have spoken as he had to Luke in public.

Luke stared at his partner and saw something of what was in his mind. He accepted Paddy's reservations. Maybe Paddy hadn't yet seen the pattern that he thought *he* saw in these killings.

On the other hand, maybe that pattern didn't exist.

"Very well," he said, brusquely, turning away. "Put him to bed. But I'm leaving someone here with him until morning."

"Can he do that? Treat Mark as a suspect?" Jennifer demanded of Paddy, who was watching Luke's retreating figure with some bemusement.

"I'm afraid he can do just about anything he damn well pleases, as long as he sticks to the letter of the law. And he knows the letter of the law, believe me. I shouldn't worry about it," Paddy reassured her. "Let's get him upstairs and into bed, shall we? Things will look better in the morning."

Jennifer looked at him and her mouth quirked. "I deserve better than that, Paddy Smith."

He grinned engagingly. "Damn thing is, it's true, you know. Things *do* look better in the morning. Something about blood sugar, or lack of oxygen to the brain, no doubt."

Together they helped a limp and whimpering Mark up the elegant sweep of the manor stairway. "I hear you took Frances out to dinner, tonight," Jennifer grunted.

"I would have," Paddy agreed, puffing a little. "She was going to meet me in town, but she couldn't get her car started. By the time I got to her place it was so late we settled for scrambled eggs on toast."

"Did Frances cook them?" Jennifer asked, in some amazement.

"More or less," Paddy said with a smile, remembering the smoke that had filled the kitchen and the eggs splattering the wall. "More or less."

CHAPTER FOURTEEN

"Sorry, Paddy," said Luke, as his partner came up to stand beside him. They watched Jennifer's car go down the drive, carefully skirting the assembled police vehicles. "That was stupid of me."

Paddy shrugged. "You've been stupid before, and I expect . . ."

". . . that I'll be stupid again?" Luke sighed. "No doubt." He turned to look back at the house. "Is he still crying?"

"No," Paddy said, gravely. "He got the giggles when we were trying to get his socks off, and couldn't stop for quite a while. Jennifer says sedatives take people like that, sometimes."

"I wonder," Luke said, impassively, and walked down the lawn toward the canvas barrier that encircled the corpse, "Did Bennett's man arrive before you left?"

"An officer arrived, pad in hand, as ordered. Do you really think Peacock will say anything worth knowing about?"

"Maybe. Even under drugs, a man who's killed his mother is bound to sleep uneasily."

"Are you serious?"

"Very. Evening, Cyril. Cold night for it."

The pathologist looked up and snapped his tape measure back into its case in irritation. "You'd think murderers would have the decency to be afraid of pneumonia like everyone else," he complained. "I'm getting too old to go crouching on damp lawns like this."

"Can you give me a tight time of death on this one?" Luke asked.

"Not at the moment."

"Can you give me a rough time?" Luke asked, patiently. "Can you tell me whether it was before or after midnight?"

Franklin glanced at his watch, then at the corpse of Mabel Peacock Taubman. "Probably before—but maybe after. Certainly around that time."

Luke looked at Paddy. "Thank you."

"Are you going to tell me that this one was pregnant, too?" Franklin asked, sarcastically.

"No, I don't think so."

"Shame," the pathologist said. "I'd like to think there was hope yet for the middle-aged. Still." He shrugged. "I press on."

"Cyril . . ."

Franklin sighed. "Yes, Luke, there is good reason to believe this is the work of the same person or persons who murdered the other two."

"Did you say persons, plural?" Paddy asked, quickly.

"I like to cover myself," the coroner said. "You never know who's listening." He continued his macabre ministrations, concentrating on the wound itself. There were small squishy noises and a brief gasp of air, as if Mabel Taubman had suddenly taken a breath. But the white, drained face, somewhat collapsed under its mask of carefully applied makeup, showed no sign of life. Luke moved away quickly, Paddy at his heels.

"I swear he did that on purpose," Paddy said, hunching into his disreputable raincoat.

"Hates to be watched at the scene," Luke said. "Always has."

PC Bennett caught up with them, and trotted alongside like an eager retriever. "We've got a psycho, haven't we?" he asked. He seemed torn between the rage of the lawkeeper over the intransigence of the criminal and a kind of morbid pride that their simple locale could produce a murderer of this calibre. He hated himself for the latter, but it did seem so extraordinary a thing to happen in Wychford. There would be no keeping it out of the national papers, now. And if thoughts of a job well done leading to promotion tugged at his attention, he turned them firmly out of his mind. Nevertheless, they left an echo. He was twenty-four, and hoped to start a family, soon.

"Could be," Luke said, noncommittally. "Have you put a good man in with Peacock?"

"No, I put in a good woman," Bennett said, but his self-congratulatory chuckle at the joke died in his throat under Abbott's glare.

"I suppose it's PC Carter, the attractive blonde who's been typing our reports and summaries?"

"Well, yes . . ."

"Get her out and put in a man," Abbott ordered abruptly. "Tell her it's no reflection on her ability—I just don't want to be left open to possible criticism from the press. They'd just love our leaving a woman alone with a drugged local Romeo, wouldn't they?" He glanced at Paddy. "You should know better."

"She's a good officer. She'll resent it," Paddy said, mildly.

"She'd resent a slit throat even more," Luke said.

"You can't seriously believe that Peacock killed his own mother," Paddy said, in some surprise. "And the other two as well? Jennifer gives him an alibi for tonight."

"You heard Cyril. Around midnight, he said. Jennifer says she left him before eleven. They booked his call to the station at twenty past midnight— over an hour unaccounted for. He could have come home and picked up the argument he'd had with his mother before he left. Say his mother found out he was with Jennifer and started an argument about it and he killed her."

"Cyril also said she died where she was found," Paddy reminded him. "If he killed her as a result of an argument, how did he get her to come outside?"

"Maybe she ran outside to get away from him."

"Taking time to put a coat on?"

"Exactly," Luke said, grimly. "Would a stranger have given her time to do that?"

"Maybe she put it over her shoulders to call the dog, opened the door, and the guy grabbed her on the doorstep," Bennett suggested, eagerly. "It could have happened like that, couldn't it?"

Luke looked at him, looked back at the doorway, sighed and nodded. "Well done. Yes, it could have."

"Is that what you're going to tell the papers?" Bennett wanted to know.

Abbott stopped his headlong charge across the lawn to the car and turned to stare at the young officer. "No. We are going to tell them a psychotic killer is on the loose in Wychford, and we are instituting extreme measures to identify and arrest him."

"Are we?" Bennett asked, cheering up immediately.

Abbott looked disappointed. "Use your head, boy," he said, and got into his car. Bennett looked at Paddy questioningly.

"We don't want to start a panic, we want to catch a killer," Paddy said, kindly. "Just put out the usual we-expect-an-arrest-shortly announcement, all right?"

"But they're going to want more," Bennett protested.

"Then they'll have to make it up as they go along, won't they? They can panic all they like, but we can't, officially or unofficially," Paddy said and went around to get behind the wheel.

Bennett watched the car head down the driveway, then turned and looked down the lawn at the circle of light haloing the canvas surround and the milling collection of forensic experts. As each man passed into the light his personal cloud of frozen breath was revealed, wreathing his head and shoulders. The night air was crystal clear, and the low voices of the men carried across the grass. On one side they were preparing a body bag and a stretcher, while across the width of the lawn a torchlight search had begun.

The press will turn this into a circus, Bennett thought, with some dismay. He shivered inside his uniform coat, and turned to glance up at Peacock Manor. The spindly poles of the builder's scaffolding made a webwork around its dark bulk, clattering and creaking eerily in the darkness. Better relieve PC Carter, then. If this *was* going to turn into a circus, the last thing he intended to provide was the lady in the spangled tights.

He'd sit with the poxy bastard himself.

When Jennifer got back to High Hedges, David was waiting for her. He wasn't awake, but had dozed off in Aunt Clodie's favourite chair before the dying fire. She stood in the doorway and looked at him for a moment, before going out into the hall again and making a bit of noise. When she re-entered the sitting room, he was awake.

"Well?" he demanded. "After you left it occurred to me that it might be some kind of hoax, so I called back to confirm. Paddy Smith answered, so . . ."

"They're all there," Jennifer said, sinking into the chair opposite him. "She's down at the foot of the lawn. Since I was there I signed the certificate for them."

"And was it the same as the others?"

"I gather so. Her throat was certainly cut wide open."

"And does that finally convince your wonderful Inspector Luke Abbott that we have a psychopathic killer at large here in Wychford?"

"No," Jennifer said, in a small voice.

David sat up with an astonished look on his face. *"No?* Are you serious?"

"It's my fault, I'm afraid. Mark was hysterical and I gave him quite a jolt of Thorazine. He went out almost completely."

"Why the hell did you do that?"

"I didn't mean to knock him out—Mark must be hypersensitive to it. Anyway, it meant that he couldn't be legally questioned, which is really what I was after."

"Why?"

"I don't know. Because they all seemed to be ganging up on him. Because it seemed right. Mark might have said things that Luke could misinterpret. He didn't get along with his mother, and yet he was dominated by her. I just wanted him to be more in control when he was questioned."

"Sounds to me like you suspect him, yourself."

"Don't be stupid, of course I don't. It was just that Luke was behaving so . . . so . . . like a policeman."

"Hardly surprising," David pointed out.

"I know, I know. At any rate, the result seems to be that he does suspect Mark of killing his mother." Jennifer's voice was oddly distant. "At least, that's how he's behaving at the moment. He's got someone watching Mark while he sleeps, in case he says anything incriminating, I suppose. He intends to ask him a lot of questions as soon as he wakes up."

David looked as if he couldn't believe what he was hearing. "Come on, Jennifer. You're just feeling defensive because of your feelings toward Mark." His brow cleared a little. "Luke is just being officious, and you've misunderstood."

"No." Her tone had become grave. She *was* listening to him, she *was* considering the matter. "No, I mean it. He thinks Mark killed his mother."

"And the other women, too?"

She stared at him, appalled. "I suppose he must. I don't expect you to believe this, but when I walked into that house I forgot about the other killings. I just thought about all the arguments Mark has been having with his mother. If Luke suspects Mark of this, he must be thinking of the other killings, too . . . and it's my fault!"

"Poppycock. Sheer unadulterated rubbish," David said, irritably. "So you put your foot in it. Unfortunate, I agree. But your guilt is making you over-sensitive, and you're probably taking things all wrong. I shouldn't have sent you over there, it was a mistake. I should have gone, myself."

She seemed to see him, again, to have come back from a journey. "Why didn't you?"

"I . . . don't know." He stood up and walked to the window, his hands in his pockets. "I suppose the situation seemed clear enough and I wanted to stay free to answer any other calls that might come in. Mrs. Clack had a mild stroke this morning, I half expected another. Then there's the Saunders baby who's putting up a good fight against bronchitis, but you know how cold that place is, even in summer." He turned back. "Mostly, I just thought you'd want to go. To be near your love in his hour of travail."

"He's not my 'love,' " Jennifer snapped.

David raised an eyebrow. "Oh? I was under the impression you'd become the Lily White Maid to his Lochinvar from out of the West." He paused. "That doesn't sound right."

"It isn't. And neither is your assumption about Mark and me."

"I meant—oh, never mind." He scowled at her. "Wasn't he dangling a wedding ring before your dazzled eyes at lunch today?"

"No, he was not. He merely said his mother's opposition to his plans had been done away with."

"They certainly have, now," David observed. "Is *that* why Abbott is so suspicious?"

"No. I think *he* thinks they might have quarrelled over me."

"My goodness, a real *femme fatale* in my own midst, as it were. Literally *fatale*, in fact." David shook his head in disgust. "He's just casting around in the dark, trying to avoid the obvious explanation, because he's afraid of starting a media riot. Or worse, having the media make him look bad because he can't catch the bastard. I don't think much of your Detective Chief Inspector Abbott."

"You made that abundantly clear the other evening," Jennifer said.

"Well, for goodness' sake, it's so obvious. It has to be random killings. What possible connection could there be between a nice, ordinary cleaning lady, a highly sexed bitch, and now a wealthy matron?" He was walking back and forth, in agitation. "None, none at all."

"There is one," Jennifer said, after a moment's reflection.

He whirled around and glared at her. "What, for God's sake?"

Jennifer's eyes were wide and dark. "The towpath. All the killings happened along the same path."

"The first woman was killed in Woodbury."

"Yes, but that same path leads down to the river and joins the towpath. I know it well, we used to go along it all the time to get up to the woods that used to be where the processing plant is, now. The highway was only a side road, then. They widened it when the motorway came near, to make a better connection. The best blackberries in Wychford used to grow up there, the bushes would be bent double with them."

"Have you mentioned this to Abbott?" David asked.

Jennifer smiled, momentarily full of memories. "Oh, he knows. We used to go up there together, sometimes. He'd remember that, all right."

"I see." David looked at her expression, then looked away and marched back to the window to glare at his own reflection. "And did you go up there with Mark Peacock, too?"

"Good heavens, no. Mark Peacock was a bit out of my reach, then. Anyway, he went away to school, he was never part of our crowd. We were town kids, Luke and I."

"So you and Abbott are old friends, are you? I thought I was wading through a few undercurrents the other night, but I couldn't figure out what they were. I see now why he was invited to dinner so quickly—Clodie encouraging the rekindling of old flames, no doubt. And in my innocence I thought it was so Wally could find out more about the killings."

"It was. You know how insatiable he is when it comes to gossip. He loves knowing all the inside details. I sometimes think that was why he became a doctor. He's perfectly discreet, he just likes knowing, that's all."

"Rather a dangerous hobby, I should have thought," David said, reflectively. "People don't like their secrets known."

"Well, he's safe enough, now," Jennifer said, standing up. "I'm going to make some hot chocolate. Would you like some?"

"Thanks." David's voice was distant, as he stared out over the lawn to the hedge that hid them from the road beyond. "What was Abbott doing when you left?"

She stopped at the door. "Glaring at everyone," she said. "Especially me."

CHAPTER FIFTEEN

A local stringer for one of the national newspapers was keeping a close eye on his patch, which included Wychford and environs. He had duly sent in a report on the killing of Beryl Tompkins, cleaner at the photoprocessing plant, spicing it with conjectures concerning the work the plant did and what she might have seen that she shouldn't have. The story received four lines at the bottom of a column. The story above it concerned a pop star's marital problems. The local reporter's follow-up story wasn't even printed, but at least he had the consolation of knowing he'd done a bang-up job for the local rag.

When Win Frenholm was killed, he sent in another story to the nationals, this time with conjectures concerning the nature and motivations of the killer and hints that the two deaths could somehow be connected, noting the similarity of the methods used. Unfortunately a government scandal had broken the night before, and there was little room for his skillful milking of the story. This time his line count reached two paragraphs, but was placed well to the back of the paper. None of the other dailies picked it up.

Mabel Peacock Taubman's death occurred before one o'clock in the morning. In journalistic terms, the evening had been dull. No film stars had been thrown out of nightclubs or flaunted a new affair, the government was silent —licking its wounds and deciding on strategy, the pound was steady, and the skies were clear. Alerted by a contact at the local police station, the stringer was at the gates of Peacock Manor less than ten minutes after the coroner arrived at the scene of the crime. He was too late for the morning nationals, but he got through to the local television night-news editors, both of whom he knew well. And the local paper took everything he had.

As Wychford awoke to a new day, bags were being packed in London. The stringer, a cynical and cadaverous victim of Fleet Street fallout, prepared to defend his territory. He was on top of a big story and intended to stay there.

Mabel Peacock Taubman was society (minor county), she was wealthy (she had an account at Fortnum's), and she was the latest victim of (wait for it) the Cotswold Butcher.

Luke Abbott listened to the local radio report, audible through the hotel kitchen doors, and gazed bleakly across the table at Paddy Smith. "Remind me to have someone clean the fan," he said.

Kay Hall stood beside Jennifer's desk, scowling. "They want to know Mark Peacock's blood type. Should I tell them?"

Jennifer looked up, startled. "Who wants to know?"

"The police. They're on the phone, now. What should I say?"

"Do we have a record of it?"

"Yes. It's A negative."

Jennifer looked at her and sighed resignedly. "Whether we tell them or not won't make any difference in the long run. They'll simply go to some other source with a court order and get it. Hospital, blood bank, whatever. One presumes Mark refused to give the police the information, or a sample."

"One does presume that, yes," Kay said, in an ironic tone. "One does not give one's blood to just *anyone*, does one? They could wait around and hope to catch him on suspicion of drunk driving—but the chances are he'd be only too willing to blow into their bag or even pee on them, and that wouldn't help, would it? It's blood they're after. As usual."

"Are you antipolice, too?" Jennifer asked.

"Only when it suits me," Kay said, grimly. There was a strange glint in her eye, seen only rarely. Someone had gotten too big for his boots, and was in real trouble. "This morning it suits me, because of some snotty little git on the other end of the phone demanding me to tell her about this blood business. When they finally get that little creep that stole Raymond's motorbike behind bars, I'll be back on their side again."

"I see," Jennifer smiled. "Logic, as usual, prevails."

"Of course. What shall I tell this kiss-my-socks madam on the phone?"

"Apologise and say—" Jennifer began.

"Damn," Kay said. "Do I have to?"

"Yes. Tell her it's a matter of patient confidentiality."

"Well, I'll leave her on hold for a while, and then I'll cut her off accidentally," Kay said. She smiled. "That way she'll have to call back."

"And you will apologise, of course."

"Not my fault British Telecom slips a cog now and again, is it?" Kay said, blithely, and went out, leaving Mark Peacock's records folder on the corner of Jennifer's desk.

Jennifer sighed. She was within her rights to refuse, of course. Luke and his people were just doing their job. She'd been foolish to make him suspicious, but no harm could have been done because Mark was completely innocent. This request for Mark's blood type was just a necessary part of the investigation. She knew what it was for—to see whether he could have been the father of Win Frenholm's unborn child. That, and the thought that he had killed his own mother, were equally ridiculous, of course.

Weren't they?

Idly she opened the file. Her eye was instantly arrested by a red inner folder under some letters. She slid it out, and opened it, already knowing something of what she would find. Red inner folders were used for psychiatric reports. And this one was quite thick.

Reluctantly, she began to read.

Luke put the telephone down and gazed across the small cluttered room at Paddy. "Cyril says he can't eliminate Mark Peacock as the father of the unborn child if he's A negative, but he needs a full sample for anything more specific."

"Damn. How do we get that?"

"We don't. Not for the moment, anyway." Luke sighed and leaned back in his borrowed swivel chair. It clicked, and for a moment there was a question of whether he would remain in it or end up on the floor, but eventually he steadied. "I wish I knew why I mistrust Peacock," he said, ruminatively. "I just can't get away from the feeling that all the time he was ranting, raving, sobbing, and all the rest of it he was watching us through his fingers."

"Hunches are inadmissible evidence," Paddy said, phlegmatically. He thought he knew why Luke disliked Peacock. It had something to do with the past, but even more to do with the present—and Jennifer Eames. It was Luke's jealousy she sensed when she'd leapt to Mark Peacock's defence the night before.

Paddy was surprised to discover Luke had developed tender feelings toward Jennifer after so short a reacquaintance, and he suspected that Luke himself would be even more surprised. Nevertheless, all the signs were there. Paddy didn't know whether to be pleased or not. Luke had been terribly lonely since his wife had died. There had been women enough, but never the right ones.

The boys didn't fill the gap, for although Luke was a loving and devoted father, he needed more immediate support than children could give. Paddy liked to think that his friendship had helped Luke through the bad time—but now, if his promotion came through, he'd be leaving Luke to a stranger. He had his eye on several promising young sergeants who would be a good counterbalance to Luke's rather eccentric approach to detection, but none of them were likely to become Luke's friend.

Their own partnership, forged over more than ten years of working together, was a good one, on both a professional and personal level. The friendship would never end, but it would change when he himself was put in charge of other investigations. Contact would become a matter of arranged dinners, formal meetings—reunions. Not the same. Not the same, at all.

"Three women," Luke finally said. "One in her twenties, one in her forties, one in her sixties—or near enough. One poor, one middle-income professional, one of a wealthy county family. One plain but honest, one beautiful and bitchy, one well-preserved and demanding. Two married and apparently faithful, one single and promiscuous. All of medium height and weight. One brunette, one blonde, one greying. One a mother of young children, one pregnant, one beyond child-bearing—although the mother of a grown son."

"Those are the differences," Paddy said. "What similarities do we have?"

"They're all dead," Luke said, tersely.

"And?"

Luke sighed. "All had their throats cut around midnight. All were attacked from behind. No sexual molestation. No mutilation beyond the single wound. No weapon found. No claims for responsibility made by person or persons unknown. All killed along or opposite the path that runs from the photoprocessing plant down to and along the river."

"You left one out," Paddy said. Luke raised an interrogative eyebrow, and Paddy went on. "All three were patients on the medical list of Dr. David Gregson."

Luke brought his feet down from the desk and stared at him. "How did you find that out?"

"I asked," Paddy said, quietly. "We knew Frenholm was, although she saw Jennifer that last time for some reason, and we know Mrs. Peacock was, too. I woke up thinking about it this morning. So I rang Mr. Tompkins over in Woodbury and asked who his wife's doctor had been. He told me she used to go to old Dr. Mayberry, but when he got ill she started seeing Dr. Gregson. So there *was* a connection." He eyed Luke warily. "What do you think?"

Luke stood up and walked to the window. The small office they'd been assigned overlooked the parking lot, and he gazed down at the colourful collection of cars below. Black and white for the marked cars, dark blue for the unmarked cars, and just about every bright contrast for the personal cars of the local constabulary. His own car was scarlet, and stood in a far corner. He was using one of theirs, so that the local police and traffic wardens would recognise it. On his last case he'd collected four citations, through a habit of parking where he damn well felt like it. Bad habit. He had a lot of bad habits, he thought. Not least of which was allowing his personal feelings to interfere with his professional instincts. He turned back to the room and met Paddy's eye.

"I think we ought to walk that path," he said, firmly.

CHAPTER SIXTEEN

The first true frost of the autumn had descended in the predawn hours of the morning, coupled with a heavy dew. In the shadows there were still traces of the silvery result, like secret spangles left from a night's illicit revel. Luke and Paddy left their car in the parking lot of the photoprocessing plant and headed toward the gap in the fence that marked the beginning of the path. Luke paused there, and surveyed the land below.

"It was the road that stole it, Paddy," he said, quietly. "Or all the roads, put together. There used to be a wood here, and the path followed a stream down to the river, where it joined the towpath. I guess the stream fled underground when they cut down the forest and built this damn factory. It wasn't really a forest—it just seemed that way to us. We could look down on the adults below and have our secrets and games to ourselves. I'm glad I left before the big roads came."

"I thought it was only the elderly that talked about how things used to be," Paddy said, briskly. "You're adding years on before your time, Luke." It wasn't often he called his superior by his first name, and then only when they were alone. He thought Abbott was very alone in that moment, and needed calling back to the present.

Luke flashed an amused glance his way. "Don't worry, I'm not becoming morbid. It's a simple fact—I'm glad I left before the changes began. This Wychford is one place. The Wychford I grew up in is another. I keep it over here." He tapped a spot behind his left temple. "Right in front of my university years, and just behind my first year on the strength." His eyes left Paddy's face and quickly flicked across the parking lot of the photoprocessing plant to where the hedge was pushed aside. "Come on, let's go."

They went through the ragged gap and began the descent toward the highway which followed the curve of the hill below them, breaking the angle of the land as it sloped toward the river. At one point the path skirted a stand of bushes, and it was here that the murder of Beryl Tompkins had taken place. Abbott paused and looked back up the hill. "The lights in the factory parking lot were on, but wouldn't have been sufficient to reach this far. The highway is lit below, but those lights wouldn't have reached up enough, either. A natural black hole. I bet the women run when they get to this point."

"Why the hell don't they go down the drive leading up to the factory?" Paddy grumbled. "There's a nice wide pavement there, it's well-lit."

"And it takes them four hundred yards out of their way, as the bus-stop is directly below this bush. They'd have to backtrack to it," Luke said. "Like water, people take the easiest way." He continued past the bush and on down toward the highway, Paddy stepping carefully behind him, as the path was treacherous with hidden pockets of frost. One caught him as he was nearly down and he skidded into Abbott's back. Only Abbott's quick reflexes stopped him from being precipitated under the wheels of a juggernaut that was thundering past at that moment.

He looked at Paddy's horrified face. "I know you're looking forward to promotion, but let's not get carried away," he said, leaning against the bus-stop sign.

"Sorry," Paddy mumbled. "Frost on the path."

"That's *your* story," Abbott grinned. "Come on, we've got a gap coming up, here." They darted across the four lanes and jumped the fence on the other side, as another juggernaut and a bus crossed through the space they'd just vacated. Luke turned to his right. "We go along here for a ways—there's the stream, or what's left of it." He gestured down at a stained and ugly concrete culvert that protruded from beneath the highway. A sluggish flow of discoloured water issued from it and disappeared into the bracken that covered the rest of the hill down to the river below. He continued to walk parallel to the highway for another five or six yards, then stopped. "Here's where the path drops down again. Pretty overgrown, not much used on this side, anymore." He turned into what looked to Paddy like an impenetrable wall of undergrowth, but which proved to be thinner in this one spot. They thrashed through it, thorns and weeds catching at their suit coats and their ill-protected ankles. Paddy, a city boy, found this progress through Nature in the raw was not exactly what he had dressed for that morning. He wiped blood from a scratch on one cheek, and trudged after Luke, who was moving slowly along the path, his sharp eyes darting everywhere, up, down, around. Paddy stopped for a moment to investigate a wool thread caught on a branch, only to realise it came from Luke's trousers. He looked up and found that Luke had disappeared. It was only Luke's sudden "Aha!" that located him. Paddy broke through into a clear space that edged the hospital grounds.

"We'll have to cut across the corner of their parking area, here, and then I think we'll find the path continues quite clearly down past the housing estate to the towpath itself," Luke said. They edged between cars, crossed the gravelled expanse beyond, then between more cars. There seemed to be a lot of activity at the far end of the lot, near the hospital, where a tow truck was surrounded by a number of gesticulating workmen. Luke paused, moved along, then straightened. "Here. I was right. At least the hospital architect had the sense to put in a gate. Must have been a local boy," Luke grinned.

"Easy walking, now, Paddy. You can stop growling at me. It's like being followed by a bear."

"Need to be to get through all that," Paddy grumbled.

"Exactly. I don't think our killer took this route, although he may have known about it. If I were still living here, I'd skip it, too, but it needed checking." They broke through the last of the undergrowth and stopped. "Good God, it *couldn't* have been a local boy who designed *this.*" Abbott was staring, appalled, at the bleak entwining of treeless streets lined by shingled boxes that was the Riverview Estates. "On the other hand, I suppose it's the best place in town to live, because it's the only place in town from which you can't see it," he added, drily.

"Now, now, a lot of young couples start their lives on estates like these," Paddy said, idiotically. Luke looked at him in some dismay.

"And a lot of young couples start their *divorces* on estates like these, where the women are isolated and the men come home feeling like drones living in a beehive. There's what I mean," Abbott said, gesturing toward a young woman who was pushing a pram on the pavement opposite them. She was slim and fresh and young—but her eyes were worried, and her baby was fretting. She gave them a wary, sideways glance. "Give me a broken-down flat any time—at least it has identity. There's more crime on these estates than in . . ."

"All right, all right, it was a dumb remark," Paddy agreed, sheepishly. "What's happened to your famous path, by the way?"

"It's been displaced," Abbott said, turning around and around. "Ah . . . over there." He started off toward a small plot of land that had been allocated for a rather dismal toddler's playground. Paddy caught up with him by the swings.

"How do you know?" he asked.

"Water," Abbott said. He strode across the patchy grass, toward a break in a tangle of old and young trees.

"Water?" Paddy repeated.

"Finds the easiest path down," Abbott went on. "Beyond this is a sloping bank . . . see? And there's the towpath. Go down here and along the towpath, and arrive at the bottom end of town, some small shops, and a bus-stop. She'll be coming this way, you watch and see."

"She'll never get that pram down the slope," Paddy said.

"Oh, yes, she will. I'd bet she does it every day," Abbott said, squinting against the sun which was now above the roof-tops. The young woman pushed the pram steadily, a carrier bag of clothing bumping gently against the handle—destined, no doubt, for either the dry cleaners or Oxfam. "Afternoon, madam," he said, gravely. "Could we give you a hand with the pram?"

She glanced at him nervously. "No, thank you."

Paddy was about to reassure her that they were trustworthy, when she adroitly twisted the pram to one side and skidded it sideways down the slope to the towpath six feet below. In a moment she'd turned it toward town and disappeared behind the hedge. Abbott smiled. "You see? Now if the town council had an ounce of sense, which *would* be a change from the old days, they'd make a proper job of this shortcut, instead of trying to fence it off." He pointed to the broken fencing pushed into the hedge, and a half hidden sign that said "No through way." "Ridiculous. Nobody pays the least attention to it, and I don't blame them, either. Presumably they're expected to wind their way through that maze of streets to the highway and then walk two miles to the other end of town. And two miles back, I might add. Try that with a squalling baby, a couple of carrier bags of groceries, and a headache. Alternatively, we have on offer here a brief walk beside the cooling river. No contest. What was Barry Treat's address again?"

This abrupt change of subject caught Paddy off guard, and it took him a minute to find his notebook. Luke kept looking around while he searched for the right page. "Number Ten Purlway," Paddy pronounced.

"Which puts him along there, I believe," Abbott nodded toward the road down which the young mother had come. "So this is the way he came, and presumably the way Win Frenholm came, too. Come on."

The young woman with the pram had disappeared by the time they reached the towpath. A few minute's walk brought them to the place where Win Frenholm had been murdered. Across the river they could glimpse the near corner of the grounds of Peacock Manor.

"So, you see, there is a linking factor," Abbott said.

"Yes—fallen arches," Paddy said grimly, easing a foot inside his shoe. "Did the killer swim the river to kill Mrs. Taubman, perhaps?"

"No," Abbott said, solemnly. "He drove or walked over one of the bridges or took a bus, which is what I propose we do, now."

"Bloody hell," Paddy moaned.

They didn't have to wait long for a bus, but it took them only to the centre of town and the bus station. There would be a twenty-minute wait until the next one departed for the hill and the photoprocessing plant where they'd left their car. Paddy was all for calling the station for a pick-up, but Abbott said no. He went into the despatcher's office and obtained the names and addresses of the men who regularly drove the latter route in the evenings, which he passed to Paddy to give to Bennett. "Tell him to find out if they took any unusual passengers up or back that way on the night Mrs. Tompkins was killed," he said. "At that time of night most of the passengers would be regulars. An unusual pick-up would be noticed, I think. There's our bus, by the way. At least we can sit down in it until it leaves."

As the bus finally left the station and wound its tortuous way through the town Abbott gazed out with fascination at the things that had changed and the things that remained the same. Some of the names above the shops were the same, but the fronts had changed. Many of the familiar High Street chains were represented. Occasionally, there would be something he remembered, something that was just as it had always been. Places where the smells would be the same, but which seemed somehow smaller than he remembered, as if time had compressed them. Pelmer's the chemists, Osgood's the sweet shop, Laine's wool shop, all brought a slight curve to his normally serious mouth. "Good way to see a town," he commented to Paddy. "A few feet above, slow-moving, it gives you a new point of view. Things look different. Not a bird's-eye view, but not a man's-eye view, either." He glanced at Paddy. "You're not impressed, I can see."

"Oh, I'm always willing to learn," Paddy acknowledged. They were coming to the foot of the hill, now. Suddenly he straightened in his seat, then turned as they passed a truck towing a car with a smashed-in front end. "Oh, God," he said, half to himself.

Luke turned, too. "What's the matter?" he asked.

"That's Frances's car," Paddy said. "What the hell's happened to it? And to her?"

CHAPTER SEVENTEEN

Frances stared up at Jennifer from the hospital bed. "Oh, Jaesus," she said, her accent considerably more pronounced than usual, in travail. "I've never been so embarrassed in my life, coming through the wall of the surgical theatre like that and Dr. Blythe looking up, scalpel in his hand, never batting an eye. 'Has that car been sterilized?' he says, and me sitting there like a great goop with the steering wheel half up my jumper and all the instruments across the bonnet like a canteen of cutlery on a barrow."

"It must have been dreadful," Jennifer said, trying to be sympathetic, and not to laugh. Frances looked at her twitching mouth and sighed in resignation.

"I'd laugh, too, if it didn't hurt my ribs. It was only that ice on the slope, wasn't it, and me locking the brakes, I was that startled when I started to skid."

The new surgical wing was built half into the ground, with a wide sloping ditch surrounding it on three and a half sides. The walls were of tinted one-way glass panels and exposed steel girders. At the rear was a service drive curving down from the general parking lot. This was on the west side of the building, and consequently had gotten no sun by nine o'clock that morning. Frances, coming in to park, had hit a thin sheet of ice created by a leaking hosepipe and had slewed down the service drive straight into the side of theatre two, where the senior orthopaedic consultant had been about to commence a complex pelvic osteotomy.

"He was lovely, really. He sent the patient into theatre three with Dr.

Marsh, and lifted me out of the car as gently as a babe, once he'd made certain there was nothing broken," Frances said. "Called a trolley for me, sent me over to casualty, and here I am. I suppose he had to scrub up again and all, but he never complained. Thank God the patient never woke up, it would have been cardiac arrest at the least. Oh, God, I'll never live it down. I'll be working here for the rest of my life, paying it off, plus having to face Dr. Blythe nearly every day, too. You know what he is for the teasing."

"I'll have a little word with him," Jennifer said. "And as for the question of payment, it seems to me you have a good case for negligence against the hospital concerning that broken pipe or drain or whatever it was that sent the water over the parking lot in the first place."

"They weren't to know it would freeze."

"In late October? They could hardly deny the possibility," Jennifer said, firmly. "No, I expect the insurance companies will settle it between them. Now, do you need anything?"

Frances was wearing a surgical collar for whiplash, and had several cracked ribs, but otherwise her injuries were mainly bruising. They were keeping her in for twenty-four hours observation. She tried to shake her head, and winced. "Not unless they decide to commit me to the local Home for the Bewildered," she said, mournfully. "It's the fairies, I tell you. They've got it in for me, and no mistake. I could just hammer the little divils."

Jennifer laughed. "I'll pick you up tomorrow after surgery," she said, waving as she went down the ward. She nearly ran into Paddy Smith at the door. "Fourth bed on the right," she told him. "Tell her you've arrested the fairies involved, and are holding them in a shoebox for trial."

"The fairies again, is it?" Paddy asked, grimly. "More likely she needs new lenses in her spectacles and a bell to warn people she's coming."

"Paddy."

"What?"

"She's fine. Bruised, not broken."

"Oh? Well, then." His relief was visible. "A shoebox, did you say?"

"I gather they're small," Jennifer grinned.

Downstairs, she found Luke waiting for his associate in reception. He had his hands jammed in his trouser pockets and was leaning against a windowsill, his long legs stretched out before him as he contemplated some mud that had stuck to the instep of one shoe. He looked up at the sound of Jennifer's heels on the lino, and his blue eyes instantly became wary.

"She's all right," Jennifer said.

"That's good."

"How did you know about it?"

"We saw her car being towed away, and made some enquiries. That's our job, you know. Making enquiries."

"I'm told you're pretty good at it."

"When we aren't hassling your friends, you mean?"

Jennifer looked down, then met his eyes. "I'm sorry, Luke, I shouldn't have flown off the handle at you last night. I was wrong."

He inclined his head, slightly. "Thank you."

"We had a request in the office this morning concerning Mark's blood type. I assume that's to help eliminate the possibility of his fathering the Frenholm baby?" She raised a hand. "Wait, no, I'm sorry, I had no right to ask that."

"Because you refused to tell us?"

She felt herself growing red. "Since Mark himself refused, I decided . . ."

"It doesn't matter. We got his blood type from hospital records. We couldn't eliminate him, but that's not saying much. We'd need a proper sample to make any closer comparisons. He's just one of a number of people we're looking at." His voice was very measured, very calm.

"Here's looking at you, kid," Jennifer said, lightly.

He considered this, and awarded it a small smile. "Yes," he said. "And what do you see?"

"Someone I used to know. Someone who's changed, or been changed, very deeply. Where's all the laughter you used to have, Luke?"

"In the grave with my wife," he snapped, then sighed in exasperation and looked away. "Sorry, that was uncalled for. And not true, because I would never burden her memory with that blame. It's the job, Jenny, the job and the victims and the need to suspect everyone, everything, all the time. It gets to be a habit."

"Then why do it?"

"Because I'm good at it. Because despite what it does to me, I like what I do. Killing people is wrong. You take an oath about that, so do I. The temptation is always there, to grow too strong, to play God, to make decisions without due care and attention, just because it would be easier all round."

"Such as not suspecting Mark because he's my . . . boyfriend?"

"Or even not suspecting *you* because Mark's mother was against your becoming involved with her golden boy."

Jenny was dumbfounded. "You suspect *me?*"

He shrugged. "Not seriously, but conscience and logic both indicate you can't be rejected as a possibility. You're medically trained, you'd know where to make the cut and how much force to use. The women wouldn't have suspected another woman, they might have turned their backs on you without fear. You're young and strong and quick."

"And am I supposed to have fathered Win Frenholm's baby, too, perchance?" She didn't know whether to laugh or kick him.

"You could have found out Mark had had an affair with her, killed out of jealousy and/or hate, then turned on his mother who stood in your way almost as much."

"Thank you very much."

He shrugged. "It's automatic. I could make a good case out for any number of people, providing certain things were true. I'm only talking about possibilities, Jennifer. Conjecture. Patterns. However, we still don't know that the deaths are connected."

"My God, what does it *take* to convince you?" she demanded. "I can see what David meant. Does this killer have to put up a sign saying, 'Catch me if you can'?"

"It would be a big help." He smiled, sadly. "You see, it's easy for everyone —the media, the local people, Gregson, you—to jump to the conclusion that it's the same man. It would be easy for me, too."

"And you don't like the easy route?"

He gazed at his shoe again. "Something like that."

"Would you *rather* believe it's three separate murderers?" She asked the question quite seriously.

"Obviously not. My thoughts now tend toward a division of one and two —but which one is separate and which two go together is the problem. The person who killed Beryl Tompkins *might* have killed the other two—or he might have killed just one of them. Or neither."

"But surely, forensic evidence . . ."

"Cyril Franklin is brilliant, but he can only go so far without a magic spyglass to look back in time. Murder is an awkward business—victims struggle, feet slip. No two deaths are *ever* exactly alike. Only similar, at best. Even if the same killer uses the same method every time, differences occur. For Cyril and for us, the best bet is experienced observation and instinct. Something bothers him and bothers me, but neither of us can decide just what it is, yet. It may not even be the same thing. Hence my suspicion of your golden boy and his rather melodramatic overreaction to his mother's murder."

"Mark is sensitive," Jennifer said, automatically.

Luke smiled. "So am I," he said.

"And the next minute, he asked me to have dinner with him, tonight." Jennifer gazed at her aunt, having presented her with a rather full platter of information over the luncheon table.

"Some doctors do have them," David said, wryly.

"Have what?" Jennifer demanded.

"Crazy friends and ardent suitors by the dozen," he answered, reaching for the coffee pot.

"I don't . . ." Jennifer began, hotly, but her aunt's cool voice intervened.

"Are you going to have dinner with him?"

Jennifer gave David a last glare, but his amused expression remained. "Yes. I called Mark, but Basil said he's still too upset to see anyone."

"I went over this morning," David said. "He may be shaken, but he was up and dressed. Mr. Taubman is being overprotective, in my opinion. Maybe if he'd had a little more reality in his life, Mark wouldn't be such a jellyfish now. First his mother bossed him around, now Taubman is stepping in."

"That's not fair," Jennifer flared. "It's a terrible shock to find anyone murdered, much more so your own mother."

"I agree. As it happens, Mark didn't look shocked," David said. "He just looked . . . relieved. They were going over plans for the conversion. They were really very absorbed."

"Basil's lost his wife, you seem to forget. He's not a man who shows much emotion in public, I gather. He's probably just trying to keep occupied, and to keep Mark occupied, too," Jennifer said. Gregson's silence was a kind of comment. After a moment, she cleared her throat. "I . . . happened to look through Mark's record folder this morning."

"Oh?"

"I didn't realise he'd had a nervous breakdown." Jennifer watched her aunt and David exchange a glance.

"It was when his father died," Aunt Clodie said. "It was more nervous exhaustion and grief than a breakdown."

"Not according to the psychiatrist's reports," Jennifer said, her eyes on David. "They wrote Uncle Wally that they found acute mania, delusions, and paranoia. I see he's been on a maintenance dose of Serenace ever since." She turned to her aunt. "You might have mentioned it."

"I thought it was just grief," Aunt Clodie said, in some confusion. "I thought it was just temporary. Wally never said otherwise. Mark was only hospitalized for a short time. I didn't think he was *crazy.*"

"He's not," David said, sharply. "There is a family tendency toward schizophrenia, it's true, but nothing more than that."

"But if Jennifer married him, if there were children . . ." Aunt Clodie was deeply dismayed.

"I never intended marrying Mark," Jennifer said. "But I can see now why he was so malleable and mother-dominated. The drugs took away his aggression."

"Fortunately," David said, drily. "And as for the rest, there's no problem as long as he keeps taking the drug, of course." He looked pointedly at Jennifer. "And he *has* been taking the drug regularly. I checked."

Jennifer felt herself flushing, knowing he had read her mind and her fears clearly. "Well . . . good," she said, lamely.

"Dear me," Aunt Clodie murmured.

David finished his coffee and stood up. "I have some notes to update before rounds. Your list is on your desk, Jennifer—Kay pulled the records for you." He smiled at Clodie and went out. They could hear his voice in the kitchen, thanking Mrs. Louis for the lunch, on his way through to the surgery.

"He never forgets to thank her," Clodie murmured. "He has nice manners."

"Oh, really? I hadn't noticed, particularly," Jennifer said, crossly.

Clodie sighed. "I wish you two would try to get along, it would make things so much easier in this house." She poured herself a second cup of coffee. "Now, tell me everything Luke said about the murders."

"I did."

Clodie looked disappointed. "You mean there wasn't anything else? Anything at all?"

"I'm afraid not."

"Oh, dear. I wonder what Hercule Poirot would say," Clodie murmured. "Or Henry Merrivale? Or Maud Silver?"

"I'll ask Luke if he'd like their assistance, shall I?"

"Don't be flippant," Clodie advised.

Jennifer grinned. "Why, will it give me sciatica?"

"No, but it will give you indigestion. You've just poured custard into your coffee instead of cream."

CHAPTER EIGHTEEN

Annabel Leigh reached up to silence the bell over the door as she entered the shop she shared with her partner. She crossed the room, her bright hair flaming briefly in a shaft of sunlight that managed to penetrate from outside. In the cluttered rear of the shop she found Mary Straker carding wool. "My God, I am heartily sick and tired of talking about Win Frenholm," Annabel said, lighting a forbidden cigarette and tossing her coat into the corner. "I've just stopped at Sam's to get these and been waylaid by yet another reporter. They hang around, take up your time, and never buy anything. They just want more scandal to put in their rotten papers."

Mary looked sympathetic. "I know. Poor Hannah has had it worst—they latched onto her right away, once they'd wrung Barry and Gordon dry. But I understand Ray Moss gave one reporter a black eye and threw him out bodily, yesterday afternoon."

"Really?" Annabel was amused. "I hadn't heard that. Maybe Ray has some good points after all. Is Barry back?"

Mary's face clouded. "No. I asked Gordon, and he said he had the flu and wasn't up to working, yet."

"Do you believe him?"

"Yes, funnily enough, I do. I don't know whether it's flu, exactly, but I'm certain that dear little Barry would have to be really ill to miss this chance to be the centre of attention."

"Oh, bitchy, bitchy," Annabel laughed.

Mary smiled. "Sorry. I wouldn't blame him for playing hooky if he wanted to, though. I feel like getting flu, myself, at the moment. Damn." The bell in the shop had rung, and she stood up to go. "I never thought I'd complain about being too busy, but, really . . ."

"We've sold a lot of sweaters," Annabel pointed out, reluctantly. "Whatever Win did or didn't do for this place in life, she's more than made up for it in death. People are coming from *miles* away, just to have a look. She's put us on the map at last. Sam's happy as a sandboy, over there, selling pies and doughnuts like a madman."

Mary nodded, and went through to the front of the shop. Annabel listened for a moment, and sighed. They sounded like browsers rather than buyers. She got up to put the kettle on, and, as she did, there was a tapping at the back door. She opened it to find Hannah Putnam standing there.

"I've closed the studio," Hannah said, her voice harsh. "I can't stand any more today."

"My God, you look ghastly. Come on in and have some coffee or something." Annabel swept her friend in and closed the door behind her.

"Oh, you've got customers," Hannah said, pausing on her way to a chair.

"Never mind, Mary's out there. They're only looking," Annabel said, negligently. "Sit down, for heaven's sake."

Hannah sank down gratefully into the rocking chair by the back door. She looked on the verge of collapse. Her fine-boned face was haggard, and there were shadows under her eyes. Her silvery cap of hair looked dull and lay flat against her scalp, as if she hadn't washed it for days. Her hands plucked restlessly at the big black shawl she wore wrapped around her against the chill of the afternoon. "I'm so tired," she whispered.

"You should have closed the studio days ago, right after Win . . . died."

"Was murdered, you mean," Hannah said, gratingly. "She was murdered, Annabel. Her throat cut . . ."

"Stop that!" Annabel ordered, horrified at the defeated sound of Hannah's voice. It was as if she were dead herself, kept upright by habit, blind and deaf to life. "Drink this coffee *instantly.*" She thrust a steaming cup into the older woman's hands. Its scalding heat seemed to jolt Hannah out of her self-absorbed misery.

"Ouch, dammit! That's hot!" she said, in a reproachful tone.

Annabel was relieved to hear this normal response. For a moment there she thought Hannah had become numb in every way. "Then it will do you good," she said, firmly, and poured out cups for Mary and herself. "Get it down you."

Hannah sipped gingerly, and spots of colour appeared in her pale cheeks. After a moment, she smiled. "Thank you. This is a really nasty cup of coffee, Annabel. May I have some milk and sugar in it, please?

"Only if you behave yourself and stop moping," Annabel said, in a tone she usually reserved for her schoolboy sons.

"I shall try," Hannah said, austerely. "I have not your resilience, my dear." She loosened her shawl and sat back as Mary Straker returned from the front of the shop waving a handful of notes.

"They bought the black-and-white bat-wing pullover," she said, gleefully. "I *told* you that would go quickly."

"Only because you've been pushing it shamelessly," Annabel grinned. "Well done."

Mary caught sight of Hannah and her smile faded. "Hi, Hannah. What's wrong, lovey? Are you ill?"

All of Annabel's efforts at bucking up her friend came to nothing, for at the warm sympathy in Mary's voice, Hannah broke down completely and began to cry like a child.

"Not well done," Annabel said in a flat tone, scowling at Mary. She went over and put an arm around Hannah's shaking shoulders. "Maybe you'd better have a good cry and let it all out, after all," she suggested, kindly. This had the almost instant effect of stopping Hannah's tears. She took some deep breaths and got herself in hand, glancing up at Mary through wet lashes.

"I can take anything but sympathy," she said to the horrified girl. "Next time you see me looking miserable, kick me in the shins. It's the only way." She smiled tremulously, took another deep breath, and firmed the smile into something resembling the real thing. "There, I've hit bottom, now. I shall be better in moments." Occasionally Hannah's European origin betrayed itself in her precision of speech. She had married an English soldier after the war, but, like the tattoo on her arm, her heritage was indelible. Another part of that heritage manifested itself as she sat upright and squared her shoulders. "I shall finish my coffee," she said, and did so.

The other two women picked up their cups, constrained, now, by Hannah's impressive powers of recovery. They glanced at one another and sat silent, hiding behind their respective mugs. Hannah put hers down and leaned her head against the high back of the rocking chair. In this position, they could see that she had lost weight over the past few days, for the bony lines of her jaw were delineated clearly beneath the translucent skin. Her habit of dressing in black only emphasised her pallor.

"I have a secret," she said, after a moment. "It is a heavy secret, and is weighing upon me. I do not know what to do."

Annabel and Mary exchanged another glance. "Is it about Win?" Annabel asked, finally.

"It is. In a way, it is. You see, I know who she was going to meet the night she was murdered."

"Good Lord, Hannah! You should have told the police that immediately!" Annabel said, astonished. "Why didn't you?"

Hannah lowered her head from its resting place and gazed down at her thin, clever hands. "I don't know. Perhaps because I didn't think there could be any connection. I assumed she had been murdered by this Cotswold Butcher person the papers talk of so much, now. Like the other woman, up near the factory. I thought he killed her on her way to meet her friend. Or afterward. But not that the *friend* killed her. Not her 'woolly lamb.' From what she said, he was not like that."

"Someone from here?" Mary asked.

"No. Oh, no. Someone from the town. Not like the others, not the rich one or the rough one. This one she . . . cared for, in some odd way. She only met him in the dark, she said. Walking, by the river. He didn't know she was beautiful, only that she listened to him talk and was kind to him. She seemed surprised herself that she could be kind to anyone. But perhaps it was a new game she played. Perhaps the cruelty would have come later. I wonder now if it maybe came that night. But even so, even if he killed Win because she was cruel to him or rejected him, I do not think he could have killed these other women, so therefore I do not know what to think, what to do."

"Tell the police," Mary said, promptly.

But Annabel was not so quick. "Have you a reason for wanting to protect him?" she asked. Hannah nodded.

"He has a certain position, and I think also a wife," she said. "This I know, and his first name, and some other small things about him that would be sufficient, I believe, for the police to identify him. Some of the things Win told me would not be of help, of course, but were only spoken of to hurt me." A muscle flickered momentarily in her cheek. "Which they did."

Mary spoke angrily. "The thing that has amazed me is why Win wasn't murdered long ago. She hurt everyone she knew, one way or another."

Hannah smiled, sadly. "Yes, now it is more easy to see her weaknesses clearly with . . . hindsight, is it? But when she was here, alive and vital and so lovely, one forgave her. One kept forgiving her. Perhaps that was what made her cruel, perhaps she didn't know it was cruelty."

"She knew," Annabel said, uncompromisingly. "Just as you know you must go to the police, Hannah. If this man is innocent, as you hope, he still may be able to help them. Perhaps he saw or heard something."

Hannah looked at her. "Then why has he not come forward himself?" she asked. "This is what I do not understand. This is what worries me and makes me think perhaps he is, after all, the killer."

"Perhaps he has . . ." Annabel said, reasonably, "perhaps he has talked to the police, and been cleared. Or even called them anonymously. But you won't know, you can't know, unless you go to them yourself."

"Yes," Hannah nodded. "I see you are right, of course." Her normally clear eyes clouded with other memories, as she absently rubbed her wrist. "But betrayal of another human being is not something that comes easily to me. It never will." She smiled, almost apologetically. "It is . . . very difficult to condemn weakness, when one is so weak oneself, you see."

"But you must."

Hannah sighed. "Yes. I must."

CHAPTER NINETEEN

Jennifer and Luke dined on roast beef and memories, with local crime forgotten in the pleasure of catching up on the life of someone who mattered—on both sides. However they had come to be what they were, what roads taken, what joys and sadnesses encountered on the way, they were pleased with the result and the moment they were sharing, too jealous of the time to waste it.

Carefully, they juggled the silences, keeping them high and light so neither could tilt them with a wrong reference, an unfortunate allusion, and drop reality back into their evening.

They were clever people. They managed the trick for quite a while. But Luke faltered, in the end, his duty too much a part of the man he was to be ignored. Their after-dinner walk in the crisp autumn evening inevitably led down the High Street and onto the river path. At first Jennifer didn't notice, too enchanted with Luke's soft laughter and tall elegant presence. Alone, and away from his investigation, she found he had retained his wicked sense of humour, as well as the athletic grace of his adolescence, so he moved easily beside her, gesturing widely to outline the shadowy figure of a pickpocket he'd encountered in his first months on the force.

"He said I was interfering with his right to work," Luke chuckled. "Said I was an example of the Establishment's determination to stamp out the liberties of the common man. It was quite a speech."

"And what did you say?"

"I said 'I agree with you totally, but you're still nicked, because that's *my* work, and *I* have a right to pursue it.' He suggested that we had reached a stalemate and wondered if we could perhaps come to some amicable arrangement."

"And did you?"

"I've always been a reasonable man. I said I'd let him escort me back to the station, and then he could let me book him. Seemed a fair division of labour. He took exception. *And* about four inches of skin off my left shin. I still have the scar."

"You're a hard man," Jennifer laughed.

"So they say. I don't think so, myself, but then, I wouldn't. Paddy says I'm like a steamroller, full of hot air and inexorable, so I flatten them all in the end."

"And do you still cry at sad movies?"

He stopped and looked down at her, smiling in the faint light that came over the rail of Martyr's Bridge onto the towpath where they stood. "Yes," he said, softly. "I still do. Know where to stick the pin, don't you?" He lifted her chin with a finger and kissed her, once for yesterday, and again for today, and then, harder, for tomorrow. "Damn you, Jenny," he whispered into her hair. "Why couldn't you have grown up ugly like you promised?"

Stunned by the warmth and sudden hunger of his mouth, she could only stammer, "Did I promise that?"

"Yes. Up on the hill, one summer afternoon, the week before your family moved away. I said I was going to find you and marry you when we grew up and you said you were going to be fat and ugly and would never get married. I kissed you and you ran away."

"I was only fourteen."

He pulled back, slightly. "So you do remember."

"Yes." She stepped away too, afraid of what he was making her feel. "I went back, you know. Hours later. I was such a conceited little brat I thought you might still be there. But of course you were gone."

"You went back." For a moment he felt a terrible sense of loss, a tumbling of the years over his head, and sixteen again. Her mouth had been so sweet, then and now. "You never told me."

"No. I think I was ashamed."

"Of what?"

She chuckled. "Of wanting another kiss."

"Have it now." He took her back into his arms.

Suddenly there was a step beside them, and a shadowy figure loomed up from the path. "All right, then, that's enough. I'm afraid you'll have to move on, now," said a brusque but sympathetic voice. "Let's just . . ." A torch flicked onto their faces. Luke released her and squinted into the light, scowling. "Oh, Christ!" came a gasp from the dark figure behind the torch.

"Good evening, constable," Luke said, calmly. "All quiet?"

"Yes, sir. Just a few walkers and courting couples, like," came the strangled reply. "That is . . ."

"That is good to hear," Luke said, gravely. "Remember to keep out of sight, won't you?"

"Yes, sir. Ah . . . sorry, sir."

"Not at all, you did right. Carry on." Luke took Jennifer's arm and started walking down the towpath, away from the bridge. The river gurgled and lapped the bank beside them. Above them the lights of the houses glowed, and, across the river, they could see an answering glimmer between the trees —the lights of Peacock Manor. Jennifer tried not to look that way, wondering if Mark could see them, which was, of course, ridiculous. As was her almost overwhelming impulse to giggle.

As they went along, not speaking, another figure appeared from behind a bush. "Evening, constable," Luke said, evenly, before the man spoke.

"Sir," came the respectful reply, and the figure fell back.

They went on, and around a bend. A night bird called, then another. "How many of them are there?" Jennifer finally asked, in a small voice.

"I don't know," Luke replied, and she could hear the laughter in his throat. "That's up to the local man in charge. I only said I wanted the towpath watched. Have I destroyed your authority in the town forever, caught canoodling under the bridge?"

"Never mind me, what about you?"

"Ten minute wonder—if they believe him at all," Luke said, dismissively. "I'm not exactly known as a Lothario." He rubbed his ear and chuckled. "At least, I haven't been. Very serious chap, I am, you know. Very dedicated."

"Yes." Jennifer's voice was still small, and he turned his head, sharply. "What is it?"

"Is that why we came down here? So you could check on your troops?" she asked.

He stopped and took hold of her shoulders. "How would you like to be thrown into the river?" he asked.

"Not very much."

"Then stop being an idiot. Frankly, I forgot why I was here at all. I just wanted to walk with you by the river. It seemed to be a way to keep on remembering, that's all."

"But something in you also remembered the real reason why you came back to Wychford," Jennifer insisted. "I'm certain of it."

He dropped his hands and sighed, looking over the river to Peacock Manor. "Yes, you're probably right. I'm sorry. I told you it becomes a habit."

"While we were having dinner and talking about old times I was also thinking about having to tell a patient the results of her cervical smear test. She has cancer—very advanced." Jennifer reached up and touched his face. "We're grown up now, Luke. Only children have the luxury of single-mindedness."

"And all times like these are stolen," he agreed. "Perhaps that's why they're so precious." And he drew her to him, again.

Dazed and somewhat guilty at his hiatus from duty, Luke returned to the hotel after driving Jennifer home. He had wanted to linger, but Gregson had been there, starting out on a house call. His brusque greeting and scowling departure had jolted them back to reality, and they had both realised that the moment was past. Whether other such moments lay ahead, neither of them knew.

The whole episode had unnerved them both.

Luke had returned to Wychford to find a killer, Jennifer to find a vocation. Neither had expected to find one another, nor to discover in such an encounter the fire that had once been set between them but never lit. They had been children—just children, then.

After David had driven off, Luke had touched Jennifer's face, gently. "We'd best be wary of dry tinder," he said. "We've both been alone a long time. We'll have to decide whether we want a blaze or a slow burning, Jenny. And we'll have to be careful not to kick the fire out."

She'd laughed. "Meaning good night?"

"Meaning good night." He kissed her lightly. "I'll ring you, tomorrow. I hope you can do something for your lady patient."

"So do I," Jennifer said, and watched him get into his car and drive away. He waved as he drove out the gate. When she closed the door she found herself shaking, and was grateful for the darkness of the hall.

The minute Luke walked in, Paddy could see that he was unsettled and restless, but made no comment, although he'd been awaiting Luke's return with mounting impatience.

"I called in at the station on my way back from the hospital, this evening," he said. "We've had a break. Two of them, in a way."

"Tell me." Luke went into the bathroom and washed his face and hands, staring at himself for a moment. He looked like a stranger, no sign of the boy he had been, little sign of the man he had become before returning to Wychford. And yet they were both within him, along with this new person they were having to accommodate. He felt very odd.

"First of all, you may remember telling Bennett to keep in contact with the dry cleaners in town."

"Routine."

"Which may have paid off. Pair of trousers brought in that seem to have blood on the cuffs and lower leg. Cyril has them."

Luke came out of the bathroom and leaned against the doorpost to look at his partner. "And?"

"And what?"

Luke smiled. "Come on—there's more, isn't there?"

"There is. Hannah Putnam, from the craft centre. Came in to make a statement just as I was leaving." He paused.

"And?" Luke was growing impatient.

"And she told me she thought she knew who the Frenholm woman was going to meet the night she was killed. Seems that in addition to fielding all comers, Ms. Frenholm was having an affair with some guy from the estate. Miss Putnam doesn't know his full name, but she gave us a lot of detail that added up to someone. We checked it out." He paused again.

"*And?*" Luke said, in a terrible voice.

Paddy smiled. "Looks like it might be a guy by the name of Fred Baldwin. He works up at the photoprocessing plant, and does week-end gardening over at Peacock Manor." Paddy started to pause again, then thought better of it. "It was Baldwin's wife who brought the bloody trousers to the dry cleaners," he concluded.

"Oh, hell," Luke muttered.

"I thought you'd be pleased," Paddy said, drily. "What's wrong, don't you want to close the case?"

"Yes, of course I do," Luke snapped. He reached backward to turn off the bathroom light. He didn't look into the mirror again.

CHAPTER TWENTY

"But I threw those trousers away!" Fred Baldwin turned to his wife, accusingly. "I put them out with the rubbish, dammit, I didn't want them anymore!" He was a stocky young man, with thick white-blond curly hair. He wore jeans and a shirt, and seemed in imminent danger of bursting out of both. He stood over his wife, who looked up at him with a mixture of fear and confusion.

"Well, I found them and they looked perfectly all right except for the mud, so . . ." She was on the verge of tears. "I thought I could save them, they were perfectly all right, just a little tear at the knee—" Tricia Baldwin said, quickly, avoiding her husband's eye, and fixing on Paddy's not unsympathetic face. "I wanted to surprise Fred, you see. To show him I'd saved them for him, because he was very fond of them." She looked at her husband and then away. "I don't understand," she said, miserably.

Fred Baldwin turned away from his wife with a groan. His eyes met Luke's and there was both fear and resignation there.

"Am I under arrest?" he asked.

"We'd like to talk to you," Luke said, carefully.

"Not here," Baldwin said.

"What is it, Fred? What's *wrong?*" Tricia Baldwin's voice was despairing. From above them, through the thin floor, came the sound of a baby, crying.

"Not here," Baldwin said, again. "I'll get my coat."

Tricia stood up. "I'll come, too," she said. "I'll call Janet to come over to Darren and . . ."

Baldwin turned. "No," he said.

"But, Fred . . ."

"No." His voice was dead serious. She seemed to crumple up before them, then sank down again in her chair, eyes wide under the urchin-fringe of blond hair, no more than twenty, until a moment ago happy in her clean house with her lovely baby and her dependable husband, everything nice about her, everything fine.

"I think it might be a good thing if you called a friend over," Paddy said to her, gently. "A bit of company for you."

"Be all over the estate in no time if she does," Baldwin said, to the air above the door. "Go to bed, Tricia. See to the baby and go to bed, like a good girl."

As they went down the path to the car, they could hear her stumbling up the steps to her child, her own weeping nearly as loud as his.

"Bastards," Baldwin said, as he got in the car. "Couldn't have waited until morning, could you?"

"I didn't kill her."

"There was blood on your trousers, Baldwin. Blood that matches hers." The report had just come through. Luke's voice was hoarse with weariness, as was Baldwin's. Luke had asked many questions, different questions, but Baldwin's reply had never varied. He had simply repeated the same thing, over and over.

"I didn't kill her."

"But you were having an affair with her, weren't you?" Paddy asked.

"I didn't kill her."

"You were going to meet her that night, weren't you?"

"I didn't kill her."

"You called her and arranged to meet her, the way you'd done many times before. To meet her on the towpath, to go to that old boathouse, where you always went." Paddy's voice was insistent, irresistible.

"I didn't kill her."

"Did she say she wouldn't be meeting you anymore, was that it? Or did she taunt you, say you weren't much of a lover? That was one of her tricks, you know. She said that to all the men she made love to, when she got tired of them. Said they bored her, said they were rotten lovers. Did she say that to you?" Luke asked.

Baldwin's head came up, suddenly. "There weren't any others," he said.

Luke leaned forward, very, very slightly, the abrupt change in Baldwin instantly erasing his weariness, bringing his mind to point. Had he found the way in? His face remained blank. Quietly, Paddy sat back, letting him take over. "Oh, but there were, I'm afraid." Luke put a slight edge of malice on his voice. A cutting edge, he hoped. "The night she died she'd made love to at least three men—we have medical evidence of that. There was a party, you see. She made herself available—as usual. Were you one of them?"

"You're lying, you bastard. You're just saying that. You're lying!" Baldwin's rage was almost total. His eyes blazed with fury, but within them was also the despair of suspicion—was it true? He was angry at Abbott for saying these things, and angry at himself—for almost believing them.

"I'm afraid not," Abbott said, with regret. Poor bastard, he thought, did you love her? Does it matter so much?

"She wasn't like that," Baldwin went on. "Oh, I'm not saying she was a saint, but she was trying to get away from all that. Men had used her, been cruel to her, poor kid. She hated them all. But not me. She didn't hate me, see. Because I never touched her . . . like that. I wouldn't. I wouldn't."

"Tell me about your relationship with Win Frenholm."

"You wouldn't understand. Nobody would." His voice was bleak.

"Try me."

Baldwin shrugged. "We talked. That's all. We talked."

"How did you meet her?"

"Walking on the towpath. It was while Tricia was pregnant, about a month before she had Darren. She was kind of weepy and short-tempered, not like herself at all, and . . . I was a bit frustrated, I guess, one way and another. You know."

"I know. Go on."

Baldwin sighed. "So, I used to get out of the house when it got too bad. Walk it off, like. So I wouldn't hurt her, you understand. I love Trish . . . I don't know how I'm going to tell her about all this."

"About all what?"

"Win Frenholm and . . . everything."

"What is there to tell?"

"Nothing. *Nothing!* We just used to talk, I told you. I found her on the towpath one night, sitting on an old piling, just sitting there in the moonlight, like some kind of . . . water fairy or something. What is it . . ."

"Sprite?"

"That's it. Water sprite." Baldwin's tough face took on a kind of luminosity that Abbott found slightly unnerving. "There she was, dressed all in silver. Shining. Just . . . shining. Said it was a kind of costume or something she'd been wearing to model in, something like that. I don't much remember, except the sight of her, there. I felt like I'd come into some kind of fairy tale or something, it was so . . . I don't know words for it." Baldwin was struggling for expression of this wondrous thing that had happened to him. "It was special, that's all. As if she'd rose up out of the water just for me. But she spoke, she said, 'Hello,' just like anyone would. Voice soft as silk, it was. Made me tingle all over."

"You mean she turned you on?" Abbott asked, and instantly regretted it. Baldwin's face lost its luminosity and returned to its former sullen lines.

"Said you wouldn't understand," he muttered.

Abbott took a deep breath. "I'm sorry. It's just that magical things don't happen to policemen very often. I think I *can* understand—a little, anyway—of what you felt. Water and moonlight have had strange effects on people all through history, after all. But she wasn't *really* a water sprite, was she?"

Baldwin became annoyed with what he considered Abbott's patronising tone. He suddenly felt he was being humoured. "Well, of course she wasn't. I was only trying to tell you how it was that *first* night, that's all. How it struck me, like. Why I wasn't myself, so to speak. Once we started in talking—she was just like anyone else, really. Well . . . not quite." Again, came the luminous expression. Abbott, to his own discomfort, recognised the emotions behind it. Touched by a little magic himself a few hours before, he felt some of Baldwin's disorientation, and understood the power of a beautiful woman in the moonlight far better than was good for his interrogation. "See, I'm not anybody special," Baldwin went on, awkwardly. "I know that. But that first time—and all the other times—I *felt* special, with her. She told me I was, and I was. Then."

"And how many other times were there?"

Baldwin looked defensive. "Not so many."

"How many?"

"Maybe . . . once a week. Sometimes more."

"More when your wife went into hospital, for example?"

Caught, Baldwin looked uneasy. "Well, yes. Visiting hours was over by eight . . . you can't look at television all your bloody life, can you?"

"Friends? Your local?" Baldwin muttered something, and Abbott leaned forward.

"What was that?"

"I *said*, it's not the same."

"No," Abbott agreed, gravely. "It isn't. And how did you get in touch with Miss Frenholm—or did she contact you?"

"Sometimes she'd phone me at work and ask me to meet her—if she felt down and wanted to talk. Once in a while I'd phone her. But mostly, it just happened. I'd go on the towpath, feeling rotten, and there she'd be. Waiting for me."

"Like magic?"

"Dammit, don't laugh at me!" Baldwin's voice rose and he began to leave his chair, fists clenched. Paddy stood up, too, abruptly, and stared him back down into his seat before resuming his own. Baldwin was breathing hard and held Paddy's eyes for a moment, a muscle working in his jaw.

"You don't like being laughed at," Luke commented. It was not a question.

"Do *you?*" Baldwin's tone was still belligerent. It was clear he had a loose hold on a short temper. Had Win Frenholm set off that temper? Clearly the relationship had been a complex one, completely beyond the man's previous experience. Baldwin was a stolid type, slow-thinking, and close to the earth. He resembled a heavy-headed ram, ponderous and deliberate. He'd been walking the towpath filled with his own troubles and frustrations, in the dark in every way. Suddenly his life had changed. Win Frenholm had appeared like something out of a dream. Quick-silver and ethereal, playing with him, literally enchanting him, with the gift of her attention and time. How she must have savoured her power. Rather than taking his body, she'd taken his mind, flattering him beyond anything he'd ever known. Not a sexual spell, but one far more seductive to a man accustomed to the merely physical. What had been in it for her? Had she been drawn to his animal strength, as with Ray Moss, or had it been a game, this magical, spiritual enchantment of a stumbling male? A game she'd tired of, in the end? Had she broken the magic at last? And paid for it? Baldwin had a powerful body, he was about the right height.

And he hated to be laughed at.

"You work at the photoprocessing plant."

"Yeah. I'm in machine maintenance, there."

"Did you know Beryl Tompkins?"

"Who?"

"Beryl Tompkins."

"Never heard of her." From his tone, he'd never heard of anyone.

"Then I take it you don't read the papers or watch television?"

"What?"

"And Mrs. Taubman? You worked for her, I believe? Week-ends. Gardening and odd-jobbing up at the hall."

"Yeah, I . . ." Suddenly Baldwin's face went blank. "Oh, no," he said. "Oh, no, you don't. You've got it all wrong. That Beryl woman—she the one that got killed up by the plant?"

"She is."

"Oh, no . . . not me. Not me. Never me, never. Never!" Panic was setting in, and he was beginning to sweat. "You got it wrong, again. You got it all *wrong!*"

"Suppose you put me right, then." Abbott's voice was calm and even, his gaze was unwavering. Could it really be that Baldwin had not, until this moment, realised *why* they were questioning him? Or was this all part of the edifice of defence he was building around himself? "Tell me about it."

"About the trousers, you mean." Baldwin was feeling his way through the quicksand. "About the blood on the trousers?"

"If you like. Start with the blood on the trousers."

"Start and finish, you mean. There's nothing else but that—believe me."

"I'll try to. Come along—let's have it all." Abbott kept his voice steady. Baldwin had already been given the cautions, and Paddy glanced at the stenographer, who caught his look and nodded. It was all going down, every word.

CHAPTER TWENTY-ONE

Baldwin seemed a little calmer, now. It was as if, by realising his true position, he'd focussed himself—the attitude of a man accustomed to dealing with emergencies. Whether he would be as successful with people as with machinery remained to be seen. He eyed Abbott, and was not encouraged.

"She called me at home, that night. She'd never done that before. Never.

She sounded upset, angry, scared, all kinds of things. Maybe drunk, too. It was hard to tell, because I was so afraid Trish would come and ask who was on the phone. Fortunately, I always answer the phone at our house at night because sometimes it's the plant with a problem, or whatever. Anyway, she called. Scared the hell out of me, thinking maybe Trish would pick up the extension or listen from the next room or whatever. I guess she didn't. Anyway, Win said she was in trouble and needed me to help her. I got the feeling she wanted me to duff someone up or something. It was funny, nothing she said, exactly, except, 'You're strong, I need somebody strong,' something like that, anyway. She asked me to meet her at our usual place. That was the towpath—the old boathouse, like you said." He glanced at Abbott's bland expression, and flushed, slightly.

"Go on."

"Well, it was late, but I told Trish it was the plant, and that one of the chemical tanks had begun to leak, so they wanted me out there right away. She didn't argue—she's good that way."

"She trusts you."

Baldwin met Abbott's eyes. "No reason why she shouldn't. I told you, there was nothing *wrong* between Win and me."

"Go on."

"I started down to the towpath, like always. It was later than usual, so there wasn't much light from the houses. I fell twice, cursed like a good 'un. Third time I fell . . ." he paused, swallowed.

"Yes?"

"Third time I fell, it was over Win. She was lying there in the path, her head over the edge. She was . . . oh, Jesus." Baldwin faltered, recovered himself. "I been trying to *forget*," he said, as earnestly as a child.

"Please go on." It took all Abbott's self-control to keep his voice level, unhurried.

"She was . . . gurgling, whooshing, sort of, and twitching like some kind of puppet. I could see her face in the moonlight—and her neck. She died right there, right then, while I was getting up."

"There. On the path. By the river's edge?"

"Yes."

Abbott allowed himself a glance at Paddy, who in turn permitted himself a raised eyebrow. "Go on," Abbott said.

"I didn't know what to do. But I couldn't just *leave* her there. I knew there was no hope, that she was dead. I tried to stop the blood, but—it just kept coming. I . . . I picked her up and carried her over under a bush, so nobody could see her like that. I didn't want anyone—anyone—to *see* her like that. Oh, God—God . . ." Baldwin broke down at last, sobbing into his hands.

Abbott leaned back in his chair and looked across at Paddy. He spoke soundlessly. That was it, his lips said. That was one part that didn't fit. Paddy nodded.

"Mr. Baldwin." Abbott's voice was gentle, now. "Mr. Baldwin, as you were coming along the path to meet her, did you see anyone else?"

"No." It was half choked.

"Did you *hear* anything?"

"I told you, I fell over twice. I heard *me*, that's all." He looked up at Abbott. "Christ, don't you think I *wish* I heard something or saw something? Or got there maybe one minute sooner? Don't you think—"

"Try," Abbott urged.

Baldwin shook his head. "No. Nothing. I looked around, I listened—just cars going over the bridge." He stopped. "A car starting up," he said, suddenly. "I heard a car starting up."

Abbott drew an invisible circle on the table with his index finger, spoke without looking up. "You're a mechanically minded man. Anything special about it?"

"Yeah. It was missing badly. Sounded like a sports car. He needed a lot of choke."

"He? What makes you say 'he,' exactly?"

"I don't know. I wasn't paying attention—I was looking at her. I touched her face, but it was cold. Cold so quickly, as if . . . as if . . ."

"Yes?"

"As if she'd gone back into the water. As if she'd flowed back into the water with her blood. Had become one with the river again, and left behind the body she'd been using."

It was probably the closest to poetry Fred Baldwin would ever come.

Two hours later, they put him in a cell.

"I'm just not certain, one way or another," Luke said, angrily. "He's had plenty of time to make up a cover story."

"He has no alibis for the other nights, either," Paddy said. "Out walking. Out with her. Hardly verifiable. And he's connected with both places—the plant, and Peacock Manor."

"Yes. You'd better chat to the personnel manager up at the plant again. I'll head over to the manor later on this morning." He glanced out the window. To the east the horizon was lightening. Soon the sky would pale and start to glow pink over the frosted fields. Already the shapes of the distant hills could be seen. "A couple hours of sleep would be welcome, I think, Paddy."

"Amen. Baldwin went out like a light the minute they put him in the cell. Poor moon-struck sod."

"Yes. It was unsettling, the way he altered so completely when he talked about her." Abbott rubbed his ear. "A psychiatrist might be able to make something of that kind of obsession, I suppose. If Baldwin is psychotic at all, having his obsession disturbed in any way might have pushed him over the edge. But that doesn't add up when it comes to the other murders." He sighed. "At least he's cleared up one aspect of it for me."

"Hiding the body, you mean?"

"Yes. That was what bothered me, why it seemed her death didn't match the other two. Both the Tompkins woman and Mrs. Taubman were dropped, literally dropped, where they were killed. But Win Frenholm's body was hidden out of sight. And, if he's telling the truth, it answers that little niggle Cyril had about there being less blood than he'd normally expect from a wound like that. Her first blood went into the river—that would have been blood under pressure, the greatest flow. Then Baldwin scooped her up and carried her over gravel for a yard or two, and she bled onto him. The rest just drained out over the grass under the bush."

"What about the wound, though?" Paddy asked. "The same, all three times."

"I know, dammit. Let's sleep on it, for God's sake. Baldwin will sleep as well in the cell as anywhere else—we'll have another think over breakfast."

"What about his wife? She'll be fretting."

Luke scowled. "She'll fret a lot more when he starts explaining our interest in him. If I remember anything about babies, they reflect their parent's moods. Little Darren will be giving her merry hell—that will keep her busy. I know our boys used to drive us up the wall when I was on a rough case and started to snap around the house." He smiled, fleetingly. "Now they just ask me for extra pocket money and promise to stay out of my way, clever little beggars."

"They miss her too, Luke."

Luke's smile hardened. "Yes. Well, let's get over to the hotel or we'll never get our heads down. I can't think straight at the moment. There's still something wrong, Paddy. Dammit, there's *still* something I can't quite work out."

CHAPTER TWENTY-TWO

Wychford woke up to a fresh autumn morning, with the smell of woodsmoke carried on the breeze. The High Street was all a-bustle when Luke and Paddy left their hotel several hours later.

"Pretty little town," Paddy observed. "Must have been nice, growing up here. Not a bad place to grow old, either."

Luke glanced sideways at him. "Thinking along those lines already, are you?"

"A man has to take hold of his life sometime," Paddy observed. "If my promotion comes through . . ."

"Then what?"

"Then . . . I'll know where I am, financially and—so on."

"Thinking of taking a wife, Paddy?"

"Doesn't hurt to think," Paddy said, calmly. "Doesn't hurt to plan, either."

"No," Luke agreed. They concentrated on the attractive prospect of Wychford High Street at ten in the morning of a lovely day.

Sleep had come hard to both of them. Each had lain awake, staring at the ceiling, waiting for some secret message from someone to say it was all right to formally charge Fred Baldwin, or release him.

"Not yet," Luke had said, over breakfast. "We need to know a lot more before I'd feel right about letting Baldwin go. We can hold him another day —and I think we should. If he is our man, let's find more evidence to back it up. The blood on his trousers puts him in at the death, but not necessarily at the kill. His explanation *could* be the true one. If he isn't the killer, maybe holding him will cause the real murderer to make a mistake."

"The real murderer?" Paddy echoed. "One murderer?"

Luke sighed. "I don't think I can fight it much longer, now that we've cleared up that point about the position of the body. Yes—it looks more and more like one murderer."

When they reached the incident room, they found Bennett and the other local people assigned to the investigation in a state of some excitement.

"You've cracked it, sir. Well done!" Bennett enthused.

"Not I," Luke said, reprovingly. "And not exactly cracked, either. Perhaps only dented. I am by no means convinced Baldwin is our man. We'll hang on to him for a bit, but I want no heavy questioning until we can have him interviewed by a psychiatrist."

Bennett looked dumbfounded. "A shrink? But, he seems pretty straightforward to me . . ."

"Not at all straightforward," Luke said. "I presume you've all had copies of his statement?" Nods all round. "Well, then, you'll see that at the very least he's a man who's undergone a most unusual experience." There was a snort from the corner of the room. "Yes, Jagger, you have something to say?"

"It's all codswallop, sir," said the broad-shouldered young constable. "He was just having a bit on the side, that's all. Dressing it up don't make it no different. Water sprite, my arse, sir."

Luke looked at him for a long time without speaking. Then he glanced around at the others. "Perhaps, when you are more experienced—and I mean no disrespect—you will come to understand that occasionally there are more than just facts to a case, and that people can sometimes appear rational and still be *extremely* strange. If you had heard and seen that statement given, you would not be so sure of yourself, Jagger. The old wive's tales of men bewitched by fairies and goblins grew from something, sometime. Caught at the right moment, in the right way, I dare say any of us could claim to have seen a flying saucer and believe it totally. Baldwin's blood type already indicates he could not have been the father of Frenholm's unborn child. I do believe the man was enchanted, to put it in the old way: obsessed, to put it in the new jargon. Obsessed with a kind of possessive, awed madness about a beautiful woman who reached some secret place inside him no one else suspected was there. They say everyone has at least one song in them. Is that so damned hard to believe? Haven't you been in love, yet, Jagger?"

"No, sir. Not *me*, sir." There was a kind of smirk on his face.

So the story had gotten around already of the kiss under the bridge. Luke ignored the smirk and went on. "Then I pity you. This is a man as vulnerable and tender as a child in one area, but in one area *only*. For the rest he is tough, practical, sane, and defensive. Going at him head on is not going to get information. Now that it's over, now she's no longer here to cast her spell on the poor bastard, he's become embarrassed by the whole thing. He hears himself talking and it's like listening to another man. In some ways, a silly man. That makes him want to crawl away from his memories, and that's the last thing we want. He will only close down completely and lose for us any chance of a lead concerning the Frenholm woman, and what really happened that night. I don't want him touched, spoken to, bothered in any way, until the psychiatrist I've sent for has had a chance to talk to him. Is that clear?"

"Yes, sir." Bennett spoke smartly, and sent a glare toward the offending Constable Jagger.

"In the meantime, I want his house searched for a weapon or anything else that might help us. I do *not* want the garden dug up or a swarm of uniforms pouring through his doors. Bennett, see to the necessary paperwork, would you? Two of you in plainclothes, one a woman, will be sufficient. His wife is young and has a new baby. I don't want any allegations of intimidation nor any stories about harassment in the press. In fact, I don't want the press notified about Baldwin in any way." He glanced at Bennett, who began to flush bright red. "You've already done it?"

"I've said we have a suspect in custody, sir. Sorry, sir."

"You're a horse's ass, Bennett," Abbott said, easily. "Did you give a name?"

"No, sir."

"Only half assed, then. Very well, but say nothing more to anyone, is that clear? All of you? I will make the announcement, if there is to *be* an announcement, myself. Now, then, reports. You first, Jagger, as you're so bright and eager this morning. What news on the Rialto?"

"Sir?"

"The questioning of the Tompkins woman's associates, lad," Paddy said. "Have you come up with anything?"

"No, sir. I've spoken to several of her closest friends, and there was no hint of anything out of the way concerning a man friend or anything of the kind. Quiet woman, they said. Good neighbour, good wife and mother, wanted the best for her kids and all. That's why she was working at the plant, as well as her other jobs."

"I see. Thank you. Who was checking on Basil Taubman's alibi?"

Constable Goodwin stirred. "That was me, sir."

"And?"

Goodwin consulted his notebook. "Constable Kinsale of the Met called round to Mr. Taubman's club on our behalf. The porter rang through to Mr.

Taubman's room and there was no reply, so he and the constable went upstairs and found Mr. Taubman asleep in bed."

"And what time was this?"

Goodwin cleared his throat. "Just before six in the morning."

"Left it a bit late, didn't they?"

"Some confusion about the message," Goodwin mumbled, red-faced.

"And Taubman was definitely asleep?"

"So Kinsale says, sir. 'Snoring like a pig' was his words." Goodwin's chin came up, defensively.

"I see." Luke stifled his annoyance. "Thank you. Who was looking into Frenholm's known sexual contacts?" Bennett raised his hand, reluctantly. "How many are we up to, now?"

"Fifteen, sir." There was a murmur and a few suppressed sniggers in the room.

"And at this party, the night she died?"

Bennett flushed, slightly. "Three."

"Tight knickers, must have slowed her down," somebody muttered, and there was a general laugh.

"All right, all right, that will be enough of that," Luke said, impatiently. "Go on, Bennett."

The reports continued, and it was some time before Paddy and Luke could go their separate ways—Paddy back to the photoprocessing plant to requestion Grimes, the personnel manager, and Luke to the manor.

"Chief Inspector Abbott to see you, sir."

Mark Peacock looked across at Basil Taubman, who sat in a chair before the fire. "Here he is, then, Basil. The dreaded 'man from the Yard.' "

Basil nodded. "So be it."

"Send him in, Jeffers."

"Yes, sir."

Mark stood up behind his littered desk as the butler showed Luke into the office. "Ah. Good morning, Chief Inspector. Take a seat, won't you? Basil, this is Chief Inspector Abbott. Inspector, my stepfather, Basil Taubman. He was in London when you were last here."

Basil rose from his chair and came across the room to give Abbott a firm, dry handshake. "Nice to meet the man in charge, at last. I was apparently only considered important enough to be interviewed by one of the local men. Unfortunately, I could offer very little in the way of assistance." He indicated a chair. "Please, make yourself comfortable." If Abbott hadn't known Mark Peacock was the owner of the manor, he would have assumed it was Taubman. He had the naturally adroit manner of a seigneur—but there had been tension in his handshake, and a nerve flickered near one eye. The man was just holding on.

Abbott sat down. The butler reappeared, apparently in response to a hidden summons from Mark.

"Coffee for three, please, Jeffers."

Abbott raised an eyebrow as the butler withdrew. "That's a new addition to your establishment, isn't it? I don't recall a butler on your staff list."

"That's right. Some good has come out of this ghastly tragedy," Basil volunteered. "Mark is now in full charge of the estate, and we have begun our planned expansion of the manor to a conference centre. Of the better kind, of course. Very discreet, nothing gaudy or commercial, you understand. We'd never do anything to spoil this perfectly beautiful place. Never. And, of course, primary to that plan is establishing an efficient staff for the manor. Jeffers comes to us very highly recommended. We have been interviewing for some while, of course—" He paused without completing the sentence.

"We have hopes of opening next spring," Mark said, quickly. "Mother would have approved of Jeffers, I'm sure. We'll be able to take more time over the selection of the rest. Of course, I'll want Jennifer to have a full say about the staff we hire."

Both Abbott and Taubman stared at him, startled. "Jennifer Eames?" Abbott finally managed. "Dr. Jennifer Eames?"

"Yes, that's right. We're engaged," Mark said. "I'm sorry, I thought you knew that, Inspector. Obviously we'll have to wait a decent interval before the wedding, but that's no reason why she can't become involved in the work of the manor, is it?" He seemed very pleased with himself.

"You hadn't said anything to me about this, Mark," Taubman said, with a rather fixed smile.

"I can't see what difference it makes. It's just a personal decision. It won't affect *our* arrangement, Basil, merely enhance it. She'll simply be taking over Mother's role." He seemed genuinely perplexed at the effect his statement was having on the other two men. "We do need a woman's touch here, you know. With Mother gone—surely this is an obvious solution?"

"Yes, well, if that's your decision," Basil said. "I agree we have to get on, Mark. We made that decision together the day after your mother died and we must stick to it. I'm sure Mabel would have approved."

Abbott raised an eyebrow. "Oh? I was under the impression that Mrs. Taubman *didn't* approve of Dr. Eames *or* the conference centre idea."

"That's not true," Mark said, quickly. "She was growing very fond of Jennifer. It was just a matter of their getting to know one another better. As for the project, she had agreed only the day before her death to the plan going ahead. She had even spoken to Heatherington, the bank manager, about it. That very morning, in fact."

"Ah, I didn't know that. Thank you." Abbott paused as the butler re-entered with a coffee tray and served them all, only resuming when the door had closed once again. "I believe the coroner has released Mrs. Taubman's body for burial?"

"Yes, the funeral will be on Monday," Basil said, and sighed heavily, taking his coffee over to the window, where he gazed out onto the lawn that led down to the river. "I still find it hard to grasp that she's dead. Being in London as I was, it seems that she's simply gone shopping or something, be back any minute, walk in the door, demanding tea and all the latest gossip. I haven't actually seen her, of course. I suppose that will bring it home to me. I expect the anger and the grief will come, then. Now, I am only rather numb." He bowed his head for a moment, and took a sip of coffee.

"Basil, please . . . don't." Mark's voice was shaky.

"What?" His stepfather turned, startled. "Oh, sorry, Mark . . . didn't mean to upset you, my boy." He glanced at Abbott and noted his expression. It seemed to embarrass him. "I'm not unfeeling, Inspector, wouldn't want you to think that, not at all. But it's no use pretending that Mabel and I were love's young dream. We met late in life, and I think we were more good companions than anything else. Yes, that's it. Good companions. I'm afraid truly savage grief is more a burden for the young than the old." His eyes rested affectionately on Mark, whose earlier composure had begun to crack, slightly. "As one grows old, death becomes less daunting. It even holds a kind of strange fascination. One is more or less prepared to lose the people one loves. Mabel was older than I am, and not at all strong . . . I knew our time together would be short. But not so cruelly short." He suddenly looked angry, and his knuckles whitened on the cup he held. After a moment he cleared his throat, and spoke with an obvious effort. "I hope I made it a happy time for her."

"I see." Abbott would not have called Basil Taubman "old," rather "well preserved." His hair was beautifully cut, his clothes were immaculately fitted to a well-shaped body, and while he was not handsome taken feature by feature, there was about him an air of style and assurance, almost arrogance. Abbott thought he would do well in the conference centre business, graciously and subtly intimidating the common folk. He certainly seemed utterly at home here in Peacock Manor. "We contacted the Met and asked them to inform you of your wife's death. I understand they found you at your club the next morning. You had spent the night there, I believe?"

"It was a shock," Taubman recalled, with evident embarrassment. "They actually had to summon one of the members who's a doctor to minister to me. Gave me something or other, calmed me down. I made a fool of myself and they made quite a fuss over me, I'm afraid. I've never made up my mind whether that is one of the blessings or one of the drawbacks of a club."

"Yes, of course. What time had you come in?"

"The night before, you mean? Let me see. Sometime around ten, I believe. I'd had a meal out with clients, lingered a bit, afterward, but I wanted a decent night because there was rather an important meeting the next morning. As it was, of course, I missed it." His tone was not aggrieved, exactly, rather overpatient, as if he were trying not to mind.

"I see. Thank you." Abbott got out his notebook and wrote in it. "Can anyone verify that you were, in fact, in the club all night?"

"I have no idea. One of the waiters served me a brandy and soda, and then I went straight up to bed. Took my usual sleeping pill, went out like a light. Always do."

Mark Peacock was growing restless. "Just what is it you're trying to get at, Chief Inspector? Surely you don't suspect *Basil* of killing my mother?"

"They always suspect the husband or the wife, as the case may be. Classic. Isn't that so, Inspector?" Basil gave him a conspiratorial glance, born, no doubt, of many a midnight detective story.

"Murders often tend to be family affairs," Abbott agreed, neutrally.

"But Basil was in London," Mark persisted. "That's almost two hours away by train, three by car—and Basil doesn't drive."

"Oh?" Abbott looked at Taubman in surprise.

"Never felt the need," Taubman said, airily. "Always plenty of cabs in London, friends with cars to meet one at the station should one venture down to the country."

"Basil's blind in one eye," Mark said. "Claims it was a flying champagne cork, but it's a war wound. He was a Desert Rat."

"Now, now . . ." Basil demurred, but he looked pleased.

"Anyway," Mark went on. "There are no trains at that hour."

"At what hour, Mr. Peacock?"

"Why, midnight. Mother died at midnight, didn't she?"

Abbott looked at his notebook. "You got back home at what time, Mr. Peacock? What time, exactly?"

"Why, I don't think I could say, *exactly*," Mark said, with an air of surprise. "Surely your records would show when I called through to the station? I hadn't been home many minutes before I . . . found her."

"Dr. Eames left you around eleven. Your call to the station came at twenty past midnight. What did you do during the hour or so between?"

Mark flushed, slightly. "I drove around."

"Just—drove around?"

Mark's chin came up. "Well, she probably told you, anyway. Jennifer and I had a bit of a disagreement, lover's tiff sort of thing. I was a bit het up and got rid of it on the back roads."

"Rather dangerous to drive when you're angry," Luke said, mildly.

"I suppose it is," Mark said, stiffly. "Anyway, no alibi, apparently. Sorry about that." He swallowed. "Isn't . . . can't they determine the time of death scientifically? I thought I heard someone say she died around midnight. I thought it said that, in the newspaper."

"You've read the newspapers, then?"

"They tried to hide them from me, but I found them, all right," Mark said, bitterly. "The papers all seem to be under the impression that my mother was the third victim of this Cotswold Butcher who killed the other two women."

"And do you think that?"

"Dear God, how would *I* know?" Mark demanded. "Obviously it would be preferable to thinking Basil or I did it, although the thought of my mother being . . . of meeting . . . of running . . . of some bastard's dirty hands on her . . ." He faltered, turned away. "Sorry."

"Can't you see you're upsetting the boy?" Basil asked, angrily. "Is there any need for this, now?"

Abbott glanced at him in some surprise. The boy he was defending so strongly was thirty-nine years old. "There will be a need for questions until we have caught the killer, Mr. Taubman. Surely, you can't want to stop us doing that?"

"Of course not." Taubman turned away, went over to a tantalus on a sidetable, and helped himself to brandy, adding it to his coffee. "But equally, if Mabel was the victim of this Cotswold Butcher, which she obviously was, then it can't have anything to do with Mark or myself. It is, in the end, much the same as if she were struck down by a hit-and-run driver. We have to live with her death and her absence, Chief Inspector. Surely we shouldn't have to live with unfounded suspicion as well?"

Abbott closed his notebook, put it in an inside pocket with his pen, drank the last of his coffee, and stood up. "I'm afraid you will, Mr. Taubman. If not mine, then that of the newspapers or your neighbours or one another. It is simply a fact of death. It will be finished when I've done my job. Meanwhile, grit your teeth and bear it. That's what I do."

CHAPTER TWENTY-THREE

"Oh, my God, they're back," Gordon Sinclair said, peering through the window, his hands frozen on the pottery he'd been rearranging.

"Who?" asked Barry Treat, from the door to the workroom.

"The police."

Barry made a small, keening sound and sank onto a stool. "They've come to arrest me, I know they have," he said, in tones of dreadful finality. First the shock of finding poor Win like that, then being questioned as if he were a criminal in that ghastly police station, then more questions here, and then, *then*, that terrible time at home, when they'd gone through Win's room and all her papers. Persecution, that's what it was, absolute persecution. And still it wasn't over, for here they were again. He just couldn't bear it. He *couldn't*.

"Well, if they have come to arrest you, they're going an odd way about it," Gordon said, briskly. "They've gone into Graham Moyle's studio."

"He's been ill, too, you know. Or he says he has. Hiding under the bed-clothes, more like." Relief and jealousy sharpened Barry's tongue. "He was one of them, you know. One of her 'conquests.' The *energy* of the girl, *quite* phenomenal. Not that it showed around *here*, goodness knows. I was always having to push her, the cow. She was lazy, lazy, lazy when it came to *work.*"

Gordon turned his back on the sun-drenched scene of Courtyard With

Important Visitors, and regarded his small partner. "Why do you think they'd arrest you? You didn't kill Win."

"I could have. There were times I cheerfully could have," Barry said.

"Wishing isn't doing," Gordon observed. "If that were the case, they'd arrest me, too. Do you suppose they've found out about the insurance?"

"Probably. God knows, it's motive enough. Eighty thousand, Gordon. I still can't believe it. What are we going to do?"

Gordon smiled. "It's not going to change our life one little bit," he said, in cruel imitation of a pools winner. Barry giggled appreciatively. "We'll leave it in the bank for a while to gain interest, then pop it into some sound investments. After all, love, we're happy here, aren't we? Doing our little thing together?"

"Oh, yes, we are," Barry said, fervently. Memories of youthful squalor in London had not faded. Nor was he unobservant of his own fading attractions. Finding Gordon was the luckiest thing that had ever happened to him. Now that Win was gone, there was dear Gordon to look after him. And he was sensitive—he *needed* looking after. At least Win had understood that, whatever her failings. He was a genius—she'd said so. She'd also said other things, from time to time, but he disregarded those. If only she and Gordon had gotten on better. Dear Gordon. He looked with affection at his partner and lover. The wonderful line of his neck flowing into those square shoulders, the long arms and strong hands, the way his hair curled. Quite inspirational. Perhaps it was time to try the portrait sculpture, again. After all, with the insurance money, they were safe whether the shop succeeded or not. He'd show that pompous Hannah Putnam that she was not the only artist with clay around here. Excitement flooded him. He'd start immediately.

He began to speak, to tell Gordon of his plan, then thought better of it. Make it a surprise. Gordon would be pleased when he saw the result. And, anyway, he was busy with all those insurance papers, now.

Best not to disturb him.

"Graham Moyle?"

The tall, thin man turned, startled. "Yes." He was a Viking/Christ figure, blond, bearded—with the high cheekbones of an ascetic, and the full-lipped mouth of a sensualist. "Can I help you?"

Luke produced his warrant card. "We'd like to ask you some questions. I presume you're well enough, now?"

"Yes." He was disgruntled to discover their identity, but there was no place to run in the crowded little studio.

Luke and Paddy looked around, and found clear places on the benches against which to lean. There were no chairs, and there were shards of coloured glass everywhere, twinkling, glinting, even crunching underfoot. Graham Moyle's hands were heavily scarred.

"You do photographic work, too?" Paddy asked, nodding toward a shelf on one wall that contained several expensive cameras, both large and small.

"I take pictures of stained-glass wherever I go, here and on the Continent," Moyle explained. "In fact, I've just done a book on it which will be coming out, soon. And I like to take pictures of the sites where I'm restoring or replacing old glass. It helps a lot."

"I see." Paddy seemed satisfied.

"You knew Win Frenholm well, I understand," Luke said.

"As well as anyone knew her, I suppose," Graham Moyle acknowledged.

"You're not distressed by her death?"

"Of course I am, but what's the point of blubbering all over the place?" the blond young man said, and turned back to his work. "Look, do you mind if I get on with this while we talk? I've gotten pretty behind what with being sick and interruptions and all, and the delivery date is the end of the week." He reached for some crimson glass and began to mark it in curves with a felt-tipped pen. He then followed the markings with a glass cutter, and broke the resulting petals free, one by one, with a quick sure tap from underneath. He glanced over his shoulder. "Hand me that blue pot over there, would you, please?"

Luke looked around, but could see no blue pot.

"On the table in front of you," Graham Moyle said. "That peacock blue glass—we call single-colour glass pot."

"Ah. Sorry." Gingerly, Luke picked up the sheet of glass, which caught the light from outside and glowed in his grasp.

"Thanks." Moyle worked swiftly and smoothly. Blue petals followed the crimson, until he had a small pile of each to hand, next to a stack of gold-coloured glass circles. He then reached for a reel of grey metal that was hung from a nail on the wall, unwound a length, and cut it with a sharp knife. He tossed the knife down on the table beside the glass shards, and then began straightening the length of lead. First he smoothed it by hand, then he bent each end at a right angle, and placed one in a vise while still holding the other. As he began to stretch the lead, Paddy moved over casually to the table, and looked down at the knife which lay there. He glanced over at Luke and raised an eyebrow, nodding almost imperceptibly.

Graham Moyle looked up at that moment, and caught the exchange. He flushed deeply, his fair skin blazing up in an instant. "I didn't kill her," he said, hoarsely. "That's just a cut-down palette-knife, good for lead, but not much else."

"It could have done the job," Paddy observed.

"Why should I kill her?" Moyle demanded. "She meant nothing to me. She was a—convenience. Cheaper than paying a whore from the town, and on the premises, too." Despite his attempt at sounding harsh and tough, tears stood in his eyes.

"She seems to have been a lot of things—to a lot of men," Luke observed.

"She was like that," Moyle said.

"So it doesn't matter to you that someone cut her throat?" Luke asked, as if enquiring the way to the nearest stationers.

Silence. "No," was the eventual reply. "No, it doesn't matter a damn to me."

"An odd point of view—for a husband," Luke commented. "Catch him, Paddy," he added, as Graham Moyle went white and began to collapse. Paddy was there, and Luke joined him. Together they eased the suddenly boneless young man onto the floor, and propped him against the leg of a table.

"How did you find out?" Moyle asked, weakly, when he'd recovered his wits.

"Just simple checking, following up some documents we found in her room. Your marriage certificate, dated some six years ago was pretty conclusive," Luke told him, drily. "But we had to find out whether there was a divorce. No record of one."

"No, that's right. Still legally man and wife," Moyle said, bitterly. "But in no other way. Not since six months after the date on that certificate. Took me that long to find out about her . . . her problem. She was a witch, you know." His voice was a whisper, his tone quite serious. "Could make you believe anything—for a while. Until she got bored with the game. She always got bored, eventually. Nobody was more surprised than me to find her down here. Even her darling little cousin Barry didn't know about her brief fling with respectability, and as far as I know, she never enlightened him."

"And you didn't resume your relationship?"

"I'd have rather made love to a tarantula," Graham said, flatly. "Come to think of it, the comparison is pretty apt."

"But according to people here in the centre, she spent a lot of time here with you."

"That's right—she did. Trying to talk me into a divorce."

"She could have gotten the divorce herself—you've been separated for more than two years."

"That's what I told her. I don't know if she went into it or not. Sometimes I thought it was just an excuse to come over here and yak at me." He blushed, again, which at least brought some colour back into his cheeks. "Not that she wanted me back or anything like that. I think she used me as a safety valve or something. I heard all her troubles."

"Did she ever tell you about a man named Fred Baldwin?"

"I don't think so. Wait a minute—he the guy she used to meet on the towpath?"

"Yes."

"God, how I felt for that poor bastard," Graham said, shaking his head. "If he could have heard how she laughed at him, he would have cut . . ." He stopped, abruptly. "I didn't mean that," he said.

"Did you know she was pregnant?" Luke asked, ignoring the apology.

"Yeah, she told me at the party, the night she was killed."

"Did she say who the father was?"

"No."

Luke kept the disappointment out of his face, but it was not easy. "Give any indication at all?"

Moyle shook his head. "She was funny about her 'friends,' called them by nicknames or codenames, if she called them anything at all. Win loved her games." He sighed, and shook his head. "Anyway, at first she was just pissed off about getting caught out. Seemed to think this guy should have known better. 'Of all people,' she said—something like that. But I got the feeling she was going to *use* the kid—you know? To pressure the guy into something." He looked from Luke to Paddy. "See, she was tired of her life, the way it was. She'd read some books, knew what she was. She said at first she was going to get an abortion, or try to 'shake it out,' as she put it—I gather she put in a busy night, that night. She could do that—go on for bloody ever, like a rattlesnake." He sighed. "But then, it must have been just before she left the party, she came over to me and she looked—different. She really did. She told me that all that evening she'd kept thinking about it in there, and the more she thought about it, the more real it got. She said she thought maybe having a kid could help her. Make her different, somehow. She'd had a bit to drink, of course, and it had made her sentimental or something. It was kind of pathetic. I said no way, but she'd got hold of this thing about changing, and I think she really meant it. Maybe that's why I got so put down by her getting killed. Just when she was going to try to get straightened out—for somebody else, mind you, for that kid—she dies. Isn't that a bitch?" He was crying, now. "Jesus, she was such a mess, but for the last hour or two of her life, she tried to be better—and look where it got her. Ah, shit." He just sat there, the tears streaming.

Luke and Paddy looked at one another and slowly, stiffly, arose from where they'd been crouching on either side of him. Paddy shook out his trouser legs and Luke rubbed his ear.

"She had an insurance policy, Mr. Moyle. Eighty thousand pounds. If you're still legally married, I'd say you cop the lot. At the moment, her cousin Barry thinks it's his. Any comment?"

He peered up at them. "Are you kidding?"

Luke shook his head. "No, I'm not."

Despite the tears running into his beard, Graham Moyle started to chuckle. Then laugh. "Oh, hell," he choked. "They'll go mad, those two. Gordon Sinclair is the most grasping, avaricious, greedy bastard in the world. He must have spent it a hundred times over, already. I can't believe it. Did she mean it to go to me? Really?"

"Beneficiary next-of-kin, that's all. Unspecified. Your lawyer will take a chunk, but odds are it's all yours."

Moyle had stopped laughing abruptly when he realised it was chance, not her personal intention, that had brought him the money. For a moment, he'd been ready to trust her, again. "Seems wrong to take it, the way we were. The way I felt . . ."

"You don't *have* to take it," Paddy pointed out.

"I'll think about it," Moyle decided. He stayed on the floor, and was still there when they closed the door and glanced over at the window of The Three Wheelers.

"The money was a surprise," Paddy said.

"Yes."

"You want to do anything about that knife?"

"No, I don't think so." Luke was looking into the distance. "He said she was a witch, she could make anybody believe anything—for a while. Do you think she was conning him about changing for the baby's sake?"

"No. I think she was conning herself," Paddy said.

Luke nodded. "I wonder how long she could have made herself believe it?" he said, softly.

CHAPTER TWENTY-FOUR

"I feel like a bloody idiot," Frances grumbled, retying her scarf for the tenth time. "How often have I told patients, 'Nobody will notice' and, 'You'll get used to it in time,' and now here I am, and you know and I know it's all a lie. Damn the ugly thing."

Jennifer smiled. Frances's surgical collar was less conspicuous than most, being of a new experimental design, but there was no denying its presence. Frances looked like an indignant turtle as she put on her coat. "Come on, you can sulk in the car."

"Now, you're sure about this?" Frances asked for the fiftieth time, as they left the ward and started down the hall. "I can perfectly well go home, there's nothing I can't—ouch—manage for myself." The "ouch" was occasioned by a collision with a trolley emerging unexpectedly from a lift. "All it needs is—ouch—rest and—ouch—serenity. Damn." It wasn't so much that the halls were crowded—more that Frances was drawn unerringly to every passing person, wheelchair, wall-mounted fire extinguisher, and open door.

"Frances, you need looking after," Jennifer laughed, disentangling her friend from a drugs trolley and a student nurse. "You never look where you're going."

"I do, too!" Frances was deeply hurt by this calumny—as well as by the edge of the door into reception.

"You don't! You're so intent on whatever new plot or character you're dreaming up at the moment, you forget everything else. You've got to learn to leave your work in the typewriter." Jennifer hated the idea of stifling an artist, but anything was preferable to the artist stifling herself—permanently. "You're always muttering, you know. And going off into a dream. No wonder you keep having accidents. In my considered opinion, the physical world has no real meaning for you—until it ups and socks you one. Uh-oh." Jennifer slowed. Coming toward them was the surgeon who'd been operating when Frances made her precipitous entry through the wall of the surgical theatre. "Good morning, Philip."

"Jennifer." Dr. Blythe was a big, bear-like man, fiercely demanding to the staff and unfailingly gentle with his patients. Frances, being both at the moment, stood uncertainly by, awaiting whatever new disaster was about to consume her. "Good morning, Miss Murphy. How are the bumps and bruises?"

"Mending, thank you." Frances looked as if she wanted to retreat into her collar.

His brown eyes were amused. "That's more than we can say for the wall of the theatre. I believe I actually heard one of the builders whinny with delight when he began adding up his tender—muttered something about going to the Canaries this year."

"Oh, God," moaned Frances.

"Not to worry—the insurance adjusters will dine out for months on it," he smiled. "I had a look at your X-rays this morning. Dr. Marsh seems happy—so am I. Are you?"

"Oh, yes . . . indeed."

He chuckled. "Liar. Hurts like hell, doesn't it? Never mind, time will do the work. Rest for at least two weeks, but we can't spare you after that. You've a way with the patients, you know." This was undeniably true, and he seemed faintly puzzled by it. "I think they feel sorry for you, really." And off he went, whistling.

"Well, I'll be damned," Frances said, looking after him. "He usually growls at me."

Jennifer smiled. "That's because you're usually on his side of the fence, and he expects of everyone the same perfection he demands of himself. Now you're a patient, under his protection, things are different. There's a lot of father in that man."

"You doctors see one another quite differently than the rest of us," Frances observed. "I wish I could put my finger on it, the attitude you have."

"We're all in on the same secret," Jennifer told her. "We all know we're scared to death half the time, and scared half to death the rest of the time. If you only knew how fragile a life really is, how little it takes to destroy it, you'd be scared, too. I think policemen know it." She paused. "Some policemen."

They emerged into the bright sunlight and blinked.

"I understand you were treating Mrs. Taubman," Abbott said, leaning back in his chair and regarding David Gregson across the crowded desk. "Would you tell me what for, please?"

"I can't see that it would be relevant," Gregson said. He had kept Abbott waiting until the last patient had left the surgery. He kept looking at the clock on the mantelpiece, fingering a stack of buff envelopes containing case notes, and was obviously impatient to be away to his house calls.

"I can't force you, of course," Abbott said, in an even tone. It was equally obvious that he intended to sit there until Gregson told him what he wanted to know. Short of violence or a slanging-match, Gregson had few options. He faced a will equal to his own.

"Well, if you must know everything . . ."

"Anything could help," Abbott pointed out.

"Gall bladder, a little arthritis of the spine and hip, general nerves."

"Nerves due to what?"

Gregson sighed. "She was just emerging from a late menopause, she tended to be a bit hysterical, anyway, and was egocentric to a marked degree. What people of her class call highly strung. I prescribed mild tranquillisers now and again, when she demanded them."

Abbott raised an eyebrow. "Demanded?"

Gregson allowed a brief smile. "My decision was based on personal survival. It was that or endure repeated and protracted reiterations of her troubles and her pains, none of which amounted to a tenth of what many of my other female patients endure. After the first five or ten visits I was easily able to discern her physical symptoms from her emotional ones. I was her 'harsh medicine,' you understand. When she was feeling vulnerable and in need of pampering, she went to her consultant—a man with far more diplomacy and tact than I possess. When she felt a bit guilty—or frightened—she generally came to me. Something told her I was good for her because I tasted bitter. A not uncommon conviction."

"Which you encouraged."

Again, that flicker of a smile. "Indeed, it saves time, generally. She knew that if anything were really wrong, I'd be there quick enough. I generally am. Not, you understand, because I am such a wonderful doctor. Rather because the practice is of a size that permits me to do a decent job."

"I was under the impression it was rather too large for one man."

"And a little too small for two, yes. Hence the conflict between Jennifer Eames and myself."

"You admit to it?"

"I could hardly deny it."

Abbott would have pursued this, but Gregson sighed. "Is there anything else you'd like to know about Mrs. Taubman?"

"What was her general health like, aside from the things you mentioned?"

"She was a strong woman. A great deal of her problem stemmed from sexual frustration, although she never would have admitted it. Women of her type never do. Nevertheless, she had a great greed for life, and always wanted more—of everything."

"When was the last time you saw her?"

"Oddly enough, the morning of the day she was murdered. She asked for tranquillisers, said she was going through a 'difficult patch.' As she looked rather peaky, I believed her, and supplied a prescription."

"She didn't elaborate on the nature of the difficulties?"

"As a matter of fact, I encouraged her to do so, but she was rather evasive and simply said she was 'nervy,' and 'on edge.' She said something about not being able to go on arguing with her son and having to give in to his wishes, lead a new kind of life, and that it was all going to be too much for her to handle. Phrases like that—nothing specific, but definite cries for help. I simply took them at face value and prescribed accordingly. I knew from past experience she wouldn't abuse the drug, in any case. Sorry. Had I known she was going to be killed, I would have made a greater effort on *your* behalf, of course."

"Of course." Abbott's face remained neutral. "And when was the last time you had seen her, previous to this visit?"

"About six months ago."

"Was that usual—a gap of that length?"

Gregson's face took on an odd expression. "Now that you mention it, no. She called in for her usual prescription renewals, but Kay, our receptionist, handled that. She hasn't asked to see me."

"Perhaps she's been feeling fragile and has gone to her consultant?"

Gregson shook his head. "No, he always drops me a note if she sees him—professional courtesy."

"So a frustrated and rather hypochondriacal woman suddenly ceases to visit her doctors. What might that suggest?"

"That she's no longer so frustrated?" Gregson tilted his head to one side. "Are you suggesting she'd taken a lover? And that her state was because the affair had come to an end?"

"I'm not suggesting anything. I'm simply gathering information, doctor. Did you ever treat Win Frenholm?"

Gregson hesitated for a moment, as if trying to remember. "No, I didn't. She was Wally's patient. After he became ill, I believe she went onto my list, but I don't recall her. I looked at the records after her death. The last time she came in for medical attention before that day was almost a year ago—presumably for the infection Wally mentioned at dinner the other night."

"And nothing more until her visit the morning of the day she died."

"As you say—nothing until that visit."

"At which time she asked to see Jennifer, not you, had a pregnancy confirmed, and made enquiries about the possibility of an abortion." Abbott watched Gregson's face closely. Gregson merely nodded. "Another long gap, doctor. A long time between drinks, as they say. And that evening *she* was murdered."

Gregson's face paled, then grew flushed. "Are you suggesting there's some connection between a visit to this surgery and her death?"

"I told you, I'm suggesting nothing. It is merely another fact. Just as it is a fact that the first woman who died was also a patient in this practice."

"Ah, but she had moved away some time ago, she should have transferred to another doctor. She was not a frequent visitor, in any event."

Abbott nodded. "So you checked her name, too, after her death."

"I recognised the name, yes."

"Dr. Eames didn't know her."

"She was before Jennifer's time." Gregson looked uneasy.

"In fact, Dr. Gregson, you didn't need to check up on her name the morning after the murder, did you? Her notes were on your desk, were they not? Mrs. Beryl Tompkins hadn't transferred herself to another practice, had she?" He leaned forward, slightly. "You'd seen her the day she died."

Gregson sighed and nodded. "All right. Yes. I made a house call. It was the same old story—back trouble. I suggested, not for the first time, that she quit her job. I also suggested that it would be easier for her if she transferred to a doctor nearer her new home."

"You could have gone on treating her, surely? It's hardly very far to go."

"Not for me in a car. But for her, on a bus, it was."

"So you were thinking of her rather than yourself."

"Of course. It's not particularly comfortable for someone with back trouble to be bounced about on public transport and then walk nearly a mile from town, just to be told to quit a job she can't afford to quit."

"She argued with you, about the job?"

"I wouldn't say *argued*. I told her there was nothing we could do to help her, other than provide pain-killers, as long as she did such heavy work. And that the problem could only get worse. Reluctantly, she accepted that. There was a possibility that surgery could have relieved the problem—it was a question of spinal fusion—but she was afraid of surgery, and refused. It doesn't always help, anyway, so I couldn't wholeheartedly recommend it. The whole situation was very unfortunate. I felt sorry for her. The pain was considerable, believe me."

"So, in each case, we have women in positions of frustration or difficulty, each seeing their doctor and then being murdered. Interesting."

"I resent the implication that this coincidence is in some way relevant to your investigations," Gregson exploded, suddenly. "Oh, you're being very bland, very noncommittal, but the pattern of your thinking is very clear."

"Is it?" Abbott grinned, suddenly. "In that case, I wish you would explain it to me, Doctor. The coincidence may not lie in the visits themselves, but in the results that such visits can bring about. When one sees one's doctor, it's usually in order to achieve something—surcease from pain, a way to go on, an answer. All things of that nature have a tendency to force decisions. Decisions have a way of forcing events and precipitating confrontations. And it's such confrontations that sometimes lead to murder. These women saw their doctors and then died, yes. Which leaves me with a question. Did you or Jennifer have something to do with the deaths—directly, or indirectly? For example, did you perhaps decide to murder the women because you felt sorry for them, or you felt they were annoying, or wasting your time?"

"Preposterous!"

"I agree it seems unlikely, but *not* impossible. Alternatively, did you tell them some fact or advise some course of action that made them bring about their own deaths?"

"I don't understand."

"It's really very simple. Say you told Mrs. Tompkins to quit her job, and after some consideration she decided to do so. She told her husband that there would be less money coming in, and he lost his temper and murdered her. Or you told Mrs. Taubman she was under too much of a strain and she decided to tell her son that she was not prepared to go through with his proposals for the manor after all—and he killed her, in order to remove her opposition. You see? Ripples going out from this particular centre. Or one thing leading to another. We find that murder is usually like that—the result of one thing leading to another. It's finding the one thing that's so difficult."

"Well, you won't find it here!"

Abbott stood up. "On the contrary, I may have done just that. Good morning, Dr. Gregson. Thank you for your time."

CHAPTER TWENTY-FIVE

"Watch out for Dr. Gregson, he's in a right mood," Kay said, putting on her coat as she stuck her head around Jennifer's office door. "Better you than me here tonight, I can tell you." The doctors handled their own evening surgery, which was by appointment, only.

"What's happened?" Jennifer asked.

"Your precious policeman happened," Kay said. "Put him into a right tizzy and no mistake. Watch out for flying potatoes at the dinner table is my advice."

"Good heavens," Jennifer said. "Thanks for the warning."

Kay grinned. "He just wants listening to, that's all. Haven't you learned that, yet? Poor man hasn't got an ear to lean on these days, what with his wife walking out and your uncle too poorly to take the strain."

Jennifer smiled. "And me too Bolshie to listen?"

"I never said that. Exactly."

"Do you think you'll ever get us straightened out?" Jennifer asked, with a weary smile.

"I don't know. I'm working on it," Kay said, grimly. "It's a bit like that chap pushing the boulder uphill, but I'm working on it. Like a couple of stubborn kids, the pair of you. Pig-headed. Good thing I'm here to keep an eye on you."

"Amen," Jennifer agreed. "See you tomorrow." She finished up her paperwork and glanced at her watch. Barely time to wash up before tea. She went through the waiting room, and looked around at the empty unmatched chairs standing at attention around the wall, the big table with the stacks of magazines neatly aligned, the soothing pictures on the walls. Beyond the window, the lawn stretched to the hedge—a single bit of sodden paper caught under a leafless bush, a scatter of gold and scarlet leaves, a bedraggled thrush hopping about hopefully. The rug was worn thin in front of the reception desk and in front of each chair. Under the big table was a box of toys to amuse restless children. Behind the reception desk the cover was over the typewriter, the filing cabinets were closed on their secrets, trays were cleared of work—ready to fill up again the next morning. If only Kay could straighten out the doctors the way she straightened out their place of work.

What on earth had Luke said to upset David? From experience she knew it needn't have been much. David was so touchy at the moment, so defensive. Perhaps she should make an effort with him, as Kay said. Somebody had to make the first move, after all. She sighed, heavily, and went back to knock on David's door. There was no response, and she opened it to look through. Either he was still out on house calls, or had already gone through to tea.

The empty office bore the imprint of the man, nonetheless. Jennifer had inherited Uncle Wally's room, and had hesitated to make any changes in it, yet. David's room was peaceful, like the waiting room. His desk was clear—unlike her own which was awash under a tide of papers, samples and literature from the pharmaceutical houses, clippings from medical journals she meant to read, odd pencils and pens. She entered, tentatively, trying to reach out to the man in his absence, and walked round his desk. She rested a hand on the back of his chair. The view out his window was bleak—just the path that encircled the house, and, almost against the window itself, the laurel hedge, closing him in. Still, the windows were high enough to let in plenty of light, and the room didn't feel enclosed or claustrophobic.

She paused beside a glass-fronted bookcase and saw that he had a collection of old surgical instruments, within. Surprised, she opened the door and examined some of them. It seemed an incongruous collection, for both the room and the man himself were modern in the extreme. And yet the brass trim and the steel blades were gleaming bright, and the wood in the handles was freshly oiled to a rich warm glow. Not a speck of dust was on anything. She wondered if Kay looked after this, too, but somehow she doubted it, for it had never been mentioned, and surely such an exacting task would have been cause for *some* comment on her part.

Jennifer picked up a particularly fierce-looking scalpel and touched the edge, giving a start when it cut her skin and drew a thread-fine line of blood. It was as sharp as a modern instrument, but much, much heavier in the hand. She went to the sink, rinsed it, carefully wiped it with a paper towel and replaced it on the glass shelf, hoping David wouldn't notice that it had been disturbed. She felt she had intruded on something secret and private, almost as if she had touched the bare skin of his body, not with a physician's objective hand but with a woman's touch, reaching more than the surface. She knew, instinctively, that he would be angry with her for it. He did not seem to be a man who wanted to be touched.

A few minutes later she arrived at the lounge to find quite a cozy group gathered in front of the fire and the tea-tray: Aunt Clodie, Uncle Wally,

Frances, Paddy, and Luke. No David. Was he still out on house calls, then? Or in his room, hiding? The thought startled her—why should she think he would hide?

"What's wrong, Jenny?" Luke asked, standing up. Her face had changed so suddenly. She had come in, looked at him, then through him, and the sensation had been almost physical. Having been kept busy all afternoon, he had forgotten how lovely she was, how tumbled and strong his feelings were for her, and how upset he had been at Mark Peacock's calm announcement of their engagement. She stood in the doorway, pale and somehow enclosed. His voice reached her, brought her back from wherever it was she had momentarily fled.

"Nothing. Hello, Luke. Hello, Paddy. Are we being questioned over the crumpets, then?" The suggestion, meant to be light, fell heavily between them.

"Of course not," Aunt Clodie said. "What an idea, Jennifer. Luke and Paddy came by to see how Frances was, and I insisted they take tea with us."

"Of course. Sorry." She flushed, avoided Luke's eye, sat on the couch, beside her uncle's chair. "Mrs. Rustle had twins, Uncle Wally. Boy and a girl, all well and happy."

"Grand. I told you she would. You and David owe me ten pence each, then, as agreed." The old man was inordinately pleased.

"Couldn't you tell from the scan?" Frances asked, puzzled.

Jennifer chuckled. "Uncle Wally told us she was having twins when she was only two months gone—long before the scan. You old warlock, you. I think you have a crystal ball hidden in your room."

"Hidden in my files, more like," he grinned. "If you'd bothered to look back in the records you'd have never taken the bet. Dora Rustle was born Dora Wentlock, one of twins, daughter of a twin. And Tom Rustle's father was a twin, too. Sucker bet, I believe they call it." He laughed at her expression. "*And* she was already showing at two months, Jenny."

"If we put our records on computer, the way David is always saying we should, it would have shown up," Jennifer conceded.

"Ah, good economics," her uncle said, sarcastically. "Spend five thousand pounds on a damned computer so you can save twenty pence bets against an old man. Try using your own brains, instead. Much cheaper."

Luke listened to this exchange, and observed the deep affection and respect between Jennifer and her uncle, evident in glance, gesture, and tone of voice. She was the natural inheritor of the old man's kingdom, a good doctor and getting better every day. What right had he to expect her to include him in that kingdom, he, a travelling knight, passing through? This was where she belonged. Even, perhaps, at Peacock Manor. Not as the wife of a copper, the mother of another woman's sons.

The thought came as a shock to him. He hadn't realised he'd been thinking that way, that far ahead. But, of course, he had. Since the previous night, since she'd returned his kisses with more than nostalgia, he'd been subconsciously committing her to his life, his heart. She obviously regretted what had happened already, otherwise why was she avoiding his glance? Her voice had been cool, she hadn't reached out to him, smiled at him, claimed him, or allowed herself to be claimed in any way.

He suddenly felt out of place, and it was damned uncomfortable, but not unfamiliar. Policemen grow used to being out of place except with other policemen. Even old friends can be uneasy in a policeman's presence. The jokes soon begin—'Uh-oh, watch what you say, there's a copper listening, now'—and the gap appears, widens, becomes a gulf, unbridgeable. Luke had always thought it was because they brought with them, unbidden and unwished for, an aura of judgement and censure. They were spectres at the feast, reminders of the wrongs that men do. And every man has wrong in his heart for someone, something. Everyone is afraid of being caught, if only by their own conscience.

He had hoped that here it would be different, that somehow Jennifer would make it different, that his long friendship with Dr. Wally would make a bridge for Jennifer. But Dr. Wally had grown old, and Luke was here investigating a violent series of deaths that involved people and patients she knew. He glanced at Paddy and Frances—the gap had not been so wide, there. A bridge was building that he thought had a good chance of becoming permanent.

He hid a smile in his teacup—that hard-headed Paddy would be caught by so fragile and dreamy a creature as Frances Murphy was as unexpected as it was satisfying. He would protect her, admit the existence of his own softer nature, and become a better officer for it.

Luke's own marriage had done that—for as long as it had lasted. With his wife's death he had been left with his softer side unprotected, and two small boys to keep him vulnerable. His hardness had been painted on in layers—it did not come from within, as it did with Paddy. He had a sudden and terrible conviction that his feelings for Jennifer would require a great deal of covering over, for he had been caught unawares, assuming he was safe as he approached middle age. He was not safe. He wondered if he would ever be safe, now.

"I understand you called on David Gregson this morning," Jennifer suddenly said, looking at him across the tea-tray. There was a sound of betrayal in her voice, a cloud in her eyes. "Kay said he was upset all afternoon."

"I'm sorry if he was upset," Luke said, evenly. "I can't think why anything I said would have distressed him."

"Can't you?" came Gregson's voice from the doorway. "It seemed rather deliberate to me." He addressed the company at large, but it was Jennifer he was telling. "According to the good and wise inspector, there is a connection between our surgery and murder. Women who come to us on perfectly legitimate visits have a way of getting their throats cut afterward. I wonder if we should perhaps post a health warning on the door—'Visits to this practice could result in exsanguination by violence.' It would make quite a selling point."

"I don't understand," Uncle Wally said, anxiously, looking from David's stormy face to Luke's deliberately blank one. "Did you say such a thing, Luke?"

"I merely pointed out the coincidental factor," Luke said. "I'm sure one could also discover others—they had all gone shopping the day before, or read the same magazine, that sort of thing. You have a largish practice in a small town—it's quite conceivable that the three women would all be your patients. Were Wychford a village it would be inescapable. There are only three other doctors in town, after all. It *is* a coincidence, but hardly a sinister one."

"At the moment, you mean. Suppose another woman dies—and *she's* one of our patients, too. What will you do then?" Jennifer demanded in a bewildered voice.

"I would respectfully request a list of all your patients and would put them through our computer to see if we could come up with any common factors," Luke said, calmly, finishing his tea, and standing up. "I'm sorry, Clodie, to have disturbed your home with my investigations. I assure you, I didn't bring them with me deliberately. Thank you very much for the tea. If you'll excuse us, we'll move on, now. Paddy?"

"Sure," Paddy said, standing up, too, but with obvious reluctance. He gave Frances's shoulder a gentle pat, then thanked Clodie and followed Luke out.

"Is there any tea left?" David asked, blandly, sitting down on the sofa beside Frances.

CHAPTER TWENTY-SIX

"What's going on between you and Gregson?" Paddy asked, as they drove back into town.

"Nothing, yet. I put some pressure on him, that's all. He seems so unnecessarily antagonistic," Luke said. "It bothers me a little—but I can't put my finger on why."

"I think he feels you're intruding on his territory," Paddy observed.

Luke glanced at him, puzzled. "Territory? You mean his practice?"

"I mean his partner," Paddy said. "It may have escaped you, and it's almost certainly escaped her, that David Gregson has a yen for Jennifer." He checked the rear-view mirror, then turned into the parking area before the station, parked and switched off the engine. "Seems to be a lot of it about at the moment." He chanced a look at his partner and saw comprehension and anger there.

"You make it sound like a bunch of tom-cats going after a female in heat," Luke growled. "My God, if I thought it was interfering with my investigation, I'd turn it over to someone else instantly."

"No, you wouldn't," Paddy said, calmly. "Once you had a chance to think about it, you'd use it. That's why I mentioned it."

Luke stared at him for a moment, startled. "And I thought you were developing a softer side."

"I am," Paddy said. "But I have an on-off switch that's still in good working order. You haven't had to use yours in a while."

"Rusty?"

"A little," Paddy acknowledged. "Nothing that can't be fixed."

"I think I'm in love with her," Luke said, quietly. "I expect I always have been, in a way."

"Memories are funny things," Paddy observed, watching his own strong, square hands clench and unclench around the steering wheel. "Your first love, was she?"

"Yes."

"And were you hers?"

"I don't know," Luke admitted. "Perhaps that's where the trouble lies. *Dammit*, I feel like a bloody idiot, sitting here, talking like some spotty adolescent about the girl at the party last night. I only realised what was happening—"

"When she walked in the door this afternoon," Paddy said.

"Christ! Was I that obvious?" Luke asked, appalled.

"Only to me. You've been edgy and restless all day, but you went totally still when she appeared, interrupted yourself to ask if she were all right. You generally finish your sentences."

Luke grimaced. "Said the warden to the recidivist." He stared gloomily at nothing, cursing his own weakness.

Paddy regarded him with some sympathy for a moment, then glanced at the station. "I wonder if the trick cyclist has finished with Baldwin, yet?"

Luke slumped in his seat, glowering at the station before them. There should have been brocade draperies gracefully suspended behind the tall windows, but instead, as the lights came on, one by one, they revealed dusty panes behind which stood filing cabinets, desks, and uniformed people going about the work of the early evening shift. Somewhere in there, Baldwin sat in a cell, alone. Luke was glad to return to the matter at hand. "First-time fathers get a rough deal in our society—all the attention is on the mother, who becomes a stranger to him sexually. She's so absorbed with the life within, and she's a different size and shape, not the girl he married at all. She even smells different. More like one's own mother, presumably. Pheromones have a lot to answer for. Some men go off the rails then—maybe Baldwin is one of them. Let's see what the psychiatrist says, anyway."

They got out of the car. "Maybe he can advise you on your own problems," Paddy suggested, with a lopsided grin.

They went in.

"I'd say no," Dr. Fernandez said. He was a sallow-skinned man, short and slightly rounded in the middle—a comforting and unthreatening shape, ideal for the work. "On balance, I'd guess Baldwin could have been pushed to kill the Frenholm girl, but not the other two. And I don't think he killed *her*, either. For what it's worth." He took off his glasses and polished them on a red-and-white checked handkerchief. "He's an interesting case, actually. One comes across these men, occasionally, in practice. Calibans, I call them. Not brutes, you understand, but living on a completely earthly level. Practical, sound, strong, steady. And yet, from time to time, they become aware of the stars and the flowers. I don't mean to be condescending, quite the opposite. They may be the only true poets God makes, because whatever rare dreams are in them spring from within, quite naturally and spontaneously, not from learning or posing or polished technique. And they can amaze you, damned if they can't. Someone should set up a bloody foundation or something to find them and nurture them."

"Got to you, too, did he?" Luke said, amused.

Fernandez looked abashed. "Hell, yes. He's a good man, Luke, you know? And, to be perfectly honest, she sounds as if she were some kind of a bitch."

"By all accounts," Paddy agreed.

"She stumbled into his dream, and once there, she used it to hold him. Not because she cared, but because . . . why?"

"Habit," Luke said. "Usually sex was her weapon, but in this case she realised she had something much more powerful. She flattered him into thinking . . . whatever he thought."

"You would be stunned at what he thought," Fernandez said, with a kind of rueful awe. "It wasn't what she did that's chewing him up, but the return to reality. I think he may seal it over pretty successfully. He's already calling himself names and trying to make jokes about it."

"Did you learn anything about what happened the night he found her?" Luke asked.

"Yes. I hypnotized him."

"Oh, God . . . that's . . ."

"Inadmissable, I know, but I didn't think you'd be bringing him to trial. He's a witness, Luke, not a killer. I'd stake my professional reputation on it. Really." Fernandez, convinced, was very convincing.

"Okay. Did you find out anything?"

"Yes." Fernandez produced a tape cassette. "Want to hear?"

"Please." Luke paused. "You did have someone in with you, once he was under?"

"PC Bennett, and PC Jagger."

"Jagger? Good. Very good. Let's hear it."

Fernandez inserted the tape into the cassette player on Luke's desk, switched it on. After the preliminary introduction and identification of witness, time, place, etc., they heard Fernandez address Fred Baldwin.

"Now, we're going to talk about the night you found Win, all right, Fred?"

"Yes." Baldwin's voice was dull, uninterested, the sheep-voice of the hypnotic subject, waiting to be directed, all self-volition suspended.

"You got her call. What did she say?"

"She said, 'This is Melisande, I . . .' "

"Melisande was your secret name for her?"

"Yes. She said it was her name in the Other World." Fernandez clicked the tape onto pause, and gave the other two an odd look, rather like the man who catches the stripper's knickers, excited, abashed, proud, but not quite sure what to do with them.

"Their relationship, such as it was, was founded entirely on a mutual fantasy, a kind of verbal game. You have to know that Baldwin's main reading matter is science fiction to understand how easily he could enter into and elaborate this kind of fantasy structure. They probably laughed a bit at first, admitted they were pretending, but then it got involved, competitive, symbolic, and very real—at least for him. Not having a chance to talk to her, I can't tell how much she had to do with it. She may have simply accommodated him, or she may have become enthusiastic about it, too. I'm telling you, Luke, pick up any stone . . . it's incredible what supposedly sane people will do when no one's looking. It took me four hours to trip into it, he had it very strongly guarded. In their fantasy, she claimed to be a being from a place they called Other World . . ." He trailed off, seeing the expressions on their faces. "It's not unusual—children do it all the time. In an adult we call it regressive play, probably a sexual substitute in this instance. Luke, you studied psychology at university—don't give me that Constable Plod stare." Fernandez's voice was getting a thin edge, and Luke grinned, relenting.

"All right, we'll buy it. Melisande, was it? And what did she call him?"

"What else? Prince of Shadows." Fernandez was protective of his latest chick. "Anyway, that's beside the point—read about it in my next book." He clicked the cassette player on again. "What did she say in the phone call— what were her exact words?" That was Fernandez's voice. Baldwin answered:

"She said, 'This is Melisande. I must confront an Evil Traveller and I am afraid. If you will stand by me when we meet, no harm will come to me, Prince of Shadows. Will you meet me on our Water Path, right away?' And I said I would." Baldwin's voice took on a strange, feminine quality as he repeated the words of Win Frenholm. Fernandez switched off the player again.

"Evil Travellers are beings who try to interfere with the passage of the Beautiful Ones from the Other World. Basically, it referred to anyone who wasn't a part of their fantasy structure. Most of the social aspects of Other World came from her, I'd say, and the more practical aspects from him. She thought up names and rituals, he delighted in working out the mechanisms for travelling back and forth, the landscape of Other World, and so on. Dammit, the detail is amazing. He went on for a bloody *hour* or more. But there was getting to be a lot about battles, struggles, and so on, toward the end. It was only a matter of time before the whole thing went sexual, I'd say. She was pressuring for it from the beginning . . . presumably she felt more secure in that area than in the fantasy thing. Anyway, this Evil Traveller she mentions could have been anyone she didn't like or was actually afraid of. Sorry I can't be more specific." He started to click the player back on, but Luke stayed his hand.

"She used the word 'confront'—interesting choice."

"Yes. I thought that, too," Fernandez agreed. He switched on the cassette recorder, and they listened to Baldwin's voice, droning on.

"I told Tricia there was a problem at the plant and went out. She wasn't very keen on me leaving her alone, and we had a bit of an argument, but in the end I went. I had to drive off in the car, because of saying I was going to the plant, but then I circled around and parked near the playground. I took the shortcut down to the towpath." Fernandez raised an eyebrow, and Luke nodded, to show he knew the geography. Baldwin was describing the night:

". . . cold. I had never met her this late, and I'd been in too much of a hurry to put on a jumper. There was moonlight, but not very much. I knew she was waiting for me."

"How did you know?"

There was a long pause, then Baldwin spoke with a slight tone of surprise. "I could hear her talking to someone."

Both Luke and Paddy straightened up at that. Fernandez, who knew it was coming, just smiled at them. "What could you hear?" said his voice on the tape. "You're there, now, going along the path beside the river. What can you hear?"

Baldwin hesitated, then went on. "The river, I can hear the river, and an owl, and the wind in the rushes. I'm cold. And I can hear Melisande's voice. She's angry. Very angry. She's around the curve of the path. 'No use,' she's saying. 'Forget it, I'll tell her myself, and then we'll see who marries whom, won't we? My baby, *my* baby will be . . .' and then she stopped."

"What did you do?" Fernandez asked.

"I stopped, too, and listened," Baldwin's voice said.

"Damn, damn, *damn,*" muttered Luke.

Baldwin was continuing. "I heard him laugh," he said. "And there's a bump, like something fell, and this terrible . . . choking. The Evil Traveller. I hear him running. I hear him and I wait for him to come around the corner, but he doesn't come. He must be running the other way. I run, too, and now I fall. I trip and fall onto the path, nearly into the water. And . . . the moon comes from behind a cloud . . . and I see Melisande. Oh, my God, my Beautiful One . . ." Baldwin was crying, now, the memories strong and clear.

There was a passage where Fernandez steadied Baldwin and brought him back to the present. The psychiatrist fast-forwarded the tape, stopped and started it a few times, then let it run, again. "Here," he said.

"A car," Baldwin said, clearly, on the tape. "A sports car, probably an MG. They have such a distinctive exhaust note, you can't miss them. Not new, either. Or not looked after. Two tries, and it catches . . . gone off, now. I'm picking up Melisande, I don't want her to stay there, where anyone . . . anyone . . . could see her, touch her. She's gone, of course, I know she's gone, but her body . . . the body she used . . . no one should touch that. No one."

Fernandez clicked off the recorder. "That what you were after?" He knew it was, and grinned at Luke.

"Yes, thanks. I thought Baldwin might be able to make more of that car. We were told he's a master mechanic, always fussing with cars and motors. Of course, the car could have been started up by someone else entirely. But even then, that person might have noticed a man running from the direction of the river. Either way, it would help us a great deal to trace the driver." Luke rubbed his ear. "All this Melisande business . . . it's going to look bloody daft on the reports."

"Oh, I can give you some great psychiatric jargon to throw in," Fernandez reassured him. "And you don't really have to go into detail, do you? Just the relevant statements should be enough. If you could avoid calling him at all on anything other than the discovery of the body, it would be doing the poor bastard a favour, Luke. Use him if you must, but if you can protect his secret world . . ." He paused, knowing he was asking something that might be impossible. "His wife doesn't know, shouldn't know. It would hurt her far more than any physical infidelity. It's not just the sex that hurts when your partner is unfaithful, it's the shared time, the laughter, the magic they've had with someone else and not you that brings the real pain."

"I know," Luke said, quietly.

"Is Bennett likely to . . ."

"Bennett's all right," Paddy said, firmly. "I can speak to Bennett, Luke." His mouth tightened. "And Jagger."

Fernandez was dangerously close to crossing the line of noninvolvement, and he knew it. They all knew it. "The guy isn't crazy, you know. Any more than a man is crazy who calls his wife snookie-ookums in bed. Like that guy, Baldwin is embarrassed to admit it. He just has a little more to admit to than most. A tribute to his rather individual imagination, in a way. The most I ever call *my* wife is . . . well, never mind. People in love aren't clinically crazy, but they're damned near it—no sense of proportion, ultrasensitive, delusional, obsessive . . . you name it, love will do it."

Luke and Paddy exchanged a quick, embarrassed glance. "So you'd say Baldwin was in love with Win Frenholm?"

Fernandez considered this. "Not in the socially accepted sense, no. She was his mental mistress, if you like, she offered him a safe release from the tensions of his marriage. He's a Catholic, you see, very strong moral attitude toward physical infidelity. Don't know what his priest would make of his interludes by the river, though."

"Impure thoughts?" Paddy asked.

Fernandez shook his head. "That's just it, they weren't impure, at least not on his part. Just the opposite—she was untouchable, beautiful and untouch-

able. That was the fascination. And, of course, that she *listened* to his soul."
Fernandez made a face. "Oh, Lord, now he's got *me* doing it." He took the
tape from the cassette player. "I'll take a copy of this, if you don't mind. I
really appreciate your calling me in, Luke. He'll make a great chapter for my
book. I hope it was worth it for you."

"Oh, yes," Luke said. "In more ways than even I expected."

CHAPTER TWENTY-SEVEN

Dinner was a strained affair.

Over the remains of tea David had explained Luke's interest in the practice, and his comments about coincidence. Uncle Wally was inclined to
anger, but Clodie said it was an understandable mistake on Luke's part.
"He's a good man," she said. "He's only trying to do his job properly."

Uncle Wally muttered something about serpent's teeth.

Neither Frances nor Jennifer said anything.

Shortly afterward, they all went their separate ways—Aunt Clodie to su-
pervise dinner preparations and perhaps snatch a moment or two at her
embroidery frame; the two invalids, Uncle Wally and Frances, to rest; and
Jennifer and David to take evening surgery.

Now, together again over dinner, they found the situation, if anything,
worse than before, primarily because David's anger had continued to perco-
late, growing ever stronger.

"I suppose he's planning to arrest *me*, next," he said, over the dessert.
"Well, let him try, that's all I can say. It would give me great pleasure to
knock that self-satisfied smirk off his face, and throw in a suit for defamation,
to boot."

"Luke isn't the kind of person . . ." Jennifer began, defensively.

"He isn't a person, he's a copper," David snapped.

"Now, now, that's not fair, David," Clodie protested. "Look at it from his
point of view. He has a job to do, he has to examine all the facts and follow
all the ways they lead. He can't pick and choose, can he? I must say, it's
bound to be difficult for him, knowing us all as he does."

"They don't usually send people who are involved locally," Frances said.
"Paddy told me Luke came only because there was no one else available. And
he *is* finding it awkward. They both are. More people than yourselves remember Luke as a boy—that makes it difficult for him to exert authority."

"I didn't notice him having any trouble," David growled.

Frances shot him an impatient glance. "As it is, he's got no clear path to follow. They're holding a man for questioning, but Paddy says . . ."

David's head came up. "Holding a man? Who?"

"I don't know, Paddy wouldn't say," Frances said. "He said he shouldn't have mentioned it at all, but . . . well . . . it was in connection with something else, anyway. I didn't press him."

"It's Fred Baldwin," Jennifer said, wearily. "His wife was in this evening to get some tranquillisers, she's in a terrible state, and the baby is acting up as a result."

"But . . . why *Baldwin?*" David seemed very perplexed by the announcement.

"Why not? His wife doesn't know, either, but she did admit to me once before that Fred often goes out walking at night—to work off his various frustrations, apparently. He started doing it during the summer, while she was pregnant, and has just carried on. He was called to the plant the night Win Frenholm was killed."

"And Mrs. Taubman? The night Mrs. Taubman was killed?" David asked, eagerly. "What about then?"

"Out walking," Jennifer nodded. She wasn't certain whether this information came into the category of patient-doctor confidence, but she was past caring. She wanted it all *over*, one way or another.

"Then this Baldwin looks like being the killer," Uncle Wally said. "I remember him—thick-set chap, short temper." His lined face lit up, slightly, as he thought of something else. "*And* I believe he works up at the photoprocessing plant, doesn't he?"

"Yes, he does," Jennifer said. "If you'll excuse me, Aunt Clodie, I think I'd like to lie down for a while. Headache." She got up and quickly left the dining room, before any further questions could be asked or arguments started.

She was confused and upset. The night before, when she had been out with Luke, he'd been taking a few hours' respite from the rigours of his investigation. Or so she thought. It had been a soft and romantic evening, and she'd welcomed what had happened between them on the towpath. They'd gone back home, and she would have invited him in, had not David been standing there on the doorstep. Invited him in and . . . who knows?

She knew.

There had not been many men in her life since her divorce, but there had been one or two. And then Mark Peacock when she'd first returned to Wychford. She was not a child anymore. The pressure of Luke's mouth had brought a quick, deep, and natural response from her that she hadn't felt for a very long time, and which was much more than sexual. She had said good night to him with regret, but had looked forward to their next meeting with considerable interest, even a kind of smothered adolescent excitement.

And then this afternoon she'd heard that he'd come to talk to David in the surgery and hadn't even looked in on her. Talked to David, even intimidated

David. Suggested that perhaps there was a connection between the practice and the murders.

Leading her to wonder whether the night before had been a night off for Luke, after all? They'd talked about her life here in Wychford, her practice, her patients—although the latter only in general terms. She tried hard to think back, to remember whether she had mentioned names, but was reasonably secure in her own mind that she had not. Luke was trained to question. Had he been questioning her, using an opening and an opportunity that were uniquely available to him and no other?

He wasn't the Luke she had grown up with. Had adored. Had often thought about in the intervening years. Had kissed before and kissed again last night.

He was a stranger.

A dangerous stranger.

As if on cue, there was a sudden flicker of lightning and a distant roll of thunder from beyond the open casement. "My goodness, sound effects and everything," she said, aloud, and got up to close the window. Beyond the glass the garden was lit, momentarily, by more lightning. Below her window was the drive, and, as she looked into the returning darkness, light came again. Not from the sky, this time, but from the opening of the front door. David, with his case in his hand, standing on the step to do up his mackintosh, glancing up at the now invisible sky. The light from the hallway caught his high cheekbones, the straight line of his nose, the top edge of his firm mouth, and his strong, mobile hands catching at the buttons of the flapping coat.

And what about David? she asked herself. Contrary to Paddy's guess, she was very aware of David's mixed feelings about her. She was not a fool. Nor was she unkind. He was in a vulnerable state, rejected by his wife, alone, working hard in a profession that needs all the support it can get while it supports others. He was lonely, and he was hungry for love and sympathy. This made him feel weak and ashamed, so his automatic reaction was to reject loudly and thoroughly she who would seem to offer it most naturally. They had never spoken about it, but they both knew it was there.

She turned her back to the window and heard his car start, then drive away through the hedge and down the street. She forced herself across the room to the mirror. After a moment's regard, she smiled.

"Come on," she said, softly. "Can you honestly think you're such a *femme fatale* that three different men are falling all over you?" Her hair was standing on end from where she had lain on the bed, her grey eyes were bleary, her full mouth looked bruised and discontented. A prize for no man. She hadn't looked closely at herself, lately. She saw, now, that new lines had appeared around her eyes and on her throat. Many of the curves that used to go up now went down. There was even some grey in her brown hair. Time to buy one of those cover-up shampoos. She was too thin—how odd to be too thin, when for years she had battled extra pounds. "You look your age, girl," she murmured. "Maybe it's time you started acting it, too."

Behind her, the lightning flickered, and the thunder was louder. A few spits and spats of rain struck the window, which rattled at the touch of the wind. The phone by her bed rang, suddenly, making her jump. "Nerves are shot, too," she told herself, ruefully. She went over to answer it, sat on the edge of the bed.

"Hello, darling," said a male voice in her ear. "How about having a drink with me?"

It was Mark.

She was downstairs in the hall, reaching for her coat, when the doorbell rang. She opened it, and found Luke on the step.

"Hello," he said, gravely. "I'd like to talk to you."

"I was just going out," she stammered, backing away from the open door. He looked so big, standing there, his coat flapping around his long, lean body.

"Oh." He considered her, the wind from the open door pressing her sweater and skirt against her. "It won't take all that long."

"Well, come in, then," she said.

"Who is it, Jenny?" came her uncle's voice from the sitting room. Jennifer looked up at Luke.

"Just the paper-boy, Uncle Wally," she called, and then whispered, "He's cross with you—no sense getting into an argument, now. Come on in here." She went through into the darkened reception room, and Luke followed, closing the door behind them. She could feel his presence in the dark, like an unanswered question, and quickly found the light switch.

"Were you going out on a call?" Luke asked.

"No, David's doing all the night calls until . . . for the moment. I was going to meet Mark for a drink."

"Oh." He glowered at her for a moment, then turned away. "I wouldn't want to keep you from your fiancé, of course."

"My what?" She couldn't have heard him correctly.

He turned to face her again. "Your fiancé. He told me very firmly that you and he were engaged to be married, but would wait a decent interval until the actual wedding."

"Oh? And when did he tell you that?" She felt rage and something else welling up in her. Something that felt very much like claustrophobia seasoned with resentment. She considered, fleetingly, the possibility of becoming a card-carrying lesbian. Out in the hall, the front door opened and closed, the brief intrusion of the wind in the hall rattling the surgery door in turn.

"This morning. I saw him this morning."

"I see. Was that before or after you saw David Gregson?"

"Before." He regarded her for a moment. "Jenny, what's happened?"

"I don't know what you mean."

"There's a classic evasion for you," he said, wryly. "What I mean is, last night and tonight. Not exactly similar, are they?"

"I don't know. Are they?" she asked. "Aren't you here to ask me questions? Wasn't that what you were doing, last night? Being a good policeman, doing your job?"

There was a long silence. Then his voice came, and despite her anger she could hear real pain in it. "I don't generally make love to the people I question."

"Fred Baldwin, for example?"

Another silence. "We released Mr. Baldwin an hour ago. Jenny, I wasn't a policeman last night. I was me. Luke. Just me. And I was very, very happy. I thought you were, too. Then, this morning, I'm told you're engaged . . ."

"I'm not engaged. I don't know what Mark was going on about, but he's mistaken. I saw quite a bit of him when I first came back here, yes, but it certainly hadn't gotten to that stage as far as I was concerned."

"Perhaps that's why he wants to see you, now."

"Perhaps."

"Well?"

"Well, what?"

"Are you going to marry him?"

"No. I don't know. What does it matter? Why do I have to marry anyone? I'm quite happy as I am, thank you."

"I see."

She turned to face him. "Look, Luke, I don't . . ." She stopped. "What was that?"

He looked tired, distracted. "What was what? I didn't hear anything." He listened for a moment.

"It sounded like . . . I suppose it's one of the cats, asking to be let in from the storm." She looked at him, tried to find the words she wanted. "Are you here to talk about your case, or . . ."

"Or," he said. "It concerns the case only because I can't think very straight at the moment. No, that's not true. Dammit, it *does* concern the case, but . . . frankly, my dear, I don't give a damn. About the bloody case, that is. Something's happening to me. Is it happening to you? That's all I want to know, Jen. One way or the other."

"I wish I knew, Luke. It's very sudden."

He smiled. "The hell it is. It's . . ." He paused, considered. "It's twenty-two years late. You should have let me kiss you again in the woods that day, Jen. Then we might know where we are now—at the end of one thing or the beginning of another."

"Which do you want it to be?" Her voice faltered.

After a moment, he spoke, softly. "Oh, Jenny—you sound so tired."

To her dismay, she began to weep. "I am," she said, the tears overflowing her eyes and rolling down her cheeks. She wiped them away with the back of her hand. "I'm tired of having to be strong for everyone else, of being expected to supply answers for everything, tired of being afraid I'll overlook a vital symptom, of fighting with David, of lying to Uncle Wally about his coming back to work . . . of simply having to stand up straight all the time. I want to go home again, Luke, and I can't. It isn't here anymore. It isn't anywhere. I'm all grown up, now, and I don't want to be. Not *all* the time. Damn—what a stupid time to start crying."

He took her into his arms as if she were a child, petted her, soothed her. "I know," he said. "Nobody told us there'd be years and years and years like this, did they? I go through life being unprepared for most of it, caught one day too early, one day too late, and thinking I'm safe when I'm not. Wrong foot, Jen, we're always on the wrong foot. That's why people work better in twos, didn't you know?" He kissed her, but lightly, even impersonally. "In about one minute I am going to turn into a policeman again. Meanwhile, what I'm about to ask you I'm asking as Luke Abbott, the boy who waited under that damned oak tree all afternoon. What are you going to say to Mark Peacock?"

She rubbed her face on the harsh tweed of his jacket, blotting her eyes. "I'm going to say yes to a Campari and tonic, and no to anything else. All right?"

"All right. That's enough for the moment." He let her go. "And now, before your very pink eyes, I'm going to turn into Detective Chief Inspector Abbott of the Regional Crime Squad, intent upon his case. What kind of car does Mark Peacock drive?"

She frowned. "An MG, I think. Some old sports car, anyway."

"Damn."

"Why?"

"Nothing. Come on—you're late for your Campari."

He refused to answer any more questions, and they went out into the hall, tiptoeing past the sitting room door, past the sound of the television set and the murmur of voices.

"That's funny," Jenny said, looking at the coat rack. "I could have sworn my mac was here. Oh, never mind, I'll wear my jacket and run for it." She took it down and put it on, then called toward the sitting room. "I'm just going out to see Mark. I won't be late."

Luke grinned down at her. "Thank you for that," he whispered.

"Thank you for not pushing me any further," she whispered back.

"I'm biding my time," he said, and opened the front door. The storm had begun in earnest, and a slashing curtain of rain blew at them. The light from the hallway showed each drop as a line of silver falling past the eaves, and spattering the front of Jenny's much loved new red Maestro, purchased only a few months ago, which was pulled up near the door.

Just beyond the gleaming red slope of the front wing, it also showed Frances Murphy, lying on the ground, arms outflung, face up to the storm, head back and twisted to one side. A spreading crimson stain flowed down her chest, over her shoulder, and into the creamy white gravel of the drive.

It matched the colour of the Maestro perfectly.

CHAPTER TWENTY-EIGHT

"On the table, there," Jennifer directed, shrugging off her jacket one-armed as she held the folded scarf against Frances's face, then switching hands to keep up the pressure on the wound.

Luke gently lowered Frances's limp body onto the examination couch, then stepped back and nearly fell over Uncle Wally's wheelchair. "Out of the way, boy, let us work," the old man commanded, his face and eyes sharper than Luke had seen them since his return. "I'll hold the sponge, Jenny, get what you need from your bag." Rolling the wheelchair closer, Wally took over when Jenny moved away.

"The surgical collar saved her life," Luke said. Uncle Wally glanced sideways at him, but said nothing.

"She went out to get something from Jenny's car," Clodie said, from the door, where she stood, wringing her hands. "It was only for a minute—her cigarettes or something had fallen out of her handbag in the car . . ."

"I'll call this in," Luke said, and went out into the reception room to phone in private.

Jennifer brought towels and draped Frances's head and shoulders, offering gauze to replace the blood-soaked headscarf they'd been using to stanch the flow from the vicious cut that ran from in front of Frances's left ear to the top of the surgical collar that had been hidden beneath her polo-necked jumper. The jumper was slashed and gaped raggedly. As she scrubbed up, Jennifer ran over what she had in her bag, and what was available in the office. She decided she could manage.

Frances's eyes fluttered open. "Ouch!" she said, her breath blowing the towel that was over her face half off. "Damn!"

"Lie still, you're all right," Uncle Wally snapped. "Thanks be to no one in particular, especially the police." This last was directed toward Luke, who had returned. Clodie had gone for strong coffee.

"Did you see anyone, Frances?" Luke asked.

Frances shook her head, resulting in a fresh outpouring of blood from the wound. "No . . ." she whispered. "I just grabbed a mac and went out to get my purse and cigarettes. I was opening the car door when somebody grabbed me from behind, cursed me, and did something to my . . ." She paused, full realisation coming to her. "I heard the thing scrape across my neck," she croaked. "Was it . . . was it . . ."

Jennifer put down a tray and told her to shut up. "I'm going to close up this wound, Frances. I'll give you something to dull the pain, okay?"

"Oh, Saints be," Frances said. "A needle, is it?"

"You know it is. Just close your eyes and go away for a while, and thank God it's no worse." Deftly, she injected a local anaesthetic.

"What did he . . . it *was* a man?" Luke asked, from beyond Jenny's shoulder. Frances said it had been, definitely, a man. "You said he cursed you. What did he say, exactly?"

"Luke, please," Jennifer protested. "Everytime she talks, she loses more blood."

"It's important, just this and one question more," Luke insisted. "What did he say, Frances?"

"He . . . called me a bitch. Said 'There, you bitch, that will put an end to your trouble-making.' That was all."

"And did you recognise the voice?"

"No. It was all . . . strained."

"Luke, *please,*" Jenny said.

"All right, all right, that's all for the moment. Ah, there they are, now." Luke went out through reception and the patients' entrance. Paddy came across the rain-swept drive on the run, his face white with fury and fear.

"She's all right, calm down," Luke told him, and outlined what had happened. "Jenny's stitching her up now. She's lost some blood and had a shock, but she's fine."

"God dammit, Luke!" Paddy said. "I want to see her."

Luke surrendered. "One look from the door and then get back here. We need to move fast." He looked around as Paddy went past him. "Bennett. Come here!"

Bennett came over at a run, and Luke gave his instructions. "Just have someone see if he's there. Don't say anything to him or anyone else. I also want someone to check on the craft centre." He went on for some time, Bennett writing everything down, when it became obvious he couldn't hold it all in his head. Paddy returned as Bennett was turning away.

"I never saw so many stitches in one wound. Little tiny damn things. She says she doesn't want the scar to show. She's one hell of a doctor, Luke." Paddy's relief ran out on a flood of words. "Frances says to tell you he also called her something like 'an evil meddler.' "

"Or was it 'evil traveller'?" Luke asked, grimly.

Paddy looked astonished. "You think it was Baldwin?"

"I don't know what to think," Luke said, angrily. "I'm thinking about twenty things at once. All I know for certain is that Frances was wearing Jennifer's mac and opening the door of Jennifer's car in front of Jennifer's home when she was attacked."

Jennifer straightened up and sighed. "There. All done."

Frances looked at her reproachfully over the top of the gauze and adhesive that strapped one side of her face. "I'm getting a little tired of all this reality,

Jennifer. It's a bit nobler on the page than in the face. That's why I've never put in about the snivelling and yelping." She spoke with some difficulty, using only half her mouth.

"Yes." Jennifer went across to wash up, while Uncle Wally, working quite efficiently from his wheelchair, set about cleaning up the scene of the surgery. "When did you have your last tetanus injection?"

Frances sighed and glared at the ceiling. "A long time ago, wouldn't you know it? Go ahead, puncture me again, I'm growing to like it. Aerates the brain."

"Frances . . . are you certain you didn't recognise the voice of the man who attacked you?" Jennifer asked, preparing the syringe.

"Yes." Frances sounded surprised. "Do you think I should have?"

"Of course not. It just might have helped, that's all." She looked down at the blood-soaked scarf she had removed from over the wound. The overhead light glinted briefly on a tiny piece of metal lying there. "When you've had a bit of a rest, I'll get Luke or Paddy to help you upstairs. You lost a fair amount of blood. Are you warm enough?"

"Yes. Fine, thanks."

"I'll just sit here with her," Wally said. "Clodie's arranging coffee or tea or something. You go off and see what the police are doing out there. I can hear them stomping around like a herd of grampuses, probably smashing up the rhododendrons."

Jennifer took a last look at Frances, who was pale but breathing evenly, her eyes closed. She went out of her office into reception, drawing the door shut behind her. After a moment's hesitation, she went as quietly as she could into David's office, put on the desk lamp, and approached the glass-fronted bookcase.

The antique scalpel she'd been looking at earlier was gone.

David Gregson returned about half an hour later, and had trouble getting his car in through the gate, which was blocked by one of the police vehicles. Eventually he scraped past and came in, half running.

"What's happened? Why are the police here?"

Luke, who was conferring with Paddy at the rear of the hall, turned and came toward him. "Ah, Dr. Gregson. I'm afraid Miss Murphy was attacked about an hour ago."

"*Frances?* Attacked? My God—do you mean by this butcher person?"

"It would appear so," Luke said. "Fortunately, the surgical collar she was wearing deflected the blade from doing any real harm. She got a nasty cut along the jaw and lost rather a lot of blood, but other than that—and shock, of course—she's all right. We've just taken her upstairs to bed. Dr. Eames is with her."

"I'd better go up," David said, shedding coat and bag in a practised single movement and heading toward the stairs.

They watched him run up the stairs and exchanged a glance. "We'll have a list of his calls, I think, when the moment is right," Luke said, quietly. "And someone to time the distances."

"Right," Paddy said.

"Now, what have you heard from PC Whitney up at the photoprocessing plant?"

"I think she may be onto something," Paddy said. "I just wish we hadn't had to go through personnel to place her."

"We couldn't be certain of her getting the job otherwise," Luke said. "And what about the men we have on Sam Ashforth, Barry Treat, Gordon Sinclair, and the others?"

"Bennett is checking with them, now. So far, they were all well away from here. Ashforth is still at the craft centre cafe, baking pies for tomorrow, and Treat and Sinclair are at home."

"What about Ray Moss?"

"Nothing on him, yet."

"And Baldwin?"

Paddy looked grim. "He was home for about half an hour, then went out for a walk. Betts lost him on the towpath."

Luke stared at him. "You're joking."

Paddy shook his head. "Wish I were. Bennett swears Betts is sharp—so Baldwin may have done it on purpose."

"Issue a general pick-up . . ."

"Already done."

Luke nodded. "Good." Hearing footsteps above, he glanced up and saw Jennifer coming slowly down the stairs. "How is she?"

"Fine. Nearly asleep." She reached the bottom and faced them, her expression set. "I think I have something you might find useful."

"Oh?"

Reluctantly but dutifully, she brought her hand out of her skirt pocket and produced the blood-stained scarf, which she had wrapped in a plastic bag. "There's a tiny piece of metal in there, which came from her wound. I think the blade of the weapon must have struck the surgical collar and got broken, or chipped. Can't your laboratory people tell a lot from something like that?"

"A great deal, sometimes," Luke agreed, accepting it. "Thank you." They were back on a formal footing, and he was aware of some distance between them. It didn't worry him as much as it had before—possibly because he had more urgent concerns relating to her. "I think you should go to bed and get some sleep yourself, Jen." He used her old nickname deliberately, reminding her who he was, giving her a line to cling to, if only temporarily.

She sighed. "I can't. I have to see Mark, remember? Although I doubt he's still waiting at the Woolsack—he must think I've stood him up or something."

"He's gone home," Luke said.

"How do you know?" She looked at him for a moment, and then her face went quite lax. "Are you having him followed?"

"Yes." He said no more than that, the bare affirmative.

"You still suspect *Mark?* Of killing his own mother—and the other women, too?"

"I suspect everyone," Luke said. "It's my job. We've been over this before, Jen. I wish you'd accept it."

"I do," she said, fretfully, pushing her hair back from her forehead. "I do, it's just that it keeps . . . coming up, like those things that jump out at you in the dark when you go on one of those tunnel rides at the fair."

"The Tunnel of Love?" Their eyes met.

"So it is," she said. "How apt."

"Go to bed, Jen," he said, softly.

"Go to bed and let the men look after things?" she asked.

"I have a good reason for asking it," Luke said. "I think whoever attacked Frances thought she was you." He deliberately kept his voice calm and objective. "And if that's the case . . ."

Jennifer stared at him. After a moment's thought, she spoke tonelessly. "She was wearing my mac, and getting into my car."

"That's right," Paddy said.

"What would you say to going to bed and staying there tomorrow?" Luke asked.

She looked at him and her mouth quirked. "Alone, presumably?" It amused her to see he was a little shocked by this.

"Jennifer, we're talking about murder and attempted murder, here," he said, irritably.

"I'm sorry, Luke. Put it down to tiredness. You want me to pretend I'm the victim, is that it? What good will that do?"

"Perhaps none, if, in fact, it was a random attack. If it was a deliberate attack on you, specifically, then it will give us time to work."

"But a lot of people know it was Frances and not me," Jennifer protested. "Uncle Wally, Clodie, Mrs. Louis." She took a breath. "David."

"Yes, well they can all keep their mouths shut, can't they?" Luke said. "I'm only talking about one day, Jen. Couldn't you use the rest?"

She looked down at the floor. "What about my patients?"

"Can't you get in a locum?"

"Not at such short notice . . ."

"I can take morning surgery," came Wally's voice from the surgery doorway. He rolled his chair forward. "I may not be up to much, but I can still tell a sore throat from a sprained ankle. For a morning, anyway."

"But . . ."

Uncle Wally looked at her with fond patience. "Jennifer, I'm still a good enough doctor to diagnose my own case, as well. I *know* I'll never work full time again, despite all the balderdash you and David and Frances keep dishing out. I've come to accept it, sitting up there in my damned room, watching all those old movies. But I can listen, dammit, and listening is a good seventy percent of what a doctor has to do. If anybody needs examining on the table, I'll send them through to David. Anyway, Kay's sharp enough to sort out the customers. I'll bet you anything you like she won't trot in a single case that requires more than an open mouth or an open shirt. Go to bed, girl, listen to what this monster says. The more we help the quicker he'll do his job and stop hanging around here."

Luke looked hurt. "I have a job to do," he said, tightly.

Dr. Wally didn't look at him. "And you don't care who knows it, do you? Bully you used to be, bully you've stayed."

"That's not fair, Uncle Wally!" Jennifer flared.

The old man looked at her. "Oh? Sticking up for him, are you? At tea-time you were sticking up for David, as I recall. Well, all right, I take back the bully part, but not the rest. You've upset things, coming back here, Luke. Upset them badly."

"It's the murderer who's upset things," Paddy said, defensively. "Not us."

"Used to be a quiet place, Wychford," the old man grumbled, wheeling himself toward the sitting room. "Used to be beautiful, and slow, and peaceful. Go to bed, Jennifer. And send David down to me—I want to have a talk with him." The chair and its grumpy burden disappeared into the sitting room. After a moment, the blare of the television resumed.

Jennifer spoke, as if the words were heavy in her mouth. "Luke, can your laboratory tell the kind of blade that bit of metal came from?"

"With luck, they'll be able to tell us the kind of blade, the kind of knife, and where it was purchased, among other things."

"Oh," Jennifer said, and turning wearily, she went up the stairs. At the top she looked down at him for a moment, then disappeared down the hall.

Luke looked down at the bloody scarf in his hand. "We'd better get this over to Cyril in the morning," he said. He glanced up at the empty hall, a puzzled expression on his face. "You'd almost think she didn't want us to have it, wouldn't you?"

CHAPTER TWENTY-NINE

"That bit of metal is on its way," Paddy said, coming back into the office. "Cyril should have it before lunch. Did you get through to him?"

Luke nodded, and tapped his fingers beside the phone. "He's confirmed his theories about the wounds. Or rather, his microscope has."

"Damn," Paddy said. "That means we'll have to keep going in separate directions. What about Frances's wound? If he could have examined that, we'd know . . ." He made a face. "She'd have bled to death, waiting for him."

"Not quite," Luke said. "But she might have complained a bit about police brutality. Has Whitney come in, yet?"

"Yes. She brought some interesting items—care to take a look?" He produced a large buff envelope, with an expression of distaste. Luke raised an eyebrow, and took it from him. He opened it and glanced down inside before drawing out the contents.

"Oh, my God," he said, in a sickened voice. "Kids."

"You got it," Paddy said. "She found them in a locker—along with a big file of negatives."

"Whose locker?"

Paddy scowled. "Guess."

Jennifer knocked gently on the bedroom door, and went in after Frances answered. "Good morning. How do you feel, this morning?"

"Now how would you feel if you were me?" Frances said, trying not to smile. "Gone, and never called me mummy—although I look like one."

"Paddy?"

Frances nodded. "He just sat here, held my hand, and looked at me."

"What did you do?"

"I looked at him."

"Poignant."

"Well, it was, actually." Frances looked self-conscious and rather pleased. "He feels terrible about what happened."

"So do I," Jennifer said, sitting on the edge of the bed. "Did he tell you Luke thinks it was meant for me—if it was meant for anyone?"

Frances nodded, not without difficulty. "That will teach me to borrow people's coats without asking. Is that why you've not gone down to morning surgery?"

"Yes. Luke wants me to lie low and say nothing—for today, at least. Whoever it was must have realised he hadn't killed you."

"I hope so. I gave him a healthy kick in the shins for his trouble."

"Oh? Did you tell Paddy about that?"

"I did. He was very pleased with the information. All he has to do, now, he says, is to ask every man he encounters to roll up his trouser legs. Should have someone behind bars by tea-time." She sighed. "Don't I wish?"

"Don't we all." Jennifer reached out and prodded the sides of the bandage. "Any inflammation?"

"Ouch. Only of the spirit." Frances pulled her head back. "Will there be a terrible great scar?"

"Not if I remembered my lessons," Jennifer said. "That's why I took so long over it. Fortunately I had some very fine sutures in my bag. I was quite brilliant, as a matter of fact. Even Uncle Wally approved, and he's a hard taskmaster."

"So pleased to give you the practice," Frances said, wryly. She looked at her friend and saw the shadows under her eyes. "You didn't get much sleep last night, did you?"

"No." Jennifer stood up and went over to the window, which overlooked the side garden. The storm had blown itself out in the early hours, and the lawn was scattered with leaves and small twigs. The trees, barer now, looked bleak against the grey sky. Winter was on the way.

"I'd like to think it was worry over me," Frances said, "but I won't flatter myself. What's wrong?"

"Why me?" Jennifer asked, abruptly. "Why would . . . anyone want to kill me?"

"I don't know. You can be very aggravating," Frances said. "Lovely to look at, of course, intelligent, witty . . ."

"I don't feel witty this morning."

"No, well, thank heaven for that," Frances smiled, then winced. "Come along, tell all. I'm just lying here, wishing for amusement. Obviously the Fates have it in for me, lately, and listening is as brave a performance as I'm willing to give."

Jennifer turned and looked at her friend. "Was it David?" she blurted.

Frances looked as dumbfounded as her bandaged face would allow. "David? *DAVID?* Who attacked me, you mean?"

"Yes." Jennifer's voice trembled. "Oh, God . . . was it?"

"No. Good Lord, no, I'm sure it wasn't. Why, in the name of mercy, would you have thought that?" Frances didn't know whether to laugh or cry, Jennifer looked so ghastly, as if her own question had horrified her, been a stowaway in her throat that had found its own violent release against her will.

Jennifer sank down onto the window-seat, her legs as shaky as her voice. She told Frances about the antique surgical instruments—and the one that was missing. "Where is it?" she asked. "What did he do with it?"

"Ask him," Frances said, promptly. "I'm as certain as I can be that it was not David who did this. He'd have to be crazy to do it."

"I know," Jennifer said, miserably. "But I can make out a good case for that, too. His wife leaving him, his antagonism toward me . . ."

"Piffle," Frances said. "That's probably because he fancies you and doesn't want to admit it."

"No," Jennifer disagreed. "What if it's part of a hidden antagonism toward all women? He was out on calls every night there was a killing. Luke said whoever did it knew what they were doing, how and where to cut. He keeps goading Luke, insisting that there's one killer, that it's a serial killer— what if he *wants* to be caught? That's just what he'd do, isn't it? Compelled by some inner madness to kill, yet, with his conscience and training, crying out to be stopped . . ."

"I think you'd better start writing the stories and I'll stick to the physiotherapy," Frances said. "Good Lord, Jennifer, you know the man, see him, work beside him every day. Wouldn't you have seen more signs of this 'inner madness'? You're trained to observe . . ."

"Six months on a psychiatric ward isn't exactly sufficient unto this particular day," Jennifer said. "And I don't see that much of David, you know, except over meals, and a quick daily discussion about the practice, which he keeps strictly business. Hardly opportunities to announce his new and fascinating hobby of murder and mutilation."

"Have you mentioned this to Luke?"

"You know I haven't."

"If you really believed it were true, you would have," Frances said, with conviction. Then, after a moment, she asked, "Wouldn't you?"

Jennifer waited until morning surgery was over. When she was certain her uncle had gone up to his room to rest and David had departed on house calls, she went into the surgery. Kay looked up from her desk.

"Gawd! You scared the life out of me! I thought you were confined to bed with what might be termed a sore throat." The relief in her face and voice were palpable. "David said . . ."

"It was Frances who was attacked, not me, but it's a secret," Jennifer said. "Luke thinks it may have been meant for me."

Kay looked more puzzled than anything else. "Why?"

"Why does he think that, or why me?"

"Take your pick."

Jennifer shrugged, and told her about Frances wearing her coat. "If he came up behind her, he might not have known. She wears her hair shorter than I do, but it's more or less the same colour. We're also about the same height, although she is a bit heavier than I am. But he wouldn't have been measuring waistlines, would he?"

"I suppose not. But who would want to kill you?"

"I don't know. Luke seems to have some idea, but . . . he's not exactly forthcoming. I think he suspects Mark Peacock."

"That one never had enough nerve to cut his losses, much less anyone's throat," Kay said, skeptically. "Doesn't make sense, anyway."

"Does murder ever make sense?" Jennifer asked.

Kay shrugged her thin shoulders. "I should have thought he'd have more than enough candidates out at that craft place, without sniffing around the manor," she said. "Mrs. Taubman wasn't exactly beloved at Monkswell, for a start off. She was trying to get the place closed down, you know."

"Was she?" Jennifer asked, surprised. "I didn't know that."

"Oh, yes, she was," Kay said, nodding. "My brother's on the council, and he says she put on a lot of pressure to have the place shut down—if it wasn't one thing it was another. Health regulations, trespass, people parking on her land . . . all sorts, she came up with. Seems her last prod was at the zoning committee and the ancient monuments bunch. Trying for sacrilege or something, Fred said. Daft old bat. Money was behind it, though. Always was. She fought it being put up, and she fought to have it brought down. *She* came down, instead, in a manner of speaking."

"But what would that have to do with the death of Win Frenholm, and that other woman up at the photoprocessing plant? And me?" Jennifer asked.

Kay shrugged again. "Don't ask me, ask your pet policeman." She eyed Jennifer, assessingly. "Not too happy this morning, are you? Got rings like a badger around your eyes. Maybe you aren't in bed, but you should be. Who doctors the doctors, I ask you? Me. Did you have any breakfast?"

"No. I wasn't hungry."

"Thought not. And not keen on lunch, by the look of you, either. What about your policeman, then?"

"What do you mean, 'my policeman'?"

Kay leaned back in her chair. "Denying everything, are you? The two of them come into town like Butch Cassidy and the Sundance Kid, one scoops up Frances, the other . . . I thought he had his eye on you, that Luke Bloody Abbott. Should have heard your uncle on the subject, this morning. Sir Laurence Olivier wasn't in it. Ungrateful whipper-snapper was the least of it, according to him." Kay's blue eyes were amused, but watchful.

"He's only cross because Luke seemed to think there was some connection between this practice and the murders. Or implied as much to David, yesterday."

"Oh, so *that's* why he was so snappy," Kay said. "Do you know how many patients we have on the lists, here? About four thousand. Aren't fifteen thousand people in the whole town. Not *that* surprising if all the victims are our patients, is it?"

"But surprising when one of the victims is me—or would have been me. It makes the connection almost inescapable. That's why Uncle Wally is angry with Luke. He doesn't want it to be true."

"But it is?" Kay looked more worried, suddenly. "Do you think it is?"

"I don't know. What have you done about this evening's appointments?"

"Dr. Gregson's got Dr. MacDonald up at the hospital to come along this evening."

"Oh. And how did Uncle Wally do, this morning?"

Kay beamed. "He did just fine. I sent in mostly the old regulars, and they were that glad to see him it did them more good than any prescription he could write. He wore down a little toward the end, but that's only to be expected. He did just great."

"Good." Jennifer glanced around. "Someone's coming up the path. I'll just slip into David's office for a minute."

"He's not there."

"I know." Jennifer turned away and left Kay wondering behind the type-writer. As she closed David's door, she heard someone's voice asking for a repeat prescription. She leaned against the door and looked around. The office was as neat as it had been the day before. David might not have even spent the morning there, it seemed so untouched, unchanged.

Save for one thing.

She looked into the glass-fronted bookcase and felt something contract in her chest. The collection of antique instruments was once again complete. The scalpel that had been missing last night was back in place, shiny and gleaming.

But without a tip.

The missing piece was tiny—as tiny as the bit of metal she'd found in the wound. Hardly noticeable, unless one was looking for it. Jennifer stood before the cabinet for a long, long time. The patient in the outer office departed, the phone rang and Kay answered it, another patient trudged up the path and made an appointment. Jennifer stood there for a long time, staring at nothing, and then, finally, she turned and sat down at David's desk. Slowly and deliberately, she picked up the phone and dialled.

By the time the police station answered, her cheeks were wet with tears and her entire body was shaking.

"Chief Inspector Abbott, please," she said, in a broken voice.

CHAPTER THIRTY

She was still sitting behind David's desk when the door opened and Luke stood there. Kay must have gone to lunch, Jennifer thought, then glanced at the clock and realised she'd been asleep in David's chair. "I came as soon as I got your message," he said. "What is it?"

"Your suit is all muddy," she said, before she could stop herself.

He glanced down, then came into the office and closed the door behind him. "I was down by the river," he said. "Last night's rain has made a mess of the towpath."

"What were you doing on the towpath?" She felt as if she were still half dreaming. He looked ruffled and a bit wind-blown, and his tie was askew.

"We're dragging the river."

"What for?"

"Fred Baldwin's body. He's gone missing, and his wife told us he stormed out of the house last night saying he was going to put an end to everything, poor bastard."

"Do you think it was Baldwin who attacked Frances last night?" Jennifer said, hopefully.

"I don't know. They said you wanted to show me something." He was impatient, and suddenly Jennifer had a sense of the investigation he was heading. Behind him was a small army, people dragging rivers, people following people, clerks and computer operators clicking away at their keyboards, questions and more questions and laboratories and heaven knew what else, lines as on a map, wires reaching everywhere, roads, telephones, radio signals, people talking, writing, checking—and he was in charge. The centre of the investigation *was* here in the surgery, but only because he was here. Touching him was like touching the edge of a spider's web—he and everything else came alive in an instant, ready, waiting. He was waiting, now, and he was in a hurry.

She wasn't.

"I don't know if it's important . . ." she began, slowly, and stopped. After a moment, he came across and sat down in the patient's chair beside the desk. She saw him make a visible effort to relax, fold his hands, wait for what she had to say. This is how you're trained, Luke, she thought. This is what you do best. If I'd gone back and kissed you under the oak tree, would all this be different, now? Better? Worse?

"Take your time." His voice was soft, and she knew that he had realised, almost immediately, that it was very important, indeed, to her.

Instead of speaking, because she couldn't say it, not even one word of it, she simply turned David's swivel chair and pointed to the middle shelf of the glass cabinet in the corner. Luke rose and went over. She watched his long, lean back and, after a moment, saw his shoulders stiffen.

He had seen it.

"What is it?" he asked.

"An old surgical instrument called a bistoury," she said. "It's very sharp—I cut my finger on it, yesterday morning."

He turned. "And was that bit at the tip missing, then?"

"No." It came out in a whisper.

"Why didn't you mention this last night?"

"Because . . ." her voice faded, and she had to clear her throat. "Because last night it wasn't there."

He swore, under his breath. She knew, somehow, he was not swearing at her. "I'm sorry, Jen."

"Oh, so am I," she said, with a sob. "So am I."

Taking his handkerchief from his pocket, he opened the cabinet and picked up the scalpel in the white cloth, carefully grasping it by the band between blade and handle. As he turned away from the cabinet, the office door opened, and David Gregson came in.

"What the hell are you doing in here?" he demanded, taking in Jennifer, and Luke, and the thing in Luke's hand.

"I'm afraid I'll have to ask you to come down to the station, Dr. Gregson," Luke said. "Just a few questions."

But David's eyes were on Jennifer, dark with anger, filled with accusation. "What have you done?" he asked, in a terrible voice.

"You'd like it to be me, wouldn't you?" David Gregson said, angrily. "That would suit you down to the ground, the mad doctor going berserk when the moon is full, I suppose."

"Nobody said anything about a mad doctor," Luke said, in a quiet voice. "I just want to ask you some questions concerning your movements last night and on previous nights, and your relationships with the dead women."

Gregson, red with anger, became suddenly pale with apprehension. "What do you mean, my 'relationships' with them? I had no relationships with them, other than doctor and patient."

"According to your receptionist, Miss Frenholm normally asked for you— but on that last occasion, she asked specifically to see Dr. Eames. Why was that, do you suppose?"

"I have no idea. Perhaps my morning list was full. Perhaps she felt a woman would be more sympathetic concerning a possible abortion."

"I see." Luke's voice was skeptical. "And other than visits to the surgery, did you have any occasion to see or speak to Miss Frenholm?"

"No."

"Paddy?"

Paddy opened a folder on his desk. "According to our information, you met Miss Frenholm on at least one occasion in the Woolsack. And left with her."

"Rubbish."

"Our witness is a local constable, who was there with his wife when off duty."

"It was probably *my* wife he saw—she's blond and rather beautiful."

Paddy cleared his throat. "It seems the constable in question had private reasons to know Miss Frenholm on sight. According to him, he was considerably relieved when she left with you."

"How does he know it was me?"

"He's a patient of yours."

Gregson closed his eyes for a moment. "Ah." He seemed, with this syllable, to acknowledge a kind of defeat. "All right, then, yes, I met her at the Woolsack—but *not* by arrangement. It just happened we were there at the same time."

"And you had a drink together."

"We had several drinks together, if it matters."

"And left together."

Gregson sighed. "And left together," he said, in a defeated voice. "And stayed together for several hours more, in the back of her blasted pottery. Damned uncomfortable."

"This was in August."

"It was. Two weeks after my wife left me for a bastard baronet with a speech impediment and a million in the bank. If she has continued as she began, by now he should be down to about fifty pence." Gregson's voice was bitter with self-disgust. "I was lonely, I was tight, I was randy, and Miss Frenholm was more than willing, she was bloody avid. Took me a week to recover."

"And did you go back for more?"

"No, I did not. Aside from not being up to her pace, she was one of my patients. Not done, Inspector. Unlike policemen, doctors are never off duty. You now have it in your power to have me struck off. Feel free. I took advantage of what was undoubtedly the clearest case of nymphomania I have ever encountered outside a textbook. I was depressed and miserable. I was a fool. But I am not a murderer."

"You could have been the father of her child."

Gregson's head came up. "I suppose I could have been, at that. Bloody hell, that would have pleased my wife. Speeded up the divorce no end. She would probably have offered to be godmother to the little bastard—once she'd stopped laughing, that is. She always maintained I couldn't get up a sweat, much less anything else."

It disturbed Luke to hear Gregson, normally taciturn, speak so bitterly and fully about something that was obviously a source of deep anguish to him. Subjected to sexual scorn in an unhappy marriage, then a willing but possibly unsatisfactory partner to a sexual predator who made no secret of her contempt for men—fertile ground for murder to flower? Or just an unfortunate juxtaposition of misery?

"Tell me about these antique instruments of yours."

Gregson shrugged. "I collect them. It's a hobby. Some of them are beautifully crafted. I intended to become a thoracic surgeon, but there was no money for me to study further in a special field. I had no option but to go into general practice. The collection is mere sentiment, nothing more."

"This particular instrument—a bistoury?"

"That's right."

"The tip is broken off."

"Yes. I don't know when it happened."

"Sometime between yesterday lunch-time and this morning," Luke said, carefully, watching Gregson's face.

"Oh?" was Gregson's response. His face remained impassive. "And why do you think that?"

"Because yesterday morning it was whole. Dr. Eames cut her finger on it. She picked it up out of curiosity and didn't expect it to be so sharp."

"I keep all my instruments sharp," Gregson said.

"Why?"

"They are proper instruments, despite their age. They deserve that respect." He thought for a moment. "She must have rinsed off the blade, then."

"She did."

Gregson nodded. "I noticed a few tiny spots of rust forming last night, before I went out. I usually keep the blades well oiled, for at that time stainless steel was unknown, and they need protecting. I took the bistoury out and put it into my bag, intending to oil it last night when I got back. Which I did."

"And did you notice the tip of the blade missing at that time?"

"Yes, I did. Those blades are very brittle—I assumed it had been chipped while in my bag. If you'll recall, my return home was at a rather hectic time. I simply oiled it quickly before I went up to bed, and put it back. I meant to resharpen it this morning, but with Jennifer off, I didn't have time." The thought of Jennifer clouded his face. "She thinks I am the killer, presumably, and that that is the murder weapon? The little fool."

"It's hardly a conclusion that has brought her any personal pleasure," Luke said. "She was very distressed, but . . ."

"Thought it was her duty as a responsible citizen?" Gregson asked, bitterly. "How admirable. And here I am being interrogated in a pointless exercise, while patients wait to be seen and treated. *What* a clever girl."

"Did you kill Win Frenholm, Dr. Gregson?"

"I did not."

"Did you kill Beryl Tompkins?"

"No."

"Did you kill Mabel Taubman?"

"No."

"What was your relationship with Mrs. Taubman?"

"I was her long-suffering GP, nothing more. She was a difficult, demanding woman. But there were no drinks, no liaisons, nothing. The same goes for Mrs. Tompkins—although she was quite different from Mrs. Taubman. A quiet, pleasant woman. She was the one who was long-suffering, not her GP."

"Would you say she was a very moral woman?" Paddy asked, abruptly. Gregson gave him a startled look, as if he'd forgotten he was there.

"A moral woman? What do you mean?"

"I mean, do you think she felt strongly about right and wrong?" Paddy said.

"I have no idea. The subject never came up. I treated her for a persistent and extremely painful back condition, plus the usual coughs and colds, nothing more. We never ventured together into the realms of philosophy."

"She was a strong family woman."

"Oh, yes, *that* was true. Devoted to her husband and children, almost obsessively so. Particularly the children."

"So something to do with children—say a case of sexual abuse—would have struck her forcibly, caused a strong reaction?"

"Undoubtedly."

"Thank you." Paddy leaned back in his chair. "Thank you."

"Did you attack Frances Murphy last night?" Luke asked, suddenly.

"No, I did not."

"You realise that you have no alibi for the relevant time, nor for the times of the other killings?"

"I hadn't thought about it."

"You were out on each of the evenings in question."

"Was I? I'd have to check my records."

"We're doing that, now."

"I didn't give you permission to do that!"

"You didn't have to. Your arrangement with Dr. Walter Mayberry is that of a partnership, you hold records in common. He has given his permission for us to view all relevant files."

"My God, he must be crazy! Those are confidential files, you have no right . . ."

"We will read only relevant files, and we will do so under his eyes. Nothing will leave your office, nothing will be copied, except with his permission, and he will personally sign every copy made."

"Does *he* think I murdered these women, as well as Jennifer?"

"Neither of them has accused you. We are simply investigating. This instrument will be given to our forensic people for comparison with a piece of metal found in Miss Murphy's throat wound. If they match . . ." Luke paused.

"I see."

There was a pause. "Tell me, Dr. Gregson," Luke said. "What is your ancestry?"

"My what?" David Gregson stared at him.

"Your ancestry," Luke said, calmly. "Scots, Irish . . . what?"

"What the hell has that got to do with anything?"

"A great deal, as it happens."

Gregson scowled, considering this. "I don't get the connection."

"Have you ever heard of a blood condition known as thalassemia?"

"Vaguely—translates as 'the sea in the blood' or something, doesn't it? Affects Mediterranean people. Read an article . . ." he paused, and then his face cleared, as comprehension began to dawn. "You had your lab people test the foetal blood, didn't you?"

"Yes."

Gregson almost smiled. "Very clever. Well, you won't find thalassemia in me, I'm certain of that."

Luke inclined his head. "Perhaps not. But we have other means at our disposal, now. Have you heard of genetic fingerprinting, Dr. Gregson?"

"I know the theory, yes," Gregson said, reluctantly. "Every human being has a unique genetic pattern in his DNA, as distinct as a fingerprint, no two people alike."

"Not a theory, anymore, I'm glad to say. By scanning the DNA in foetal blood, we can now get a genetic fingerprint which, using established comparison techniques, can prove conclusively the paternity of a child. No percentages, no good guesses, anymore. It can be done with total certainty."

Gregson swallowed, only too aware of how fast technology moved these days, and of how little time he had to keep up with it. "I don't believe you," he said.

Luke smiled. "Care to bet ten milligrams of your blood on it?" he asked.

CHAPTER THIRTY-ONE

Kay had spent the afternoon cancelling and rearranging the evening appointments. She was deeply upset by David Gregson's detainment by the police. She had worked with Gregson for five years, now, and although she was fond of Jennifer, she had worked with her for less than one year.

She glanced over at Jennifer, who was seated out of sight of the waiting room, behind the bank of filing cabinets that held patients' records. Constable Bennett had come and gone with his notebook, working with Jennifer and Dr. Mayberry, writing down everything they'd give him about the people on Abbott's list. They didn't answer all of the questions, only as many of them as they thought fit or relevant. Co-operation, not revelation. Even then, there were some conflicts and arguments between the two physicians—partly professional, partly personal. Now Bennett was gone, and Dr. Wally had gone upstairs for another rest, looking drawn and exhausted.

Kay, protective of the old man, felt Jennifer was to blame for this latest unfortunate development—and yet common sense told her that she was unfair to pass judgement. Certainly Jennifer looked as badly off as her uncle.

Jennifer seemed to sense her disapproval, and looked up. "I had to do it, Kay. What if David is ill? Couldn't help himself? If I said nothing, more women could die. I'd rather be wrong like this than that."

"I suppose so. But you could have talked to him first about it, couldn't you?"

"If he is the killer, he tried to kill me last night, remember? Would *you* want to accuse to his face someone who wanted you dead? I'm not that brave."

"Do you really, seriously, believe David Gregson wants you dead? Why, he's half in love with you."

Jennifer shook her head. "What he feels for me isn't love, exactly, and it could even be hate. They're very similar emotions. It's indifference that's opposite to love, not hate. I've been forced on him by Uncle Wally, and he resents that, he's been badly let down and humiliated by his wife—I could see a reason there for him to detest women. Whether he's made a leap into homicidal psychosis—who can say? I agree, it does seem far-fetched. But those knives . . . have you *seen* all those knives he keeps so damned sharp?" She sighed. "I want everything to be the way it was before these killings began. I want to go on learning how to be a good family doctor, I want to build a life here, be of use, look after Uncle Wally and Aunt Clodie, come home again."

"What about Mark Peacock? He part of your nice life?" Kay asked.

"I don't know." She ran a hand through her hair. "I feel absolutely rotten about Mark, as well as David."

"And Luke Abbott?" Kay asked, pointedly.

Jennifer looked across the office at her and managed a grin. "My God . . . it's getting out of hand, isn't it? It's ridiculous. I mean, I'm divorced, approaching forty at about a hundred miles a minute, committed to a career—why should any of them be interested? Mark wants a chatelaine for his precious manor, David wants someone to bind his wounds and make him whole again, and Luke . . ." She paused.

"Luke is different?" Kay asked. "Or are you different where Luke is concerned?"

"I don't know. Luke . . . cares. It's getting in the way of his investigation, it's throwing him. Me, too." She looked at Kay in some bemusement. "I think Luke is wonderful," she said, simply. "And I think being a family doctor is wonderful, too. What do I do?"

"Nothing, until you hear from me," Kay said, with a wry smile. "Is Luke Abbott asking for a decision?"

"No, of course not. It hasn't got that far. He may not want that, anyway. I might just be a—distraction, for old time's sake."

Kay saw this possible explanation of Luke's behaviour was haunting her. Still bruised from her divorce, Jennifer wasn't ready to trust again. "Well, then—leave it alone," she advised. "See what develops. As you said, you're not a dewy-eyed teenager, or even a fresh young thing. You're an old bag, Jennifer. Face it. Old bags are allowed to take their time about making up their minds—what they have left of them." She glanced at her wristwatch, and grimaced. "Doesn't look like Dr. Gregson's coming back before dinner, does it? I'd better use the answering machine and refer night calls to Dr. Calgary—Dr. Wally called him earlier and asked if he'd stand in, tonight. We did it before, when he first had his stroke and Dr. Gregson was run off his feet before the locum could come in. Worked out all right."

Jennifer watched her as she put the message on the machine and connected it to the telephone. She felt listless and depressed. Kay clicked the last switch and let out a long, relieved breath. "Nearly time to go home and peel potatoes. We career women do have these fascinating demands on our time, don't we?"

"We do." Somehow, Jennifer managed a smile.

With Kay gone the surgery seemed too quiet, too like a tomb. Jennifer went out to the kitchen and talked to Mrs. Louis about dinner, then to the sitting room for a word with her aunt, back at her embroidery again. Then she went upstairs to face her uncle.

"Be angry with *me*, Uncle Wally, not with Luke. It's not fair, blaming him."

"Always was bull-headed, even as a boy," Uncle Wally grumbled, perversely, his eyes firmly on Robert Donat, who was mouthing silently on the turned-down television set. "Fishing, studying, cricket—Luke Abbott always went his own way, wouldn't listen to anyone. I suppose I should have seen he'd become something like a copper."

Jennifer sat on the edge of the bed and took one of his hands. "About David . . ."

"What about David?" He scowled at her. "No more a murderer than I am. The whole idea's ridiculous. What do you think he does, drink some potion in the silence of his lonely room, then dash out to slaughter the first female he comes across—just because he objects to you joining the practice? God save us, Jennifer, you don't know him at all. Not at all." His eyes went back to the television set. "His wife's a doctor, you know."

"Oh." Jennifer was taken aback. "I *didn't* know."

"Well. There you are. She is. Consultant, dermatology, private practice only, over in Milchester. That's how she met her precious baronet, by all accounts. Probably came to her with his semiroyal boils or something. And what has she up and done—just dropped her entire practice, that's what she's done. For 'love.' Do you wonder David looks on female doctors with a wary eye? Must admit, I'm beginning to see things his way."

"You mean, you want me to leave the practice?" Jennifer asked, dismayed.

"No, I don't want you to leave the practice," he said, mimicking her feminine tones. "But I can't say I take kindly to your accusing your—our—partner of murder, either."

"Uncle Wally, somebody tried to kill me last night."

"Rubbish. And anyway, it wasn't you who suffered, it was Frances. I can't say I've ever taken kindly to her pushing me about the way she does, but she's a good gel, I like her, she's under my roof, and it was damned unfortunate. Don't see why *you* have to make such a fuss. Don't see any stitches in *your* neck."

"Perhaps if there were you wouldn't be so stubborn, yourself," Jennifer said.

"Nonsense," he said, but his voice was affectionate, despite his best intentions to remain stern. He loved Jennifer, but he was very fond of David, too, and he didn't like this situation one bit. Personal feelings aside, it was professionally damned difficult. "Naturally, I don't want anything to happen to you. Least of all have you turn into a dried-up old maid. I'd hoped you and David would . . . get along."

"Yes, I know you did," she said, wryly.

"And here you are, mooning after Luke Abbott, instead."

"I'm not mooning after Luke Abbott!"

"Then why this mother-lion act about my blaming him, hey? I can see what's going on under my nose over a dinner table or a cup of tea. Cow-eyes, quick look, quick look away, pulses throbbin' and all that. Lord, Jenny, I've had a stroke, not been struck blind and stupid. You were sweet on him as a girl, and you still are. But he's a police officer, now, not the captain of the cricket team or Lochinvar come out of the East. Only came from Milchester, for crying out loud. He's got a job to do, and by God, he'll do it. This turning David over to his not very tender mercies—why, it's ridiculous, like some offering to a god. Look how clever I can be, Luke. Look at me. A cat bringing home a mouse, looking for approval. You've let me down, girl. I'm cross with you. Turn up the TV and let me rest."

Jenny was enraged. She stood up. "Why, that's not fair! That's wicked, to think I'd be like that. David has all those sharp knives . . ."

"Always *has* had them—why should he turn to murdering now?"

"One was gone from the case last night, put back this morning with a chip out of it. A chip about the size of the one I found in Frances's wound . . ."

"Circumstancial . . ."

"And he keeps insisting that the killings are done by one person, as if asking to be caught . . ."

"Psychological flimflam . . ."

"And he has no alibis for the relevant nights . . ."

"He's a hard-working GP . . ."

Jennifer's guilt over what she had done, mixed with outrage and confusion, made a volatile mixture. Moreover, it had the odd characteristic of being able to strangle normal speech. All she could manage was a choked "Oh!" before storming out of her uncle's bedroom.

He watched her go, relieved to be done with the scene he had been dreading, glad to be able to build up his strength for the inevitable scenes which lay ahead. David was bound to have a great deal to say about being turned in like this, forced to waste time answering questions and defend himself when there was so much to do in the practice. Perhaps he'd even refuse to work with Jennifer again. *That* would make a pretty mess.

Of course Luke would release David, there was no question about it. Even if the chip of metal *did* match the gap in the point of the bistoury, surely it could only mean that someone had stolen it and slipped it back. David was no killer. True, he'd been a little odd of late, but that was due to strain, and was quite understandable. Perhaps he'd even taken a pill or two to keep going, and then another to get to sleep. Many a doctor has done the same under stress—he'd done it himself, during the war. But that was no reason to worry.

Absolutely not.

Mind you, there *were* some damned odd pills about these days. And people *did* have adverse reactions, sometimes. And it *was* getting late, and David not back, yet. But that was no reason to worry. He looked down at his hands.

No reason to twist the coverlet up like that, either.

CHAPTER THIRTY-TWO

"PC Whitney has just phoned," Paddy said. He'd been summoned from the interrogation room, where they were questioning David Gregson, by an agitated PC Bennett. After talking to Whitney, Paddy had gone back and called Luke out. "Our man is there, right now. Hard at work, she says. Wants to know what we want her to do."

"Damn!" Abbott glanced at the door of the interrogation room, where Gregson sat with a local officer from their investigative group. "He would pick tonight." He looked at Paddy. "Well, this is your baby. What *do* we want to do?"

"I want him, Luke," Paddy said.

"All right. Take Bennett and whoever you need. I'll go on working on Gregson. And for God's sake, be careful. No telling which way he'll jump when you confront him. He has everything to lose."

"That's why I want to take him," Paddy said, grimly.

He went to Bennett and explained what he wanted, who he needed. The young officer never blinked an eye, but simply wrote it all down, and then did it. Paddy thought that if he did ever come down here, Bennett would be the one he'd want on his team. He might even want to move him over to Milchester, when he had the authority. They hadn't had a chance to become acquainted, so he didn't know the lad's personal situation, but he recognised promotion material when he saw it. So did Abbott, who had already commented on his potential. One more good thing to come out of this rotten case. Who'd have believed it possible?

When all was ready, they left in the unmarked lead car. The others would follow and be deployed around the parking lot in case their target made a break for it. A lot of dark and rough country, still, around the plant, Paddy thought, as Bennett drove through the evening streets. Maybe it would have been better to let Luke do this—he knew the land. But it was Paddy's chance to show his colours, and they both knew it.

Had to go right, first time. Had to.

Bennett parked the car across the front entrance to the photoprocessing plant, and the other cars following spaced themselves around the perimeter, the men stationing themselves in between. It was fully dark, now, but the moon was rising. They moved in silence, with only an occasional low mutter into a lapel radio.

Paddy and Bennett glanced at one another. Paddy nodded, and they went in through the main entrance. The reception area was only faintly lit. They could hear the voices and laughter of the cleaning women in the plant itself, mops cracking against the bases of machines, the hum of a floor polisher. There was movement in the shadows, and PC Whitney, a trim, pert-faced blonde in loose clothes and a wraparound coverall, emerged.

"Upstairs, sir," she said to Paddy. "In the small laboratory where they do special orders. He's alone. There's only two doors, both open onto hallways. I'll show you."

"He's actually processing negatives?" Paddy asked.

"Yes, sir. Or he was when I left to call you. He's still there, his car hasn't left the lot."

"Good girl. Come on."

They went up the stairs, listening in case he took the lift down, but there was no sound from the mechanism. The upper hall ran from a small foyer down a long, unlit hall which went around a corner at the far end. Halfway down, a square of light spilled out of windows set high in double doors.

"That's the special projects lab," Whitney whispered. "If you go around the hall at the end, you'll see the other door—just a fire exit, really."

"Bennett?" Paddy said. Bennett nodded and moved off.

They waited for a moment for Bennett to take up his position, then Paddy pushed the door open and entered the lab.

"Working late, are we?" he asked, in a loud voice, meant to startle and unnerve. The man bent over the lab table jerked upright and dropped the photograph he'd been holding. It caught a draft and skidded away from him. He made an automatic lunge for it, but it eluded him.

Bennett, coming in the other door, picked it up, looked at it, and scowled. He came across and handed it to Paddy. "Lousy composition," he said.

Paddy looked at it and his jaw clenched. "This isn't very nice, Mr. Grimes," he said. "Not at all the sort of thing one puts on the wall of one's office, is it? Wouldn't go down too well with the rest of the jolly old chaps, would it?"

"Oh, my God," Grimes moaned. "You weren't supposed to be on to-night," he said to PC Whitney, accusingly, as if it were all her fault.

"Volunteer work," Whitney said, grimly. She had seen the photograph, too. "I have a generous heart."

"Is this what Beryl Tompkins discovered, Mr. Grimes?" Paddy asked. "Did she accuse you, say she was going to the police about you and this filthy stuff? She had children of her own, Mr. Grimes, she didn't take kindly to this kind of thing, did she?"

"You don't understand," Grimes said, weakly, his smooth face suddenly pale and overlaid with an oily sheen of perspiration. "I love children. These are only art studies . . ."

"Come off it, Mr. Grimes. This is paedophilic pornography under any definition of the act, and you are guilty of causing it to be sent through the mails to others of your kind. You've used the equipment here, without permission . . ."

"I had permission," Grimes said, drawing himself up.

"Not for this kind of thing," Paddy said. "I checked."

"You've talked to . . ."

"I've checked," Paddy said, again. "I repeat, Is this what Beryl Tompkins discovered, Mr. Grimes? Discovered the night she was killed? Is that why she left before her work was finished, telling the others she had a headache? Ran to catch the earlier bus? But it didn't do any good, did it? You anticipated her, you waited by the bush. We checked your army record, Mr. Grimes. You were in the photographic section only in the beginning of the war. You were transferred, trained in commando techniques, and sent behind the lines to photograph Nazi military installations. That kind of training doesn't go, does it? Faced with discovery, you did what you were trained to do—kill silently and run. You're finished, Grimes."

"I don't know what you're talking about," Grimes protested, his voice shrill.

"Then we'd better go somewhere and discuss it, hadn't we?" Paddy suggested. "Whitney, go downstairs and get a couple of the men up here to gather up this filth as evidence."

"I'll do it, sir," Whitney said, in a calm voice. "I have a strong stomach—and I didn't have any dinner tonight."

Abbott emerged from the interrogation room when he heard the protesting tones of Grimes coming down the hall. The ride to the station had given the personnel manager a chance to gather his wits, and he was demanding a solicitor, justice, understanding, his wife not to be told, a cup of tea, and anything else he could think of.

"Got him?" Abbott asked Paddy, who grinned.

"With the ink still wet, you could say. I think he'll break in about an hour, maybe two. Want to have a go?"

"Don't mind if I do, thanks very much," Abbott smiled. "I'm not getting anywhere with Dr. Kildare in there. Make a change." He glanced up at the clock on the wall. "Looks like it's going to be a long night. How about some coffee? Bennett?"

"I'll organise it," Bennett said.

They watched the young officer move quickly down the hall, looking for a victim to make the drinks. "Going to ask for him when you get promotion?" Abbott asked Paddy.

"I think so."

"I saw him first," Abbott pointed out.

"Yes, but my need is greater," Paddy smiled. "You can work with anyone. I'm a sensitive creature."

"Balls," Abbott said, chuckling. He glanced down the hall at the farther interrogation room, where Grimes sat waiting, and the smile faded. "Let's go get this one settled—then we can concentrate on number two."

CHAPTER THIRTY-THREE

Grimes broke at just after 4 A.M.

Tougher than either Paddy or Luke had suspected—another leftover from his wartime training, perhaps—their steady cross-questioning had finally brought him to the end.

"Yes," he said, his head in his hands. "Yes, I killed her. She was going to tell. I would have lost my job, my wife . . ."

All of which he had certainly lost, now.

And a blameless woman dead in the bargain. Neither officer wasted much time feeling sorry for him. He was fed into the legal machinery and left to his fate. They felt no real relief, for they were still left with the other two murders unsolved.

"At least we can stop trying to find the common denominators between all three," Luke said, rubbing his eyes and trying to bring some semblance of alertness back to his brain. The questioning of a suspect can be as hard on the officers involved as it is on their victim. They not only have to watch and listen to him with full attention, they also have to keep up a rhythm of exchange between themselves and read one another's intent as they go on. They had worked together a long time, which made it easier.

But never easy.

In the end, they opted for a few hours' sleep before starting up again with Gregson in the morning.

"This is driving me crazy!" Jennifer moaned, looking down from Frances's window-seat over the path that led to the surgery. "That was Mrs. Bennett who just went in. *I* wanted to tell her the final pregnancy test was positive. Now Uncle Wally will get to do it. Damn!" She turned away from the window. "She looked awfully pale—I hope she hasn't had any trouble. They've been trying for years, she told me, without luck. I was just about to send them to a fertility clinic. I was nearly as excited as she was when she skipped a period."

"Sit down, for goodness' sake," Frances said, with some difficulty. Her face had stiffened up over the past twenty-four hours, and the stitches were pulling. "If this is the way you behave when you're away for a day, Lord knows what you're like when you take a holiday."

"Oh, that's different," Jennifer said, morosely. "You can *organise* for holidays, get loose ends tied up, follow through on lab reports, all that. But to be taken out with no notice—and there's nothing *wrong* with me. Poor Uncle Wally down there, wearing himself out all morning again . . . and just because Luke Abbott has taken it into his head that I'm in danger, even when they have David in custody. If I *am* in danger then it's because he didn't do it. In which case, why are they still holding him? I've called the station several times this morning, but they keep saying Luke's busy. Paddy, too. I didn't want to talk to any of the others." She sighed. "Are you *sure* you can't come up with a clever solution to all this?"

"And why should I?"

"I don't know. I just thought with your writing and all—"

"I don't write detective stories," Frances said, regretfully. "What does your aunt say? She's read the lot."

"She doesn't know, either," Jennifer said. She walked back to the window, and slowly, watching the patients arrive and leave, her fists clenched. "Oh, God, why doesn't Luke call? I left a message for him to call," she wailed, in sudden despair. "You'd think he could take a *minute*, wouldn't you? Just a *minute?*"

"Twenty thousand!!" Gordon Sinclair was incensed. "A measly twenty thousand? You must be mad." He glared at Graham Moyle.

Moyle shrugged. "I talked to the insurance company about it. They said you also have partnership insurance which will give you another fifty thousand. I don't have to give you *anything,* according to them. In fact, they advised against my giving you anything. So did my solicitor. But I want to be fair."

"What partnership insurance?" Barry Treat asked, in a thin voice.

"I still don't believe you were married to Win," Sinclair expostulated, stalking around the shop. "I simply cannot believe it."

"The police have the marriage certificate," Graham said, calmly. "You can always get another copy from Somerset House or whatever the place is called, now. We never divorced."

"Ah, but how do you know?" Sinclair whirled around. "She might have divorced you for desertion in the meantime."

"The police have made enquiries. They say there has been no divorce. Win was still my legal wife when she was killed."

"What partnership insurance, Gordon?" Barry asked again, more loudly.

"What about abroad? Win lived in America for a year—what about that?" Sinclair stormed on, ignoring the rising voice beside him. "You can't know but that she might have got a divorce over there."

"My address was never a secret, she always knew where I was, even if she didn't do me the same courtesy," Graham said, refusing to be drawn by Sinclair's rage. "They would have had to send me papers to sign—my solicitor was very clear about that, too."

"But why? *Why?* She wasn't the marrying kind!"

"She thought she was pregnant—and I thought she loved me," Graham said, with thin dignity. "She wasn't, and she didn't."

"Then why didn't you divorce *her?*" Sinclair demanded, striking out where he could.

"I had no one else, and I had no money. What would have been the point? I've never had enough money—until now. No matter what she was, I'll bless her every day of my life," Graham Moyle said. "And since you don't want the money . . ."

"I didn't *say* that!" Gordon shrieked. Graham looked at him for a long time.

"Yes, you did," he said, quietly, and went out the door without looking back.

"What partnership insurance, Gordon?" Barry asked, again. There was a steely edge to his voice, now. He wanted an answer.

"Oh, it's nothing at all, really," Sinclair said, negligently. "One has insurance in case a partner dies, that's all. For the good of the business. Just a formality."

"I don't remember signing anything about that."

"Well, you did," Sinclair said, turning away and trying to look busy. "What about these orders . . ."

"If *I* die would you get money, too?" Barry asked. "And if I *had* gotten Win's insurance money, and *then* died, would you have gotten both lots, Gordon? All of it?"

"You don't understand, Barry, love—it's just business, that's all." He approached and put an arm around the stiff, narrow shoulders of his partner. "Let's not go on about death and money and all that anymore, shall we? An artist like yourself shouldn't concern himself with sordid matters . . ."

Barry shrugged off the encircling grasp. "I want to see all the papers I've signed, Gordon. And I want to see them *now.*"

Sinclair stared at him. Barry Treat's face was pale and determined. Sinclair tried a smile.

It was not returned.

"She was overjoyed," Uncle Wally was saying, over lunch. "I gave her a prescription for iron tablets and put her down for our antenatal clinic. Her husband is a policeman—working with Luke Abbott and your Paddy, Frances."

"But she's all right?" Jennifer demanded.

Her uncle put his knife down and looked at her over his glasses. "She's fine," he said. "Don't fuss."

"I told them what to do," Jennifer said. "I told them about the ice-water treatment, and it worked. That's *my* baby, too, dammit!"

This time he put down knife *and* fork, and smiled. "Well, well. So you've become a family doctor at last, Jennifer. I was beginning to wonder when it would happen, you and your textbook theories and your quick referrals to the consultants."

Jennifer looked confused. "I don't understand."

"She was mazed as a sheep this morning, watching the patients arrive," Frances commented, understanding him perfectly. "Nearly fell out of the window."

"Difference between hospitals and us is simple," Uncle Wally said, leaning back. "Hospitals treat cases, we treat people. Some might say that's obvious, but it isn't so obvious to a new doctor coming along from the wards. I know you've been scared, Jennifer, thrown in at the deep end with my illness, not getting along with David so well as you might—but in the last couple of days I've been getting a pretty good chance to see how you've been doing from the patients themselves. And from Kay, who does not give her approval easily. Those were *your* patients, weren't they? You wanted to see them *yourself*. You've got family doctoring in your bones, now, girl. Never get it out. Marked for life, you are, thank God. I can rest back easy, at last. Still help out in the rush hour, of course—when you want me."

"Were you worried?" Jennifer asked, still feeling 'mazed as a sheep' at these minor but all-important revelations.

"Yes, he was," Aunt Clodie said, smiling. She looked at her husband affectionately, then the smile thinned. "He still is."

"Not about you, Jennifer," Uncle Wally said. "But about tonight and tomorrow and all the rest. About David. If we haven't heard by the end of lunch, we'll have to call up the Family Practitioner Committee and see if they can fetch us out a locum, fast. We can't trade on the good will of our various colleagues much longer, when we're not in a position to return the favour. God knows who the FPC will come up with—last one was older than I am, one before him hardly wet behind the ears. If David is charged with murder, we'll have all kinds of problems. I hate to think about it, but think about it we must. They'll want to know why we didn't spot it before . . ."

"Because it wasn't there to spot," came David's exhausted voice from the dining room doorway. He leaned against the doorpost, white-faced and dishevelled, his eyes on Jennifer's, holding her immobile. "I'm sorry to disappoint you, Jennifer, but the police have come to the conclusion that I am not a psychopathic murderer after all. The laboratory said that the chip from Frances's wound didn't match the missing chip from my bistoury, which, by the way, Luke Abbott then found in the bottom of my bag, with the help of a ten-penny children's magnet. They checked back over the people I saw night before last, and timed my journeys. They're very thorough, very careful. At the time Frances was attacked, I was bandaging Mrs. Carey's phlebitic lesion. She told them I was as gentle as a butterfly with her poor leg, which, as you know, had burst that evening, again. I had arranged for her to be admitted to hospital this morning. I hope she went in all right." His voice was a hoarse monotone. He'd clearly been awake and talking most of the night, and his needle had worn.

Nobody at the dining table moved or spoke.

He took a long ragged breath and let it out. "I now propose to go to bed and sleep for several weeks. If Calgary can take emergency calls again this evening, it would be a help. No, Clodie, I don't want anything to eat or drink, thank you." He turned and they heard his slow step cross the hall and start up the stairs.

"Well, Jennifer?" asked Uncle Wally, but she was already up and running.

"David?" He turned and looked down as she climbed up the stairs to him. "Dear God, I'm so sorry. So very sorry. I was really afraid . . ." She paused. His face was unreadable. "I had to tell him. Do you understand that? I had to tell him."

"Oh, I understand that very well," David said, softly.

"Please . . . please don't hate me for it," she whispered, aghast at what her precipitate conclusions and action had done.

"I don't," he said, bleakly. "I might have done the same, in your position. Of course, I can't say for certain, never having *been* in your position. I had to *earn* my place, here." He turned away and finished climbing the stairs, leaving her to stand there, staring after him.

"Did you get to see Jennifer, this morning?" Basil asked, as he stood with Mark on the terrace overlooking the sweep of lawn and the twinkle of the river between the willows. The once smooth turf was criss-crossed with trenches and heaps of dirt, and workmen were everywhere, like ants.

"No. They told me she was 'resting,' and couldn't see anyone," Mark said. He turned away and began to walk around in agitated circles, waving his arms. "You'd think they'd let her see her own fiancé, give her a bit of comfort and so on, but oh, no. And when I demanded to see Gregson they said he was 'out on calls.' Offered me some damned locum or other. Stupid receptionist. I told her what she could do with her locum, by God I did." Mark laughed, with some triumph.

"What I can't understand is why they didn't send her to the hospital," Basil said, finishing off his gin and tonic. "She must have lost a lot of blood. Still, I suppose, with all those doctors in the house, they figured they could look after her themselves."

"I don't know." Mark didn't seem to care, now. His mind was back on himself. "I could have seen Dr. Wally, but I wasn't about to, no thank you. Don't get on, we don't. Never did. *Never* did." Mark rubbed his temples. "Wish I had, now. Got another of those ghastly headaches."

"Grief, dear boy. It's simply the tension of grief and overwork. Perfectly natural, under the circumstances," Basil said, gruffly. He rested a hand on Mark's arm. "You'll have a good night's sleep tonight, I promise. You can have a couple of my own sleeping pills. The hell with the quacks. Don't worry yourself. Tomorrow everything will look much better."

"I don't know how I would have managed to get things organised without you, Basil." Mark was grateful. "It's been very good of you to drop everything in London and pitch in so much." He turned away again and paced the length of the patio, gesturing around at the scaffolding and the men working, the hum of the cement mixers and the thudding pound of a hammer. "There's so much to *do*, God, so *much*—and yet, I know I can do it. I *do*. I feel as if I were in some kind of dream, able to do what I want at last. It's almost like being drunk," Mark said.

"You have to let me do more, take more off your shoulders," Basil said. "I mean to say, this is all a big project—one of England's most glorious houses, brought back to the state it deserves, made a showplace and a byword. Exciting stuff. But it's too much for one man. We're family, Mark, family and partners. We'll go on well together. You'll see. We make a marvellous team."

"And Jennifer, too," Mark said, eagerly, and then scowled, suddenly. "If only I could get to her. How *dare* they keep me from her side? All this terrible murder business, this man walking about attacking women the way he does, and those damned policemen everywhere you look. Everywhere you look."

"Now, now," Basil said, reassuringly. "Just be glad Jennifer is still alive. I'm sure she'll be up to seeing you, soon."

"Yes, I suppose so. I want to talk to her. I *must* talk to her and get everything settled." His voice was fretful. "I *hate it* when things aren't *settled!*"

"Speaking of which, have you finished with all those papers you asked the solicitor to bring over this morning?" Basil asked, turning toward the French doors. "Must get the financial side shored up, dear boy, or the bank won't play."

"I'll do it now," Mark said. "Would you get me a couple of aspirin and ask Jeffers and one of the others to come along in to witness my signature?"

"As good as done, dear boy. As good as done." Basil strolled off to perform his good deeds.

Mark stood on the terrace for a minute more, looking down the torn-up lawn to the place where his mother had died, where her life had drained into the land of Peacock Manor. Her blood was all that she had ever given to the estate. For the whole of her time here it had been take, take, take. She had killed his father, in the end, with her demands and petty tyrannies. Now she was gone. One by one, all the problems were going. One by one he was dealing with them. One by one was the best way to do it. He was in charge, at last. Everything, *everything* was his.

A smile touched his mouth, a smile that twisted into a grimace as pain shot through his head like a javelin. Where the *hell* was that stupid Basil with his aspirin?

CHAPTER THIRTY-FOUR

"I can make a case for each one, but not for both, no matter who you put up," Luke complained to Paddy. He pointed his pencil at the list. "This one had both motive and opportunity to kill Frenholm, but no reason in the world to kill Mrs. Taubman." He moved the pencil down to another name on the list. "*He* would benefit from Mrs. Taubman's death, but had no connection with the Frenholm woman."

"And yet Cyril says the forensic evidence puts them together, that they were copy-cat killings by the same person. This person imitated Grimes's murder of Beryl Tompkins, which the local crime reporter covered only too well in the local paper," Paddy said.

"But *neither* of them have any rational connection with the attack on Frances. Or if it wasn't meant for her, with Jennifer—except that she was their doctor."

"Which could still be coincidence," Paddy reminded him. "Or which, on the other hand, could be an indication that this is, maybe, a *random* copy-cat killer, God help us. Take your pick, dammit." He scowled at Luke, at the list, and out the window, at the late afternoon sun.

"I really thought we might be onto something with Gregson," Luke said.

"You went after him hard enough, before Cyril's report came through," Paddy said, in a slightly disapproving tone. "Not your usual style, at all."

"Sorry," Luke said, briefly. He pointed the pencil again. "What about this one?" The point touched sculptress Hannah Putnam's name.

"Don't see it, myself," Paddy said. "I admit she's strong enough to have done it, but again, no connection between them. Unless Mrs. Taubman was a lesbian, which doesn't seem likely, from what I've heard. Aging coquette's more like it. Anyway, Ms. Putnam seems to have herself under pretty strong control, in my opinion."

"Perhaps too strong," Luke said. "Might snap rather than bend, under pressure. Cyril said a short-bladed triangular knife. Sculptors use all kinds of knives and tools."

"So do carpet layers, craftsmen, carpenters, and home handymen. He said it was most likely a Stanley knife, or something similar. Pick one up in any DIY shop. Short, strong blade, very sharp. Baldwin laid some new carpet in his baby's room only last month."

"So you still think it's Baldwin?" Luke was surprised.

"Until we find him, dead or alive, we can't discount the possibility, can we? Maybe the connection is that Mrs. Taubman was out walking that bloody dog of hers the night Frenholm was killed on the towpath, and saw it all, across the river. It's not all that wide, there. The sky was mostly clear and the moon was full, that night. If the killer was somebody she knew—like Baldwin—she might have recognised him. And he might have recognised her, too."

"Ah," Abbott said, leaning back. "Nice one, Paddy."

Paddy grinned. "Nice one, Aunt Clodie Mayberry, you mean. She suggested it on the phone this afternoon. Said she'd read something like it, once."

"I understand Mark Peacock's been trying to get in to see you," Luke said to Jennifer. Evening had fallen, warm and soft after the sunny last fling of the afternoon, but with a crisp edge that said enjoy it while you may. They were walking in the garden behind the house.

"Yes, so Kay mentioned. He came in this morning in a foul temper, apparently. Called her some awful names. He's very nervy, she said. Told her he had a right to see me as he had 'every intention of making me his wife'—as if I were some kind of pet he were adopting. He's changed since his mother's death. I don't understand it. It's almost as if—" She paused.

"As if what?"

She shrugged. "As if his old trouble were coming back." She glanced up at him. "You knew about that."

"Yes, your uncle explained. But we checked his record and he's been having regular prescriptions of his drug right along. We also checked with Pelmer—all the prescriptions have been regularly filled. I imagine it's just the freedom of having his own way, at last. Lord-of-the-manor syndrome."

"I suppose so." She turned her head to look up at him, a tall, lean shadow beside her, his features barely distinguishable in the darkness. Was he telling her the truth, or did he still suspect Mark? "Have you really, finally arrested someone?"

"We have a man in custody, yes," Luke said, carefully.

"And is it all over at last?"

"Not quite. A lot of loose ends to tie up."

"Is he crazy, this man you've arrested?"

"I'm not qualified to say." Luke looked up as the tops of the high hedge moved fitfully in an errant breeze. They seemed to be waving to someone. "He's not a very pleasant person. Perverted sexual tastes. Driven by ego to survive at all costs, as all murderers are. They kill because they're convinced they're more important than their victims. Other than that, you can't generalise."

"Then please, sir, can I have my life back?" Jennifer asked. "I've gone nearly crazy having to hide my face and sit around. Did he admit to attacking me?"

"No, not yet. We're still questioning him. He's only confessed to the first murder, so far."

"Oh." She was quiet for a moment. "Still, I suppose you'll get it out of him in the end."

"I'm not so sure," he said, hesitantly.

"Well, I can't go on living like a nun forever!" Jennifer said.

"I'll be glad to alter that," he offered. "Purely for medicinal reasons, of course."

"Oh, very funny." Frustration put an edge to her voice she hadn't intended. "Nothing has happened since Frances was attacked, and nothing will. Tomorrow I'm going back to work as usual."

"I'd rather you didn't, just yet."

"But *why?*" she demanded. "You've caught your killer, haven't you?"

"We've caught *a* killer. We're not certain he's responsible for all the deaths we're investigating. We're still working on several lines of enquiry . . ."

"You're doing this deliberately, aren't you?" she snapped. Suddenly the romantic evening was not so romantic. Suddenly he was not wonderful, but simply infuriating. His slow, stolid way of talking, his caution, his practicality, his damned *calm*, made her want to scream. He had never been like this as a boy. Mercurial, fast-moving, quick-thinking, decisive, aggressive. Where had he hidden all that—under a rock, somewhere in Upper Woods? "You want to lock me up, don't you?"

"All men secretly want to lock up the woman they love," he said, deliberately. "Keep her in a velvet-lined box, to be taken out only for personal delight. It's damned hard, suppressing our chauvinist impulses in order to be acceptable to today's feminist-oriented society."

"Oh, shut up!"

"Yes, ma'am."

"And stop laughing at me." Had he said 'woman they love'?

"Yes, ma'am."

"And I won't be locked up like a . . . like a . . . bauble."

"All right. Then I'll just have to put a guard on you and the house. I would have thought you would have been more sensible, Jennifer." The laughter had gone from his voice. He sounded tired. "If I had a broken arm, I'd take *your* advice. Why won't you take mine?"

"Because you've got your killer and because it doesn't make sense, that's why." She peered at the shape of him in the darkness. "Or is there something you aren't telling me?"

"There's a great deal I'm not telling you."

"Why not?"

"Because I'm not certain of it, because it will cost you very little to do what I ask and it might cost me a great deal to make a mistake at this point."

"I'm going in," she said, abruptly. "I'm cold."

"Jenny . . ." he began.

But she was gone, only the sound of her feet, marching angrily down the gravel path, only the shadow of her, passing before the lighted windows, and the slam of the surgery door.

Then nothing but the rush of the breeze through the high hedges that surrounded the garden.

"Oh, hell," he muttered, and went back to the station.

Night fell on Wychford.

One by one the lights that had burned through the evening winked out, and soon the shops showed their wares to empty streets where the three traffic lights blinked on and off and on and off for no one.

The River Purle gurgled and chuckled its way beneath the bridges and through the rushes along the banks. The trees, having lost so many of their bright leaves, made clacking, creaking conversations as branch rubbed on branch, twig against twig.

In the lovely houses and the small cottages, warmer blankets had been brought out against the autumn nights, and hot water bottles reappeared from the backs of cupboards. Teeth were brushed, milk was warmed. Wychford slept early.

At Peacock Manor only two windows showed light. In one of the darkened rooms a radio muttered. The trestles and scaffolds of the builders gave forth strange clanks as ropes moved against them in the wind. There were large mounds on the lawns where the workmen had heaped stone, bricks, sand. Trenches temporarily gashed the once flawless lawn with dark wounds.

At the police station, many lamps burned late. The night shift began. There were new instructions, and more reports to be filled in. The coffee urn was refilled and someone had to go home for extra tea-bags and milk. And then back again for sugar. There was talk of sandwiches.

At Monkswell lights burned late only in the pottery, the lithographic shop, and behind the cafe. When Hannah Putnam drove out of the parking lot at ten o'clock, there were still four cars there. In one of them a dark figure looked at his watch and wrote something in a notebook, then reached for his radio.

At the housing estate Tricia Baldwin held her baby close in the big double bed, and wondered whether she should ask her mother to come down. She couldn't go on alone like this, waiting for the worst to happen. She couldn't.

Gradually the night gave way to the secret sounds of the hunters, large and small—an owl over the meadow, a fox in the woods, a cat at a mousehole, a rat in a dustbin.

And a killer, sharpening a blade.

The wind picked up a little, then stopped as night wore on. Clouds obscured the moon from time to time. The temperature continued to drop, until the first delicate fronds of frost began to form on the tips of grass and leaves.

At High Hedges, the phone began to ring.

CHAPTER THIRTY-FIVE

"Calm down, Basil," Jennifer said, into the phone. "Are you certain he
. . ." She listened to the agitated voice at the other end of the line. "I see.
Yes, it does rather sound like that, doesn't it? Similar circumstances." The
voice went on. And on. "Well, it sounds as if you would really do better to
ring 999, you know. Two strong ambulance men might be a better bet." She
listened a little more. "Yes, well . . . all right, I'll come. No, I'm fine, really.
No problem. Tell him I'm coming—it may help."

Jennifer put down the phone, turned, and nearly jumped out of her skin.
Frances stood behind her, a robe thrown on over some rather alarming pyja-
mas, the white bandages around her face gleaming in the faint light from the
open bedroom doors.

"What's wrong?" Frances hissed, in a stage whisper that might have wak-
ened the dead, had there been any around. Fortunately, everyone else slept in
the farther end of the house. Only their two rooms were here at the front,
and Jennifer had been quick to get to the phone, as she hadn't been asleep.

"Apparently Mark is having a recurrence of his old trouble," Jennifer said.
"He had a breakdown when his father died, and now—with his mother dead,
the whole thing seems to be coming back. Basil says he's practically climbing
the walls over there. He took some unnamed sleeping pills of Basil's, but they
seem to have made him worse, not better. The drug he's on might account
for that, I suppose, but—" she paused, uncertain.

"That does happen, sometimes," Frances said.

"Yes, I know. It happened the night his mother was killed—after I gave
him a shot to calm him. I didn't know he was on haliperidol, then. The two
might have set up an adverse reaction, although if anything I would have
thought . . ." She sighed, impatiently. "My God, when will people learn
you can't just give drugs to people willy-nilly? Basil is a fool."

"He was probably only trying to help," Frances protested.

"Yes." Jennifer was considering. "I'm just wondering if dear, dim old Basil
has done this before. Given Mark pills to make him sleep that actually make
him—" Her voice faded. She swallowed, hard. "Worse," she whispered.

They stared at one another. "Maybe you'd better call Luke," Frances said.

"Oh, no, I'm *not* going to make a fool of myself accusing people again
before I know what's happening," Jennifer said. "I want to get a look at
Mark, first."

"You'd better wake David," Frances said, nervously.

"No, it's all right. I can handle Mark," Jennifer said.

"I'm going with you, then," Frances said, firmly. "Why did Basil call you, by the way? The answering machine should have turned him onto Calgary."

"He apologised for that. He said Calgary was out on a call, already. So he used the private number, expecting to get David, I suppose. Or even Uncle Wally, although what he thought *he* could do is beyond me. The number was in Mark's diary."

"That's the trouble with living in a small town," Frances muttered, scuffing toward her bedroom as she untied her robe. "Everybody's got your number."

"I want to put a WPC onto Jennifer," Luke said to Paddy.

"We've already got a patrol going by every twenty minutes or so," Paddy reminded him. "We just haven't got the manpower, what with everyone spread so thin over all the suspects—"

"I know. It's not someone getting in that worries me so much as her getting out. She's getting restless, and says she intends going back to work tomorrow."

"Wonderful." Paddy's expression was resigned. "Shall I send one of the cars over now?"

Luke glanced at the clock. "No, I imagine she's safe in bed at this hour. Morning will be good enough. They've got someone else taking night calls, anyway." He thought for a moment. "Can you ask the patrol to stop and take a good look around on their next pass?"

"Will do."

"I mean—just in case."

"Of course."

"I'll put Whitney on the bodyguard detail—she's been assigned here until the end of the week. It will make a change for her from using that waxing machine up at the plant. She says her shoulders will never be the same."

"Fine. Anyway, I don't think Jennifer would do anything foolish, do you? After all—*Frances* is there."

They looked at one another.

"Is Whitney at the hotel?" Luke finally asked.

"Yes."

"Maybe you'd better wake her up."

"I don't *believe* we're doing this," Frances muttered, slouching down in the passenger seat. She wore a dark woolen scarf over her head and around her neck, but in the glow of the Maestro's dashboard lights the white edges of the bandages were visible along her cheek. She looked like a grumpy nun. "If this were one of my stories, fine, but it's real life, it's the middle of the night, and it's cold. No sensible woman should be out in it."

"I have never claimed to be a sensible woman," Jennifer said, grimly. "Have you?"

"Frequently," Frances said. "And every time a lie."

"There you are, then."

"So what are we doing, flying along here?" Frances demanded. "Surely be to God you should have called the riot squad at the very least, if Mark Peacock is swinging from the trees?"

"I'm expecting to call them, as soon as I've verified the symptoms," Jennifer said, through tight lips. They were tight because she was using them to keep her teeth from chattering.

On the way down the High Street, they passed a patrolling Panda car going up. "I used to hate the sight of them," Frances observed. "Now, I can see they're not so bad. Family, sort of."

"We've gotten ourselves into something, haven't we?" Jennifer said. "With the two of them?"

"I've only gotten into something with one of them," Frances said, demurely. "Your personal excesses are of no interest to me."

"Uh-oh," Jennifer said, as they turned into the drive that led up to the manor. It looked like a festival was in progress. Every light was blazing, and a great wedge-shaped carpet of light flared out from the open double front doors onto the gravelled drive.

"I think you should *definitely* call Luke and Paddy," Frances said. "Or somebody."

They got out of the car and looked around. After a moment, Basil appeared out of the darkness and came across the gravel toward them, carrying a torch. "Thank God you've come, Jennifer. He's got out, he's in the grounds somewhere. Jeffers and the other servants are looking for him. I'm certain they'll all give in their notices tomorrow morning. The boy's mad—simply insane with grief."

"I'm going to call the police," Frances said, firmly, and started to march up the stairs to the open front door. Basil looked after her.

"Who is that?" he asked Jennifer.

"A friend. What happened, Basil?"

"Why is *she* all bandaged up like that? I thought *you*—"

"It's a long story. Tell me what happened with Mark."

"I'm not certain, to tell you the truth. I went to bed and I thought Mark had done the same. We've been working very hard and we were both exhausted. He's been having trouble sleeping and so we made it an early night." Taubman's hands were shaking, and the light from the torch wobbled across their feet, back and forth. "I'm sorry about the pills—"

"Never mind. Have you given them to him before?"

"Well—" Taubman looked uneasy. "A few times, yes."

"When?"

"Well—" There was a sudden shout from the darkness toward the river, and they both jumped.

"We'll sort that out later," Jennifer said, unnerved by the sound. It had been Mark's voice, no doubt about it, but wild and uncontrolled. "Tell me about tonight."

"I was almost asleep over my book. The next thing I knew, Jeffers—that's our new butler—was knocking on my door. Mark, he said, was in the lounge, behaving peculiarly. He—Jeffers, that is—had gone down to investigate a noise, and found Mark . . . dancing, in the lounge."

"Dancing?"

"That was the best he could do for a description. Sort of jogging about, apparently, as if to music. But there *was* no music. He'd knocked over a small table, but didn't seem to have noticed. Jeffers spoke to him, but he didn't hear him, just went on with his dance. So Jeffers fetched me. I tell you, Jennifer, it was a most eerie sight. Terrifying, really, when you know how well-controlled Mark usually is. He behaved as if he were quite, quite mad. I spoke to him, and he heard me and whirled about and began to talk about all the colours."

"What colours?"

"We'd been talking earlier about the colours of the various function rooms of the extension we're going to build out the back. All in keeping with the house, you understand, even to using old reclaimed stone . . ." He stopped. "That's not relevant, of course. Sorry. Then he went on dancing about. That's when I called you."

"And then called Calgary."

"What?" He looked at her. "Oh, yes . . . but he was out. So then I rang your private number. I hesitated, knowing you were unwell, but I thought Dr. Gregson would be there, you see. I was most surprised when you answered."

"Dr. Gregson was out, too," Jennifer said. Out like a light, more like it, she thought. My fault, again.

There was another sudden cry from the direction of the river, this time a savage howl that shook them both. Frances, coming back down the steps, crossed herself involuntarily. "Jesus, Mary, and Joseph," she muttered. "The Hound of the Baskervilles."

"Don't be ridiculous," Jennifer snapped, although her own reaction was much the same. The whole situation was so bizarre. Was she supposed to believe this was staid, sedate Mark Peacock, whooping and screaming in the dark? It didn't make sense. "What happened after you called me, Basil?"

"I went back into the lounge and tried to get him to talk to me sensibly, but he wouldn't. He *talked*, my goodness, yes, he talked as if he'd just discovered his voice—but it made no sense, and came out so quickly, there was no way of following what he was getting at. I sent Jeffers away, I was so . . . embarrassed for Mark. We'll have to get new servants, of course," he added, half to himself. Obviously the situation was telling on him, as well. "At any rate, about five minutes ago, he suddenly turned rather nasty, called me names, called his poor dead mother even worse names, screamed dreadful things about women and . . . about you . . . and then shot off outside. If I'd been able to stop you coming, then, I would have, but by then, I discovered—"

"That the phone is out of order," Frances said. "I just found that out, myself."

"Yes. Mark pulled it out of the wall," Basil said.

"Isn't there another phone, perhaps in the kitchen or servant's quarters?" Jennifer demanded.

"No. We're waiting to have it put in. We never had need of it before . . . never had live-in servants before." He straightened up. "That's it, we'll send one of the servants into town for the police. Jeffers! Jeffers!" He shot off into the darkness, the light from his torch bobbing up and down over the lawn. After a moment, it disappeared around the far wing of the house.

"Do you ever suppose they keep gin in that house?" Frances asked. "I had a quick look, but I couldn't spot it."

"It's a drug," Jennifer said.

"I know, but I'm not proud at the moment," Frances said.

"I meant Mark. It's a drug reaction, it has to be. Or such a violent recurrence of his mania that the maintenance dosage of his usual drug simply wasn't sufficient to cope."

"Fine," Frances said. "Let's find the gin. You can play Dr. Kildare later on, when they've got him tied up hoof and mouth."

"It's almost as if he were on a trip," Jennifer went on.

"Well, if he is, he's not gone far. You can still hear him laughing, down by the river," Frances said, nervously.

"I'm going down there," Jennifer said, turning back to the car and rummaging in her bag. "If I can get close to him . . ." She filled a hypodermic syringe by the light from the front door.

"Holy Mother of God, are you as crazy as himself?" Frances demanded, becoming more Gaelic with every moment.

"I've dealt with drug abuse cases before, in London," Jennifer said, calmly. "Once you realise what the problem is, it's not frightening anymore."

"Well, I know what it is and I'm that scared to death my legs think I've left them behind," Frances mourned. "Indeed, I wish I had. And myself with them."

"Wait here."

"I will not."

"Then come along—and bring your legs with you."

They started down the lawn, past the mounds of building materials, looming in the dark. Once beyond the glow of the lights from the manor the night was pitch black, cold, and still. As they drew closer to the river they could hear the gurgling of the water. And another sound. Giggling, purling laughter, as continuous and meaningless as the flow of the river itself.

"Mark? It's Jennifer," she called.

The giggling continued. There was a thrashing in the bushes, first on one side, then on the other. They froze there, not knowing which way to go. The lights of the manor seemed very far away. "Maybe you're right about leaving it to the police," Jennifer said, suddenly regretting her decision to come out here unescorted save by Frances, who was quivering like a jelly.

"Definitely," Frances agreed. "In fact, I think we should go for them right now, myself."

"I agree," Jennifer said, and they turned as one and ran back up the lawn. In the dark, they lost track of one another, largely because Jennifer dodged around a hole in the ground, and Frances fell into it.

Jennifer heard Frances yell and turned back, stumbled, and fell against a tarpaulined mound of what felt uncomfortably like bricks or stones. She picked herself up, and felt a stab of pain in her thigh. Reaching down, she touched a sticky patch that hurt like hell. She began to curse, feeling even as she did the first stiffening of the wound. She was so annoyed at her own clumsiness as she limped on toward the light that she never even turned at the sound of footsteps behind her. She assumed it was Frances. "I think what you've got is catching," she grumbled.

And then the arm encircled her neck, and she heard the low, vicious voice in her ear. "Bitch, bitch, bitch . . ."

She screamed.

And began to struggle.

As she struggled, she heard the roar of a car engine starting up. She supposed Frances had reached the car, and prayed that she would go for help. "Mark, Mark . . . please, let me go . . . please . . ." she gasped as she wrenched herself away.

She had taken a course in self-defense years ago, while still a medical student, as she was thinking at the time of going into psychiatric work. The first month on the wards had dulled that particular ambition, but the course had left her with some memories. She tried to put them to use. Unfortunately, her instructor at the time had been co-operative.

The man she was fighting was not.

"Mark . . . *please* . . . it's Jennifer . . ." she said as he grabbed her again. She side-stepped into a mound of sand that shifted under her feet, throwing her off balance.

She staggered, and fell with heart-stopping suddenness into one of the trenches. For a minute she lay, winded, at the bottom. Then a dark figure loomed above at the edge of the trench, outlined by the lights from the manor, and she could see the blade in his hand. He bent as if to jump down to her.

Jennifer scrambled backward down the trench, clawing the sides as she struggled to her feet. There was a thump, and she knew he was there, in the trench, with her. No one could see them, no one could hear them.

They were alone.

In the distance she could hear police sirens, but oh, so far away. She backed off, her feet slipping in the loose earth. She could hear him, panting like an animal as he came after her. And though it was invisible, she knew the knife was there, too, in front of him. Coming closer and closer to her.

"Mark, listen to me, you must listen to me, dear . . . you must let me help you. Please let me help you."

He laughed. It was a low, intimate chuckle, as if over a shared secret. And the secret was that there was no help for him, or for her. He liked what he was. He was a killer. He was going to kill her. He knew it. She knew it. Jennifer felt sweat pouring down her body, despite the coldness of the night. The sweet stifling smell of freshly dug earth was all around her.

Like a grave.

Abruptly, as she backed away, she became aware that the ground was sloping up to the end of the trench. As soon as she realised it, she turned her back and began to claw and drag herself up the slope. She felt a hand close on her ankle, and she kicked, involuntarily, freed herself, and struggled on. He was only inches behind her, so close she could almost feel his breath on her. But she gained the surface once again, and began to run, dodging between the heaps and mounds, desperately trying to avoid falling into yet another trench—into another grave.

She knew she was between her attacker and the house, knew that she was visible while he was not. She tried to hide, but there was nowhere safe. And she could not summon the courage to run toward the river again. Into the dark. Into the whispering shadows.

He kept on coming. It was uncanny, as if he could see in the dark. Wherever she moved, he moved, as if they were connected with an invisible thread, as if she were a fly in his web and he could feel every movement, every trembling of her terror. She couldn't see his face, he was a black, panting presence in the night—except for the flash of the blade in his hand. She looked back, once, and saw it catch the light. A short, angled blade, gleaming.

And all the while, muttering and cursing her in a hoarse, animal voice, vicious hate pouring out of him like poison, he came on. "Bitch, she-dog, with your dirty body and your dirty ways, sucking and vile, stinking and soft . . ." On and on, words she knew, some she didn't. She ran on, her chest filled with pain, her throat closing, trying to get out of the light . . . but the light followed her, which didn't make sense. The light followed her wherever she went.

And then she realised the light came from the headlights of a car—her own car. Bearing down on them, faster and faster, weaving nimbly between the huge mounds of sand and rock, rounding the small bulldozer that stood beside them, coming closer and closer, the horn blaring all the while. Jennifer kept on running, and the panting thing ran after her—but she was not fast enough.

Jennifer felt herself struck a glancing blow, screamed as she fell face down into suffocating sand. At the same time, there was a harder, heavier thud, and a thin, fading cry of "Bull's-eye!"

There was a roaring in her ears. As she turned over, she was just in time to see her new Maestro bounce off a bush, scrape the support out from under a corner of the scaffolding, and plunge its front wheels into a trench with a terrible rending of metal.

As it went over the edge under a cascade of iron piping, she saw it was Frances at the wheel. Frances, who had driven her car across the lawn and straight into a pedestrian. Frances at her worst. Only this time, *this time*, she had *meant* to do it.

Jennifer stood panting on the lawn, dazed, looking around her as men ran up with torches, flashing them over, under, and around, like searchlights in a wartime sky. They fell on the car, out of which Frances climbed. She teetered for a moment on the edge of the trench and then righted herself with a triumphant wave.

"Wasn't that driving, then? Can I not do it when I have to, I tell you?" she shouted, staggering forward. Then she stepped, cheering, onto a sheet of tarpaulin that lay on the ground. It lay over a hole. Slowly, still waving, she descended out of sight. And slowly, very slowly, the tarpaulin slid in after her.

The lights of the torches found Jennifer, who was standing there, bleeding and shaken, not sure if this was a drug dream or that reality that Frances had warned her about, a hundred years ago.

The lights also fell on a still figure that lay on the lawn some distance from her, arms outstretched, legs at a peculiar angle.

"I got him, I got him," came a shout from the direction of the river. Some of the beams of light turned to the sound, and into their glare came a giggling Mark Peacock, held firmly in the burly arms of Fred Baldwin. "I got the bastard for you," he shouted. "I've been waiting for him to show himself and here he is."

Paddy had extricated Frances from the hole and was brushing her down, holding her close, listening to her laughing and crying explanations. Luke was by Jennifer, almost afraid to touch her, for she was as rigid as a statue, staring down at the broken body of Basil Taubman.

And at the knife that lay inches from his outflung hand.

CHAPTER THIRTY-SIX

"You can't blame the media for their deaths—only for the manner of their going," Luke said.

It was the evening of the next day—a day that Jennifer and Frances had slept away, that Luke and Paddy had worked through.

Dr. Wally, Aunt Clodie, David Gregson, and Jennifer sat with Luke in the lounge of High Hedges. They were fresh and curious, he was weary and sad. His voice was growing harsh, but he wanted them all to know the truth before he let go of this case.

Paddy had taken Frances off to celebrate her triumph, a heroine at last, deserving, he said, of a wonderful meal, wonderful wine, and anything else that occurred to him. It was left to Luke to explain.

"Taubman's only intention, for a long, long time, had been to kill his wife," Luke went on hoarsely. He took the brandy Uncle Wally proffered, and sipped it, wincing. "Bit by bit he worked out the where, and the when—he'd always known the why—but the how had remained unsettled. Sometimes it was poison, sometimes strangulation—he passed many a happy hour thinking about it."

"He told you all this?" Aunt Clodie asked.

"We haven't really been able to stop him," Luke said, drily. "He'd worn out two stenographers before tea, and was starting on a third when I left." And thank God for Bennett, who seemed to have summoned reserves of energy and enthusiasm from somewhere and had taken over the interrogation. Not that he had to ask many questions.

"Taubman is crazy, I suppose. We'll leave it to the psychiatrists to decide that, but he sounds insane to me," Luke said. "Apparently he didn't fall in love with Mabel Peacock—he fell in love with Peacock Manor."

"Ideal match," David Gregson said, in an ironic tone. "It would never talk back, never walk away."

Luke smiled, just. "It seems he met Mabel at some party in London. Thought she was rich, played up to her mostly out of habit. He came down on a week-end—would go anywhere for a free meal, he said—and became obsessed with the house on sight. He married Mabel Peacock simply to get into the line of inheritance, not realising then that the house belonged to Mark. When he found that out, he knew he had to work another way. It was his idea, planted very skillfully, to turn the house into a conference centre. It was his idea to go into partnership with Mark, once Mabel was dead."

"But why kill Win Frenholm, then?" Uncle Wally asked.

"Oh, she was in his way, too," Luke said. "She was carrying Mark's baby. Or, at least, she *claimed* it was Mark's baby. And if Mark married her, or even acknowledged paternity, the question of inheritance would have become a rather muddled one. Actually, you know, it *was* Mark's. We've proved that with blood tests. Mark has a rather rare blood condition called thalassemia, inherited from his mother's side of the family. It usually occurs in people of Mediterranean stock, and his maternal grandfather was Italian, apparently. And comparative scans on the genetic fingerprints made it absolutely certain."

"So Mark had an affair with her," Jennifer said.

"In August, it seems."

Aunt Clodie nodded, sagely. "While Jennifer was away in London."

"But not only Mark," Luke said. "There were others. She simply decided that Mark was the best man to nail with the paternity. She rather liked the idea of being lady of the manor. Her ambition crossed Taubman's."

"You said the media could be blamed for the manner of their going," David Gregson said.

"Yes. You have a very good local reporter, and some rather loose-mouthed local coppers." Which won't happen again, he thought, grimly. "The reporter published all the details he could get—and they were quite a few—on the death of Beryl Tompkins. Taubman read the report in the local paper, and decided this was the time to put his great plan into action. He only intended to kill his wife, even then, but Win Frenholm came along. She had been phoning the manor all evening, getting progressively drunker and angrier each time she was told Mark was out."

"Where was he?" Uncle Wally asked.

"At the Woolsack, arguing. Apparently the landlord has a large circle of friends and elastic views on closing time," Luke said, in a neutral tone.

"So he does, so he does," Uncle Wally said, smiling reminiscently. "Good old Bomber."

"How did Basil come into it?" Aunt Clodie asked, with an indulgent look at her husband.

"Well, the last time she rang it was quite late and she got Basil, who had been told of her repeated calls and was the only one still up. Basil has a way with women—even on the phone. He got the story out of her—or at least enough of it to set his internal alarm bells ringing. He arranged to meet her."

"On the towpath?"

"Yes. She was too drunk and angry to be cautious. Anyway, as far as she knew, he was a gentleman. On the other hand, she must have had second thoughts a bit later, and therefore called Baldwin. Unfortunately, she didn't give him enough time, and Taubman was quick, too. He simply walked across the lawn and over the bridge. He listened to her story, and then killed her." He paused, thinking back to Taubman in the hospital, making his statement, cold as ice, as quiet as the blade of the knife he had used. Just an ordinary lino-cutter, found in a tool box. "He said it gave him an opportunity to practice the technique."

"Dear God," murmured Aunt Clodie, and took Wally's hand.

"When the media spread the word that there was a maniac in the vicinity, a mad killer who'd now claimed *two* victims, he knew his plan for killing his wife would have an even sounder basis—she'd be bound to be named as victim number three."

"But he was in London when she was killed," Jennifer objected. "He was seen at his club at ten o'clock, and he was there in the morning, too. There were no trains, and he can't drive. How did he get down here and back again in time?"

"By the oldest road in England," Luke said, softly. "He came by water."

"By *water?*"

Their astonishment made it almost worth the telling. Few pleasures accrue to a copper at the end of a case—mostly he is sick of death and sicker still of mad excuses for it. In the innocent amazement of his listeners he found some solace. But not much.

Uncle Wally wheeled himself to the decanter and carried it over to replenish Luke's glass as well as his own. "Well, get on with it, then," he said gruffly, and that was as much apology as Luke ever got for the old man's temporary rejection.

"He signed in at his club at ten—true enough," Luke explained, after soothing his raw throat once more with brandy. "Then he went to his room, waited for a quiet moment, and slipped out the fire escape. All classic stuff. Took a taxi to Paddington, and caught the ten-thirty train to Milchester."

"Milchester? But that's twenty miles away."

"By river, only seven," Luke said. "He'd taken the trouble to buy a small boat and rent a mooring there some time ago. Under a false name, of course. It was a moonlit night, but he could have managed it in the dark, once his eyes grew accustomed to it. He had a small outboard motor, and he came down the Purle as smoothly as you please. Arrived just before midnight. Tied up, strolled up the lawn, and let himself into the house. He knew Mark was going out with Jennifer. There were no live-in servants at that time, remember. Mabel was quite alone, and delighted to see her darling husband. He told her the moonlight was beautiful, and took her out to see it. No doubt he made her giggle like a girl, all romantic and unexpected." Luke's voice was bitter, for whatever Mabel Peacock Taubman had been, she had been murdered for gain by a cold and calculating bastard. It was his job to catch the killer. Contempt for the killer was a private affair, always to be kept inside, according to regulations. But he was tired, tonight. So damn tired.

"He killed her," he said, simply. "Then he got back into his little boat and carried on downstream to where the Purle joins the Thames, and then to Reading, where he tied up at a boatyard and walked to the station. He had rented a locker where he kept a donkey jacket and cap. He caught a train around four, with some other working men, and arrived at Paddington in plenty of time to dump his disguise, and catch a cab back to the club. His luck—and killers always need luck—was the confusion in our communications with the Met. They didn't arrive at the club until six, giving him just enough time to get back into bed and start 'snoring like a pig.' In his original plan, he hadn't expected the body to be found until morning, of course."

"Would you have got him, eventually?" David asked.

"I'd like to think so, yes."

"But, why me?" Jennifer asked. "Why did he try to kill me—and nearly kill Frances, instead?"

"Because Mark had announced he intended to marry you. Taubman had killed twice to eliminate women who stood between him and the manor, and saw no reason to let another one get in his way. He'd lost no time once Mabel was dead, remember, in getting Mark to agree to making the manor and estate into a limited company, with him and Mark as the two directors. If Mark died, it would be all his."

"Would he have killed Mark, then?"

"It's very possible. Right after Win Frenholm's murder, when the whole uproar about the maniac began, he got at Mark's medication. Emptied out the capsules, substituted sugar. Mark took them regularly—but they did him no good. Gradually, under the stress of our investigation and then his mother's death, Mark's condition worsened, as Taubman had intended it should."

"Mark had started to get full of himself and a bit pushy," said Jennifer, remembering how he had been at luncheon.

"I gather he was arrogant and impatient with the builders, and servants, too. Then he decided that you would marry him, and announced your engagement as a *fait accompli*. He couldn't imagine you refusing him, I suppose," Luke said. "So Taubman tried to kill you—and failed, thank God. The failure worried him. He was afraid you (or Frances, as it turned out) might have recognised him. And so he decided it was time to end the game. He got Mark into a particularly excited state, talking about the plans for the manor and so on, then put LSD or something similar—he has some very odd friends in London—into a couple of his sleeping pills, and gave them to Mark. You saw the result. Taubman knew that when Mark was inevitably put away the deaths would stop, and assumed we would draw our own conclusions about who the Cotswold Butcher had been. I have no doubt that when Mark was 'cured' and released, he would finally have been eliminated. Perhaps a 'suicide,' out of remorse? Taubman would have managed it somehow, and achieved his end at last. He loved the house beyond anything. *He had to own the house*, owning it obsessed him. He didn't care about anything but the house, and getting his own way. Even to killing whatever stood between him and his desire. After the first death, what did it matter? It gets easier, you see. Easier to kill, each time." Luke looked at them, bleakly. "We can't have that," he said. "That's got to be stopped."

"Why was Fred Baldwin there, last night?" Jennifer asked. They had left the others inside, and were walking in the garden. Jennifer was ostensibly seeing him to his car. They were taking the long way round. And round.

"*He* thought *Mark* had killed Win Frenholm," Luke said. "He'd worked it out—because of the car he'd heard start up. He knew Mark had an MG, and he decided—from the line of our questioning—that Win had had an affair with Mark. He tried to convince himself it wasn't true—but in his heart of hearts he knew what she was, all right. Funny thing is, the MG he heard *was* Mark's. Mark was driving off from in front of the Woolsack as Basil ran back up from the towpath to the High Street. Basil recognised the car, and decided there and then that Mark was the ideal one on whom to pin the murders. The fact that Mark had been so near the scene at around the right time was one of the many good reasons I suspected him, as it happens. Anyway, Basil stood in the shadows until Mark had passed, then went back over the bridge, across the lawn, and in through the back door in time to greet Mark coming through the front. Luck of the devil, they call it, I believe."

"Poor Mark," Jennifer murmured, remembering his confusion and fear as the ambulance doors had closed behind him.

"Yes, well, Fred Baldwin had formed this idea about Mark killing the Frenholm woman, and wanted to confront him. Maybe even kill him—but I doubt that. He's a decent man. I think he would have beaten him up a bit, and then brought him to us. But Mark never came out into the grounds alone—until last night."

"And then he came out with a vengeance," Jennifer said, sadly.

"At least he's not really crazy, just unbalanced through being deprived of his normal medication, plus the dose of LSD. Fortunately, it was a happy trip for him, according to the consultant at the hospital. He'll recover," Luke said, evenly. "And when he does, there will be plenty to keep him busy." He chuckled. "Including getting your car out of the dry moat."

"Wasn't Frances wonderful?" Jennifer said.

"I wish I'd seen it," Luke agreed. They walked on companionably, neither wanting to end nor change the situation just yet. It was Jennifer who spoke, eventually.

"You know, Frances told me this morning that she thought it had all been about love, really," Jennifer said, reflectively. "Different kinds of love—possessive love, obsessive love, perverted love, frustrated love, love going wrong, getting twisted and changed, destroying things, destroying people. It's very sad. Love shouldn't be like that."

He stopped abruptly and took her into his arms. She was shivering. "You should have worn a jacket."

"I don't feel cold inside," she said, into his shoulder. "Quite the opposite, in fact."

He tilted her chin up with a gentle finger. "I can't tell you how glad I am to hear that. So I'll show you," he said, and kissed her.

After a moment, she pulled away. "Luke—we have to talk."

"That sounds ominous," he said. He kept his voice calm and natural in the darkness, but her tone, her words, and the hesitation in her body told him things he had hoped never to know. Still the dreamer, aren't you? he scolded himself. Duck—here comes reality.

"After what's happened—about my accusing David and all—I don't know whether I'll be able to go on working with him. He came back exhausted, and so resentful. Oh, I'm not blaming you, I'm blaming me, entirely. But if we had differences before, they're nothing to what I've created, now. The trouble is, I *want* to go on working here. Uncle Wally must retire, and the practice is growing."

"I want you, Jenny. I want to marry you."

"Yes, I know. And a great deal of me wants to marry you," she said.

"What do I get?" he asked, trying to keep it light. "Nose, ears, and elbows?"

"Heart, mostly," she smiled. "It's my head that's causing the difficulty."

"The same head that made you run away from me twenty-two years ago?"

"Same head. I'm a doctor, and I never want to stop being a doctor."

"That's no problem."

"But I want to be a doctor *here*. I want to work things out with David. I'll never be settled until I've made that work."

"*That's* a problem," he agreed, reluctantly.

"So—can we just—wait a bit?"

"Could you be more specific?" he asked. "What exactly has to wait? The wedding? Fair enough. You and I? Not so fair, Jenny. I'm no plaster saint."

She came up to him and gently touched his face, rested her head on his chest, subservient in this and only this. "Neither am I," she told him. "And Milchester isn't so very far away, after all. Don't you get days off?" She paused, delicately. "Nights off?"

He stood very still for a moment, and then he sighed, relief and regret mingled with a smile. "This is going to cost me a fortune in petrol," he told her.

It was a kind of capitulation.

The River Purle murmured between its banks, glinting here and there with the reflection of the waning moon between racing clouds. The water's surface was ruffled by a fleeting wind that danced away and then came back, stronger every time. Later, rain would come.

In the High Street the display of bath salts and bile pills in Pelmer's glowed under the fluorescent lights, one of which was flickering and would soon go out.

The lights of the houses in town went out, too, one by one. They were already out in the craft centre, at the manor, and in Frances Murphy's flat. In the hills above the town, an owl swooped across a rustling field. Moments later a mouse shrieked and was still. The clock in St. Mary's tower struck midnight, then one, then two.

Wychford slept.

At peace.

At last.

About the Author

Paula Gosling was born in Detroit, Michigan. Her first novel, *Fair Game*, won the John Creasey Award in 1978. She now lives in Bath with her husband and two daughters, and writes full time. THE WYCHFORD MURDERS is her third novel for the Crime Club, following *Monkey Puzzle* and *The Woman in Red*.